Marauder

Marauder

Marauder Book I

D.W. Roach

"To all those who ever stood by me.
For my family.
For my brothers in arms.
For my love.
I am forever grateful."
~ David

Professional Acknowledgments

A sincere thank you to American Novelist and Best-Selling Author Cara Lockwood. You are a fantastic Editor and an insightful guide that helped make this project possible!

To my cover page designer Miguel Parisi, thank you so much for the amazing cover! You have brought visual life to my novel and helped to fuel the imagination of my readers.

Contents

1   Blood and Iron   1

2   What Lurks Below   22

3   A Hero's Welcome   38

4   The Great Hall   55

5   Vengeance, Honor, Glory   77

6   In the Presence of Death   96

7   Surrounded   111

8   A Dangerous Host   126

9   Against All Hope   141

10   The Hounds   158

11   Trust & Deceit   176

12   We Were Mortal Once   192

13	Exposed	208
14	The Puzzle	221
15	Thief of Hearts	242
	Preview of Book 2 - Valhalla Unleashed	261
	About the Author	278

One
Blood and Iron

The great heavens, so constant and unwavering in their path for hundreds of years, now began to growl and rumble in furious anger. No longer could we navigate the great expansive oceans by the glowing sparks in the night time sky. We were lost, set to wander aimlessly from island to island by All-Father, Odin, and his offspring. For when the gods bicker and scheme against one another, man will inevitably suffer the consequences of their indignation.

These were the dark times the Volva and Seidr had foretold of, the age before the last and final battle promised through the eons, the Ragnarok. Violent men led countless raids upon the lands of the frigid north. The snows melted from the great fjords and the glaciers once again receded as far back as Helheim itself. The power of the local Chieftains had all but ceased during mid-winter by the falling snows, howling winds, and deathly cold, but now winter's grip had loosened at long last and I welcomed its departure. With summer's return, the war bands, fierce and merciless tribes of fighting men, gained in strength and moved freely throughout the land. At land's end, longships were eagerly readied and brothers gathered, sharpening their weapons against the stone wheel. War was not beckoning to the lands of the north, it was already there...

From the fog came a shadowy and sinister creature. It was a dark and ominous behemoth, spit forth from the bowels of Helheim; the long-necked two-headed serpent stretched high into the sky. The creature glided atop the water, searching stealthily for its prey. Bearing gleaming razor-sharp fangs for all to see, the beast appeared ready to strike at a moment's notice; its teeth dripping with murky salt water. A silent hunter indeed, this stalker brought death and destruction to every shore it visited, for it carried upon its back the most deadly and destructive creatures this realm had ever known, the white foreigners, the death-bringers, Norsemen.

"Get the oars up. Shut your mouths. We're getting close now," Rurik quietly commanded from the rear prow.

The men guided their heavy oaken oars back into the longship, the wood sliding effortlessly along the rails with little or no noise. We waited patiently for Odin to send a mighty gust of wind to send us to shore. If the current and winds were against us, it could slow our advance, giving our prey ample warning and time to rouse their warriors for a sufficient defense. Halldis steadily fixed his gaze on the dark skies, keeping close watch of the weather vane atop the mast for any movement or sign of favorable winds. "My lord," said Halldis "the winds fail us, but the tide is in our favor. We should move with haste, my lord, before the Aegir in all his power changes his mind."

Rurik turned swiftly towards me and the men placing his hands on his hips. "Brother Halldis says it is time to attack. What say you?"

We stood to our feet and raised our weapons to the sky, "Aye!"

Rurik tugged on his long braided auburn beard. "Very well, brother. Then it is to battle and glory. Bring down the sail, oars out. Start rowing you stupid bastard sons of dogs." The men pulled at the ropes and secured them to the decks. We whispered orders back and forth, moving silently on the ship's deck quickly gathering our weapons: axe, spear, shield, and sword. Like a serpent skimming across the water, the ship moved through the dense fog, inching closer to its victim.

"Row quietly now. We wouldn't want to give them early warning," said my brother Jareth as he steadily worked his oar. Rowing no more than the length of several ships we were once again ordered to pull the oars back in as our longship drift towards the shore.

"Ready your blades men and wait for the signal," commanded Rurik.

"No sudden movements until I give word," Halldis quietly repeated Rurik's' order to the men while walking between us up and down the center of the ship. Our hearts pounded, palms sweating, gripping our weapons, waiting for the proper moment to strike. The long and agonizing winter of the North had left us anxious to return to the glorious rituals of battle. Gripping a bone knife handle, my hand bounced and shook anxiously in place; the time for battle was nearly upon me. Well into manhood, this was my fifth season raiding with Rurik and his crew. I waited impatiently for Rurik's order; stroking my dirty blonde beard and cracking my neck from side to side. The harsh and unforgiving winter months had left us fat and lazy with no one to challenge, no glory to deliver unto our Gods and our people. We craved blood at the end of an axe, silver and gold in our coffers, and this night we would have it all or dine in Valhalla.

Halldis strode to the rear prow to speak to the young ones, their first raid, merely boys no older than thirteen. "Listen here, you little shit kickers, out there is your glory, your chance to become men. If you fall behind, I will kill you. If you fall down, I will let you die. Be fearless, be menacing, and show no mercy upon your foe for they will show you none. If All-Father Odin sees fit that you shall live this day and you fight with honor, you will become one of us. Until then, you're fucking worthless."

Halldis stepped up onto a foot locker next to the mast and clung to it with one hand. "Know this," he said pointing towards the shore, "those sons of whores out there want you dead, to spill your guts on the beach like a pig to the slaughter, so who's it going to be? Who's it going to be? Some of you boys are cowards. You're scared. I can see it in your beady little rat eyes. It's time to become men." Halldis spit on the deck in front of the young ones and walked back to his station. The young ones said nothing and barely moved for fear of reprisal from Halldis. The dread in their eyes was perfectly apparent. The thought of ending up impaled at the end of a spear point sent chills down their spine and the brief taste of vomit crept into their mouths as they swallowed nervously.

I turned my head and looked at Jareth standing next to me, our eyes met and we each nodded at each other, no smiles, no fear, just the bloody rage that now flowed in our veins. Jareth removed his seax that was tucked under his leather belt and made a small cut upon his arm. "Jareth, what the hell are you doing?" I asked. Jareth opened his free hand wiping the dark red blood onto his palms and smeared it across his face making a long bloody streak. I quietly chuckled seeing my brother now turned into a demon like creature. Extending my hand I said, "Lend me your blade."

"So brother Audan, I'm not so foolish after all?" Jareth warmed at the idea of being clever. I made a small cut on my forearm, the blood dripping out like tears, one pouring through after another. Catching them into my hand I dragged my fingers straight down my face and neck, the blood still warm against my cool pale skin. The very sight of our faces must have been frightening and gruesome to even the most hardened of warriors. Jareth extended his hand; wiping the blood off the knife onto my pant leg and I happily returned his property. We drifted into a small channel lined with tall grass passing several torch lights along the shoreline. The village beach, our enemy, lay just ahead.

Standing on the front prow Rurik placed a brown leather helm upon his head and lifted his arm straight into the sky. "Get to your fighting positions, let's go, quickly now. Rocks! Brace yourselves!" The ship came to a sudden and blaring stop on the beach head throwing most of us forward. Rurik fell to the ship's hard wooden deck but stood up quickly, gazing at the foggy horizon for signs of resistance. Halldis stood higher at the prow, his eyes scanning the far horizon in darkness. "Halldis?" asked Rurik. Halldis took one more look at the shoreline and shook his head; there was no sign of resistance. Rurik lifted his arm once more into the sky, signaling the archers. Two dark hooded men quietly stepped forward, lifting their yew bows skyward, and drew back their strings, ready to unleash their stingers upon our awaiting victims.

"Give me fire," Halldis commanded. A warrior quickly stood and handed him a recently lit torch. Halldis waved the fire under the arrows that were wrapped with cod liver oil soaked cloth. The arrow heads now ablaze, lit the rock covered beach below and the tree line in front of us. With the drop of Rurik's arm the bolts of fire roared as they streaked across the sky, casting moving shadows and rained down hot iron tearing through the straw of the village hovels just beyond our sight. The signal to commence the carnage had been given.

"There they are, men! Attack! Get off the ship!" Rurik yelled as he wildly lifted his heavy bearded axe into the air. Warriors arose swiftly from their stations, shields clunking, chainmail clanking, thrusting a thunderous battle cry upwards to cut the heavens. Bodies jumped into the shallow, dismal water below, one by one, each splash was a messenger of death inching its way closer and closer to shore. Warriors filed into two lines working towards the front prow so not to drown in the deeper waters in full kit. Reaching the front prow it was my turn to take the leap; I looked down at the black murky water that lay below and without hesitation, plunged in. Like a million stabbing knives, the cold water soaked my leather armor and pierced my skin down to the bone, my lungs momentarily robbed of their breath. Tripping over a rock beneath the water's surface, my brother in arms picked me up by the back of the neck as one would pick up a dead rabbit.

"Don't die yet, little brother; we may have some use for you yet. Besides, if you drown, who will watch your back in Valhalla?" Jareth said. I smiled briefly, picking up my spear and moving forward to the beachhead. The water weighed down my clothes; I grunted and forcefully lifted each leg as I marched to the beach with my shield in front of me at the ready. Reaching the pebble-laden shore I shook off the water like a stray dog and removed the hair from my eyes.

"Take formation on the beach! Take formation on the beach! Shields! Shields!" shouted Mar the Lesser as he feverously repeated his orders. "Lock your shields and make ready to move forward." Warriors knelt digging their knees into rocks, shields and spears forward at the ready awaiting the next order. We locked our shields together making a solid defensive wall. Archers formed up behind the wall of shields, quickly scanning the beach, moving our heads left to right, searching for signs of resistance. Alas, there was nothing but darkness and the outlines of small village hovels that lay ahead. The ground was frigid, hard, and unwelcoming under our feet. Muffled screams could now be heard in the distance followed by the sounds of rustling brush, but the warriors had not yet challenged us.

Mar stood next to Rurik bearing his blackened teeth. "It's an ambush my lord. There's no sign of the enemy and yet they must be here."

Rurik smirked. "Of course, it's an ambush. It's always an ambush. Get the men forward. We take this village tonight, Odin willing." Mar nodded and looked to the men. Rurik moved to the front of the formation with his shield forward he turned and looked back at us, "Sons of Odin, what makes the grass grow and the rivers flow?"

We replied in unison, "Blood, blood, blood!"

"And how do we get blood?"

"Kill, kill, kill!"

"For glory!"

"You heard your Chieftain! Forward, you dogs! If our enemy does not wish to welcome us with open arms then we shall make ourselves at home," commanded Mar. All at once, as if one man, we stood and marched forward atop the loose pebbles, increasing our speed as we got closer to the village. Dark shadows moved in the distance and as we approached, our adversaries gradually became visible, taking refuge behind a wall of earth and mud.

Swoosh, swoosh, thwack! Arrows flew invisibly in the darkness. Their deathly shriek could be heard all around us, striking shield and dirt. The villagers were prepared; perhaps they had been attacked before in previous raids. "Keep your shields up lads unless you want to eat iron stinger!" said Rurik. Chieftain Rurik ordered open ranks to break up the concentration of arrow fire. We split up and charged forward, swords and axes drawn. The tip of my ear bent forward, arrows from our archers just behind us passing by my head giving us support to move onward.

"Aaaaaaahhhh!" The piercing shriek from the first kill. Vallis the Ruddy stood up, placing his large foot firmly on the chest of his now dispatched victim. He pushed his foot deep into his victim's cracking ribs and pulled his sword from the villagers' motionless body. Dark blood dripped profusely from his blade. Vallis looked at his cutting edge intently as if to see if his weapon was satisfied with the meal it had feasted upon. Looking back at his Chieftain with a devilish grin, Vallis then returned his attentions forward to track down his next victim. "Valhalla awaits!" yelled Vallis as he charged forward into the darkness.

Thunk! His victory was short lived. A stray arrow pierced Vallis's throat. He grasped his neck tightly around the arrow, desperately trying to keep the blood from rushing out of his body. The sound of blood rushing into a man's throat, gurgling, as he fought for air was like watching a fish flop about on dry land, longing for the water. Reaching outwards for some kind of comfort from his brothers, Vallis stumbled. Quickly succumbing to his wound, he fell, like a cut tree to the earth, eyes still open as he took his final breath. Rurik, our Chieftain, looked down upon the dying Vallis and kneeled next to him. "We will meet again in Valhalla brother. Heimdallr will show you the way." Vallis' comrades continued to move forward under the relentless hail of arrow fire.

Jareth and I stayed at each other's side; once again we merged our shields to move forward on several peasant archers taking refuge behind the wall. Their arrows hammering at our shields endlessly, volley after volley, littering the ground with broken stingers. *Schunk, thwak, shud!* With one last yell, we reached the wall throwing our spears into the mass to break up their defense. The villagers braced themselves and were knocked back as the spears struck heavy upon their poorly assembled shields. Jareth reached over his bright blue shield with his battle axe, striking one of our foes, separating his collar bone from his shoulder. Jareth gripped both hands on his axe handle; his shield now hanging by a strap from his arm and severed the archer's head from his body. I kneeled picking up my spear and thrust it at the archer next to him, but it was deflected by his bow, which smacked it away. Lifting my shield, I struck his chest with the front end, robbing him of air and stunning him just long enough for a fatal blow. The archer leaned forward over my shield and I cleaved my spear's edge over his back as he fell. Sinking the blades into his spine the archer's body tensed and became rigid, a brief shriek emerged from his mouth. I pulled and pulled at my spear but could not remove it from his now lifeless corpse.

"Leave it. Get your axe! We need to keep up with the others unless you wish to join Vallis in the afterlife," said Jareth. "Vallis is pleasuring himself in Valhalla as we speak. I wonder how he's going to get that arrow out of his throat?" Jareth said with an asinine grin. We all knew that when you journeyed to Valhalla you looked as you did in death. We all hoped in vain for a clean death knowing full well our fates would someday match that of the butchery we now proudly inflicted upon our enemies. Jareth was always known for making fun at the poorest moments, but no warrior could have a better comrade in a pitched mêlée. He was as skilled with his words as he was with an axe. He would often confuse those he quarreled with after several horns of mead by spouting some long deep-thinking argument just prior to pummeling him with the nearest object.

Soon we found ourselves in the epicenter of the village. Bodies and random belongings of village life strewn about, huts burning to a cinder leaving nothing but ash in our wake. Where were the rest of the villagers? The warriors? Jareth kneeled in the dirt. "Look there, brother. Their tracks lead outside the village. They've ventured east. We won't be able to catch them without risking our ship."

"We need to retire from this raid. They may warn others and send reinforcements to avenge them," I said hurriedly.

We split up and began searching the small earthen huts for treasure, weapons, or anything of value that could be traded back at home. This village was full of simple people, mostly farmers and fisherman; there would be few great treasures here. Approaching one hut that was only partially burning I lifted my right leg and kicked in the door throwing my weight into the blow. I fell forward nearly falling to the ground on the other side as the timber gave way. When I stood upright I saw a simple home with four beds and a smoldering fire in the center of the room; smoke was slowly billowing into the hovel and it was difficult to see. The walls and corners were barren; someone had already cleared this place out before making a hasty retreat leaving their simple meals strewn about the floor. The beds appeared undisturbed and I became suspicious as I walked toward them. I placed the underside of my axe under the gap between the wool bedding and the makeshift wood deck lifting it upward. A glimmer appeared in the dim light and hiding underneath were several iron daggers and a small silver jewelry piece. I placed them hastily in my leather satchel that rested on my hip and headed back to the courtyard to meet Jareth.

"Did you find anything of worth?" Jareth asked.

"Enough for a month of food and drink. And you, brother?"

"I found maille hiding beneath the floorboards and a sword I picked off a corpse! He no longer had any need for it." Jareth smiled wickedly as he held up his trophies in hand.

"You shit, how do you always come upon the good treasure?" I asked. Jareth just continued to smile and without delay we headed back to the ship to regroup with the men.

From the longship, fire arrows were unleashed and landed on huts and piles of straw creating quite the blaze. The Norse archers were relentless in their bombardment, showering the remaining villagers with fire and metal. The village quickly gave way to our warrior horde. Those not running in terror were already dead, an easy victory this day. Our spearman plunged over the earthen walls and traded their spears for sword and axe in close quarters combat as they slaughtered the remains of the resistance. As we walked among the burning hovels and lifeless corpses a woman villager came running out of a burning hut screaming, in fear that the flames that now engulfed her home would consume her as well. Her gaze fell upon Halldis as she rounded the corner and without hesitation plunged a dagger into his thigh.

Halldis groaned in agony for a moment, stood upright, raised his arm and backhanded the terrified woman, the magnificent crack of bone, her jaw now broken in several places. She fell to the ground and curled into a ball screaming in pain, her blood soaking into the dirt. "Take that creature to the ship. We may have use of her; perhaps as a thrall," said Halldis in a vengeful tone.

"Or a worthy sacrifice to All-Father Odin!" sneered another Viking.

The woman screamed with blood flowing from her lips, pleading with her captors, we barely understood her words, "No, no, I beg of you!" The warriors just smiled and laughed, picking her up like a sack of grain, throwing her over his shoulder and disappearing to the beach.

"She has spirit this one! She will make an excellent thrall!" hollered Mar. Our warrior brothers gathered their captives together; placing leather collars around their necks tightly and ropes to bind the hands. They were now lifetime servants of the Jarl and would serve at his pleasure until death released them. At any moment their master could choose to take their life without reprisal. Keeping thralls seemed to be more trouble than it was worth. I grew up with many slaves in my lifetime. They fed me, clothed me, and sheltered me as I became a man. In return we clasped them in irons as you would a dog and even branded their hide. It was the ultimate form of disrespect to the families of our fallen enemies and those who would stand against us.

"Rurik, the village resistance has fallen, but the peasants may be warning a nearby settlement, sending reinforcements. What are your orders my lord?" asked Mar with sincere concern in his voice.

Mar was second in command, the personal bodyguard to Rurik. Mar the Lesser as he was known; he and Rurik had fought in numerous battles over the ages. Mar was much taller than Rurik but lacked the intelligence to lead and influence those around him. Rurik, on the other hand, was charismatic, well-liked amongst his peers and respected by those he ruled over. Unlike other Chieftains, Rurik considered himself a shepherd to the people, responsible for their safety and wellbeing. It was the raids that kept his people clothed, fed, and living in modest comfort. As Mar waited impatiently for Rurik's answer he wiped the sweat from his shaved head and crossed his arms.

"Take what provisions you can, load them on the ship, then burn the rest," ordered the Chieftain.

"And what of the prisoners my lord? What shall we do with them?" asked Mar the Lesser.

"Execute the men. Keep only the strongest of the women and children as thrall. Let loose the old and the weak to fend for themselves like wild dogs." Rurik turned away and walked back to the ship.

"You heard him!" Mar repeating the order of Rurik as he pointed to the captured men. "Get those dogs down to the beach. Today they meet whatever god they so choose."

Six men now knelt in front of their Viking captors, knowing very well their failure would lead to death. Our Chieftain walked away and Mar ordered his warriors to execute the prisoners at once.

"But we have family! Children! Show mercy! Please, I beg of you! We are but humble merchants and farmers. We are not warriors like your kind," cried one of the prisoners. Halldis leaned forward on his good leg, punching the man in the face and sending him to the hard ground.

Mar resting his palms on his hips looked upon the six men with great indifference, their lives dangling in his hands. "They will join you soon in the afterlife," replied Mar. Turning his back he motioned to the men to execute the captives.

With evil bloodthirsty grins, each Norsemen drew their sword or axe, steadied it from behind the bodies of their soon to be victim and brought them down with great force. The familiar sound of iron cutting through flesh and bone echoed over the water's edge. Blood splattered dark on the sandy shore, flowing downwards towards the gentle waters. It's no easy task removing a man's head. It requires hitting the right edge of your blade, using enough force to break through flesh, tendons, and bones. All but one head fell, the younger of the executioners hadn't had enough practice, and it took three strokes of his blade to sever head from body. With a disgusted look the young Norseman hacked away until his victims head fell into the water. The other men laughed and pointed at him as Jareth and I stood by watching with arms crossed.

The young warrior scoffed. "Cowardly fool," he said, clearing his throat he spit on the man's corpse and kicked it several times in spite of him. Then the boy bent down and picked up the floating head and kicked it as far out into the water as he could. Jareth laughed loudly at the young man.

"Learn to swing a sword young man. Kicking a corpse does not a Norseman make!" The men burst into laughter once more at the boys expense.

"Fuck you Jareth." The young warrior shouted as he walked away with the look of embarrassment on his face. Jareth took no offense to the boy's insult and merely continued to laugh.

As they walked away from fresh corpses the heads of their victims could be seen floating in the current as if mere driftwood. Perhaps a stern warning to others who would attempt to cross us. The warriors gathered food, drink, valuables and weapons before boarding the longship. As they waded back to our vessel, the blood on their clothing washed away in the salt water, staining the beach crimson. Bodies were scattered about the beachside and the potent smell of death filled the air, its putrid scent sticking to the back of our throats as the fires raged in the distance.

As we loaded up the ship, we began to laugh, sing, and make jokes to calm the nerves. Within minutes we pushed off from the rocky beach and disappeared into the thick grey fog. The sound of our oars slapping the water echoed through the haze, becoming quieter and quieter as we moved further into the distance. *Drums, drums, drums, silence.*

"Now where do we go?" asked Jareth as he rowed in unison with the men.

"The next village I imagine, or perhaps our homeland. Rurik will decide. He always decides," I reluctantly replied.

Village raids were a way of life for us. I could have been a farmer or fisherman, alas, this way of life called to me. We were soldiers, warriors, merchants and marauders. Treasure was of great importance to us, our lifestyle, and we took everything we could to raise the standing of our households. Gold, silver, and weapons were the most valuable. If none of the three were to be found we took trinkets that could be bartered with at market, tools, fish netting, anything of use. Often times I found myself trading farmer's tools for small amounts of food and drink. Not every year of raiding for me was a good year.

"Man your oars! Do not shirk your duties! We need to get out of this damn channel before more warriors arrive to revenge their fallen," Rurik blared at us. Getting in to the rivers and raiding a village was easy. Leaving the channel unscathed was less so. Our ship was now weighed down with treasure, slaves, and the weariness that comes from battle. My limbs shook uncontrollably from excitement and yet I pushed and pulled at my oar as did each man among us.

"Row, row, row!" shouted one of the men. The longship picked up speed. We would reach the end of the channel soon and be back to the wide-open plains of the ocean; the kingdom of Aegir.

In the distance we noticed a single light dancing in the darkness. "My lord, look. Is it a lantern?" whispered Mar. The light moved, bounced, and quickly multiplied.

"Oh shit! Fire arrows! To your shields! Shields up!" screamed Rurik. We dropped our oars and unlashed our shields from the side of the ship bracing ourselves. Looking through a small hole in my shield I could see the arrows coming. Silently they moved through the black sky and murk, their glow lighting up everything around them. The red death of stingers poured down upon us ripping everything in its path to shreds and setting it ablaze.

Shunk! An arrow landed next to my foot, just slightly missing my large toe. I picked it up by the fletching and threw it over board. "Aaaahhh!" one of the men took an arrow to the thigh near the front prow, another to the shoulder.

"Get the arrows, put out the fires." Rurik sounded calm and composed despite the hail of fire. The longship drifted closer and closer to the end of the channel. Although the relative safety of the see was near our foes could now see us clear as day with the fire arrows lighting up our decks. *Whoosh, swoosh, sssshnap.* The archers continued their barrage from the shoreline. With our ship now well-lit, fire arrows became a moot point. There was no warning now as the unlit iron hurled passed and in-between our bodies. I grabbed another lit arrow from the deck and turned to throw it over board hoping to lessen our ship as a target.

Looking over my left shoulder I saw Nias sitting next to me lying there still in the chaos. An arrow had pierced the top of his skull, his hair set ablaze. "Audan! Get him overboard or we will all burn," Rurik hollered at me.

Pushing Nias over, I dragged his corpse by his arms and rolled his flaming body overboard. With a splash the fire was extinguished and our comrade floated face down to the open sea. A passing thought, that could have been me instead of Nias, but it wasn't. I grinned at my luck and turned back to my station. Our enemy was well behind us now, lobbing arrows aimlessly into the sky hoping to get just one more kill. The fire arrows were extinguished and we were finally out into the open sea disappearing into the night.

So much for heading to the next village, I thought to myself.

We were in no shape for further raids. We needed to head back home to allow the wounded to heal, recruit more men to replace the dead, and resupply our provisions. This was our fourth raid this season, and the most fatal thus far. It's customary to lose several men in a raid, but not a fourth of your crew. I looked about the ship, the blood soaking into the grain of the wood deck. The stains of blood never leave our ships; they merely darken along the planks lines, and are a constant reminder that one day we all die. Odin willing, it's an honorable death in battle. I looked over my shoulder towards the rear prow and noticed several of the thrall we had loaded on board died as well, only three souls remained: two deathly pale women and a child who stared blankly out into the abyss.

A short and stocky Norseman, Eric, threw the dead slaves overboard and then tended to the living, making sure they didn't escape, grab weapons or sabotage the ship. "Are you injured?" asked Eric not in concern for their well-being, but in the interest of protecting our assets. The thrall hesitantly shook their heads and looked down at the ships deck.

Rurik quickly regained his poise and returned to the rear prow to man the rudder. "Back to your oars. Healer! Tend to the wounded, place our dead in between the men so they may receive a proper ceremony at home as heroes that will be welcomed into Odin's home, Valhalla!"

The men cheered and raised their arms in celebration at the thought of our dead comrades ascending to Valhalla, home of slain warriors. Only those who die an honorable death, a warrior's death, may hope to enter Valhalla. Its halls are said to be made of gold, with columns of stone towering on high to rafters of spears and a roof covered in the shields of fallen warriors. Its casks of mead never run dry, its spit of wild boar is forever giving and plentiful.

Orbrecht the Healer quickly hopped over bodies moving his thin figure to the rear of the ship. He fetched his remedy sack, which contained mostly clean cloth and several jars filled with herbal remedies. Orbrecht grabbed my arm, "Audan, start a fire for your friends, you're going to help me clean the wounds." The healer looked up at me with a mischievous grin and you could tell that although he was a caretaker, he took much delight in causing us pain.

I reached under a woolen tarp and grabbed a small iron bowl placing it next to Orbrecht. Reaching into my pocket, I removed my fire kit: several small fibers, tinder, and a fire rock with fire steel secured by cloth. The fire steel wrapped around my hand with a perfect fit allowing for a quick strike to the fire rock. *Chack, thack, chack, thack.* The sparks and embers flew setting my hands a glow. I adjusted the direction of my strikes so as to get the sparks to hit just right on the tinder. Smoke and embers at last, the fire started. As I blew slowly on the embers, the smoke grew and moved up the kindling like a serpent climbing a tree. I slowly added more tinder; careful not to suffocate the fire and added bigger pieces until smoke and ember became flame.

"Get it red hot," Orbrecht scolded as he rubbed his hands together. "You wouldn't want them to die of disease, would you?" He stared at me intently for a moment as a discomfort came of me and I reached for my ribs. "What is this Audan? Are you injured?"

I looked where the healer had motioned. The left side of my tunic was soaked with blood, dripping onto the deck. "Lift up your tunic, and let me see." I lifted the woolen cloth just enough to see where the blood was coming from. "Ah, a flesh wound," he smiled, "that will need treatment."

In all the excitement, I hadn't noticed that an arrow grazed my rib cage. The stinging started to set in and bright red flesh could be seen beneath the skin. The cut was clean and neat, no jagged edges. "Fucking stingers. They always go so damn deep," I complained to Orbrecht.

"The arrow barely touched you, quit whining like a child." Orbrecht the Healer scoffed as he went about his duties and provided instruction to me along the way. "Keep working on the fire, Audan. I will treat you last." A chill ran up my spine, closing my eyes I turned my head to the side to shake off the thought of the coming pain to cure my wound.

The Healer moved from man to man, applying a green paste like herbal remedy and salves of leaves to their wounds. The fire began to roar and crack, hot embers now coated the bottom of the bowl. "Heat up your seax and follow me." There was only way to clean these wounds; with scorching fire. They had to be burned shut or else be open to infection followed by an excruciating death. A painful experience, most men fainted at the agony and smell of their own burning flesh. Kneelingnext to a wounded man the healer held his thigh next to his wound and looked back at me. "Bring it here, we will start with him." Reaching over the fire, I grabbed my blade; it glowed red hot under the evening sky. Lifting the poker from the fire, embers flew and were carried off by the wind into the darkness. I followed the glow with my eyes being careful not to touch anything else with it.

"Quickly now." Orbrecht placed a bloodied rag in the man's mouth, and with a slight giggle, the Healer muttered, "Now, this is really going to hurt. Are you ready?" The warrior nodded and looked away closing his eyes.

"Do it," he mumbled to me. I placed the hot iron firmly on his thigh. His screams made me jump back but the seax stuck to his smoking flesh. I quickly composed myself and leaned back in towards the warrior so not to tear his flesh further. "Don't just leave it on top, move it around a bit. We have to clean everything or he won't heal properly." I twirled the seax back and forth watching Orbrecht for further direction.

I hadn't noticed but the warrior's head had already slumped over, at present passed out from the pain and atrocious smell. I removed the dagger and placed it gently back into the fire for the next man. I don't know why, but before I did, I smelled the smoke coming off the tip of the blade. A man's burning flesh, not like the smell of any beast you would eat, it was putrid, bitter, and offensive to the senses. Leaning against the mast I saw Jareth casually manning the rudder. Not a scratch on him. I didn't know how he always managed to remain unscathed in combat; lucky bastard.

I grew up with Jareth; our fathers were great warriors together during much of the Eastern raids. Jareth lost his father at a young age to a battle with the Finns. His fathers' body never made it home. Rurik, my father, ascended to become the leader and Chieftain of our clan. We took Jareth and his mother in as family. Jareth was always a skilled with his tongue. He had a talent for courting even the most happily married of woman. Those who understood him well, knew not ever to bet against him in a game of chance. Even if he loses, he will somehow talk you into returning his winnings through some grand scheme he had envisioned. He was gifted that way.

"It's your turn, Audan. Sit here and whatever you do, don't move." The Healer reached into a jar with his fingers and removed something green and wet, like a paste, swiftly placing it into my wound.

"That smells awful!" I said with disgust on my face.

"Good, that means it will work well." Without regard for the pain he would cause, Orbrecht placed it deep within my wound.

"Ah!" It already started to sting.

"Quit your whining, we're not even to the fun part yet." He stood up and reached for the hot seax. I grasped an oar nearby to steady my arm. "Are you ready Audan?" He shoved the cloth into my mouth and told me to look away.

"AAAAAHHHHHH!!!!!" The searing pain, I could smell my flesh, the heat radiated through my entire body. What passed by in mere moments felt like an eternity. Orbrecht the Healer twisted and turned the dull hot blade in my wound, closing it off. I couldn't stop screaming. At long last, he removed the seax and placed it back into the fire. I looked at him with pain and hatred in my face.

"You didn't faint?" the Healer said with a surprised smile. "You should have fainted brother Audan."

"No shit, you fucking pot licker." I clinched my teeth and closed my eyes. "Why am I not fainting? I thought I was supposed to faint!" I exclaimed as beads of sweat ran down my face into my eyes.

The other men looked on and laughed at my anguish. I guess if I was them, I would have cackled as well; it's just another scar to add to the countless others. You'd think after all this time that I'd be numb to the pain, a stick still bruised, a rock still crushed, and a blade still cut. You could count the number of battles I'd been in by the scars marked on my young body. Barely the age of twenty-five, my bones ached and cracked like that of much older warriors. Rurik was famous for the scar that cut across his right eye. They say he stopped an axe with his face in a pitched battle; that his skull was made of iron. We all knew better, he was but flesh and blood like the rest of us, tougher than most, but he still bled.

"Drink this, you child. It'll make a man of you," Rurik said. He pushed a ram's horn into my shoulder. I grabbed it with my right arm, as my other limb would not move, I was so weak. I put the horn to my lips thinking it was water. I took a quick sip to test my palette, and Rurik was good enough to give me his ration of golden mead from his personal cask. I drank it quickly and heartily. The mead flowed into my body, giving some minor respite from the pain. He smiled and returned to Jareth who was standing smartly at the rear prow.

"How long until we reach Bjorgvin?" Rurik asked Jareth with crossed arms,

"About two days sail my Chieftain, if the tide and Aegir is with us," he replied.

"Two days!" Rurik exclaimed. "By Thor's hammer, can we not get there any faster? Mead is waiting for us in the Great Hall."

"And the women, my Chieftain, don't forget about the women." Jareth smiled from ear to ear, probably looking forward to telling his tales of glory, death, and self-sacrifice.

"Are you going to lie again about the size of your cock or do I have to show you up again adopted son of mine?" Rurik and Jareth laughed gleefully.

Practically father and son, they enjoyed competing with one another for the affections of a lady. Jareth always won over the younger of the women, Rurik however had strength, power, and wisdom attracting the more mature or eager types, hoping to supplant Rurik's wife, Kenna. My mother was a striking and graceful woman in her mid-forties. She was beautiful, tall, with fair skin and a tough nature about her. She'd have to be tough to be married to Rurik. Of course, their wedding was arranged. Rurik was the bravest and strongest in the clan so naturally he had his choice of the lot. He chose Kenna above all others. Kenna was a shield maiden once; it was said that she would join Rurik on the raids, cook food, tend to the wounded, and even join in battle when they were faced against a larger force than anticipated. She was not one to be trifled with.

Gazing upward at the clearing in the fog, and beyond the mast I could see the heavens and gods shining clearly above. The wind was picking up now and at long last caught our sail. We now crossed the North Sea, sailing slowly back to our homeland, back to Bjorgvin. When we began our raids, we were forty-two men strong, now we were thirty-four. The ocean came to life as we made our way home. The longship slapped gently against the waves, the sea relentlessly sprayed our faces, and the ocean's salt stung deeply in our wounds.

Two
What Lurks Below

The open boundless sea, a Norsemen's second home. We ventured north by northeast for Bjorgvin, our sacred homeland. Men tended carefully to their bloodied and cleaved bodies, cleansing their wounds with the sting of sea water, they drank heartily of golden mead to dull the pain. Those not injured sat grinding stone against their weapon's edge, staying ready for what dangers lurked around the bend. Orbrecht the healer tended to Halldis, who had been wounded by a knife to the leg. His lesion was small but badly infected by the rusty blade. The Healer leaned closely over the wound and breathed deep into his chest. The awfulness of the smell made Orbrecht gag and cough. "Cheese...damn," he said under his breath.

"What the hell does that mean? Is he going to be alright?" Jareth asked. Orbrecht looked at Jareth with a heavy heart and dull unflinching eyes.

"It means disease has set in to his wound flowing into his veins, and he is in the hands of the gods now." Halldis was now with a dreadful fever and death was moving ever closer.

With no way to help his brother, Halldis, Jareth sat with his knife angrily whittling a small piece of drift wood. "If he dies now, he'll never ascend to the glory of Valhalla. It is not a warrior's death. There is no honor in it." Looking down and shaking his head, I saw that Jareth felt nothing but pity for Halldis, pity that he would be forsaken a life in Valhalla with the gods from mere disease.

"Hold your tongue, young man. His fate is not determined yet; he can still pull through this if the gods will it to be so. Perhaps the Valkyrie Eir will show her mercy upon our brother and descend from the heavens to cure his ailment." The healer took a damp rag and wiped down Halldis' forehead, keeping the beads of sweat from his eyes, trying to knock the fever down. Orbrecht looked across the deck of the ship and pointed at me. "Audan, fetch me that blanket, his body needs to stay warm if he's going to fight this off." I stood quickly grabbing a woven blanket and gave it to Orbrecht. He draped the cloth over Halldis' body and tucked it in tightly to keep the cold at bay.

Staring out into the infinite ocean, I drifted away into my own thoughts for a moment. By now Obrecht's Valkyries were long gone, battle had not been seen for nearly a day and Halldis had been wounded in a most dishonorable fashion for a warrior. A woman! *What a terrible way to go*, I thought to myself. I'd rather take my own life than die at the hands of a woman. Halldis had seen many epic battles in his lifetime, killed many formidable foes, and now he stared blankly into the abyss. Halldis was an intimidating figure, taller than most men, long hair as dark as ravens feathers. His voice was deep and commanded the attention of all men in his presence. Halldis carried no shield with which to defend himself, only a giant bearded axe with the stains of blood from fallen enemies.

We called the axe *Crusher* because of the way it killed men. It wasn't the cut of the blade that killed them, as the axe was too dull, it had not been sharpened in many years. It was the great force that Halldis placed behind it. Halldis would literally crush a man's head until it entered his chest cavity and smile while he did it too. We all looked up to Halldis and wanted to see him die a brave warrior's death so he could feast in the golden halls. Even the look in his eyes was frightening to me now. His once dark brown eyes had turned to a deep black. What was he staring at? Could he see Helheim perhaps? Did he know his coming terrible fate? Perhaps he was already absent of our company, leaving his mortal self behind.

I thought back to my early battles as a younger man. Long ago, I saw a Valkyrie amidst a battlefield. A neighboring war clan was challenging ours over possession of a local lake and the right to all wealth that inhabited it. The dispute caused one man to stab another in the back. The coward aggressor tried to run and was killed himself by a flying spear that pierced his chest. A pitched battle ensued between the war clans. A silly thing it is to die over fresh water and fish, but the laws and honor of our people must be maintained at all costs. We were unprepared for this battle and I was terribly inexperienced as a youth.

I recall the horde charging towards me at great speed, dark figures in loud clanking lamellar armor, screaming and yelling, wildly swinging their swords and axes in the air. They banged their shields simultaneously, over and over, howling and yelling. Several warriors even bit and chewed at the edge of their shields spitting chunks of wood from their mouths trying to intimidate us, trying to break our spirits. Spears and arrows flew from all directions filling the sky, cutting men down like crops before the plow. The full might of a flying spear would not merely send a man to the ground, but would fling his body backward, plummeting into his brother's swords behind him. I froze, staring straight ahead, staring at nothing, not at the enemy but through them. I leaned back and looked away; suddenly, I felt weight pulling down on the end of my spear.

My adversary, so enraged had charged forward and impaled himself upon my spear point. I opened my eyes and looked into the emptiness that was a dying warrior's face. His body slid down my spear shaft swiftly. I could feel his warm blood running between my fingers and soaking my clothes. I stared at him intently, waiting for him to say or do something. The light vanished from his eyes as they rolled into the back of his skull. Stepping back, I allowed his body fall to the ground, lifeless, glorious, worthy of Odin's open arms in his Great Halls. I felt like such a coward for killing such a worthy opponent. It was at that moment that my courage was further robbed from me: I looked up, and there she was, a winged vision sent from Valhalla itself, chooser of the fallen, a corpse goddess, a Valkyrie.

A hand reached out and gripped me firmly by the shoulder. I turned with my bloodied spear raised up, ready to make my first honorable kill, to make up for the one I did not earn. Yelling at the top of my lungs I focused on my opponent and stopped just short of plunging my spear point into his throat. It was my father. "Audan, are you okay son?" My expression quickly turned from fury to gratefulness that I did not kill him. I nodded repeatedly. "Good! Then fight boy, fight!" I charged forward, with my newfound courage and never looked back.

Axes fell, bones shattered, spears found their mark. I stumbled forward and barely deflected a sword thrust. Finding my way to my feet, I drove my spear through my enemy' belly and into his chest. A short shriek exited his throat followed by a river of blood that shot out like a river, flowing down his chest. Watching this man die, he stared at me with great hatred, gripping the spear in his body, slowly falling to his right knee, then his left. He was trying to say something but could not get his words past the blood, then, he smiled at me, turned his head, and said "Thank you child, thank you." It was as though he saw something that I could not: perhaps he gazed upon the rainbow that we all longed to one day cross.

That battle was many seasons ago, and now as a man I still think back on that day. You see, many men claim to have witnessed a Valkyrie on the battlefield, always described as the most beautiful and kindest of creatures to exist, but I know better. Valkyries are vain, deceitful, conjurers of tricks and sorcery. They sneak about in the shadows to carry out their own bidding, to treat us mortals like mere play things, often fornicating with mortal men and killing those who dare to cross them. They lure living warriors to their death by briefly appearing in battles as cloaked creatures, distracting a warrior for a brief moment when they could have stopped the fatal blow.

Those who fall for their trickery do not die a warrior's death and are denied entrance into Valhalla. At the end of a battle, the Valkyries remove their cloaks, red like the blood of fallen warriors, trimmed with gold stitching, and reveal their god-like nature to the dead. Adorned with glorious lamellar armor that shines like Sol's summers sun, magnificent chainmail, and silken padded cloth, just the finest armor ever in existence. Their swords, shine like Mani's reflection on the water's edge during a clear evening sky. No weapon forged by man can come close. Not even the mythical sword of King Dainsleif himself whose blade by merely unsheathing it would wet the ground with his enemies' blood.

It was slowly becoming light outside but the sun was nowhere to be seen. Fog crept in and surrounded the longship, engulfing us in its dark, cold shadow. The salt water soaked our blood-stained clothes. "Audan, get over here!" Jareth called to me. "You're on watch until sun down. Try not to screw anything up," he said jokingly.

"Thanks for your vote of confidence. Fucking sheep shagger," I said under my breath with a smile. I hadn't slept since before the raids and now I was about to stand a twelve-hour watch. The air was so cold, always so cold. Looking up at the sky I called to every god I could think of to make the sun break through the clouds but the sun light never came.

Ships watch was an important but agonizingly boring task for a warrior. With my callused hands I held the rudder in place to reach home, sometimes fighting against the wind and waves, looking out for other war clans that may have set off on early morning raids. The wind was with us this time, and the seas favorable. The currents guided us home effortlessly. The sails were tight and pulled our ship steadily forward along the coast line; overall a good day for sailing. Our tired and wounded rested while Orbrecht the Healer continued to tend to their injuries. I grabbed my coat and placed it over my head to keep out the cold. It was a shiny and smooth brown fur coat of a bear I had hunted when I was very young. It always kept me warm and made me feel at ease and at home when out to sea.

Out of the corner of my eye I saw a dark figure, Kormak, crouched down next to me, smoking a pipe he covered carefully with his hand to keep out the sea spray. The smoke billowed through his fiery red beard and slowly rose to the sky long after he was done smoking.

"You did well today, boy, but next time, try to kill a few more of those bastards. My mother could slay a man faster than you," Kormak said with a smirk.

"I was too busy protecting Jareth's backside. And where were you? I never saw you beyond the beach head," I jested trying to bait Kormak into an angry frenzy.

"Hmmph," he scoffed. "Your shield sees more battle than your spear point and your tongue moves faster than your axe. You would do well to speak more often to Brother Thor. Then maybe he would grant you the power of big balls like mine!" Kormak laughed long and hard, slapping me on the back to reassure me that he was only making light hearted discussion.

I always enjoyed conversations with Kormak. He was a veteran to our great war clan. He had been in so many great battles alongside my father throughout the years. Together, they conquered Bjorgvin and most of the surrounding coast line from a former Jarl whose name we were forbidden to utter. They were young in those days, short-tempered, quick to fight, and according to them, always painfully outnumbered. Norsemen had a habit of grossly exaggerating the odds in combat, but it always made for an epic tale.

"Did I ever tell you about the campaign in which we raided villages for two, no, no, three months straight?" asked Kormak.

"Yes, old man, you did," I replied rolling my eyes.

"Well, what about the time we found ourselves surround by one hundred, wait, no, one hundred and fifty Berserkers of Germania?" Kormak crossed his large tattooed arms, clearly impressed with himself.

"Yes, and somehow you two managed to light a whole forest on fire and pick them off one by one in the billowing smoke. Isn't that how the story goes uncle?" I said sarcastically almost word for word.

"There you go again, Audan, doubting the greatness of our fighting skills, courage and cunning. If you were fearless like us perhaps you would have some great tales of your own to tell."

"Oh no, I have no doubt of that. I only doubt the weight of numbers in your tales dear uncle," I replied.

Kormak the Large, my uncle, could no longer run into battle. He injured his leg when a flying spear found its target many years ago. His thigh bone was shattered and my father dragged him to safety under a hail of arrow fire. Kormak begged my father to leave him so he could fight, die, and be carried by the Valkyries to Valhalla. Since that day, Kormak has been eternally loyal to our family and his brother, acting as one of Rurik's' bodyguards, friend, and mentor to me.

Halldis could be heard moaning in the background. His fever had brought on chills, aches, and deliria. Orbrecht worked tirelessly to cure Halldis of his ailments.

"Odin! All-Father!" shouted Halldis, gazing at the sky "Have mercy, do not take me now. I have not killed my last warrior," he said while coughing and hacking. Halldis reached his arms upward, hoping that Odin could hear his plea so he could fight and die to earn his place amongst the sacred halls.

Orbrecht urged Halldis to calm himself and drink water. "If you do not drink, then you will die and you will not see Odin. Is that what you want? You want to die like a coward? Like an old man in his death bed pissing and shitting himself?"

Halldis refused drink, his eyes rolled back into his skull and he slept once more. "You see that?" Kormak asked calmly. "That is a true warrior, caring not for himself, but only the manner in which he dies. Watch him closely, boy. If he goes, it will not be easy." Kormak's pipe glowed against his thick crimson beard; appearing to dance like specters wafting over him.

Orbrecht stepped back from Halldis and moved toward Kormak and I. "He is going to die you know," said Orbrecht. "His fever is too hot and he refuses drink. Stubborn bastard, I'll force it down his throat if I have to."

"You best do what you can to keep him alive. My father will kill you if he dies in your care," I said to Orbrecht as a friendly warning.

Rurik, stepped forward. "Move aside, fools." He ordered. Rurik forcefully pulled the cup from Orbrecht's grasp. "Halldis, you will drink this or you will never see battle again and you will not join me in the halls of Valhalla. Do you understand me, brother? How will I prepare for the Ragnarok without your guidance and strong shield by my side? Now drink, old friend, and stay with us a moment longer." Halldis gazed at the cup offered by my father and forcefully drank until the cup was empty. It took the thought of the Ragnarok just to get Halldis to drink; the Ragnarok would be the last, greatest, and most epic battle of all time. The gods and dead warriors would descend from the heavens for a final battle and in the process, Midgard, all that we know, would be destroyed in its fiery glory.

Rurik stood up, turned quickly and grabbed Orbrecht by the neck. "Listen to me, you scrawny little worm, if he dies, I will have your head on a spike! Have I made myself clear?"

"Yes, my Chieftain. Halldis will make it home. Upon my life, I swear it," Orbrecht said shakily.

"Ensure that he does. I do not care to explain to his woman how he died," Rurik replied. Father released his grasp and Orbrecht scrambled to the mast rubbing his neck coarsely. My father was a stern but fair man. His concern was for the welfare of his people and he looked down upon cowardice, laziness, or inattention to the task at hand.

"I hope you're all hungry," Urd said. Urd had been cooking up a stew. This was one of the few times we could not stay and enjoy our food after sacking a village. Urd used what we brought for the voyage, a Norse treat!

"What are you serving us today?" I asked Urd curiously.

"Cured shark meat, it'll make you strong and put hair on your balls!" Urd lifted his arm and flexed his bicep. Jareth took a small portion a quickly bit into the flesh.

"Did you poison this Urd? It tastes like shit!" Jareth complained.

"It will get you through the voyage so you best put it down your suck hole and shut your mouth, you ungrateful shit," replied Urd. Cured shark was made by cutting the premium pieces of the shark off into smaller pieces, placing them into a small wooden box and putting it in the ground for several weeks. Done right, it tastes fantastic, but time always ate away at the quality of this preserved food and in this case, time had taken its toll. Urd's nickname was Leftie, considering he was the only warrior amongst us that fought left handed. It was odd but in many ways it gave him advantages in combat, always getting his weapon to the enemy first. He was also a good cook on long voyages but sometimes supplies were limited and we were forced to consume what rations were available. Urd traded and bartered with passing ships to pick up new foods and spices. Every so often, we were treated to what you could consider a Norse cookery delight. This usually meant food that wasn't rotten with some form of spice dabbled atop of it from foreign lands.

"Fog?" I cursed under my breath. A mist had crept up on the rear prow of the ship. It engulfed us like an ashen plume from a volcano. Nobody saw it coming and now our clear path to home suddenly seemed much longer.

"Audan, to the horn, sound every few moments to announce our presence," commanded Rurik.

"Yes, father." I reached down for the rams horn and blew to alert other ships. If another ship was near they would respond with their horn so we could avoid a collision. *There was no response to our call, so we must be clear,* I thought to myself. I placed the horn back in its place and quickly returned to my post. Kormak ordered two warriors to the forward prow to keep watch for land or other hazards.

Orbrecht kept a watchful eye all around, holding his own hands he muttered, "This fog has cursed us. The gods do not wish us to return home."

Rurik responded, "Nonsense, quiet your tongue and mind your duties. I will not have a mutiny on this ship because you couldn't keep your wits about you. It's just bloody fog."

"I don't mean any disrespect, my chieftain, but it's well known that monsters frequent these waters. It's the fog, Rurik. The serpent creates the mist with its fiery nose touching the water's surface." Rurik looked at Orbrecht intensely but did not argue his knowledge. The water beasts were real, though none of us had seen one. It was a constant threat of death and a reminder of the beast that the gods had unleashed on our home. Just as Orbrecht finished talking, a splash was heard on the starboard side of the longship.

I quickly ran towards the sound to investigate thinking someone must have fallen overboard. Searching the waters over the rails of the longship, I saw calm silver water breaking from the ship's hull. I saw my reflection in the water and something more, something moving, shiny, and fast, very fast. A school of fish, I hoped. "Kormak, come look at this. What do you see just there? Is it a fish? A whale?" I pointed in the direction of movement.

Kormak looked over the railing, his eyes trying to focus on what was in front of him while pointing his spear at the moving water. Kormak then let out a loud laugh. "It's a school of fish. Have you never seen fish before? What kind of mariner are you?"

"I don't think that's fish Kormak. Look again," I replied. Slightly shaken and gripping the rail tightly, I backed my head away from the water. *Could it be?* "It's under the ship," I shouted.

The ship was violently knocked and rocked in the water. The mast swayed back and forth. Every able-bodied man stood to their feet alarmed, swinging their heads from side to side.

"Have we struck land?" shouted Rurik as he too gazed upon the waters for a sign of what we had collided with.

"There isn't any land for a day, my Chieftain, perhaps a shoal, or sunken ship?" said Mar.

"The oceans are hundreds of fathoms deep here, that's ridiculous," Jareth protested. The water became calm, motionless, and the fog engulfed the ship with more intensity. Suddenly the ship stopped violently in the water.

We were flung forward, bracing ourselves on whatever we could find. Kormak looked at the ship's deck and calmly uttered, "Arm yourselves, men. There be monsters in these waters." Panic set into our eyes, as the ship became a flurry of activity. "I said 'arm yourselves!' Get the spears. Circle formation! Get your shields!" Kormak shouted.

We quickly unlashed the spears from the ship's deck one by one. The men faced outward, shoulder to shoulder, spears readied. We stood our ground, eyes searching the horizon and water below for any movement.

"Have you fought a sea monster before?" I asked Kormak in hopes that he may tell me things are not as bad as they seem.

"Once, off the northern coast. It came without warning, much in the same way this monster is here. They came in quietly and picked us off one by one," he replied.

"They?" I asked, attempting to hold back the slight hint of fear in my voice.

"Aye, they. Three, there was," Kormak replied.

"AAAAAhhhh!" a scream erupted followed by a splash. A warrrior had been pulled from the ship's deck into the murky depths. The men ran frantically to the ships side looking over the rails to locate their missing comrade. Bubbles rose from the black water.

"I can get him!" exclaimed one of the men.

"No!" shouted Kormak. "The beastie is using him for bait."

We had to restrain him to keep him from jumping into the water. "What? Are you mad? You'd die with him. Take hold of yourself," Jareth yelled at him. We looked everywhere, the silence set in and we waited. "Look, look there!" shouted Jareth, as he pointed upwards at the mast.

The serpent emerged, rising from the water like a god. Its serpent-like head was turned away from the ship, eyes squinting at the sight of dim sun light peeking through the clouds. Pale green like a rotting corpse, slimy, and full of teeth as sharp as knives, it turned about searching for its prey. Its eyes pointed like daggers and pale as the snow. When the monster finally spotted our ship, we leaned back, hearts pounding, hands gripping our weapons. The serpent's nostrils flared, spines rose from its neck and the beast turned sharply to meet our gaze.

"Get ready, boys. She's coming this way! Lock your shields!" shouted Rurik.

The serpent leapt forward and smashed itself against the front prow of the ship again and again, as if playing with a toy. Spears flew forward, striking the beast in the neck and back. I charged forward with a small ships axe hacking at its fins and spine. The rage coursed through my body.

"Die you wicked creature! Aaahh!" I slashed and ripped at the beast's flesh. Black blood seeped from the beast's wounds and she shrieked with rage, such a shriek as I've never heard before. The men reached for their ears, the sounds piercing their skulls. Everyone pressed their hands against their ears in pain and I too fell to the timbers.

"Make it stop, make it stop!" screamed Urd. Rurik did no better as he dropped to one knee covering his ears as his skull stung and popped.

"Look out! Get down!" Rurik hollered. The beast's tail struck the ship's deck with a mighty blow, swiped to the left and knocked several men overboard into the water. A spear flew from the hand of one warrior and sunk into the shoulder of another. Back the serpent went into the depths, picking off men who were struggling to swim in the water, trying to get back to the ship. One man managed to get his chain mail off and swam back to the surface; it was Kormak.

"Swim, swim for your life!" I shouted. I knelt down and grabbed an oar. Reaching over the edge of the ship, I used the oar to pull Kormak to safety. "Get in, old man!" Kormak flung himself over the railing and dragged himself onto the ship with his brother Rurik lending a hand.

Jareth reached for a long bow, firing arrows with speed and precision. Two arrows pierced near the beast's left eye, the third arrow ploughed straight into her other eye. The creature let out a terrible shriek. The beast violently swung its head and neck left to right as if to shake off the arrow. White fluid spewed from the monster's skull to the deck of the ship below.

"Jareth has blinded the beast! Kill it! Kill it! Attack, you fools!" Kormak ordered. All at once, the men threw spears over the ship striking the beast over and over again. Their morale raised once more, the men were now fearless, hurling body and weapon at the beast.

"Jareth, fire arrows!" Rurik screamed. Jareth lit his arrows ablaze and struck the beast in the face. The flame, smoke, ember, and ash removed all senses of the beast.

"Quiet men. She can't see, smell, or hear us. The beast is blind. To your oars. Row, row for your sorry lives," Kormak whispered with urgency.

The men went back to their oars, and gently place their weapons in front of them. As we began to row, you could hear the sound of the oars smacking and cutting through the ocean water. The longship slowly gained speed.

Jareth kept us at pace while he quietly muttered, "Row, row, row." The serpent quickly turned its head and followed the sound of the oars.

"Oars back in, don't make a sound," Kormak quickly ordered. The men brought the oars in immediately and froze. The serpent stopped and listened. *Clank!* A warriors seax fell from its sheath onto the deck of the ship. The serpent let out a great scream and leapt towards the ship.

"Spears! Get the spears! Audan, grab the net," Rurik roared at me. I climbed the mast with a fishing net to get above the creature. "Throw it boy, throw." I threw the net as hard as I could; it landed directly over the head of the sea serpent. "Get the ropes, pull men, pull."

We pulled the beast in closer and closer to the ship. "Bring her down! Bring her down! Spears, axes, everything you've got," Rurik called out to us. Jareth relentlessly fired arrows, making their mark on the creature's face. Spears and axes stuck out of the monster's flesh. It screamed relentlessly attempting to free itself from the fish net but to no avail.

"Get those ropes tied down! We're going to kill this beast and bring it home." I climbed further atop the mast, the serpents neck swaying in front of me, and with several mighty blows of a bearded axe, I gouged a fatal wound into the monster, covering the men below in dark blood reeking of salt. Rurik yelled aloud,

"Odin owns you all!" he was ready to give his life in order to kill this monster. The beast's head swayed back and forth until finally, it fell into the water with a great splash.

"Tighten those ropes, were not going to lose this beast. This is our prize for victory! The rest of you collect the dead and injured. Back to your oars." Rurik was not about to let such a monster escape our grips. We secured the beast to the rear prow with fish netting, ropes and rowed for home. A trail of endless blood flowed in the wake of our longship leaving a trail for the gods to follow.

Rurik reached over the ships railing into the beast's half sub-merged mouth and cut one of its teeth out with his dagger and eagerly gave it to me. "This will make a fine trophy," he said, patting my back with pride.

As we sailed away sharks and all manner of sea life followed our ship trying to feed on the exposed flesh of the beast. Our only hope was that some of it would be left once we got home, to prove our tale of epic battle. My arms were heavy, hands still shaking from the fight that had just ended. I tried to look away from my fallen brothers and focus on the sea ahead, but each time I turned away my neck pulled me back and I found myself staring at the bloodied and crushed corpses of my friends. *Oh no*. I breathed in with my nose and caught a whiff of rotting corpses. I gagged; throwing my head over the rails, I emptied the contents of my belly into the ocean.

"What's your problem, boy? You act like you've never seen a dead body," Rurik said.

"It's not the sight father, it's the smell," I said, feeling shame.

"You're too soft, Audan, too much like your mother. You might fight like a Norseman, but Norsemen don't piss them-selves after killing men. You better get a hold of yourself or you'll be tending to the livestock." Rurik pointed at me, turned his head away and marched back to the rear prow.

Jareth looked at me with a smile and giggled. "Baaah, Baaah!" he exclaimed like a sheep.

The rest of the men jumped in "Baaah, Baaah!"

"Shut it, you assholes," I said under my breath. The sun was now sinking into the frigid waters, gleaming across the horizon turning everything to gold. We were not far from home now.

Three
A Hero's Welcome

The dark stretching shores of Bjorgvin, of our homeland, were in sight at long last. "Light the torches and sound the ram's horn. Let our loved ones know their sons have returned home victorious from battle." Rurik commanded gleefully.

Mar repeated the order to the ships watch. "You heard your Chieftain, step lively now, make it happen!" he snapped. The ships watch moved quickly to retrieve the ram's horn from within a chest on the ship's deck.

Rurik turned to Mar and said, "Tonight, old friend, we will feast heartily, once again giving thanks and praise to All-Father, Odin, for a successful raid."

Mar smiled and warmed at the thought of freshly cooked meat, golden mead, and familiar loose women. "That we will, my Chieftain. But our celebration this night will pale in comparison to the bounty our fallen brothers no doubt are enjoying in Valhalla this very night."

Rurik nodded and placed his hand on Mar's shoulder. "That it will, old friend. That it will. Each of them has earned their place amongst the gods and will certainly look down upon us this very night in pity that we were unable to join them." Rurik turned upward, looking at the sky as if he was searching for the smiling faces of our fallen comrades. A crack in the clouds revealed the bright nearly full moon, casting a light on Bjorgvin and the dark waters below.

We lowered the sails, working the rigging eagerly, and set out the oars to row safely into the dock. Mar continued to bark orders with pride, "Handsomely now, we may be home but that's no excuse to be lazy sons of bitches. This ship is your home away from home. Treat it as such. Show her the respect she deserves!" As second in command, Mar was the caretaker of our ship, ensuring maintenance and proper care at all times. Mar obviously took great pride in this responsibility, always standing proudly at the rear prow maintaining a close watch on all.

The ship's watch stood at the front prow, grasping the wooden dragons head from inside its mouth and leaning over the water he blew the rams horn twice signaling that a friendly ship was approaching the harbor. The sound bawled and bounced off the cliff's edge, an eerie vibration in the darkness of the fog. In the distance a slender shadowy figure could be seen at the end of the dock with shield and spear. The watch at the port responded with his ram's horn, blowing four times, signaling for a safe approach. *Drums. Drums. Drums.* The ship's watch helped us keep pace as we rowed slowly and eagerly to shore and the safety of the fjord.

"We're home brothers, victory and glory is ours! Make your people proud, backs straight, chins up," exclaimed Mar as he raised his right fist into the air. Some of us were still bleeding upon the deck of the ship, but despite our pain, we showed none to our people. No weakness, no sign of discomfort, only pride as warriors returning gallantly from the fields of battle. Our oars moved effortlessly through the water as we rowed anxiously to find land and see familiar faces of loved ones.

As we approached the dock several more dark figures emerged from the warm village dwellings of Bjorgvin. One tall and slender figure with long chestnut brown hair raised her hand into the air, waving slowly back and forth. "Welcome home, exalted sons of Bjorgvin. We have missed you greatly in our hall as of late," the woman's gentle voice said. I quickly ran my fingers through my hair and pulled my beard down to tame the long locks. I wanted to be presentable before the ladies of Bjorgvin caught a glimpse of me.

Bjorgvin was a scanty fishing village off the coast of the Northern Territories which was ruled by a Warrior King of the Northmen. While the place seemed too inhospitable to most, we carved a home and a lifestyle completely our own out of this rugged terrain. Surrounded by beautiful mountain passes that cut across the land like black curtains, thick dark forests, said to contain ghastly trolls, flesh-eating hob goblins, and spellbound witches. The village homes were nestled amongst the sheer cliffs that rose into the sky dotted with snowcapped mountains. Usable farming land in Bjorgvin was limited, so many of us struck out during the raids to make our own fortunes elsewhere. Even our leader Rurik could see the disadvantages and lack of resources in our homeland. Many of our brethren ventured far beyond our lands and never made their way home. We all dreamed that perhaps they settled down somewhere in a new glorious land abundant in riches, mead, and women. More than likely, they were killed, or drowned by the sea god Aegir.

Our damaged longship littered with arrow heads and ash smacked boisterously against the harbor and those few of us uninjured eagerly jumped to the dock. You could hear the loud bangs and thuds from the weight of our bodies slamming against the wooden planks. *Many thanks to Odin*, I thought to myself. I had finally stepped on familiar ground and death had not come over me on this campaign. We quickly tied the ship to the dock, working the wet ropes against iron crosses until the vessel moved no more.

Emerging from the Great Hall, a group of women approached the dock in a very organized fashion, almost ceremoniously: two lines, with one woman behind the next. These women, these hardened women, were striking, slender and physically fit. They walked with pride and a great sense of purpose everywhere they ventured. Their sharp focused eyes, fair skin, and dark long flowing hair was such an astounding site that foreigners often asked if they were Volva, clearly unbound by the laws of any man. Norse women were well known to be equal and in some cases greater in status, coin and property than their male counterparts. It is even said that a Woman Queen once existed in the lands long ago forgotten, lost to the great ice for eternity. The Woman Queen's husband passed away and with the support of his followers, she ruled until her dying day. I cautiously laughed at the thought, considering the company that was about to greet us.

"Get the ship unloaded, move our spoils and slaves to the Great Hall so we may share our prizes of battle with our brothers and sisters," Rurik commanded with his arms in the air.

"And what have you brought for me this time, my love?" a woman's voice called.

Putting down his axe, Rurik gazed beyond the port watch and men unloading the ship. He saw his bride, Kenna, waiting patiently.

"What did you bring me, my love? Treasure, thrall, land perhaps?" asked Kenna. Kenna and Rurik have been together for nearly twenty seasons and were no strangers to being apart during raid season. Kenna often kept herself busy hunting and foraging while the men were gone. It was the duty of the women to not only to provide for the village and keep them well fed, but to preserve its safety in absence of its protectors. It was not unusual to see the women as they were now, spear in hand and shield on their backs.

"For you, I present another thrall, to toil in cold while you enjoy the fruits of life that you so rightly deserve." Rurik tugged harshly on a rope from behind his back. A small slave girl bound by the wrists moved forward whimpering with her eyes fixed firmly to the ground. Kenna stood there silently staring at the slave girl with contempt. Once free, now a thrall, she was no more than the age of nine.

"Slave girl, give me your hands at once," commanded Kenna. Without hesitation the slave girl reached out her hands and showed her palms to Kenna. "Just as I thought, not a single callous. She's spoiled, perhaps a once-wealthy child. I can't use her in the fields! She's useless to me." Kenna was clearly disappointed with the lack of hardiness in the young girl.

"Calm yourself, love. She will do just fine. The young ones can always learn new tricks." Rurik gave the rope to one of his men and the slave girl, frightened and alone, was dragged off for safe keeping. "And this," Rurik said, removing a gold bracelet from his pocket, as he grasped Kenna's slender wrist and slid it down her arm until it gently stopped against her smooth milky white skin, "is a gift for you my love." Kenna smiled from ear to ear, the crows' feet briefly showing her age. The bracelet was unlike anything she had seen from the artists and craftsman of her realm. Engraved with the name of it's now deceased owner, Esja, depicting inscriptions of flowers and leaves. Perhaps a moment in time captured in gold and now claimed by its Norse overlords. Kenna moved her long chestnut brown hair behind her ear to have a better look.

"It's beautiful, my love, thank you. Freya has truly blessed me to have a man such as you." Kenna placed her hands on Rurik's shoulders to look upon his body. "And how do you fair, my husband? Are you injured? Did you bring everyone home safely?" asked Kenna as she moved her hand slowly across Rurik's face tracing a fresh wound.

"Aye, just a scratch to my leg. Several of the men were fortunate enough to bravely journey to Valhalla this night. We will honor our warrior brothers with a proper burial ceremony at tomorrow's dawn. They fought bravely as warriors of Odin and so we must honor the gods." Kenna looked down at the wound Rurik was nursing on his leg.

"You're injured!" exclaimed Kenna. "Come with me, we will treat that immediately before you catch sickness." She tugged on his fur cloak.

Rurik stepped back. "Not now, woman. I can't appear weak in front of the men. Wait until we are done unloading. Then you can nurse anything you wish," Rurik said with a smile. I laughed under my breath watching the old married couple banter back and forth. Their playfulness always kept the village in high spirits. As much as I favored Kenna as a caretaker, she was not my blood mother; that woman had died giving birth to me long ago. Kenna was from a neighboring tribe, the Jarl bartered peace by having Rurik marry the Chieftains daughter. Luckily for me and the village, it was a good match.

"Stubborn old fool, you are. Mark my words, your pride will be the death of you." Kenna leaned over and hugged her husband gently. Tilting her head on his neck, her face cringed and she quickly stepped back. "And before you come to bed, take a hot bath my love. You stink of death." Kenna smiled.

Rurik ignored Kenna's remarks and turned towards the men, standing straight and proud with both hands placed firmly on his hips. "Bring up the beast!" he commanded pointing towards the rear prow.

Kenna slowly cocked her head to one side. "Beast? What beast?" she asked with sudden wonder. Rurik just stood there and smiled. I ran with Jareth to the rear prow alongside the dock. Kenna scrambled after us to see what we were doing. Orbrecht the Healer tossed us several ropes from the ship and we dragged the Serpent of the North Sea to the dock's edge. Kenna shrieked. "In the name of... what the hellheim is that gruesome thing? Where did it come from?"

"From the icy depths. From the deepest depths of Aegir's kingdom ," replied Rurik.

The beast was too heavy to pull up on the docks. We dragged the net along the back side of the harbor towards the rocky shore. I stared at the creature intensely waiting for it to suddenly come back to life and swallow me whole. Its eyes, wide open, were darkened and reeled in the back of its skull. The creature's body reached the shore and we pulled together dragging its immense corpse closer to Rurik.

A crowd of excited village people began to gather and Rurik placed his hand on his sword in case the beast returned from deaths embrace. "That's it, boys. Lay it out here and remove the net." Rurik motioned to a place on the shore near my feet. Several men arrived on the beach with spears readied. "That's it, stretch it out; I want to see this beast for what it is. Let the Gods and people of Bjorgvin know that we, brave men of Bjorgvin, slayed this beast!" The villagers looked on in terror and disbelief, some covering their faces for fear of what this creature could unleash upon them. I gripped the netting tightly, the lines pulling at my skin, and stretched out the beast along the shore with Jareth's help. The creature was massive, twice the length of the longship and nearly as thick. As I reached the tail end, I could see several small sharks had attached themselves to the hideous beast; they had chewed away at the monster's skin, leaving only fragments of what used to be a tail along the shore. The only thing still fully intact was the head and upper body.

"Jareth, fetch several torches. I want everyone to see what their sons have brought home for them. This is a trophy to be admired, not just by our people but the Gods as well!" Jareth ran up the shoreline and fetched two torches from the ports watch. The light of the torches reflected brightly off the slimy and smooth skin of the beast. It was no lizard, nor fish, nor shark. Its skin was completely smooth like a newly made sword, devoid of any scales or imperfections. "Gut this beast. I want to see into this creature's belly." Rurik was determined to understand this creature. Jareth tapped my shoulder and handed me his axe. I lifted the blade behind my head and swiftly struck the beast's gut. The axe stuck in place with a dulled thud. I pulled, cut, tore, and slashed at the serpent's flesh until the innards could be seen.

"Knife! Get me a knife!" I said as I stretched out my hand and Jareth handed me his blade. Reaching into the dark carcass I grasped the giant fleshy ball that was the sea creature's stomach. Despite being dragged in the sea for hours, steam rose from the fresh wounds and the innards were warm to the touch. I stabbed and tore back and forth until fluid and undigested food spewed forth. Out of the creature's belly came fish, seaweed, and the badly spoiled bodies of several of our brothers. I gagged, the smell was vile. "What a stench!" I exclaimed holding back my own vomit. The men's bodies had been partially digested, unrecognizable, just pieces of rotting flesh.

"Axe." Rurik extended his arm and Kenna placed a finely decorated bearded axe into his waiting hand. "Look here, people of Bjorgvin! Your sons have raided faraway lands to bring you wealth, riches, and in our journeys we slayed this beast, this foul creature sent upon us from Helheim itself. Your sons fought bravely, many dying in an attempt to be the first to claim the glory of ending this creature's reign over the sea. United, we conquered this beast, but it was Audan, your brave son, who gave the final blow that ended this creature's terror. I sever this beasts head in his honor and in honor of the victorious fallen!" Rurik turned away from the crowd staring down at the serpent. He hacked and hacked at the beast's neck, peeling skin and flesh back like an onion until its skin gave way to bone. Rurik struck feverishly, yelling and spitting until finally the monsters head rolled off its body; axe piercingly striking the pebble laden ground below.

A cheer rang out from the men. "Audan, pick up your prize and carry it to the hall for all to see," my father told me proudly. Looking below upon the head of the beast, I reached down and grasped it by the spines on the back of its head and lifted it high. The jaw dropped open exposing its sharp fangs. The village people stepped back quickly, gasping in panic, but the men just laughed.

"So much fear for a dead thing! Perhaps we should kill it again and bring it with us on our next raid?" Jareth mused. "Come, brother, take your march of victory." I walked up towards the halls with my prize, the head of a dead monster, ready to hang it where it could be seen by all.

Kenna's expression went from that of happiness to seriousness. She motioned to some of the women to help with unloading the ship. Kenna's girls nodded and quickly moved towards the longship grabbing anything they could carry back to the hall. The men ceremoniously carried the bodies of the dead off the ship and lay them gently on the dock, one by one. "Keep their feet pointing north; we wouldn't want the Draugr to take hold," remarked a superstitious Mar.

The Draugr, as it is foretold on the ancient runes of Bjorgvin, was an old myth of undead Norse spirits who take hold of those whom are not properly buried. The warrior corpses were dry, ashy and pale, each one displaying the injury that had led to their death. Thrall came down from the village with a litter for each of our fallen, the broad wooden planks making it easier to transfer the bodies for preparation of their final journey. A male slave grasped the sword of one deceased comrade; he carefully placed it on the warrior's chest and wrapped his arms around it.

One by one, the bodies were removed from the docks. "Kenna," Rurik said in almost a whisper. "See that the bodies are properly prepared for their burial ceremony. Some of these boys were bastards. They will need a mother's touch to see them on their way." Kenna bowed her head in obedience to Rurik's wishes and followed the slave girls to a long house next to the Great Hall.

As Rurik's wife walked into the long house and saw that the bodies of the fallen warriors had already been properly laid down, feet facing north. The bodies were prepared immediately to be ready for the morning's rituals. Each one bathed in water, oils, and perfumes, then a cleansing of its wounds. Kenna motioned to one of the young slave girls. "Fetch some fresh linen. I'll not have our men eating in Valhalla with blood stained cloth. They must be properly dressed when meeting All-Father Odin."

The slave girl nodded "Right away, m' lady." Kenna watched over the preparations intently and with great care; ensuring that no details of the funeral rites were over looked.

Each slain warrior lay in a small fishing boat barely longer than their bodies. The thrall adorned the boats with flowers and vines from the dark forest. Their shield, sword, and spear lay proudly upon their chests, as if heading back into a glorious battle. The slave girls carried over food and earthen jars of mead that the warriors would take into the afterlife, to present to All-Father Odin in Valhalla as tribute, and placed them carefully in the boats. A large tree trunk of a man, Bear, walked into the long house pulling six young slave girls tied one after another to a rope.

"What is this?" asked Kenna.

Bear replied with a deep raspy voice, "Sacrifices for the glorious dead." Bear stepped forward, tying the rope to a wooden column and walked outside to return to the Great Hall. A human sacrifice, a retainer. Each girl would be sacrificed on top of their dead men and sent with him on his voyage to the afterlife. As they served in life, they too would serve in death. The slave girls were giggling, laughing, and appeared disoriented. They had been given mushroom tea to calm their nerves and to prepare them for the final journey.

"Very well, girls. Fetch a fresh and hardy supper for our retainers. They must eat well this night. It's their last meal amongst the living." Kenna grinned for a moment at the young slave girls, as if to show them some comfort but quickly turned away to avoid any attachment and left for the Great Hall.

* * *

Striding confidently up the cold and wet stones, we could hear a merry echo carried aloft on the chilled winds. Passing several small hovels, I rounded the corner and was greeted by a warm glow. The Great Hall, standing before us, shown brightly in the dark of night. I grinned at the familiar sights of our home, as did my brothers. Their spirits immediately lifted by the promise of food, Bjorgvin mead, and women.

"Come on, lads, we don't want to keep them waiting!" Jareth said as he pulled me back and ran ahead like a child.

The colossal door to the Great Hall towered over our heads, solid oak slabs adorned with decorative iron and rune inscriptions meant to drive away evil spirits and welcome the favor of All-Father Odin. We pounded merrily on the door and a loud, raspy voice called from inside, "The Great Hall demands that formalities be observed. If ye be a friend of Bjorgvin then what be the words that will give safe passage to enter?" We looked at one another visibly confused because we knew; there was no password to get into the Great Hall. The Great Hall was meant for all people of Bjorgvin.

"And whom am I answering to?" I asked with an authoritative tone. The large wooden door unlocked slowly, the sound of iron bars sliding against one another until the door opened. The large raspy voice called out once more and an axe, broad and shining suddenly appeared in the doorway.

"Who dares to challenge me? Who thinks himself to be a better man than I? Show yourselves or do you not have the balls to do so?" We quickly jumped back and reached for our daggers ready to fight. Then, the loud and raspy man's face became clear and familiar in the light of the Hall.

"Bear! Is that you old friend?" I asked, hardly able to contain my excitement. The axe dropped to the ground with a loud bang. Laughter erupted within our party, as we released grip on our daggers and gave hearty handshakes to all. Bear, for obvious reasons, was called Bear because he was the largest and hairiest Viking in the whole village. He stood one and a half men tall, with thick, dark, wiry hair and a beard that fell all the way down to his belt. Bear was also known to be a hugger. Not something that most men of the village were fond of, but when Bear hugged you, there was no escape. He quickly extended his arm in the direction of the hall.

"Welcome friends, welcome, welcome. By Odin, arrived just in time. The newest batch of mead has been delivered! We've been drinking all day."

"Undoubtedly, old friend," replied Jareth. Jareth stepped forward and tapped Bears shoulder causing the behemoth of a man to sway back and forth until he found his balance. "What's the occasion?" asked Jareth.

"Occasion?" Bear roared into a deep laugh that started in his belly. "Who needs an occasion to drink the milk of the gods? You've been at sea far too long, brother. Come inside and drink with me. We must celebrate our great victory!"

"We're happy to see you old friend. How fair you this fine day?" I asked.

"There is singing, laughter, feast, Bjorgvin mead and Bjorgvin women. I have no grievances this day, old friend," Bear replied. "And you, my friend, you seem to be in a celebrating mood? Did you return from your raids a wealthy man?" he asked.

"Wealthy in treasure no, but wealthy in fame…" I held up the Sea Monsters head proudly displaying it to Bear who was too drunk to notice I had been carrying it the whole time. Bear stepped back and eyes widened at the ghastly sight spitting his mead into his beard.

"By Thor's hammer, what the Helheim is that thing?" he shouted.

"We were attacked by this monster as we crossed the North Sea. I gave the killing blow that ended its murderous rage." Bear, evidently impressed, smacked me on the back sending me forward two or three steps.

"Well done, my boy, well done indeed! Tonight, you drink on me. No hero of Bjorgvin should have to sacrifice his coin while he celebrates such a heroic victory." Bear lifted his arm into the air. "Ingrid! Ingrid! Damn you wench, where did you run off to? We require drink!"

The Great Hall was a sight to behold and a festival for the senses. Carvings of gods and ancient battles littered the walls of the hall. As you entered, the nose was visited by the scent of a wood burning fire, dried cod fish from the docks, and a goose slowly roasting in the middle of the hall atop a glorious fire pit. Various animal pelts, particularly black bear, lined the walls and benches. The kin who had been there for some time paid no mind to us, perhaps too drunk to care. As we walked further into the hall cups were handed to us. Drink began to flow and our weary party found the strength to chase the women about. Bear eagerly escorted us to an empty table.

A short and curvy woman blessed with ample bosom approached our table. "Ingrid, clear this mess, would you darling? These fine warriors have been at sea far too long and are ready to feast and celebrate their glorious victory!"

"Welcome home, boys. We're glad you made it back safe. Did anyone get hurt on your travels?" Before we could reply Ingrid could see the worn looks upon our faces. "I see. Well then, you better sit down and rest your bones. I'll bring round some food and mead." Bear reached over to the table next to us removing a large jug and placing it at our table. Ingrid quickly grabbed a rag, wiping down the table and filling our wooden cups. Tired and weary, we eagerly sat down and dropped or weapons to the floor. Our swords and shields made a crashing sound as they met their resting place. We reached for our cups and drank heartily. Rare an occasion it was to drop our weapons to the floor, often burdened by their weight and always at the ready for a fight.

"So, shall we drink to your glorious kill, Audan? I have not seen a beast like that since your father and I were children off in the woods killing dire wolves. I thought perhaps all the monsters of old had been killed off years ago by brave warriors such as yourself," said Bear.

"All but one my friend." I looked up at our company and stood to my feet. "You did well, men, you fought bravely. Drink to Vallis, for he surely is drinking in the halls of Valhalla, surrounded by gold, food, and women."

"To Vallis!" the men repeated, loud and excited.

"To Vallis!" The warriors at surrounding tables, having heard our tribute to our fallen warrior brother began to pound their fists on the timber. Rurik walked in behind us and sat at our table.

Father looked over the table and the bench I was sitting on. "Do you have it? Do you have the head? Let me see it." I reached down and placed the head on the table. The green skin of the monster was beginning to dry and turn pale. "Now that is a sight. Stand up my boy." Rurik held up the monster's head in the air, grabbed my left hand and held it to the air as well. "Brother and sisters, look upon the head of the beast, slain by none other than our son, Audan! A kill worthy of a hero!" The crowd broke out in cheer and pounding of fists commenced once more. Rurik placed the creature's head at the footsteps of the Chieftains throne so he could see it upon arrival. I was proud this day but felt a warriors guilt, knowing that others had fought more bravely than I. Being recognized at home was a humbling experience and not one I would soon forget.

"Brothers and sisters! Children of Odin, let us celebrate and rejoice the return of our brave warriors, and let us ask of Odin, the Splendid Ruler, to allow our fallen brothers into his home, the halls of Valhalla!" Rurik raised a horn of mead into the air and drank heartily. The villagers cheered and warriors raised their fists into the air. "Celebrate my brothers and sisters. I have a gift for you, milk of the gods! Drink, celebrate, honor these Great Halls." Rurik took the first drink and willingly passed it on. Milk of the gods indeed, a powerful herbal remedy made by Kenna. It makes men fearless on the battlefield, turns cowards brave, drives womankind into a carnal frenzy and for most, bring about strange visions.

A stunning stranger approached me from behind and placed her slender hand on my shoulder. "Will you drink with me, brave warrior?" I turned to find Sada standing over me. Sada handed a simple drinking horn to me. I looked down at this concoction carefully; it seemed like murky water and smelled of animal shit. Probably the best batch Kenna had brewed in several seasons. Leaning back my head, I drank quickly to avoid the taste. It burned going down like fire in the pit of my gullet. "Here, drink this." Sada handed me a horn of sweet mead to chase down the remedy.

Wiping the mead from my chin, I slammed the horn on the table. "You are too kind to me, woman; a prize greater than any slain beast!" The concoction worked quickly. I stared at Sada and thought to myself how beautiful she is. Her long brown hair and big brown eyes were unmatched. I often found myself drowning in her gaze, losing all sense of time and place.

"You look love struck, or is it the brew taking hold of you already?" Sada's words sounded blurred to me. I chuckled under my breath and began to sway in place. "Come; let us sit down before you hurt yourself. Let the drink settle." Sada grasped my arm and guided me to the ground outside for fresh air. Leaning against a bench and staring up to the heavens above, I could catch a glimpse of the gods shining brightly in the sky. Sada leaned into my shoulder and placed her lips gently against my ear, and whispered, "Will you join me alone my love? It's been too long that you have been away at sea and I have need."

Cocking my head to the left, I found myself drowning again in her big brown eyes. She began to run her finger tips up my arms, and without noticing they were on my lips, moving gently back and forth. Her fingertips were soft like a gentle breeze. I pounced on Sada like a wolf would its prey, rolling in the dirt causing her to shriek and giggle. "You brute," she blurted. Stopping against a log, we grinded and trembled against one another. "Not here. Come, follow me," Sada urged. I stood up extending my arm to help her up; each of us wiping the fallen leaves off our cloths. "This way." She motioned in the direction of the woods and then ran to them.

Running slightly downhill, Sada disappeared behind a cloak of thick trees. I treaded cautiously until I saw a glow against the forest. Sada had a small fire and provisions waiting for us. "You always think ahead, don't you?" I said to Sada with a look of desire.

"I try, like I said, it has been a long time and we have much to catch up on." Sada laid out a pelt of a wolf on the ground, slowly arranging herself on top of it for me to admire. With her full brown eyes staring in love and wonder, "Does this vision please you, my love?"

"Can you not tell, woman?" I said and then she pulled me down with her.

"Now, where were we?" Sada said as she grinned that wide smirk of hers as she pulled me between her legs. I grasped underneath her knees tightly and ran my hands upward to feel her soft skin. I pulled her skirt up, exposing her smooth creamy thighs. Sada's body tensed and pushed back against me.

"So, it is that how you want to play?" I asked as I pinned her hands down by her wrists.

"Please stop playing and just take me already. I can't wait any longer!" Sada freed her wrists and grasped my trousers, pulling them down just far enough to leave me exposed. She reached down and grasped me firmly. "So, you did miss me," she said before she grabbed the back of my hair and tugged tightly to pull me into her lips. It had been so long since I'd had the sweet taste of her mouth in mine, I felt at that moment if I had gone any longer I may have forgotten it. Sada freed me for a moment, making me wonder if something was wrong. She reached up to her chest and uncovered her beautiful breasts, so supple and luscious.

Without hesitation, I began sucking on her glorious bosom, using my hand to caress the other. Sada squealed out in bliss, begging me to ravage every part of her. "You want it that bad, do you?"

"Oh please, I need you my love," she cried. I tore the remainder of her clothes off as she finished pulling my bottoms completely down and wrapped her lips around my manhood.

"Aaggghhh!" I moaned out in pleasure. I couldn't take it anymore. I pulled Sada away from me and turned her around so she was laying facedown. I climbed on top of her with the softness of the fur surrounding our bodies. I pulled one of her legs up at the knee to expose her privy area. I touched her there for a brief moment to feel if she was ready for me and she flinched in excitement. I thrust forward, delving into her from behind, and Sada wailing out in sheer joy. I began kissing her neck, re-membering how much she enjoyed the feel of my beard on her skin. As we moved together all the feelings of love and devotion came flooding through me. How I cared for this woman and she for me.

Four
The Great Hall

The next morning, I awoke lying beside a sleeping Sada with a pounding head; that damn brew had taken its toll. *Nothing a little more mead won't cure*, I thought, as I sat up and looked around. I realized somehow, we had made it back to our hovel; not quite sure how or when that happened. *Fucking brew!* I stumbled from bed, looking for my clothes.

As I dressed I heard, "And where do you think you are off to, my love?"

I cleared my throat. "To see the Chieftain," I said under my breath.

"You mean your father? About what might I ask?" Sada asked, sounding suspicious.

"About business, woman. It is none of your concern," I said as I shoved a small piece of dried fish into my mouth ready to make off for the day.

Sada stood up quickly, a fur skin draped over her naked body. She delicately dropped the fur to the floor, walked over to me and pressed her warm skin against mine. "Are you planning on leaving me again? I don't know how much longer I can keep waiting for you." I looked away, rolling my eyes and waiting for her woman banter to be finished. "I see," she said looking down. "The decision is already made."

"I need you to understand, the Chieftain is our chance to elevate ourselves, to riches and reward. Isn't that what you want?" I exclaimed.

Sada grinned. "Yes, but…."

"Then let me go about my business. I'll be back before supper. Keep yourself busy."

Sada reached her warm hands down my trousers. "Are you sure you don't want to stay just a bit longer? I don't think you have finished with me yet." Sada quickly jerked me to one side. My grimace turned to a smile as I looked over my shoulder at Sada's eager eyes.

"I have to go, but I'll be back for you shortly." I kissed her lips, wrapping my hands gently around her neck.

"Are we forgetting something?" she asked. I stopped in my tracks annoyed until I realized we had the funeral ceremony to attend to.

"Fucking brew!" I said rubbing my forehead. "Get dressed, we're already late." Sada quickly dressed and we made our way down to the shoreline.

As we reached the stony shore, we came across a sleeping Jareth, covered by two naked women. The fire pit from the night before was still smoking; no doubt containing some small remnants of embers. I headed over to Jareth who was remained buried deep in breasts and covered in woolen cloth. Reaching down near the fire pit, I picked up a bucket of water and hurriedly threw it onto his face for a laugh. Jareth sprung straight up. "By the gods, I'll see you burn!" He opened one eye with his wet hair covering the other to find me standing in front him with a grin on my face and a bucket in my hand. "Fucking cock! What did you do that for?" exclaimed Jareth.

"Did we enjoy our night of mead and women?" I said still laughing slightly.

"Oh, did I Brother." Jareth retorted with a smirk.

"Time to rouse yourself; we have fallen brothers to honor." Jareth threw the arms and legs of the women off him before he stood, exposing his fully naked body to Sada and I. "For the Gods sake, cover yourself Brother!" I yelled in disgust. Sada giggled. "We will see you at the ceremony."

At the beachhead our Gothi and Seer, the holy man, arrived dressed in raven feathers and carried a scepter with a ram's head adorning the top. He looked at each of the slave girls and asked them as a group, "Are you ready to be sacrificed? Do you give yourself willingly to join your masters as they venture to the gates of Valhalla?" The girls continued to giggle and laugh even at the seriousness of such a question. The Seer slammed the bottom of his scepter on the ground. "I'll ask you again. Are you ready to be sacrificed? Do you give yourself willingly to join your masters as they venture to the gates of Valhalla?" The slave girls straightened up this time, their faces and demeanor became serious, unnerving. The fear in their eyes became apparent as one of the girls dropped to her knees wailing and crying. The other retainers looked on, so intoxicated from the tea they knew not how to respond.

"Please no. I don't want to die. I want to go home." The girl on the ground pleaded. The Seer struck her on the back with his scepter, sending her body crashing to the ground below. He kneeled down using his stick to balance himself.

"Console yourself woman or I will ensure your sacrifice is long and arduous. Drink the tea, it will free you of your fears and speed your journey to All-Father. Do you understand child?"

The girl in pain and panic replied with tears and spit dripping from her face, "Yes Seer." The old man stood, raising the girl to her feet and placed a drinking horn in her hands. The girl looked down at the tea, raised it to her mouth and drank hurriedly. It would all be over soon.

"Then, I bid you farewell on your journey. May Odin watch over you and welcome you with open arms to his Great Hall." The Seer removed his ceremonial blade from its sheath and one by one swiftly slit the throats of each slave girl. Their bodies fell to the ground as the life began to escape them, shaking and trembling, blood pouring out, until there was movement no more. As the village people cheered and danced, other thrall picked up the bodies of the slave girls and placed one in each of the funeral boats. *What a waste of life*, I thought to myself. These girls could have lived long happy lives, instead we hand them over to our angry and vengeful gods. I don't think I will ever understand it.

Rurik stepped forward to commence his speech honoring the dead. "People of Bjorgvin, today we honor the glorious dead. Fathers, sons, and brothers slain in magnificent battle. There is no better way for a warrior to die than to meet the Valkyries head on and ascend to Valhalla, hall of the honored dead. Gaze upon their now lifeless bodies knowing they will be welcomed with open arms by All-Father Odin. Until the Ragnarok!"

The village erupted repeating Rurik's call. "Until the Ragnarok!"

Norse warriors stood knee deep in the water holding each boat, awaiting the placement of the girls' bodies. After the fresh corpses were loaded, the warriors pushed them out to the open water. The outgoing tide carried the boats swiftly further and further away from the shore. "Archers," Rurik commanded. Ten archers raised their bows in the air with flaming arrows and sent the balls of fire falling atop the funeral ships. They caught a blaze and glowed a magnificent red atop the water. What a glorious site to behold. The flames roared consuming everything in sight. We continued to watch until the bright lights flickered to nothingness, disappearing over the horizon.

Once the ceremony had concluded I turned away to address overdue business with the Chieftain. Walking through the village courtyard beneath a brilliant sun, I passed the blacksmith who was busy at his trade. "Good day, Audan. How find you this morning?" asked Njord cheerfully.

"I find myself very well, friend, and you?" Njord the blacksmith pounded his hammer upon an anvil and hot iron. Sparks and embers flew all around, and the fire cracked with each strike of the hammer.

"I am well, Audan. The gods have smiled upon me this day. No doubt they have sent you my way me for a reason." Njord placed down his hammer and turned towards a large earthen furnace. "Come and have a look Audan at what I have created." I was hoping it was breakfast, for my stomach growled and I felt famished. Knocking back some stones, Njord dug into the furnace, pulling out hot coal with a shovel until finally reaching a stone pot surrounded by hot embers.

"What is it?" I asked with much curiosity. Njord grasped his hammer and broke open the cylinder pot until a glowing round piece of metal could be seen.

"This my friend, is our new weapon against our enemy."

"A new metal? Is this a kind of iron?" I asked.

"Yes, Audan, a very special kind of iron. Made from the same iron base but forged together with coal. The coal pulls the impurities from the iron. It will make a sword of the finest quality. It will bend to great angles and will not break as easily as iron weapons." Njord was unmistakably excited about his great discovery.

"How did you come to find this, Njord?" I asked. Njord's eyes grew wide and his smile wider.

"It came to me in my sleep. In a vision, Brother Thor appeared before me with the great hammer Mjolnir pounding on an anvil and guided me on how to create a superior fighting weapon with which to defeat our greatest of foes." With a puzzled look on my face I had a trying time finding the words to describe my doubt for Njord's astonishing claim of divine intervention. I respected the beliefs of others and respected the gods as much as I had to in order to get by; but after everything I've seen in my lifetime I found it hard to believe that the gods were involved in as much as people would lead you to believe.

"Thor, the god of lightning and thunder, showed you, Njord the Blacksmith of Bjorgvin, how to craft possibly the strongest metal in existence?" I asked, not masking my disbelief.

"Yes," he replied sternly, bothered by my doubt. I placed my hand on my belly and began laughing hysterically. Njord was offended. "You doubt me, brother? Have I ever led you down a crooked path?"

I laughed deep from within my belly until I caught my breath. "No, Njord, I don't doubt your skill as a blacksmith, but Thor; come now. It was just a dream, a vision in your sleep. How do you know it was the gods? You must have drunk from the same bowl that I did last night. I swear I saw a flying goat."

Njord smirked out of one corner of his face. "Then would you be willing to place a wager on the quality of the sword?"

"What kind of wager do you suggest?" I had little coin to spare but thought this to be an easy bet in my favor.

"My finished sword against your iron sword in a test of strength; should it be my weapon that fails, I'll pay you its worth in full, but if I win, you pay me twice its worth." The smile from my face quickly faded and turned to the seriousness of losing a wager to a man who knew everything there is to know about swords.

"You're serious?" Njord placed his hammer down upon his anvil and stood up straight.

"Dead serious. Is it a wager, brother? I don't have all day. Patrons, you know." Njord extended his large coal covered arm for an agreement. I paused for a moment but pride won me over. I extended my arm and grasped Njord's forearm shaking it confidently.

"It's a wager then," I said only half confident.

"Excellent, be sure to have your money ready, Audan, and no bartering. I have all the skins, pots, and daggers I need. Coin only this time. Unless you're willing to barter with that lovely young thing in your hovel?" said Njord jokingly. I scoffed and smiled at his bold statement.

"When will your new blade be ready for its trial?" I asked.

"Tomorrow; on Woden's day before the setting of Sol. Meet me here, and bring some of your men to witness my victory. I'm always looking for new patrons and I think they will be interested in what I have to show them. A good blacksmith is also a good merchant you know." Njord's confidence started to worry me, but if what he said was true, purchasing a weapon like that at twice the price of my own was probably worth the loss in coin.

When I arrived at the Great Hall, I saw several of my brother's asleep inside, no doubt their heads still pounding like mine from the night's celebration. Stepping over half draped naked bodies, I laughed in amusement until I heard a voice from over my shoulder. "Audan, come sit with me, son." It was my father sedentary in his Chieftain's throne foot mounted atop the sea beast's head. The green skin was dry and pale. "What a sight— a kill worthy of a hero," Rurik said to me looking pleased.

"It pleases me to make you proud, Father. I could not have brought the beast down without the help of the men and the blessing of the gods," I said to him with a slight hint of gloom.

"Why are you not more pleased with yourself? This is a great victory that will be celebrated by our people through the ages. You are a hero!" he said in response to my obvious upset.

"Father, what of Orbrecht? Do we allow him to live?" I asked.

"He did his duty as our healer, it was not his to decide if our men live or die. We will need Orbrecht on our next voyage. Our brothers fought bravely and died as a North Man should; with his eyes open and a blade in his hand."

We were celebrated by our people as great warriors returning from battle. But the truth was, we fought few warriors. In order to keep our families and clans well supplied, we would leave home to raid the villages of neighboring countries. People defending their homeland would be met with the fierceness and the violent nature of the Northmen. From time to time, we found ourselves battling soldiers or village guards who could put up some resistance, but none could match our skill and thirst for blood. "Speed, intensity, and violence," Rurik would preach to us each night as children. Indeed, it was an effective method.

The Norse tactic was simple: attack from the sea, swiftly, and quietly. Make our way to the nearest village, sack it for goods, treasure, slaves, weapons, women, and destroy what we could with fire, disappearing into the fog. At home we were regarded as heroes bringing fresh supply and riches to our people. But I knew better. Not all our conquests were filled with riches and glory. Some were filled with death, despair, and the wonton destruction of entire families. Some of these villages were filled with people just like the ones at Bjorgvin. Sons, Daughters, Fathers, Mothers, Brothers, and Sisters. Families defending their homes and almost always, to the death. *Maybe one day there will be a better way*, I said to myself.

"No matter, my son. You will still die in battle and go to Valhalla with our fallen brothers," Rurik declared.

Suddenly, the towering doors of the hall burst open with a loud bang. The drunken and half asleep lifted their heads to the crashing sound. The cold wind blew inside and just beyond the door was the shadow of a dark and grim-looking stranger. The man stumbled forward into the light, moving awkwardly toward the guards. The room fell silent, waiting for the stranger to say something, anything. The man stood straight now, staring at the room with his large black eyes. His mouth opened, "We are under siege…" the stranger whispered. He fell forward onto one of the guards. The guard reached around the man's body to brace him from his fall, but what the guard thought would have been the man's back, was a dagger, protruding from up high.

The guard placed the stranger on his stomach as he exhaled his final breath. The watchman from the docks ran into the hall.

"To arms, to arms! Finn raiders are sacking the village!" screamed the watchman. Every man immediately sobered up at the thought of an epic battle. Spears, swords, shield, and axe flailed about as if a wild herd of boar bristling with tusks of iron. I strapped on my helm, unsheathed my axe and ran outside with the other men. My armor immediately weighed down upon me and I loathed having to put it back on so soon. Not more than a day's time had passed since I had been home and dropped my armor in the hall. Rushing outside I looked around, not a sound could be heard; the entire village had fallen silent.

In the distance I spotted Jareth and Bear running towards me. I turned and pointed. "Jareth, Bear, you come with me and stay close," I commanded.

"To arms, to arms!" the men shouted inside the Great Hall. Swords, axes, and spears were retrieved from the weapon's rack; men clamored to the docks and sprinted down to the homes along the shores and winding banks.

As we approached the beach, fires burned brightly atop long houses and hovels, as I heard screams of pain begging for help from the flames. We needed to help our people; I ran towards burning thatch and kicked down the doors. I stopped quickly and the dirt fell out from under my feet. A scream came from just around the corner. A woman stood in terror watching her home burn. "My child is in there! Please, somebody save her!"

Placing my shield in front of me, I leapt at the door and bashed down the burning timber. "Where are you?" I yelled out. Flames were everywhere spreading on the lumber, smoke traveled into my lungs, the black taking over. Embers flew into my eyes, and I could barely see anything. Coughing nearby, a child could be heard whimpering in the corner. "I've got you. Let's get you out of here." I picked up the child like a sack of wheat, threw her over my back and ran quickly for the door. A beam fell behind me striking the ground and the roof collapsed just as I leapt outside. Dirt and dust filled the air choking my breath. I could hear the mother screaming but could not yet see her. I stood up and walked towards the noise still holding the child tightly. The smoke cleared and I returned the little girl back to her mother.

"Thank you, brave warrior. Thank you so much. Gods be praised!" She hugged her half alive daughter, wiping the dirt from her face and chasing the tears with her fingertips.

"Look, to the docks!" a man called. In the mist, a Finn longship could be seen moving slowly away with oars pounding at the water. The mysterious ship carried a crimson flag with crossed axes, and as they rowed away one man yelled from the dark and fading ship.

"Vengeance for the loss of our brothers! For their honor and glory!"

I sprinted down to the water's edge and waded in the water up to my knees. "Come back and fight, you fucking cowards!" I yelled across the water. The earth beneath my feet began to rumble and shake. I turned back to see men on horseback flowing into the village. The warriors carried the Jarl's standard, a one-eyed wolf. Steinar, the Jarl leapt off his labored steed and angrily approached Rurik.

The Jarl grabbed Rurik by the shoulder. "Did you leave them alive? Did you take it upon yourself to spare their lives?" he asked in a desperate tone. The Jarl could not believe the look upon Rurik's face.

"A few children escaped our swords during our raid; they must have made it to the next village and alerted their kin." The Jarl dropped his head in grave disappointment of what Rurik had done.

"You brought this upon us. You fool! You know the law. If you are seen then you must hunt the ones who may warn others. How could you be so careless? This is on your head!" The Jarl demanded answers.

"My lord, the lower village is gone. Everyone is dead," a watchman reported. The Jarl dropped to his knees, and then leapt into a rage.

"Rurik, you will get the men back onto the longship, chase them down, and finish them or I will have your head. Do I make myself clear?" demanded Steinar.

We all knew what this meant: back to the cold, the harsh, and the wild. Rurik gazed at me with empty eyes and spoke softly, "Audan, gather the war council. Jareth, get provisions to the ship for an extended voyage. We're going hunting." Jareth gathered several of our war clan and headed down to the dock.

* * *

Later that afternoon men filled the Chieftain's Great Hall and we awaited the arrival of Rurik. Kenna entered the room first, and all fell silent. "Men of Bjorgvin, food and drink will be served during the gathering of the council, for now I present to you, Chieftain Rurik." All stood at this very formal presentation of our Regent.

"Sit, sit," said Rurik to the council. "I want to thank all of you for assembling on such short notice. You all know why we are here and I think that each of you know what must be done in light of this travesty."

Bear stood up and pounded his fist on the table. "We need to strike back and strike back hard. Kill every one of those bastards! Let the crows pick at their flesh and the wolves gnaw on their bones!" The room broke out in a cheer and clash of voices.

"Silence! Your Chieftain is speaking!" Jareth yelled standing from his wooden stool. Rurik placed his thumb and index finger on his face pinching the top of his nose in frustration.

Speaking with his eyes closed, Rurik used a tactful and deliberate tone. "We must strike back. Our laws demand retribution. There is no doubt that the wretched band of cowards known as the Finns must pay for the crimes they have committed against us, against our people. This cannot and will not go unpunished."

An older man stood, using a twisted cane to prop up his frail body. "Then it is decided. The few men we have left will go out and bloody themselves for reprisal against a raid that we started. Is that what I'm hearing? This battle would not be vengeance; it is a continuation of a family feud. We have but two choices, settle this dispute diplomatically or fight towards extermination. So, what will it be *hmmm*, what are you willing to give up for the people of Bjorgvin?"

The room once again fell silent as many sunk into deep thought. Mar stood and pointed at the old man. "It would be cowardly and dishonorable for us to wait or discuss this further. We must have vengeance and they must die. All-Father Odin wills it. Vengeance must be had! The Jarl himself has already given order." Mar slammed his fist on the table, spilling his mead, which trickled down to the stone floor.

Rurik stood and lifted his open hands to calm the room. "My brothers, my brothers, please. I have no intent to mull over this much longer. However, the old man is right. We risk much by setting off on another voyage. With so few actual warriors remaining we must be assured that victory will be ours. Otherwise, we leave our people defenseless to a counter-attack. Our wives will become thrall and be raped by the very men we intend to kill. We must gather more warriors from the neighboring clans, increase our strength in numbers, perhaps even recruit those we would normally leave behind due to youth or great age."

Orbrecht the Healer stood and nervously raised his hand. "If I may, my lord, I wish to volunteer to gather reinforcements for this voyage. I can leave on horseback immediately, with your permission of course." Orbrecht bowed his head and looked up slightly for Rurik's approval.

Rurik thought for a moment and tugged gently at his beard. "Very well, but take one of the slave boys with you. Should you return with less than one ship of men you would do well to not return; for I will be unkind to you. Do you understand? We cannot afford failure. The Jarl demands our success in this." Rurik dropped his head and looked up through his brow.

Orbrecht bowed. "I understand my lord, I shall return in two days' time with news of our reinforcements." Orbrecht turned and headed swiftly out the door.

The glow of the fire lit up Bear's menacing face as he stared at me. "What say you Audan, son of Rurik? How shall we best serve our enemies demise?" I was caught off guard while drinking my mead from a ram's horn. I choked for a moment, grasping the edge of the table. I quickly composed myself and stood uneasily, looking at the eager gaze of the men amongst me.

"The bastards must pay, there is no doubt about it, but we must wait for reinforcements. I'll not leave our women and children to fend for themselves in the next winter." I quickly sat down hoping that my answer, though short, would satisfy their need.

Kenna gracefully entered the room once more. "Men of Bjorgvin, food is served." Women entered from the rear walkway of the hall. The smell of fresh fish, shark, and seal wafted into our noses, making a delightful aroma. Out of the corner of my eye I saw Sada walk into the room. She smirked at me and headed straight over to deliver my meal.

"Sada," I said looking up at her enticing figure.

"M' lord," she said, as she gave a slight bow. Sada placed the meal in front of me and quickly retreated.

Kenna could be seen whispering into Rurik's ear and they both stared intently at me. What did they have planned this time? Rurik stood with half his meal in his mouth. "Audan, a word." Rurik turned and walked out of the Great Hall. I rose and took a handful of fish with me, I was starving.

Stepping out into the fresh air, I could see Rurik facing the sea with the sun at his back as it slowly set behind snowy mountains. "Come here, son. Do you see that?"

"See what, Father? The sea?" I didn't quite understand what he was looking at.

"No, son, it is your destiny, out there amongst the sea and unknown lands. Even the Seer seems to think that you are destined for greatness. I fear however that this conquest, this war that we are about to wage, will change everything. Steinar, our Jarl, in all his wisdom is sending us on a campaign that he does not expect us to return from."

"What makes you say that, Father? Is the Jarl not an honorable man?" I asked. Rurik scoffed under his breath and kicked a patch of dirt at his feet.

"Honorable?" Rurik whispered. "Honor is for men like us, son, men who have little to gain in this world. Our status in life will not elevate beyond that of warrior. Therefore, we fight, we provide for our families, and Odin willing, we die an honorable death with a blade in our hands. Men like Steinar, well, let's just say that Jarls do what must be done to maintain their place in this world. I am one of nine Chieftains in his territory. He would barely blink an eye to lose me. He could hand these lands to whomever he wished."

"Then why are we following his orders? We can fight back," I replied.

"My son, you are still too good for this world. You see things as black and white, good and bad, not the complexities that truly lie before you. If we were to refuse the Jarl's order, he would merely take our lands, our title, starve our families, rape our women and claim our children for thrall." Rurik stood atop a small boulder. "Refuse, no. We must be clever, my son. We must be strong, and wise, and everything the Jarl is not. Do you understand?"

"I think so, Father."

Rurik placed his hand on my shoulder and looked at me with steely eyes. "Very well, my son. Go about your business. We have a campaign to plan for and I need you well rested." I returned to my hovel where I hoped Sada and I would enjoy a late night of long pleasures and sleep until very late into the morning. As I entered our shelter, a bronze plate flew past my head. I quickly dodged and ducked.

"Back to sea! You are going out again, and this time not just on a raid, but to wage war on the Finns, are you mad?" Sada yelled and screamed throwing everything within arm's reach.

"Calm yourself, woman. It has to be done. Rurik has ordered it, the gods demand it and the Seer foretold it," I explained.

"The Seer? You're going to listen to that old fart and go off and die because an old man told you it was the right thing to do?" Sada fell to the ground now crying into her hands; she was inconsolable. I knelt by her side and grabbed her by the shoulders.

"You need to take hold of yourself and find your courage. This will be a dangerous voyage and an even more dangerous battle. I'll not go knowing you're angry with me. What would Frigg think of your actions?" Sada paused for a moment wiping the tears from her cheeks.

"I'm sorry, I just don't understand. You just returned from raiding their village and they came after us for retribution. There is no honor in this, just more killing." Sada, in her own way, was right but the words of the Seer taunted me, perhaps guiding me to a fate that I could not escape, no matter what decision I made in the coming days. I looked at Sada with nothing but love in my heart.

"We have little less than two days' time before Orbrecht returns with more warriors for the battle. Until then, I am yours and you are mine. Let us make the most of the time we have remaining together and not waste it on pity or sorrow. You are so beautiful, my love, and I am a fortunate man to have you at my side."

"Yes, you are." She had composed herself and brought back her stony demeanor. "How long are you expected to be gone this time?"

"We are not sure. One week's sail and perhaps a day or two of fighting. Perhaps three weeks, maybe a month." Sada stood, placing her hand on my shoulder and guiding me to a bench. "Sit here, I'll fetch the mead."

* * *

The next day when I awoke Sol already hung high above the tree tops and so I retraced my steps to Njord's forge to see how far along he was with this new sword, for if he truly had made a better weapon, now would be the time for it. "Good afternoon, brother," Njord said cheerfully. "Did you bring me my coin? I've been dreaming of the many ways in which to spend it," He said cheerfully as he banged away with his hammer.

"Whether it is your coin remains to be seen. Where is the blade?" Njord moved to the back of his forge, grasping a leather cloth from the top of his work bench he gently peeled it back revealing his creation. The surrounding men looked on in disbelief.

"I give you, a sword worthy of a god." Njord lifted the sword to the air with both hands. Its shine almost blinding in the dim sunlight.

"I've never seen anything like it," I exclaimed.

"Look at the shine," Another said in awe.

Njord stood atop his anvil. "My brothers, I give you a superior blade to serve any warrior proudly."

I stepped forward to get a closer look at this blade. "What sort of magic is this brother? I've never seen such qualities in a sword," I asked Njord.

"It's the work of the gods, thanks in no small part to Brother Thor. We can conquer the world with this blade," Njord said confidently. "Now, to the matter of our wager: bring your blade forward, brother." I moved closer, and slowly removed my sword from its sheath, keeping the blade pointing down. "Brothers, we shall conduct three trials, one of strength, one of durability, and one of cutting power. Firstly, the blades ability to cut." Njord placed a small log in front of me. "Go ahead, Audan. Cut the log." Njord stepped back to give me room to swing. I braced myself for the swing to come, placing my leg behind me alongside my sword. A long swing, my iron sword started at my rear leg, following over my head and down upon the log. *Thunk!* My sword sank two inches into the log and stopped.

"Keep going Audan, strike until the log is no more." I dropped my blade atop the log over and over again perhaps a dozen times until finally my sword broke through. My body followed and fell to the ground with my blade. Njord stepped forward and placed a new log down. "Just to prove it is the strength of the sword and not the man I'm going to let you cut at this log as well." he said. I wiped the mud from my brow and composed myself. Getting back into my stance I braced myself and dropped the blade onto the log. *Schunk!* A single cut, the sword effortlessly cut through the log. I stared for a moment in great disbelief and looked up at a very pleased Njord.

"Excellent job, brother. Now to the second test: durability. Brother Audan, if you please." Njord motioned me towards him and handed me my iron sword once more. "Do you see that shield? I want you to hit the helmet that is behind that shield without going around it."

"I'm not sure what you are asking me to do," I responded confused.

"I'm asking you to hit the top of the shield and have your sword bend enough to hit the top of that helmet." Now I understood, but I did not see how it could be done. "You have three chances," instructed Njord. I stepped forward and threw all my weight behind the sword, but the blade would not bend. Three times I struck the shield but never did I strike the helmet. Njord now handed me his sword. "Try again, brother." Njord stepped back. I hit the shield and the sword tapped the top of the helmet that lay just beyond the shield.

"You see brothers, my sword can be bent to great angles, striking a target behind a shield," he said proudly. I looked down at Njord's sword, already convinced of its superiority and worried about my wager.

"I see I'm going to lose this wager, should we even commit to a third trial?" I asked Njord sarcastically.

"Of course, the people need to see what they are about to purchase. Men, gather around for one last trial, the test of strength. Here we have a large boulder and two anvils. Each sword will be held up by the two anvils with a gap between them. I will smash the stone into the middle of the sword to see which one breaks. We will start with mine."

Njord placed the sword atop the two anvils, looked at me and then pointed at the stone. "Use your legs, Brother Audan. We wouldn't want you to hurt your back."

I scoffed and knelt to lift the boulder. It was the size of my chest and just as deep. Showing no sign of weakness, I held my breath and lifted the boulder to my shoulder. "Give us a count now." Njord lifted his arm. "One, two, three!" I dropped the boulder and watched it bounce and fall off the sword.

"Intriguing," I said under my breath.

"You see, noblemen, my sword has passed all three trials. Now it is time for the iron blade. Audan, your sword if you please." I knew I'd lost this bet and now he was going to break my sword for certain. Once again, Njord placed the sword atop the anvils and pointed at the boulder. I knelt down and once again lifted it to my shoulders, my thighs shaking under its immense weight. "Give us a count now." Njord motioned to the crowd once more. "One, two, three, throw!" I dropped the boulder atop my blade and watched the metal splinter into several pieces flying in every direction. The crowd of villagers cheered and raised their arms in amazement.

This was truly a sword sent from the gods. "I believe you now. Only a god such as Thor could have revealed to you how to build such a blade."

Njord smiled from ear to ear. "You don't have to believe me, Audan; you just have to pay me." Njord chuckled and held his hand out for his bounty.

I reached down to my belt and untied my coin satchel, dropping it into Njord's eager hand. Njord tested the weight bouncing it in his hands a few times, and then opening it to inspect the contents. "Looks about right," he said as he bit into a coin to ensure it was not a lesser metal.

"So, tell me the truth of it. Was it really Thor that came to you in a vision or did you pick this up from another merchant or fellow blacksmith?" I asked with slight doubt in my voice.

"Do you distrust our God Thor?" retorted Njord. "In any case, you just bought yourself a new blade. Use it well, take the utmost care of it and it will serve you well." Njord handed me the sword. I grasped the handle with a sense of excitement. Njord removed several coins from the satchel and lifted them into the air. "Mead for all my spectators, and while you're drinking yourselves stupid, I'll be taking your orders for new swords!" The men cheered and happily headed to the Great Hall.

Despite losing the bet, it felt much like winning. I needed a name for my new blade, something to honor the gods, I thought to myself. It will come to me shortly, perhaps after its first battle. I proudly sheathed my new blade.

* * *

Two days had now passed and true to his word, I spotted Orbrecht along with the slave boy returning to the village. The ground shook and sounded like thunder, horses of all colors mounted by Norse warriors rode valiantly into the village. Mar stepped out of his hovel and quickly ran to the Chieftain's Great Hall. "My lord, come quickly," said Mar. Alarmed at Mar's urgency, Rurik stepped outside and picked up an axe bereft of his trousers. Orbrecht rode directly to Rurik.

"Good morning, my lord. I have your new army, as commanded. Each one ready to meet Odin in his Great Hall." Orbrecht jumped down from his horse smiling and exalted.

"Well done, Orbrecht. You have out done yourself and proven your worth to me once more. Go to the hall. Kenna, fetch Orbrecht food and drink, as he must be weary from his long travels."

"Right away my lord." Kenna bowed, then stood upright reaching for Orbrecht's hand and walked him back to the Chieftains Great Hall.

A thin pale rider with long blonde hair and a colorful tunic came upon Rurik. "Greetings, Rurik, Chieftain of Bjorgvin. I am honored to be your guest and fellow warrior on this great journey."

Rurik lowered his axe and asked curiously, "Who are you, young warrior?"

"I am Fiorn, Chieftain of Myrlende and son of Bjarni. These soldiers that you see are loyal to me and me alone." Rurik placed the head of the axe on the ground and his hands atop the handle like a walking stick.

"You're a bit short to be a warrior don't you think?" Rurik said with a grin. Fiorn jumped down from his horse and stepped forward to Rurik; Fiorn was nearly a head shorter, with a thin build. He gazed upward at Rurik confidently with large brown eyes and a crooked smile.

"That I am my lord, and yet, here I stand. Scarred after many a battle but still taller than those I slaughtered." Fiorn replied wittingly.

"And, where may I ask, do your loyalties lay Fiorn, Chieftain of Myrlende and son of Bjarni?" asked Rurik.

"Why, you, my lord, of course. I am humbly at your service as long as my men and I receive our fair share from the raids," Fiorn said while tipping his head. Rurik was pleased.

"Then I welcome you to my village. Make yourselves at home. We leave at first light for battle and glory."

"Yes, my lord, and thank you for your hospitality," he replied. Fiorn pulled his horse forward and signaled for the rest of his men to dismount in the village. More horse hooves could be heard in the distance riding towards Bjorgvin, and Rurik turned his head and saw the Jarl accompanied by several well-armed riders.

"My lord." said Rurik, clearly surprised.

"Rurik, what the hell are your men still doing in town? I thought I told you to get back on that ship and follow the Finns!" The men surrounding the Jarl held their sword handles firmly with grim faces.

"Yes, my lord, you did. I thought it best to procure more supplies and men so we could..." Rurik was interrupted.

"You thought? *You?* I gave you no such order. Nor did I grant permission for you to wait for two days scouring the countryside in search for reinforcements. You bring dishonor upon us, Rurik. My word is law!"

"Yes, my lord. I humbly apologize and beseech your forgiveness. It won't happen again, I swear it." Rurik now kneeled on one knee in the mud.

"See that it does not or I will cut out your gizzard while you watch and feed you to my hounds. I will speak with Fiorn now regarding the plan of attack. With or without Fiorn's troops you will sail tomorrow morning to hunt down the Finns and return honor to our people. Is that understood?"

"Yes, my lord," replied Rurik. The Jarl angrily stormed off and made his way into the village to meet with Fiorn in a private council.

As Steiner walked away he glanced over his shoulder back at Rurik and spoke with malice in his tone. "Oh, and Rurik," said the Jarl.

"Yes, my lord?" responded Rurik quickly. He was clearly frustrated with the Jarl and his endless demands.

"If you don't defeat the Finns, don't bother returning home. You won't have a home to return to." Steiner coldly strode away without a care in the world.

"Yes, my lord." Replied Rurik. Anxious and angry he headed to his hovel to calm his nerves and prepare for the battle to come.

Five
Vengeance, Honor, Glory

The ocean waves, like rolling hills, rose and fell gracefully before us. A dozen mighty longships set sail with the fiercest warriors of Rurik and Fiorn's clans. I found glory in this epic scene; drums beat, men made ready their spears, sword, shield, and axe. Our oars hurriedly cut through the ocean waves. "Row you dogs, row! We go to war!" cried Rurik. "Man your oars! Steady now, men. I can already taste victory!"

"Row, row, row! You lazy sons of bitches, put your back side into it. My axe thirsts for blood," bellowed Bear. We prepared our hearts and minds for the coming battle, for blood, for death, for Valhalla.

The clouds slowly dispersed exposing blue sky and glorious sunshine from the heavens above. *Perhaps an omen from the gods, from All-Father Odin himself*, I thought. Smooth sailing was a rarity in these frigid waters that so often took the lives of wayward mariners. I could count the number of fair wind days upon one hand. Looking back through the rolling waves we could still see the dark figure that was our home; slowly becoming smaller and smaller in the great distance. We set sail before mornings first light with twenty-six men aboard, toting blade and bow in hand. Our colorful war-painted shields lined the ships rails making an intimidating sight for any who would challenge us. I gazed upward and watched fondly as the ships sail moved steady and held tight with the wind, proudly displaying Fenrir, the Giant Wolf of Loki, the World Eater.

"Keep the sail and rigging tight, handsomely now," Mar proudly commanded from the rear prow. "Oars in! Bring your oars in! Let the winds do their work." The wind had now taken over entirely pulling our ship effortlessly across the great ocean. We rested our tired arms and aching backs, taking a moment to stretch and recover. I eagerly slumped against the wooden rail to settle in for the long voyage and perhaps sneak in a short nap.

I looked up at the blinding sun to get my bearings; we were still heading south by southeast back to where our last fatal raid had transpired. Rurik at the rear prow motioned for Mar who quickly responded, "Yes my lord?"

"We must make haste, old friend. I sense a bad omen from the gods on this forced excursion of ours. We are ill-prepared and must use the element of surprise if we are to crush our enemies." Rurik placed his hand on Mar's shoulder. "This may be our last voyage old friend. Let us make it a glorious one." Mar looked down and slightly bowed his head in reverence to Rurik.

"Tighten the rigging," Mar ordered with hands raised in the air. "We need to arrive there before the next day light or all will be for not. Let's go, move you salty dogs! Move with a purpose."

Mars constant bawling was eating away at Jareth's patience. "That high and mighty half-troll. Who the hell does he think he is? Always yelling at us and calling us dogs. I should cut his tongue out and feed it to the sharks," Jareth said, while making a stabbing motion with his dagger.

Half asleep I barely lifted my head. "Easy, brother. Mar means well and has a job to do. Besides, we are on our way to battle. Let the Finns kill him for you." Jareth grinned and laughed under his breath.

"It would do him well to have a spear shoved up his arse! I'd pay good coin to see that." We laughed together until we caught a glimpse of Mar gazing angrily at us. We looked away so not to call any more attention to ourselves.

Fiorn's longships led the way taking most of the beating from the waves and wind, his ships proudly flying their clans standard, the Green Sea Serpent. Fiorn's eleven ships maintained a "V" formation, keeping our ship in the middle of the "V." We carried a heavy provision of equipment, food, and drinkable water. Rurik was fortunate that Fiorn had convinced the Jarl to allow us to sail at the same time. If not for Fiorn, this would have been a suicide mission. Why my father did not merely turn on the Jarl was beyond my understanding.

The battle plan was a night time raid to catch our enemies by surprise. We were small in number and our adversary would be ready this time. "Sharpen your iron and make quickly your final wishes to Odin. By tomorrows early morning, many of you will carried on high by the Valkyrie's and resting comfortably on the warm shores of Valhalla." Mar shouted.

"That cock sucker Mar is going to get us killed," said Jareth. "He's never pushed us this hard before." Jareth kept playing with his dagger, stabbing at the ship's deck over and over again digging a small pit next to his boot.

"He's merely passing on the will of Rurik. We have much to lose in this campaign," I replied to Jareth. "Just keep your head low and do as you are told. Father will let us know his mind when the time is right. Mar is just a puppet." Some men smiled at Mar's remarks, others scoffed in contempt of the idea of death.

"Why do you think the seasoned warriors laugh?" asked Jareth.

"Because they look forward to the sweet embrace of death. The embrace of the Valkyrie and their final journey home," I replied.

"But how do they know? How do they know what will happen to them when they die?" asked Jareth.

"They don't, they only believe. You should stop asking so many questions about our gods. Thor might drop a ball of lightning right on top of us." Jareth stuck his tongue out to the sky, tempting Thor to drop a bolt of lightning into his mouth.

Rurik stood at the rear prow a few lengths from where Mar had barked his orders. "Audan, Jareth, come here. We have important affairs to discuss," Rurik commanded. Jareth and I looked at each other then looked at Rurik.

It must be vital, perhaps a battle plan? I thought to myself. Ducking under the ropes we walked down the open aisle until we reached my father. Almost in unison Jareth and I both said, "Yes my lord?"

"Sit down you two." Rurik motioned to the deck of the ship. We sat with legs crossed, flexing our stomachs fighting against the rocking ship to sit up straight.

Rurik began to speak, "Listen closely lads because I'm only going to say this once." Each of us leaned eagerly forward, as Rurik stared at the deck of the ship, a look of worry hovering on the wrinkles of his forehead. "Fiorn's men will lead the attack on the Finns. They have light infantry and a sufficient number of archers to breach the defenses. We will be out numbered: there is no doubt about that. The plan is to hit and run, so no heroics – do not break the line and do not get far away from the rest of your men. Do I make myself clear?"

"Yes, my lord," Jareth and I replied.

"We want to taunt the Finns, force them into open ground where they will be exposed for the kill. We will be on their home territory and they will have defenses prepared far in advance of our arrival." Laying in front of Rurik on the ship's planks were several small pebbles representing our ships and the enemies fortress. Taking hold of the dark pebble Rurik swung it out to the left of the largest pebble. "Once we locate the Finns stronghold we will swing out to the far side and attempt a silent landing. If we time this correctly, Fiorn and his troops should already be engaged with the enemy keeping their eyes and focus away from us." It sounded like a solid plan, but as with all plans, it was meant to change.

"How will they know we are coming?" I asked.

Father placed his hand on my shoulder. "It is the warrior code, my son. Blood must be repaid with blood. There is no other way, no other law of the land. If we do not attack, our lands, our people, could become subject to the will of the Finns."

"So we mean to flank them? To what purpose and end?" asked Jareth.

"We are to sneak in the rear of their fortification, take out their Commander's guard, and capture the Finn Commander for ransom. Then we must return him to our Jarl. A promise for his safe return will catch a handsome sum of coin."

"Capture? But why when we could just kill him and take what is ours? I thought this was a raid of retribution for our village, not coin," Jareth asked angrily.

Rurik began to pull at his beard, contemplating on how best to answer Jareth. "The Jarl has his owns plans. Fiorn has assured me that he will keep the Finn forces at bay while we make good our orders. It is my belief that the Jarl has plans to take the Finn people as his own and rule both territories."

"Is he mad? It would take decades, even generations of our people to control such a vast expanse of land. The Finns will never yield to a foreign ruler. Father, we can't be a part of this," I said in protest.

"Audan, Jareth, I understand your trepidations but the Jarl will not budge on this. He considers this to be the debt repaid for the loss of the lower village, for our carelessness. We do not have a choice in the matter. Your fates, the fate of your men, are tied to mine and that of the wishes of our Jarl." Rurik shook his head wearily.

"The Jarl is a delusional old fool! Fuck Steiner!" Jareth said with great insult. Rurik leaned forward and grabbed Jareth by his collar pulling him in closely.

"Silence your tongue, inherited son of mine. As much as it displeases me to relinquish these poor tidings, I'll not have you spouting offenses that would leave you a dishonored and rotting corpse." Rurik slowly loosened his grip. "Look out for your brother and take care of the men. They need to be in high spirits before we arrive and I expect both of you to see to it. Despite our feelings towards Steiner this is his command and we must carry it out."

"Yes, Father," we both replied.

"Good, then it is settled. Now let's get on with it and kill those bastards." Rurik stood and took his post once more at the rear prow. Jareth turned to find Mar glaring at us intently.

Was he watching us during the exchange with Father? I wondered. Perhaps Mar was not privy to the details of this campaign and as second in command he should be. Mar turned away and looked towards the open ocean without a word. Jareth quickly tapped me on the shoulder.

"You need to watch out for him."

"Who?" I replied, not realizing he had heard my remarks.

"Don't be daft brother, you're keener than that. Mar, you need to watch out for him."

"What concerns you, brother?" I asked.

"When a man in his position is left out of what is rightfully his, jealousy can overcome him. Take hold of his heart and mind. You need to earn his trust and respect or you may find a blade in your back side."

"So you think Mar envious of us? Do you think him a traitor to my father's cause?" I quietly whispered.

"If there's enough coin in it, every man has a price. The question is, what is his?" replied Jareth. I took Jareth's words as an omen and hoped to somehow gain Mars trust and respect. The man had served my father for so long through so many battles. Perhaps he too could one day serve me as a trusted ally.

I lay down to take a rest, my sword pressing uncomfortably in my side, I removed my belt to settle in and fell into a deep slumber. The warm darkness had come over me. It seemed that no more than a minute had passed when Jareth awoke me. "Wake up brother, we're here." Slightly startled, I rose to my feet quickly rubbing my eyes until I could clearly make out the familiar shoreline. Hours had already passed. The ocean breeze carried us quickly back into the stream where fire arrows just recently took the lives of many brave warriors. It had been no more than two days sail that we reached the fort.

"There it is, brothers. Our glory awaits us!" said Mar pointing ahead at the Finn encampment. Jareth walked down the center aisle kicking the men awake.

"Get on your feet. It's time to be vigilant, brothers. We have work to do and throats to slit," said Jareth cheerfully. Reaching Bear, Jareth pulled his leg back further, kicking Bear in the gut with a loud thud. Bear grabbed Jareth's leg and dragged him swiftly to the ground.

"You foolish boy!" Bear pummeled Jareth's chest with blow after blow. "I ought to knock your teeth in you smart little fuck." Jareth laughed wildly as he blocked Bears powerful blows.

"Mercy, mercy," Jareth jokingly begged. Bear stood rubbing his face with both hands. "What's wrong, Bear, had enough of the mighty Jareth have you?" Bear leaned back in to Jareth raising his fist in the air until Rurik snatched it.

"Save your strength for the Finns," commanded Rurik. Bear slightly bowed his head and stepped back. Jareth stood up right and looked ahead. A well-fortified beachhead lay in front of us. Two main embattlements in front of the beach, supported by a rear stronghold, the keep made of stone and wood. We had nothing like this tower back at home. Bear helped to pull down the sail while the rest of the men made ready their oars.

"Keep silent, row steady now. Our enemies still slumber in their beds," Rurik said quietly. We kept a watchful eye on the lit torches, hoping not to be spotted by anyone on the stone tower. The longship began to sway violently back and forth. Suddenly our oars could not keep up with the water as the current pulled us in. "We need to slow down or they will hear us crash against the beach," Rurik said sternly. "Quickly now, turn yourselves about and row against the current, row for your lives." Every Northman warrior quickly rose and changed sides pulling their oars against the speeding current. I pulled and tugged, each time I removed my oar from the water we seemed to move faster.

"Row men, row to battle, let's kill those bastards. Let's not keep the Finn dogs waiting any longer," said Jareth as he pressed his legs against the ships rail putting his body's weight into the oar. Hearts pounding, blood racing, we rowed but we were too late.

Bear threw his oars to the deck. "To hell with this!" Lifting his axe from the deck of the longship, Bear rose to his feet, turned and climbed the dragons head prow. "Get me closer!" Bear kept yelling pointing at the shore as the current pulled us in.

"Everybody hang on!" I yelled. Our ship smashed and crashed loudly in to the shore, stopping violently against a patch of dirt and grass. The Tower guards were alerted, pointing and yelling in our direction.

"We're under attack! We're under attack, wake up!" a guard yelled from the fort. A flurry of activity could be heard over the walls as men popped up one by one on the palisades.

"Damnit, we've been spotted! Arrows! Get to your shields lads they're coming for us!" commanded Rurik. We looked up from our oars and beheld the bright red feathered death that filled the sky, whistling and screaming towards us. "Drop your fucking oars, shields, shields!" We reached quickly for our shields, unlashing them from the ships sides placing them over our heads bracing for the flying stingers.

Thunk, thunk, thunk. A scream let out on my right side, a young one, he was still unlashing his shield and caught an arrow at the top of this skull, pinning his head to the railing; his jaw twitching open and shut like a fish out of water. The current continued to push our ship hard against the shore leaving us off balance. The ships bottom slid and skidded against the pebbles. "Dismount! Dismount! Get off the ship!" commanded Rurik.

"Let's go!" I said to Jareth pulling him off the deck. Holding the rail with my left hand I leaped over the edge of the ship and landed into the murky water below trudging along to the shore. Banging my axe against shield I yelled, "Rally to me. Rally to me, brothers!" A stinger whistled passed. "Aaahhh!" grasping my neck, I looked at my blood-soaked hand. The arrow had just grazed my neck. The sight of blood enraged me, encouraged me to fight and push forward.

"Audan, are you alright," asked Jareth hiding under his shield. I nodded.

"I'm fine," I replied as I wiped the blood onto my sleeve.

"Then let's go, brother. The Finns are waiting for us," he said. "Rally, rally!" We formed up together in a wall of shields; Rurik took up the rear of the formation to give out commands.

"Alright, men, on my order we move forward." Stingers continued to bombard us but could not penetrate our shield wall. Rurik lifted his shield arm. "Ready men, forward, move, move!" commanded Rurik. We moved forward together, chanting with each stride.

"HAH, HAH, HAH, HAH, HAH, HAH, HAH!" The beach was covered in wooden spikes forcing us to disperse our formation into several smaller groups.

"Try to stay together, watch your brothers back side," Rurik yelled over the chaos. The arrows were relentless, hitting harder than the force of an axe against our shields. Rurik let out a terrifying battle cry. "My hand! Shit!" An arrow pierced his shield and went straight through Rurik's hand. His initial look of pain quickly turned to anger. Rurik broke the arrow in half and pulled the shaft out of his hand. "It will take more than that you cowards! Forward men! They thirst for our sword points!" Rurik let out a thundering battle cry once more and forged ahead.

Behind the battlements you could hear the Finn Captain furiously giving orders. "Focus your arrows on their flanks! Group them together! Pick off those bastards! Don't let them reach the walls or we're done for!" The archers were thus far ineffective, picking off maybe two of us and wounding two others. Their rate of fire was just too slow to maintain enough pressure to slow us down.

"Forward, forward! We can't let them pin us down." I urged our brothers to keep moving. The sandy beach was uneven, torn, but we would not be deterred. Looking over my shield, I could see the fear in the Finns eyes. They stopped taking their time with their shots, firing faster with far less skill and accuracy.

"Faster men, we must reach the wall!" Bear hollered, a man so large he carried two shields up the beach head to shield us from the rain of stingers.

"Get behind me, brothers. I will keep the arrows at bay," yelled Bear. We formed a double column behind Bear and sprinted for the wall. The other ships began to land behind us. Arrow cover increased from overhead and the Finn archers could no longer sustain their rate of fire on us alone.

"Look men! Fiorn's troops have landed! Victory will be ours this day. Fight, fight you worthless sons of whores!" Mar was mad with rage, running wildly with no regard for his safety.

Rurik looked about; the Finn archers had shifted to focus on Fiorn's troops. The distraction was working. "Now men, break formation! Get over the wall!" Rurik ordered. We charged forward into the breach. We could see the enemy now, their faces filled with fear looking down upon us.

"Get over that wall! Jareth give me a hand," I yelled. We scaled an earthen wall standing on each other's backs. Jareth kneeled and gave me a boost. I kicked and pulled to get to the other side. Once atop I was met with a spear point. Quickly moving to one side I grabbed the spear shaft and pulled the Finn over the wall. *Crack!* The Finn soldier fell on his neck and was no more. Jareth reached the top of the wall deflecting an incoming sword to the right but when he turned to swing his sword again as a Finn's spear came whizzing by. Caught in his chain mail the Finn pulled back and forth trying desperately to skewer Jareth. Jareth reached into his belt and removed his boarding axe. With a mighty blow, he decimated the Finn. He buried his boarding axe deep into the warrior's skull. Blood spewed forth and splattered Jareth in the face; his eyes and mouth closing just before being painted a dark crimson. Jareth knelt and hastily removed the axe from the Finn's pale corpse.

Jareth climbed to the next level of the earthen wall. "Audan," Jareth said, reaching his arm out, Jareth pulled me to the other side. We looked back to find Bear waiting just below us. Laying down on the timber, it took both of us to pull Bear to the top of the rampart.

"You fat swine!" I exclaimed while heaving up Bear. Once atop, Bear took over the heavy lifting pulling men over two at a time.

"The rampart is ours, the rampart is ours!" Jareth yelled excitedly. Mar stretched out his arm and was pulled up by Bear; his steely cold gaze meeting mine once more.

"Move forward, I'll protect your back," said Mar. My spine went cold; I didn't trust him. Jareth's words had stuck with me. Was Mar going to stick me in the back? Pretend I was a casualty of war? I needed to get away from him, but there was no time to argue now.

"Fine, will lead, you follow," I said. Looking down, I could see Finns making their way to the rear tower. "There brothers! Look there! They flee, the cowards run for their lives. Give chase!" I shouted. Violently working our way down a trench we turned a dirt corner, archers stood ready for our attack and opened fire with a hail of stingers. Rurik pulled us both from danger throwing us on our backside.

"Keep your heads on boys! They still have some fight left in them." Rurik stood and turned the corner throwing his bearded axe sideways; knocking down two and killing one archer, severing him at the neck. The archer fell, gripping his wound and bled out in seconds on the dark and cold ground. Rurik drew his sword and charged forward, stabbing the downed archers until they moved no more. "We will make short work of the Finns," Rurik said wiping the blood from his blade.

Looking upwards, I could see the stone tower and the ramparts that surrounded it were now ablaze. The plumes of smoke became thick; we began to breathe ash and rubbed it out of our eyes. Charging out of the trench we reached another wall, archers stood up and rained sharp iron upon us. Rurik took another arrow, this time to the leg.

"Go help him, get him to cover. He's no good to us chewed up," Jareth yelled. I lunged forward and slid in front of Rurik with my shield just in time to stop more arrows. Jareth grabbed Rurik and dragged him by the collar of his chain mail. We pulled with all our might, struggling with the dead weight of Rurik and his armor. I leaned my back into Rurik, pushing and digging my heels into the soft ground.

Urd arrived grabbing on to Rurik to help pull him to safety. Another volley of arrows whizzed by and Urd was pierced in the back several times. He turned towards the archers, sword drawn and stepped forward to attack his foes. Two more stingers ripped through his chest, he coughed up streaks of blood, and without making a sound, fell to the dirt.

"Urd! No!" We pulled Rurik behind a small wagon with a broken wheel. I lunged outward to grab Urd but Jareth was there to stop me.

"What are you doing, you fool? He's dead. Do you want to get yourself killed? Stay here with father until I can get help," he said.

Reluctantly, I listened to Jareth and turned my attention to my father. "Are you okay, Father?" I asked.

"I'm fine, boy, just let me back after those cock suckers!" Rurik attempted to stand, but his loss of blood was too great, his leg giving out under his full weight of arms and armor. "Shit!" Rurik exclaimed as he removed his shield and helmet, trying to lighten his burden.

"You need to rest, Father, you can do no more good here." Jareth returned out of the ashes of chaos with Orbrecht the Healer.

Orbrecht pulled open his leather sack or remedies. "Leave him to me, boys. Off you go now!" The Healer, despite his slender build pulled Rurik quickly back to shore behind the first fortification which was now heavily defended by Fiorn's war band, bristling with sword and spear. Rurik could be heard in the background still shouting orders at the men. Orbrecht quickly treated Rurik's wounds, wrapping a clean cloth around his hand and leg tightly to stop the bleeding.

Rurik, clearly infuriated, angrily pushed Orbrecht back. "Get off me! There's killing to be had. I need to get back into the fight! Odin commands me!" said Rurik. The Healer grabbed Rurik's wounded hand and pushed in on the wound pouring blood on the dirt below. Rurik groaned in pain and quickly sat back down.

"Wait until I have treated your hand and leg, then you can catch an arrow with your face for all I care." Rurik reluctantly sat down and waited for Orbrecht to finish. "Stubborn old man! You're no use to them now. You're going to get those boys killed," Orbrecht remarked. Rurik allowed his head to fall back against the earthen wall and took a moment to rest.

Gulls swooped and cried overhead, diving onto dead bodies, feasting, pulling, and tearing at human flesh with their beaks until they could feast no more. Ripping meat from bone, their once yellow beaks had turned red, their white feathers stained; the blood thirst had taken over. The wolves would be well fed tonight at the end of this battle.

Mar darted across the embattlements like a man crazed. "We can't stay pinned down here forever or we all die. Follow me!" Mar charged forward lifting his sword in the air. Motivated by this display of courage we all lifted our weapons and charged bravely ahead into the fray.

The Finn Raiders met us at the front gates, sword, shield, and bone crashed making the most deafening bang. We slashed and hacked our way to the courtyard. Jareth became entangled with two warriors, both armed with swords and shield. They traded blows back and forth, sword and shield, shield to buckler and back again. I leapt forward in midair, shield in hand and knocked both men to the ground. Jareth seized the opportunity and plunged his sword into one man's chest; his victim grasping the blade of the sword with his bare hands; his torso heaving upward; the blood exploding from his mouth. I was pulled to the ground by the second Finn; we wrestled, pulled and pushed, each trying to get a blade into the other.

I swung my body behind the warrior digging my feet into the ground, placing my axe handle against his neck, pulling tighter and tighter. My enemy shuffled his feet in the dirt, his face turning red, then purple. The Finn fought and clawed even trying to bite me. The harder he fought the weaker he became and soon succumb to a lack of breath, until his body went limp entirely, eventually suffocating him. Letting my adversary's body fall to the ground I stood stumbling and looked at my enemy for a brief moment before lifting my axe into the air and plummeting it on his neck, a clean cut all the way to the dirt. I lifted my axe into the air once more and shouted, "Odin owns you all!"

Fiorn's men flooded the front gate and poured in with arrows flying forward pushing back the enemy. Fiorn stood atop a barricade directing his men. "Archers to the parapets take over the high ground and pick off your targets. Spearmen; shield wall formation, shield wall formation, and follow me!" Fiorn seemed supremely confident of his troop movements through the village; there was no hesitation in sending his men forward through the smoke. Jareth, Mar, and I led our men forward just behind Fiorn's troops.

"Hold!" Mar commanded. I stopped and wondered why? We had the enemy on the run.

"Mar, what is it?" I asked.

"Look ahead, brother, can you see Fiorn's men? We don't know what lies behind here. The bastards were ready for us, they set these fires," Mar said cautiously. I looked about, slightly disoriented, unable to determine where the shore was.

"Hold fast, take cover until the smoke clears," I commanded. I caught Mar's gaze upon me as he bounced his sword in hand. He nodded at me with a devilish grin and looked away. *What was going on in that head of his?* I scooted to the right to put more distance between us fearing he may stab me once in the thick of combat.

The Finnish Raiders looked out at the beach and their toppled fortifications. The Finn Commander ordered scorched earth tactics. "Burn it, burn it all to the ground. Leave nothing for any survivors," he said.

"Yes, my lord," a Finn Captain replied.

The Finns lit fire arrows and aimed towards all of their remaining fortifications, setting them ablaze creating a wall of smoke. "Fire!" The Finn Captain commanded. Choking and coughing, losing all sense of direction, we waited for the smoke to clear. An eerie silence fell on the battlefield.

"Have they retreated, are we victorious!?" Jareth asked.

"I don't know. Let's have a look, shall we?" I suggested. We moved round and looked over the earthen structures. In a clearing between the plumes of smoke we could see the stone tower ablaze. "We did it. The cowards retreated and set fire to their own tower to cover their retreat. We did it!" The men stood and cheered.

"Wait, silence yourselves!" Mar said placing his hand in the air.

"Do you feel that?" The ground began to shake and rumble. "Brace yourselves!" shouted Bear. Dark shapes quickly emerged out of the billowing smoke, the Finns, yelling and screaming with spears bristling from end to end, had flanked us. Like pin-cushions; our men's bodies fell onto the spears. The trench was jammed with fighting men with hardly enough room to swing a sword. Stepping over our fallen comrades and fallen enemies we threw axe, spear, even shield and stabbed wildly at everything that moved. Another roaring yell came and the Finns lunged from behind us as well. The clash of iron, flesh, and bone was deafening. Mar fiercely shouted orders, but none could be heard clearly in the fray.

Outnumbered and without the strength to carry on, fathers, sons, and brothers, fell one by one into the blood soaked sands. I looked up and could see the Valkyries, like buzzards hover-ing overhead, waiting for the carnage to clear. "Perhaps this is the day," I said to myself softly, wondering if this would be the day I would die. How would it happen? Would I see the blow that would end my existence on Midgard or would I simply slip quietly into the next world? I thought of Sada back home; that dreaded vision of leaving her in this unforgiving place alone.

Our attack was falling apart, shield splintered, buckler fell, axe broke, spear snapped. What was left of the war band fought with sword, dagger, and if necessary, tooth and bone. Mar traded his round shield for another sword found on the battlefield. Leaping into the carnage, Mar vanished from sight. The hand to hand combat was visceral and brutal, men gouging out each other's eyeballs, ripping and biting at each other's flesh for a chance at survival. Jareth and I came up from a defensive pit to find the last of our comrades being pin cushioned by a wall of spears.

"We need to get out of this trench," Jareth urged. Pushing shields forward we fought our way to higher ground and found our way out of the billowing smoke. Bodies were strewn about the burnt landscape. Ash, ash everywhere. The smell of rotting and burning corpses filled the senses. I fell to the dirt, gagging on my own spit and vomiting on the ground. Jareth with his blood-soaked arms, pulled me up. "We don't have time for that! Here, take these." Jareth handed me some small pieces of cloth that were rolled up. "Place these in your nose. It will keep the scent at bay." Putting the cloth in place the smell was gone and now only the taste of ash remained.

We retreated over the fortifications and further down the beach, as a path cleared outside the smoke we could view the sea once more. "Look!" Jareth pointed looking towards our long-ship where we saw survivors, our brothers and Fiorn's men, but they were fleeing.

"Where are you going? Come back you cowards!" I yelled. Jareth placed his hand over my mouth and dragged me to the ground.

"Silence brother, there are too many of them. We cannot fight them like this. We need to stay alive," said Jareth. "We need to go. We're no good to our brothers as dead men."

"No, we stay and fight to victory, or die with our brothers," I argued in a feverish rage.

"If you die now there will be no avenging our brothers, let's make good our escape!" Jareth dragged me back from the fighting. I was lost in the fog; simply staring into the meat grinder that lay just before us. Piles of blood, bile, and body parts mixed with the dirt creating a bog of carnage.

"We need to regroup to fight again. Today was not our day to die. They will surely notice we are not aboard," I said. We turned and walked along the beach in the direction of where our ship had crashed earlier. We waved and attempted to signal our brothers once more, but they did not turn back. No sign, no signal of hope that they would come back for us.

Looking for an escape to safety, Jareth spotted a hill just beyond the burning village. "Quickly, up the hill. If we gain the high ground we might have a chance to fight them off." Scurrying up the hill through the trees and ferns, we moved like demons. Nothing would stop us, not pain, nor weakness, nor fatigue would slow us down. Our shields and swords were heavy; they weighed us down. Our clothes soaked in sweat and blood hung low and dragged on the ground. At one point the hill became so steep that we crawled like animals on our hands and knees to make it to the top, to safety. "We did it," said Jareth.

Laying down to catch my breath, I rolled over and looked backed down the hill. "Where are the Finns?" I searched the horizon and looked through the trees for any sign of the enemy forces.

"There, down there, the southern path." Jareth pointed. The Finns armor was too heavy to make it up the steep part of the hill. They made their way round to a more gradual slope, their armor clinking and clanking with every step. The Finns could be heard for miles.

"Quickly, this way. We have to keep moving, brother," Jareth urged with mad purpose, our legs burning more with each step. Running down the back side of the hill we plunged into a dense and thick forested valley. The trees were tall, dark, almost mysterious looking. Finally reaching the bottom of the hill we looked forward into this dark forest, this dark valley. No more than two ship's lengths could we see, the forest was so thick that it appeared as night. I paused for a moment, reaching out slowly to a dark curling branch. With my touch the branch turned to ash before my eyes, I stepped back in astonishment.

"Audan!" Jareth shouted and strained his voice. "What are you waiting for, they are coming!" Jareth waved his arms and motioned me towards him. With survival at stake, we made our way forward, always listening and looking back for our pursuers, but none came. The Finns reached the top of the hill and searched the horizon for us, but we were already too deep in the Forest to be spotted. The Finn soldiers gave up chase and headed back to the beach head to collect their war trophies from our fallen brothers.

We continued to hobble through the forest until we found a small cave dwelling along a cliffside.

"We will hide and recover here tonight," said Jareth. "You'll need to clean those wounds before they become diseased."

"And you, brother, what of your wounds?" I asked. Jareth was cleaved in the shoulder.

"What this? It's just a scratch. A little fire should do the trick," remarked Jareth.

Lying against a rock, I began to get lost in my own head, thinking back at the carnage we had just witnessed. My heart still raced, my hands shook and trembled. My mind wandered and my focus dulled. *How could we be left stranded here?* Were we some of the last few to survive an ambush that nobody saw coming? I thought back to the cold hard gaze of Mar, the advice from Jareth. The sting of betrayal crept into my mind and poisoned my veins. Could Mar have led us astray? Did that bastard set us up? Anger quickly wore me down, hate turned to exhaustion. The cold damp cave provided a kind of comfort, my head began to fall, my eyes closed, and the dark warmth came over me.

Six
In the Presence of Death

Time had passed quickly as Jareth and I slumbered uneasily, snoring loudly in the cliffside cave, our blood staining the granite floor beneath us. In my dreams I found myself in my hut, hearing the steps of Sada coming closer. I slowly began to awake and realized the sound of footsteps were not in my dream alone, but could be heard in the distance just outside the cave. I gently woke Jareth and we managed to stand and make ready our weapons. "It only sounds like one," whispered Jareth.

"Well, it only takes one to warn the others. Quickly, get behind the rock." We dove behind a large boulder and opened our ears. I could hear my heart pounding in my chest. I needed to calm down. *Breathe*, I thought to myself, *breathe*. The footsteps slowed and came closer. I peeked over the rock and saw a hooded figure, tall and slender walking about the cave. *This was no Finn Raider, so who was it?*

The figure moved closer and removed his hood. Long blonde hair fell on the figures shoulders and uncurled from the hood. The figure turned and revealed a women's glowing beautiful face.

"Jareth," I whispered and frantically grabbed his shoulder. "Jareth, look." He pulled himself up the rock and peeked over.

From out of the dark, a tall, slender figure stepped forward. The woman was like none I'd seen before. Her long, blonde hair flowed wildly, illuminating the cave. The figure turned and revealed her face, glowing as if it held the sun. *It can't be*, I thought to myself. She's not mortal, is she?

"Audan," the woman gently called. "Audan, are you here? I mean you no harm, reveal yourself and all will be well." Jareth and I looked at each other with doubt and shock. I wondered if this could be a Finn trick of some kind. There was nowhere for us to run, and nowhere to hide.

"Let us see what she wants," I said to Jareth. "Perhaps she can help." Jareth just nodded. "Together then, let's stand." Slowly, we stood and made ourselves visible to the creature before us.

"There you are warrior. I have been searching for you," the strange woman said softly.

I was suspicious of her intentions. "Immortals only search for dead men to bring to Valhalla, so why do you search for me? Do you think me dead?" The striking woman laughed and smiled, tilting her head back and then gazing back into my eyes, making me uneasy.

"Of course not, Audan. You are not destined to die today; you have too many challenges that lie before you. You as well, Jareth."

"Who are you?" I asked her reluctantly.

"I am Sigrdrífa but you may call me Sigr. I have an urgent message for you."

"A message? From who? No one knows we are here! Don't try and fool me you foul thing, I know what you are." I snarled and snapped at her knowing full well what Immortals do with living men. I would not be taken a fool or used for their misdeeds. She could be a witch, a demon, or a mischievous Valkyrie. Whatever she was and however she found us I did not think it wise to trust her.

"Audan, there are many of us; like you mortals, we come in all types, evil and good. Do not judge me by the misdeeds of my sisters," Sigr said softly. Her voice was gentle and pleasant, almost mesmerizing.

"And what of this message?" Just as I finished speaking a crow flew into the cave, swooping over my head and then back onto the waiting hand of Sigr. She stared into the crow's eyes.

"What is that sound?" Jareth asked, I was startled at the sound of his voice, forgetting he had been next to me. A faint whisper, dark and mysterious could be heard echoing in the cave.

"Thank you," Sigr said to the crow. She ran her hand down its back as the crow cawed and then took off once more out of sight. Sigr now turned her attention back to me. "There is another like me who wishes to meet with you, but she cannot do it in your realm." I crossed my arms.

"Can't or forbidden? Who is this other? How am I supposed to manage that feat? How is that possible without death?"

Sigr looked at Jareth, "Does he always ask so many questions?" Jareth smiled and blankly stared at Sigr. "Audan, it is not possible without death. You must pass on in order for this gathering to take place." Silence came over the three of us; the wind outside the cave could plainly be heard whistling between the trees and rocks. I cleared my throat.

"You expect me to die, in order to see this other Immortal?"

Sigr dropped her arms to her sides leaving her palms open. "Yes. That is the only way we can deliver you to her realm but she will return you to your body. It is not your time to go to Valhalla as an honored warrior. You will be unharmed, you have my word on that."

"Unharmed! Unharmed? Are you daft? I'd be dead! A corpse!" I grew furious, my fists balled up and teeth clenched.

"Deliver me to her? Her who? Who is this Immortal in search of me?" I looked down at the ground contemplating the many ways that I might be expected to die; *taking my own life?*

Sigr looked at me intently and with distress in her voice said, "No, we don't expect you to endeavor this alone, nor would we ask you to take your life."

I quickly stepped back, shocked: *she read my thoughts.* "Yes, Audan," said Sigr. "We can read your thoughts, feel your emotions, and anticipate your next move. I already told you that you are in good hands. Stop trying to control your fate. It has already been determined for you by the ones who breathed life into you in the first place."

I found it nearly impossible to let go of the thought of not controlling my own destiny. "Who has decided my fate?" I demanded. Sigr stepped forward quickly, authoritative.

"The gods decide the fate of every mortal, no matter how insignificant. You just happen to be of particular interest to them." Arguing seemed hopeless, standing before me was a demi god, my body and that of my friend Jareth were beaten and bruised; we stood no chance in a fight.

"What shall we do?" I asked Sigr. She removed a small blue leather pouch from her slender waist and removed three crow bones from it.

"Take these to the dark forest. There you will find the burial ground of the dishonored dead; plant them before the dark rune. Your answers will be revealed and only then can you meet your destiny." Sigr placed the bones on the ground in front of me. I knelt down to retrieve them and curiously stared at the simple bird bones.

"How will I know when it has worked?" An intense gold light shined and beamed throughout the cave. Squinting and blocking the light with my arm I looked up and Sigr was gone.

"Where the hell did she go? She's just vanished," Jareth uttered in astonishment. "This can't be real. This can't be happening."

"I do not know, brother, but it does not matter. We have our task ahead of us and we must fulfill it as the gods' wish." I replied to Jareth who was now in full on revolt,

"Why? Why must we do as she says? Just because some wench shows herself in a cave, pulls a few tricks and says she is sent by the gods we must take a pile of bird bones to a burial ground that we don't even know how to find? To meet another Immortal? She could be a witch, Audan!" Jareth paced back and forth swinging his arms wildly in protest. "I say we find a ship, hijack it and get the hell home. Gods be damned, even Brother Thor abandoned us in this battle."

My heart and mind battled for control over a decision to either take us home or take the path given to us by the Immortal. No doubt Sigr already knew the decision that lay in my heart. I turned and looked at Jareth with regretful purpose. "We go to the dark forest, brother. We don't have a choice in the matter."

"What do you mean we don't have a choice? We always have a choice in matters," Jareth argued. I looked up at Jareth's mud covered face, standing and extending my arm.

"Will you follow me brother? Will you follow me to our deaths and back again?" I asked.

"Of course I would. You know I would, but Audan this is different. This is madness. We're warriors, soldiers, and treasure hunters. Not emissaries to the gods to do as they please, as they wish."

"Jareth, that's enough, we've sufficiently mocked the gods for one day. If the Immortal says this is the way then this is the way. I know I don't believe in the gods as you do, but I believe what I see. How else would Sigr have found us?" I crouched down against a rock, rubbing my hands nervously trying to anticipate the hardships that lay before us. Jareth sat down angrily, laid down, and then sat back up abruptly pointing rigidly at me.

"If we perish on this errand of yours, and we go to Valhalla, I'm killing you when we get there." Jareth smirked trying to hold back his laughter.

"It's a deal, brother."

We rested in the cold and damp cave for several more hours before setting out on what we thought to be morning. With the dark trees and fog it was hard to tell the hour. We headed in the direction that led us away from the Finn encampment. We did not wish to take chances running across them and heading to Valhalla before our task was complete. The rain had stopped but the cool mist and fog darkened our view of what laid ahead. "Damn this cursed fog! I can't see anything!" Jareth tiredly protested.

"Just keep moving and stop complaining. We'll get there when we get there," I replied. We continued onward, and onward, and onward. Minutes turned to hours and hours into what seemed half a day's time had passed. The trees began to blend together; the trail of the forest floor seemed unchanging.

"Look!" Jareth exclaimed. "Footprints. Someone else is here with us."

I kneeled down to get a closer look at the steps in the mud. My tired eyes focused and saw something familiar about this foot print. "Jareth," I said shaking my head.

Jareth looked over at me with frustration, "What?"

"Give me your foot." Jareth extended his leg. I grabbed it by the ankle and placed his foot just above the print. "It's your footprint, you ox! We've been going in circles!" Devoid of breath, our chests pounding, and hearts nearly beating out of our skin, we fell to the ground in a small clearing. "Let's rest up here," I said. Winded, we rested, eagerly dropping shield and sword to the dirt. I leaned against a tree and looked up at the sky. "Do you see that, Jareth?"

"See what?"

"That's my point, there's nothing to see, brother." At the top of the canopy there was no clearing, no sunlight, the tree tops simply disappeared into what appeared as a black mist. The very air we breathed was heavy and stale. The forest, once green and lush, now appeared to us dark and unnatural. Hollowed-out trees stared at us angrily. Shadows moved and crept slowly over the beaten paths.

"What time of day do you suppose it is? It couldn't possibly be any more than mid-day." Jareth laid down flat on the dirt and stared up at the black ceiling above.

"It's not possible brother, it hasn't been daylight for more than a few hours." Strange sounds began to echo through the woods, as the darkness filled the voids of the forest. The tree limbs creaked and cracked. A deathly chill crawled ever so slowly up my spine as I looked about for any sign of movement.

"Cursed this place is, we should not be here brother. This forest will be our undoing," Jareth said.

"Better to be cursed than be dead for the time being." I replied. "Do you think anyone else made it out?" I asked reluctantly. Jareth looked down, shaking his head and frowning.

"We remained with our men until we were the last ones. There were just too, too many. We were completely outnumbered," Jareth said. I felt ashamed at myself, angry for still being alive I looked at Jareth with disdain.

"Why did you pull me away brother? I could have saved them!" I exclaimed.

"If I hadn't pulled your sorry ass out of the fray you would have just walked into that meat grinder. No, Audan, my brother, you would not have saved anyone! You would be dead! You would be lying in the dirt with your bowels strewn about the mud and your body picked apart by the crows!" my disdain turned to fury.

"You fucking coward! Do you doubt my courage? I'm not the one who wanted to run to save his own hide. We could be in

Valhalla as honored warriors feasting with our brothers." Jareth extended both arms and pushed me to the ground.

"Contain, your pride, brother! I saved your life, now we must carry on. Do not tear us apart just as the Finns did. We need to stick together on this and see this through to the end." I blinked rapidly, gathering my thoughts and calming the coursing blood in my veins. Jareth extended his hand in kindness. "Take my hand and get up. We need to find a way out of here." I accepted this gesture and gripping his hand stood up right.

"I apologize, brother. The moment took hold of me. It won't happen again. I fear this forest is taking hold of me." I was ashamed once more.

"See that it doesn't, you sheep shagger." Jareth smiled and lightly popped me on the back of the head.

Just when we thought things could not get any worse, the rains began to fall gently overhead. "Shit, did you feel that?" I lifted my hands in the air catching several rain drops.

"Storm's coming; we best seek shelter." Cold, tired, and bloodied we could not merely stand in the rain. I looked about and pointed towards a denser part of the dark forest. "There, we may be able to seek shelter there for the night. Gather your weapons."

"Well what are we waiting for?" replied Jareth. We tread heavily through the mud in our blood soaked rags. How miserable it was to be stuck in the wilderness in such a way. How easy it would be to let the elements take hold and die of fever.

"Here, take my weapons," I directed to Jareth. I began picking up the driest tinder I could find and protected it by wrapping the leaves and twigs under my shirt.

We arrived at a small mound topped by trees and a jagged rock that jutted out just far enough to give us both cover from the freezing rain. We sat back and rested only for a moment. "We need to get the fire started, give me my axe." With great effort, a tired Jareth handed the axe to me. I positioned the tinder into a small ball on the dry moss covered ground.

"Get down here and stop being lazy." I needed Jareth to blow on the embers while I struck a small piece of steel against the iron axe. I hit the edge of the axe at a steep angle, over and over. With every third or fourth strike, sparks would fly into the air. "C'mon, light damn you." The embers flew wildly until one finally landed on the tinder. "That's it, keep it alive." I exclaimed. Jareth cupped his hands around the tinder to protect the small spark from the elements. The small glow was the greatest sign of hope we had seen all day and then, like the battle at the beach head, hope faded and died. I yelled, swinging my axe wildly into the dirt. "Damn you, why does it always have to be so difficult? Why can't anything just work!" I stared intensely at the sky for answers.

"Calm yourself, brother," said Jareth in a soothing tone. "Get over here and help me with this fire. It's not going to light itself." I lay prostrate on the ground, frustrated and angry. I stood reluctantly once more. "Now strike your axe, Audan." I aimed my blade and struck the edge; embers exploded and plunged into the small tinder of Jareth's hand. "That's it, keep going," said Jareth as he blew slowly into the embers. Smoke began to billow wildly from Jareth's hand. "That's it, that's it! C'mon, keep it going." A small flame burst and danced atop the timber. I leapt for joy. Jareth still cupping the tinder in his hand slowly lowered it to a small hole we had made for the fire. "Get the kindling, Audan, were going to have a fire tonight."

I reached behind my back where I had placed a small pile of broken twigs. My forearm ached and stung like fire; the wound from battle had closed but stretched painfully at my every movement. Slowly and softly, I built a structure atop the flame. As the heat built and burned into the twigs, I would add another. Finally, a comforting familiar sound; the crack and splitting of burning wood. Jareth walked several feet away to gather some larger pieces of timber.

"We need to eat. Did you bring anything with you?" Jareth asked returning with a bundle of timber in his arms.

"Food? No. I expected us to be half way home by now, or feasting on what our enemies left behind. I didn't expect this." Jareth frowned and then looked up giving me a reassuring smile.

"Go find us something to eat, I'll keep the fire burning," said Jareth.

Just barely dried off, I grabbed my battle axe and set off to find some small game. "If I'm not back in an hour you leave without me, do you understand?"

"Now you're giving me orders?" he asked.

"One of us needs to make it out of this alive and let our kinsman know what happened here. I will return shortly." I set off over a small incline and down into another valley. Still within shouting distance, I spotted a small hare feasting on frost flowers. I slowly knelt down to the ground. The wet grass soaked my knees. I followed the hare as it disappeared into the ferns; I crawled through the dirt and mud, the leaves running across my face obstructing my view. I was close now. I stopped just momentarily, the sound of my heart thumping loud as adrenaline pumped at the thought of a fresh meal. I closed my eyes to relax and calm my nerves; I could hear the munching of the hare no more than an arm's length away.

I waited, patiently, for what seemed like an eternity. The hare hopped and moved directly in front of me now. This was it: now or never. I leapt upward so quickly the hare was stunned with fear. It was over so quickly that I did not even recall seeing the blow that struck down the small creature. Blood trickled down my face. I wiped it with my sleeve and retrieved my still dying meal. *Snap!* "It's better to put you out of your misery." Like a twig, the small hare's frame cracked in half; with his body now lifeless I returned to Jareth.

When I arrived Jareth was half asleep, exhaustion was catching up and a meal would do us both some good. Slightly startled

Jareth sat up straight once he heard me approaching. "So you found us supper after all. Well done, brother. Hand it over and I'll prepare it." Jareth removed his dagger from his boot while holding the hare upside down by its legs. Cutting straight down from the belly to the neck and just a cut around the feet. Jareth peeled the skin off the hare as one would take off a shirt. Handing Jareth a stick to cook our prized meal from, we each watched impatiently for our food to be ready.

"Praise Odin. We live to fight once more," I muttered.

"We're going to need to steal a ship you know. There's no getting home without one." Jareth pulled the now cooked hare from the fire, cutting a large piece and giving it to me. "It's hot, be careful.

"Stop worrying so much. We got this far. Well find a ship, I don't care who we have to kill for it." We both smiled as we ate our meal right down to the bone. "I suppose your gods forgot about us. No word from Sigr." I said condescendingly.

"The gods have their own plan. I'm sure Sigr will follow through in her time." remarked Jareth.

"You're so damn sure of them aren't you? I'm not ready to die Jareth, I won't allow it." Jareth laughed heartily.

"I don't want to argue with you. Just get some rest. We can kill each other over it in the morning."

With warm bodies and full bellies, we fell into a deep sleep. But it was not destined to be so for long. Only an hour had passed before the resounding *crack* of a tree branch breaking could be heard, echoing in the forest. Jareth and I awoke and became alert very quickly. Jareth lifted his head speaking softly.

"What was that?" he asked.

"I don't know," I replied.

"The Finns, maybe? Do you think they saw our fire?"

"Let's find out." Looking into the dark forest the trees appeared to shift, even move. We rose slowly from the ground picking up our weapons and shields ready for anything. "Perhaps, it is the Finns, maybe they found us?" I said. Moving through some thick brush we hacked and cut our way to the sounds we heard. Moving several branches a clearing was seen just straight ahead.

Jareth's tired eyes focused in on something dark ahead. "Stones?" Jareth questioned. I cleared the brush from my sight. Looking over Jareth's shoulder, I could see the graveyard that now laid before us. We looked about the many scattered standing stones, their markings worn from centuries of exposure to rain and wind.

This was an ancient graveyard; no living man had stepped foot on this hallowed ground since last the bodies were buried here long ago. We treaded lightly being mindful of our footing as to not disturb the dead in their sleep. The grave stones were cracked and covered in moss. Some appeared as if they had shifted in our presence, many of the stones lying against one another as they came loose in the soft dirt. Just beyond the mass of grave stones was a much larger stone structure, nearly the size of a man. We approached cautiously, not knowing what to expect or if someone was watching us.

A frost-bitten air rolled over our skin triggering the hairs to rise on the back of our necks. "Be ready for anything, brother. Do you feel as I do, like you're empty, as if something took the very life out of your bones?" Jareth asked seeming nervous. Raising my hand in a fist, I stayed silent, urging Jareth to stop and listen as well.

"I see something," I said softly, pointing my sword forward to what looked like a fire.

"What is it?" asked Jareth.

"I can't see it plainly. Get down before they see us." We crouched behind a grave, leaning against the ice cold stone. Footsteps could now be heard, moving slowly in the distance, getting louder and louder. Sweat dropped from our brows; if this was the Finns we would be outnumbered and surely die.

We gripped our weapons tightly and listened intently. The steps ceased, the silence became so great our ears began ringing painfully, desperately waiting; waiting, for another sound. The black mist that hung at the tree tops now appeared to push downward upon us; the air was heavy and stale. The tree branches creaked under the weight of the mist, their leaves nearly reaching our heads.

"Trespassers…" a voice called quietly in the wind. I swung round quickly, blade extended from my hip.

"Did you hear that?" I asked Jareth.

"I didn't hear anything, Audan. You're clearly shaken up; you need to get your wits about you."

The voice called out again, whispering and moving over my shoulder. "Cowards…" echoed in my ears.

This time, Jareth heard it too.

His eyes widened. "Very well, brother, I heard that. Show yourselves! How dare you call us cowards! Reveal yourselves at once!" Jareth was scared and felt stupid for yelling at something he could not see. Standing back to back now, we stepped closer to the fire.

"Jareth, look at the fire," I said. The flames suddenly died and left nothing but mere embers. They began to glow and fade, glow and fade, as if to signal us. "Show yourselves or by Odin, All-Father, I will strike you down!" I yelled.

The graves were quiet, no birds, no beast, nor wind. "We need to leave, Audan," Jareth said. I stared down at the stones below the archway that lay before us. "What does it say?" I looked at the inscriptions, one familiar and one in a language I recognized but could not read. I began to read aloud.

"Here lies the legion of Tranucus, sons of Rome."

"Romans, why would Romans be here? No Roman has been seen here in generations. Our Fathers drove them all out," Jareth said with curiosity in his tone.

"They're not here, Jareth. These graves are old, ancient even. These men died long before the time of our grandfathers. This may have even been the site of their fort." *Snap!* Another twig; we both turned towards the noise and there we saw a faint green glow in the darkness. "Jareth look. What in the name of Odin is that?" I exclaimed. All we could see were eyes, green glowing eyes. We stood ready to defend ourselves.

"Come forward creature, we mean you no harm," Jareth said. I looked at Jareth as if he was crazed.

"Are you mad? This thing is going to kill us if we don't kill it first." The creatures stepped forward slowly hobbling, and spoke in a language unknown to us.

"Timidi homines," the creature said over and over again.

"What do you say, I do not understand?" I asked, confused. More of the creatures stepped forward and now we could see them plainly. A chill ran up our spines, fear and terror gripped our hearts, caging our souls. The creatures flesh was rotten and exposed, eyes a wide deathly green, like fire. Their teeth were sharp and long. They carried swords and armor unknown to either of us.

"Timidi homines!" The creature spoke louder this time and more aggressively as it banged a strange sword against a cracked man-sized shield.

"These are the undead! We must run, Jareth. They are the undead warriors, sent upon us by hell itself." In a panic we searched for an escape, but the creatures were everywhere, dozens of them. Leaves fell from the trees above as the undead pushed their way towards us. Some of them were missing limbs or still had weapons lodged into their bodies. They began to chant, repeating the same words over and over again.

"What are they saying?" Jareth shouted.

"I don't know but I don't like the sound of it."

"Mortem! Mortem! Mortem! Mortem! Mortem!" Their chants become louder and louder. Jareth and I stood back to back again preparing to defend ourselves. Suddenly, the undead fell silent and ceased once we were encircled. A single creature stepped forward pushing his way through the others. His rotting flesh hung loose on his cracked bones; twitching and moving erratically he reached for his dagger and raised it quickly. With great surprise, he turned the dagger upon himself and cut at the stitching that kept his mouth closed. One by one the stitches popped and the frightening creature released a foul stench.

"You do not belong amongst us, warm blood!"

Seven
Surrounded

Surrounded by a Roman legion of the undead, the mist of the dark forest seemed to push upon our chests, the very air we breathed burned, causing our bodies to ache inside. "You should have remained outside the dark forest, warm blood. Now you must perish for disturbing our slumber," the creature said, pointing at us with long, bony fingers, while his other bony hand grinded back and forth against his sword handle. This undead however, was different from the others; he spoke our language, even carried our arms and armor.

"Are... are you one of us?" I asked the black-bearded creature, uncertain if he would respond. The creature's blank stare fixed upon me as he turned his creaking neck.

"We are beyond this world now. The lands of Midgard no longer contain us. We are what our master commands us to be," the creature replied.

"Brother, we are just humble warriors; can you not convince your brethren to allow us safe passage? Surely you are a warrior of the north and understand the plight that we have faced this day. Many of our brothers have died in battle not far from here and we are a long sail from home." I slightly lowered my sword point, hoping to win over the foul creature.

"It is not your fate to walk away from this place; in death you will become one of us, a loyal servant to the Dark Queen." The undead Roman Commander now stepped forward and signaled the others by raising his rusted sword. They circled around us, scores of undead with bristling sword, spear, and axe. Valhalla, it seemed, was only moments away, as we were painfully out-numbered.

"Mortem! Mortem! Mortem! Mortem! Mortem!" They chanted fiercely for death, for blood, and they would have it.

My pulse quickened to a mad run, and sweat poured down my brow and the back of my neck as I stared at the dozens of deathly instruments pointed towards me. *It was now or never,* I thought to myself. I turned and looked at Jareth. With a steel resolve I spoke softly, "Are you prepared brother?"

Jareth reached up and anxiously tugged at his beard with sword in hand, his feet bouncing back and forth.

"To the end. Now let's kill these bastards," he replied as he banged his sword against shield.

I hastily dropped my shield to the ground, raising axe and sword high above my head. "Fight brother, fight to the death! Aaaahhhh!" I charged forward moving swiftly and slashing the undead Roman Commander in half; so intense was my charge that I fell into the undead and on to the ground. Their bodies were soft and weak, like slaughtering a dry dusty husk in the fields. Jareth lunged forward and blocked the heavy blow of an axe with his shield and buckler. *Chunk! Chachuck!* The axe head buried itself deeply in Jareth's shield. Off balance, he lunged, smashing his shield into the undead face; flesh, bone, and tooth took flight forcing his gruesome head back and breaking his neck. The undead reached up, grasping his head and snapped its neck back into place with a terrible crack. It charged towards us once more. Again, Jareth smashed his shield into the undead, this time with the bottom edge, severing the creatures head from his body; it rolled past us, leaving a patchy trail of black blood in its wake.

From within the undead fallen head; the green ghostly glow of the eyes took flight as an apparition, a faint whispering sound echoed in the forest. The green light flew into a dark rune monument and disappeared. "Take off their heads, that's how you slay them," Jareth shouted.

Three Draugr's quickly lined up with their giant faded red shields and moved forward on us, spears stabbing methodically back and forth. Without regard for my own life, I leapt over the spear-tip-laden shield wall, knocking the beasts to the ground. Partially dazed and lying on the floor, I swung my blades to each side of me, knocking their shields back and hacking the monsters as they tried to get back up. Jareth ran towards me, retrieving a spear from the ground and placing its point squarely into a Draugr's eye. Puss, blood, and fluid streamed from the creature's face; Jareth placed his foot on the creature's chest as he swung his already bloodied sword and hacked at the beast's neck. Swing after swing, hack after hack, Jareth's arm began to tire, until the creatures head finally rolled from its body, the ghostly green light quickly escaping its corpse.

In the midst of battle, I recalled the stories Rurik had once told me about the Draugr's. "Don't let them tear into your skin with their teeth, or they will disease you and you will become one of them!" I yelled to Jareth. The ground below shook and rumbled, the rotting hands of Draugr's burst out of the soil and climbed upwards from their resting places wielding all manner of weapon. So numerous were they I could no longer see the forest floor beneath us. I swung my sword and axe wildly all around in a frenzied panic, nearly striking Jareth. Jareth leaned back, gritting his teeth, barely missing the tip of my axe as he grabbed my arm.

"Calm yourself, brother. We can make it out of this! Stay focused!" Out of the corner of my eye came a swift dark shadow;

my sword had been knocked from my grasp, and a Draugr pushed my left shoulder and heaved me to the ground. With my other arm, I swung my axe forward, but the Draugr was too quick. He leapt on top of me like a spider ready to consume its prey, pinning both my arms to the dirt. Stretching his decrepit neck outwards, he snapped his jaws at me over and over again as I pushed back; his breath was rank with the rot of decay and death. His sharp yellow teeth gleamed and dripped of spit, the thirst for man flesh was overpowering for these creatures of the darkness.

"Ahh, get off of me you foul, repulsive creature!" We wrestled and shuffled in the dirt, as a cloud of dust consumed us. I pushed the Draugr up with my left hand, and with my right hand finally free, I sent my axe crashing into the back of the Draugr's neck. "Ah, ah, ah, ah!" I yelled as I hacked at the beast until the head came clean off and I witnessed the ghostly green glow disappear into the dark rune monument. Out of breath and getting to my feet I quickly charged at two other Draugrs headed for Jareth, hacking left, then right, trading blows until I dropped to one knee, severing an exposed leg. The Draugr fell to his face, now bereft of a limb continued to crawl, screaming, as he grabbed me by the ankles attempting to pull me down.

Jareth leapt forward and before the Draugr could sink his sharp, yellow teeth into me, my brother severed the beast's head, a dull thud as his sword dug into the ground. Jareth said nothing; he just looked at me with relief and nodded.

The rage had now overcome me. "C'mon, you stupid bastards! Fight me, fight like men!" I swung my axe back and forth keeping the undead at a distance, my arms were now weak and slow. Jareth remained low, blocking spear thrust after spear thrust with his splintered shield. No matter how many we slaughtered, the Draugr continued to mercilessly advance upon us as they exited their graves.

Pinned in the dense forest, it became difficult to swing our weapons, with each missed blow we struck a tree. The Draugrs intensified their attack and reached for us in angry desperation, their arms, hands, and fingers, littering the graveyard as we cut them to ribbons. An incoming spear point deflected from the top of Jareth's shield, and grazed my forearm; I felt the sting of sharp iron and loose metal slivers pushing their way into my skin.

"Aahh! Shit!" I exclaimed in pain, grasping my injured forearm. Looking at the wound only briefly I knelt down quickly and reached into my boot, removing a dagger. Gripping the rough blade, I flung it forward watching it fly past Jareth. He turned and with wide eyes watched the dagger barely missing his ear, and sinking deep into a Draugr's open mouth. The monster gripped the dagger's handle and removed it from his mouth, coughing up ghostly green orbs; he threw the dagger back at me hitting me with the handle.

"What a shot! Are you alright?" asked Jareth. as he cut the beast down with a blow across his shoulder.

"It's just a scratch! I'm fine," I said, not knowing full well how serious my injury was.

"Do you have a plan? I don't know how much longer I can hold them off?" Jareth hacked and stabbed ferociously, his arms stained black from the blood of the undead. His shield became a splintered piece of wood in the never-ending melee. I looked about desperately for higher ground we could defend from, but, alas, none could be seen.

"To the dark rune! It's our only way out of here. We must quickly bury the crow bones and figure out why we are here!" I yelled. We ran between the stone columns that lay at the head of the dark rune, the Draugr howling and screaming as they gave furious chase. We pushed our bodies to the very back of the rocky monument and made our stand. The Draugr's crushed and squeezed their frames into the small opening, their bones shifting as they pushed their way through; only two could funnel into the monument at a time.

As we slashed and hacked to keep them back, bodies began to pile up at the entrance, slowing their ferocious onslaught. One by one, Jareth and I lay waste to the undead, knocking them down, severing their already decaying and mutilated bodies. Blood splattered the walls of the monument and soaked our faces to the point of barely seeing, until the last one fell to the ground and moved no more; spectral green orbs filled the monument all around. Jareth collapsed to his knees in exhaustion, digging his sword into the ground to brace himself as he violently vomited on the pile of undead, his body heaving in uncontrollable exertion.

Attempting to catch my breath, I looked downward and laughed heartily. "What in the name of Odin was that? Are you unwell, brother? Are you injured?"

"It's not the sight of them, it's the horrid stench," Jareth said, clearly trying to hold back the bile in his gut. Suddenly a gasp for air erupted within the monument, gurgling and labored. I looked across the corpses strewn about the entrance. One Draugr still had life or perhaps death within him. His chest rose and his body squirmed in place, knocking the other bodies about the floor. I strode over quickly and placed my axe upon the neck of the Draugr, it was the undead Northman.

"Speak demon or I will end you now! What drives you to seek us out? Why did you attack us? We brought no ill will upon you or your kind!" Jareth stood wiping his mouth drawing his sword, the point placed directly under the creature's mutilated chin.

"Speak now, beast, perhaps you can do some good in this realm before we send you back whence you came. And if I were you, I would pray that All-Father Odin accept you into his halls, lest you find yourself in agonizing Hellheim with this gruesome lot," Jareth said with anger and vengeance in his eyes.

The Northman Draugr slowed his breathing, swallowed, and began laughing deeply. "We were awoken by two, two there were, and no more. We have no more to say. Now finish us so we may return to the dark place once again."

"Who! Who is the one that seeks me out?" I gripped the Draugr by his collar pulling him in closer, his stench of rot over-powering to the senses. I turned my head to the side, clinching my teeth. "I don't have to cut your head off. I can skin and peel your skin back slowly like a hunted deer and watch you scream in agony."

The undead creature coughed sending his supernatural green essence into the air, he was near his demise. "Your threats are empty and carry no weight, warm blood; we no longer feel the pain of mortals. The world of men will be owned by two realms. Helheim will be unleashed upon Midgard and the Dark Queen will reign supreme for all eternity. Join us mortals, or die like dogs."

"How do we stop this madness?" I demanded. The undead Northman turned and grinned.

"It's too late, you're too late son of Rurik. Either she will kill you, or find a way to bring you to her side. The realm of men will fall. We will end you." The creature began to laugh uncontrollably once more. The sound enraged me, drove me to madness!

"We shall see about that you traitor!" I replied as I lifted my axe high above my head and dropped it upon the beast's neck, severing his head from body. The last of his green essence left his rotting corpse and entered into the dark rune stone.

"Audan." Jareth grabbed me by the arm. "What does this mean for us? We cannot go against the will of any one god. If they want us dead then we are dead men." I placed my hand atop Jareth's shoulder in defiance.

"Gods be damned! I'm not going to sit here and take what may come. We can make allies of others and hold off our fate as long as possible. Are you with me on this?" Jareth slowly nodded yes.

"Odin, why would you create such creatures?" Jareth stood and let out a yell. "Valhalla!"

"Jareth, look!" I pointed to the center of the stone monument where the inscription lay. It glowed green, like the eyes of the Draugr's.

"What does it say?" asked Jareth.

"It's a poem of some kind. It reads,"

Brave they were, to the very last they fought, by their desecration evil will wrought, and darkness eternal will fall upon this place, until all have a proper grave.

"You mean we must bury them? All of them?"

"They were warriors once, like us. Their foe did not see it right to give them a proper burial. We must see to it." One at a time we gathered the bodies and severed heads, dragging their rotted lifeless bodies back to the holes they came from. As we picked up the undead their limbs were dry and rough to the touch. The bodies were properly laid to rest horizontally, their shields placed atop of them, weapons gripped in their bony hands. Jareth and I knelt saying a final prayer to Odin and Thor.

"I don't think they will be coming back this time. Perhaps they will travel to whatever gods they pray to," I said. We gathered our things and returned to the task at hand.

"They are in our land brother. If they died like warriors, they will go to Valhalla. Odin will welcome them with open arms."

"Do you have the bones?" I asked Jareth. He reached down into his pocket and removed the small blue pouch Sigr had given us. Opening it up and reaching inside, Jareth removed three crow bones including the crow's skull. "I'll do it." Jareth gladly handed the bones over to me.

Stepping in front of the dark rune, I knelt down and dug a hole with my hand. "I suppose this is as good a spot as any." Extending my arm I turned my hand over dropping the bones into the hole, gently covering the bones with dirt.

"So?" asked Jareth.

"Don't look at me, brother. I don't know what's supposed to happen any more than you. She said to bury the bones at the dark rune right? So we buried the damn bones." Frustrating seemed an inadequate word to describe what we felt at this moment. Where were our answers?

"There's no sense in us standing around. Let's get the hell out of here. This place is evil," remarked Jareth. Without direction or bearing, we picked a path and walked in a straight line, hoping to find a way out before the forest swallowed us whole.

"Look, there's a way out." We could see a light cutting between the trees at the edge of the dark forest. Startled by a sound we looked back at the forest behind us. A shrill scream echoed from the darkness.

"They're coming, run!" The Draugr moved tirelessly through the dark forest, though slower than us, they never tired, never rested. I grasped my forearm and gritted my teeth; blood flowed between my fingers as I tried to cover my wound. The flesh pounded and burned. Pain… I guess that means I'm not dead yet.

"We're almost there just keep running," said Jareth. The sounds of Jareth's voice started to lower and muffle, until all I could hear was my own breathing. "Were almost there, brother, but you have to keep moving." Down I went as I tripped over a rock, breathing harder and harder.

"We can't stop now, they're catching up." Jareth knelt down and threw my arm around his shoulders. He groaned lifting my dead weight upwards. "You're going to make it, just a bit further!" The rustling of the Draugr became louder and louder, as they clawed their way toward us. Jareth looked over his shoulder, the panic in his eyes apparent as he caught a glimpse of glowing green eyes in the distance. He looked down at me. "It's okay, we're going to make it." His reassuring words could not hold back the darkness, darkness everywhere.

"Don't die on me, wake up," Jareth pleaded. The Darkness closed in on me, so warm, I wanted to let go.

"It's alright, brother, I'm… just going to…close…my eyes." The Darkness was warm, like being wrapped in furs. No pain, no fear, peace. A voice called to me.

"Wake up, Audan." A women's voice? *My love, is that you?* I thought to myself.

"It's time to wake up, Audan. You have many great adventures ahead of you, now is not the time to sleep. Wake up, Audan. Wake up…"

Exiting the Dark Forest the Draugrs gave up their murderous chase as they could not leave the place that gave them their power. We reached a clearing just outside the forest where Jareth laid me down for a moment's rest. He stood with eyes wide and looked about for any danger. Jareth's ears began to ring; all was deathly quiet now. Kneeling down, Jareth looked over my wounds.

"Are you alright?" asked Jareth.

"I'm fine. I just… I just lost a lot of blood and it's making me weak." Jareth reached down and grabbed me by the arm once more, throwing it over his shoulder.

"Well, then, let's move on. We need to find shelter on the other side of this hill." Jareth helped me hobble my way towards the hill, making progress slowly.

Once at the top, Jareth and I surveyed the beach down below and could see fires lighting the shore. The Finns were working hard to construct temporary shelters and fortifications. Surprisingly, half of their fort had been unscathed in what we thought was the fire that engulfed all. "How many men do you see?" asked Jareth. I squinted, wiping dirt from my eyes, the fire pits giving my vision some trouble in the darkness.

"It looks to be fifty, maybe a few more. The Finn Commander already has his tent set up. Look there, in red." I pointed at a brightly colored tent that glowed warmly in the cool night.

"What about prisoners? Do you see any of our kinsmen down there?" asked Jareth. I scanned the camp once more, kneeling and pushing the tall grass out of view.

"I can't tell, brother, all I see are soldiers. We need to get closer to have a better look."

"Closer? Are you mad? They will have scouting parties everywhere. They will find us," replied Jareth.

"Get some rest; we will need our strength for the killing to come." Jareth put his hands behind his head and leaned into the thick grass, covering his body as best he could. My stomach twisted and turned. So much killing, blood and death. When will it end? I just wanted to return home, to Sada. Back to the life and people I love. I laid my head down, covering my body with mud, sticks, and grass. The ground was cold and hard, so uncomfortable, but I didn't care.

Looking up at the sky, I could see a small crack in the clouds. Sunlight... The rays touched my face, like a familiar hand of a loved one. I felt an itch on my hand and opened my eyes to spot a small brown spider crawling to my thumb. It stopped and turned as if to meet my gaze. I cocked my head to one side and smirked. *Perhaps, it's one of the gods*, I thought, it may be unwise to slight him. Moving my hand down to the dirt the spider turned and grasped a blade of grass, leaping away. Sleep approached quickly and came over my already exhausted body. The warmth came over me again, beckoning me to sleep. "Good dreams." I uttered under my breath, and fell fast asleep. The day passed quickly as we slept soundly in the tall grass. Evening fast approached, the setting of a blazing sun and the rising of a red stained blood moon.

"Wake up."

Startled awake, I tried to focus my eyes. "Calm yourself brother, it's just me." My eyes focused and I could see the dark silhouette of Jareth.

"You shit, why do you always do that!" I was agitated, cold and angry.

"Well, what would you expect, maybe a little tickle?" Jareth joked.

"Shut up, you oaf. Are they asleep yet?" I asked.

"Almost, there are still a few by the fire, and a night watchmen there, and the Commanders tent is there." Jareth pointed out all the guards and their patrol routes.

"How long have you been up?" I asked.

"Long enough to fashion you some pig stickers." Jareth handed me a handful of small primitive spears, essentially sharp sticks. Not the most effective tool, but they would get the job done. I bounced the sticks in my hand.

"I'll make it count. Two, maybe three kills." Jareth smirked.

"Three kills, feeling confident are we brother? That's the spirit." He grabbed my arm and lifted me up.

"We're going home now, Audan. Let's kill as few of these bastards as we need to and get the hell out of here. The odor of this land offends me."

We crawled down to the beach, slowly, methodically, careful not to move the taller brush so not to alert our foes. A soldier! I reached out and grabbed Jareth by the ankle and motioned him to stop with a closed fist. The watchmen walked by, his feet digging through the sand. He didn't even turn his head to look. He had no idea what was lurking in the grass, what was waiting for them when they let their guard down. I reached down and grabbed more dirt, covering my pale skin to keep from sight, Jareth did the same. The night watchmen sat down next to the fire and leaned against a log. His eyes grew heavy, he began to yawn and stretch.

"Audan?" asked Jareth.

"What?" I replied.

"I have to pee." I cracked a smile.

"So pee in your pants, you already smell like an oxen." Jareth winced at the thought and suddenly became very quiet. Steam could be seen rising in the air and I fought back the laughter that came forth.

"Do you find this amusing? It's not funny brother."

"It is from where I'm sitting." Fighting back the laughter, I could see the night watchmen's head bob up and down until finally he moved no more. At last we could hear snoring over the crack of the fire. The guard was sound asleep. I hit Jareth's shoulder to let him know it was time. We squatted down, moving silently and swiftly between the grass next to the encampment. Reaching the fire, I grabbed the watchmen's Dagger, stepped behind him, covered his mouth and slit his throat. He struggled briefly as the warm blood ran down my other forearm. Then, he went slack, falling over.

"Take his weapons; we will need them to take the ship." One dagger, one axe, and one shield. We moved between the tents using the shadows to conceal our presence until we reached the final tent where we could gaze upon the ship. Jareth pointed at the soldier that was supposed to be standing watch, he was hunched over the ships rails, dead asleep. This was too easy, how is every one of these fools asleep?

As we stepped out from the shadows fisherman's net flies through the air and came crashing down on us. Jareth and I yelled and swung our arms wildly trying to free ourselves. Finn Raiders appeared at all sides. Iron pointed in all directions. "Jareth," I said. "Stop moving."

"Drop your weapons or we will gut you where you stand!" My heart sank into my stomach; reluctantly, we let our weapons fall from our hands. Soldiers crept in and removed them from our reach.

"Cowards! Fight me fair, I challenge you to single combat!" I yelled at the soldiers. "A large black-bearded Finn stepped forward.

"I would gladly accept your challenge, fool, but I was given orders to bring you back alive." He stepped forward and hit me over the head with a club. Blood splashed on Jareth's face.

"What the fuck? I thought you were supposed to bring us back alive?" Jareth yelled.

"My master said to bring you back alive, he never said anything about unharmed." Jareth was pummeled by several clubs and fell unconscious. That was all I saw before another blow hit me and I blacked out, too. I came to several minutes later and tried to lift my head. The Finn Raiders dragged us through the dirt like dogs. I was too weak to fight back or attempt escape, so I listened.

Looking to my right, I could see Jareth still unconscious, his limbs sticking outside of the net dragging on sticks and rocks. The terrain was not kind to our bodies, nor were the raiders concerned with the state of our preservation. Jareth came to and tried to sit up.

"I'll kill you, you cowardly bastards!" Jareth bawled. A raider turned round without hesitation and put Jareth back into his slumber. *Poor bastard, he's going to be in a lot of pain when he wakes up.* Suddenly the Finn raiders turned their attention to me; a boot quickly knocking me in the teeth; sending me back to that dark place.

"I said wake up, you DOG!" the Finn soldier kicked me in the chest. I was pulled away from the darkness; it was cold, stinging, pain! I gasped for air, gripping my chest. Opening my eyes, I saw we were back on the beach. "I said, 'wake up.' " He kicked me again. I gasped for air, blood squirting out of my mouth. "On your knees. You are a slave now, servant to the Finns. Do you understand, boy!" The soldier pulled me up by shackles around my wrist and placed me on my knees. A body brushed against me, as I slowly looked to my side and saw Jareth in chains. He smiled at me.

"We made it out of the dark valley brother." Jareth started laughing. The soldier backed-handed Jareth, knocking him to the ground.

"Silence, you dog, or I'll cut out your tongue out!" A swift kick to Jareth's rib cage forced the air from his lungs. Dragged away like a fresh animal kill, Jareth and I were now prisoners, soon to be dead at the hands of our enemies, or worse, a lifetime of slavery.

Eight
A Dangerous Host

"Brothers, this is no way to treat our new guests. Clean them up, feed them, and send them to my tent immediately." A large man with a bristling red beard ordered the soldiers to cease their torture. The soldiers dutifully lifted us to our feet. I flinched when they grabbed me, expecting a punch or a kick to my already bruised and bloodied body. Every part of my essence ached down to the bone. We were led between a row of tents and makeshift shelters; Finn soldiers glared at us as we walked past until reaching the large red Commander's tent.

Inside the tent, we found the Commander washing his hands. He looked towards us and began to laugh happily. "War is a messy and fun affair is it not? All the killing, the bloodshed, the lives lost. There must be a more civilized way we can come to an understanding of each party's needs, yes?" We looked at each other puzzled by the commander's kindness. "Well, don't be modest, you must be famished. Eat, drink, you are welcome here, as friends and honored guests. Guards, remove their shackles at once." The guards did as they were told without any hesitation, even a sense of fear could be seen in their expressions. *Why do they not fear that we will run or attack them as soon as we are freed of our bonds?* "So you are brave warriors yes? From the land of Bjorgvin I take it?"

Jareth and I stared at each other for a moment, pausing to think what action our captor would take on our answers. "Yes, my lord, we are," Jareth mumbles. "And you are?"

"How terribly rude of me; I am Jorma, son of Thaine and Commander of these well-armed men you see before you. I am told your names are Audan and Jareth, am I correct in saying that?"

"Yes, my lord," I replied.

"Wonderful, please eat. I insist. If you don't eat it the dogs will. It would also be terribly rude to refuse my generosity in such a precarious situation. After all, you did kill some of my guards." We cautiously bit into a plank of fish and ate it quickly. The red-bearded man looked at us eagerly seeing the desperation and intense caution in our eyes. "Are you thirsty? Would you care for some water or is your drink of choice mead? What a silly question. Guard, fetch me my mead, only the very best for our guests. Odin demands it." The guard left the commander's tent, only one guard remained blocking the exit. I glanced at the guard's sword, instinctively knowing that this could be an opportunity to escape, and then I looked up. His eyes met mine; he knew what I was thinking.

The guard approached me swiftly and leaned in next to my ear. "If you're looking to escape, I would advise against it. You see, in here, we can be civilized and follow his lordship's orders. In here, we can be men of virtue. But beyond this tent, my men are ravenous dogs and they would tear at your innards just for the pleasure of bathing in your blood." He stepped back; his hot rancid breath still lingering on my neck left me with an uneasy feeling.

The Commander smiled and began to laugh once again. "I don't think we have anything to worry about because you are going to stay here, eat, and listen to my proposal, are you not?"

"Proposal, my lord?" I asked.

"Yes, you know, you killed many of my brothers, evaded them in the woods, and even took out some of my best guards on post. None of my men could do that, they fight as a team. But you two, you two fight as if you have nowhere to go except a better afterlife. Perhaps you have spoken with Odin personally?" The Commander snapped a chicken's thigh bone in half and placed it on the table.

"We were trying to save our lives and the lives or our men, nothing more," I said.

"And what about this proposal... my lord?" Jareth asked. Jorma stood placing his hands on his hips.

"Do not trouble your minds with this now. You must be exhausted and if you are going to discuss terms I will have you well rested. Eat, drink, and we will discuss this in the morning." Jorma turned to walk out of the tent and stopped abruptly, meeting our gaze once more. "Oh, and you don't mind if I leave my scraps with you do you?" *Scraps?* We thought to ourselves. "Girls." Jorma clapped his hands summoning a harem of women. The fur cloth draped over the entrance was opened by the guard and four slave girls entered wearing colorful robes, jewelry, and decorative flowers in their hair. "These are four of my finest slave girls, each one handpicked by me. They will stay here with you tonight and tend to your, every need," Jorma said with a grin. "And Audan, Jareth, I do mean, EVERY need. I am tired from battle and need my rest. I leave you in good hands." Jorma stretched out his arms and exited the tent with a skip in his step. The guard nodded at us.

"The tent will be surrounded all night; do not attempt escape, unless you want to join your brothers earlier than anticipated." The guard lifted his arm and motioned the girls towards us slowly.

"Is he not going to torture us? Is this some sort of trick?" I asked Jareth.

"I say we thank Odin for these generous gifts and ask questions later. Whatever he has planned for us he intends on keeping us alive in the short term. I suggest we accept these gifts up front and talk in the morning," said Jareth. "Girls, girls, bring the mead! Let's have a drink, shall we?" Jareth took the shorter of the four slave girls and placed her on his lap. Holding out his glass, she filled his cup with mead from a large clay jar. I ignored the girls for now, feasting on the food in front of me, taking some bread and hiding it in my sleeve. "Audan, what are you doing? Take a moment of rest and let the girls feed you. We shouldn't waste gifts from our generous host." I looked over at Jareth, who lifted the dress of a slave girl, running his hand up her thigh.

"No brother, we should not waste gifts of our host." I lay back upon a soft cloth with a woman at each side. The slave girls looked so similar, it was hard to tell them apart. Each one had soft, milky white skin, eyes blue like the glaciers, and long, slender bodies. I relaxed and ate the food that was given to me, fed by delicate hands. The girls rubbed their hands up and down my body while they fed me food and drink. I found it difficult to hide my arousal. So long we had gone without food, without heat or comfort, and now we had everything. The girls to my left placed her mouth next to my ear.

"What do you wish of us, my lord? How can we please you this night?" I was exhilarated at the thought of being able to command beautiful women to do as I pleased. At the same time I was terribly conflicted thinking of my love who lay across the sea, Sada, who was hopefully at home waiting for my return.

"Do not be shy. Our lord has ordered us to take care of you and do as you wish. We are at your command," said the slave girl. Jareth wasted no time, already tearing his clothes off under a sheep's skin he tossed about with his two slave girls. Tearing off their clothes bit by bit and throwing them across the room. The girls giggled and screamed in delight. Jareth had not a care in the world, so why did I find it so hard to relax? I continued to drink and feed, making little conversation with the girls until I could eat or drink no more.

"Let me help you with your shirt, my lord," a slave girl said.

"What?" I asked.

"Let's take off your shirt, my lord. I see you're terribly shy. We can help you relax." The girls placed their hands on my ribs, I lifted my arms and they removed my shirt expeditiously. "Turn over and lay down, my lord."

What the hell? I have nothing to lose, I thought. I might not get out of here alive, and may never see Sada again. Lying face down, I felt the girls massage my back and shoulders as they ran warm oils on my body. Never had I had such care been taken before. The slave girls knew which muscles to rub and how much pressure to use. The oils worked their way into my skin, easing every last tension down to the bone. I closed my eyes, still able to hear Jareth having a romp with the other girls. Jareth grunted and groaned while the girls moaned. The sounds faded into darkness with each stroke of the slave girl's hands on my scarred back until I became so relaxed, I fell asleep.

That was the last I remembered.

The next day, the Commander burst joyfully into the tent. "Good morning, Audan and Jareth. I trust you both had a joyful evening. Yes?" the Finn Commander said. We sat up from our slumber with Jorma standing in front of us. Jareth pulled the arms and legs of the slave girls one by one off his body while I wiped the drool from my face. "Wonderful. Get yourselves cleaned up, we will dine and talk business." He clapped his hands twice; the slave girls rose out of Jareth's bed, donned their clothing, and left the tent quickly. "I'll leave you just momentarily while you awaken yourselves," said Jorma as he walked out into the cool air.

"What do you suppose he's going to ask of us?" Jareth asked.

"I don't suppose anything good, but you can be sure, that whatever it is, it's not going to be in our favor. He has his interests and he will use us to his benefit." I looked down at the ground and considered deeply what he might ask. Jareth kept looking at the bright side of things with a shit- eating smile.

"Well, if he keeps throwing women and mead at me I might pledge my undying fealty to him," Jareth joked.

Several minutes had now passed. I was done donning my clothing and began to pace back and forth while Jareth treated his hang over with a copious amount of water. Once more, Jorma burst into the tent, this time in uncontrollable laughter. "Audan, my slave girls tell me that you failed to, rise to the occasion, last night." I looked up, only half embarrassed.

"They know how to take care of a man, my lord; they were merely too much for me to handle, I suppose."

The Finn Commander chuckled loudly.

"Good man, good man! And you, Jareth, I hear you're quite gifted." Jareth stood proudly now puffing out his chest; clearly his ego had been stroked.

"Odin did bless me with a splendid tongue my lord. It has yet to let me down." The Finn Commander chuckled once more.

"Well-played, lads, well-played. Please, sit, sit. Food is being prepared and will be here shortly. I think that perhaps we can discuss business while we wait? We have much to discuss and very little time."

"Of course, my lord," I said but what did he mean by little time? What was the rush? I worried about what plans would now unfold for us.

"Wonderful, wonderful." Jorma sat down at the head of the table and stared at his fingers as he cleaned his nails with a small dagger. "I see that we are all honorable men here, and we all have our vision of what we want the future to be. Audan, what do you want out of life? I mean, what is it that drives you? Clearly, you are a man of vision and great strength to make it as far as you have."

"I'm afraid I don't understand, my lord?" I replied.

"Oh, come now, Audan. You sailed across the sea just to sack my fort. There must something you want for yourself? What is it? Fame, money, land, title? All men want something, Audan, beyond your current state, so what is it that you want?"

I pondered Jorma's question while he stared at me with positive curiosity. Jorma turned to Jareth with one hand open and the other pointing a dagger. "What of you Jareth, what do you want? Are you as difficult and deep in your thought as Audan here?" Jareth smiled and quickly replied.

"No my lord. You have already given me all I can ask for my lord." Jareth leaned back placing his hands behind his head, obviously satisfied.

"A simple man, I like that, women and drink are the price of your loyalty. What of Brother Audan, he still contemplates his answer. Can you not sway his decision?" Jareth gave me a momentary defense for my delayed response.

"Audan is reserved in most cases and cares only for the sake of his kin. I'm sure he is grateful for all you have bestowed upon us. Are you not brother?" Jareth insinuated.

"My Lord, at this time it seems the gods or what we perceive to be the work of the gods, have given us great purpose and we need to be on our way to Bjorgvin." I hoped to persuade him. If he was a superstitious man, this may very well work.

"Oh? The gods is it; and what purpose may this be." Jorma asked wide-eyed with great curiosity.

"I, we, have been forbidden to say, my lord." He's too clever, what was I thinking?

"Perhaps I can change your mind. Audan, Jareth, I have an offer for the both of you that I think you can agree is not only more than fair, it is downright gracious and Odin himself would have a difficult time conjuring up such an offer." Jareth listened intently; his night of fornication bought more loyalty for the Finn Commander than I had thought.

"We're listening," said Jareth with great anticipation.

"I want both of you to be generals in my army. Join my ranks; lead my men into battle and the riches of victory shall be yours for the taking. I will give you lands, men to command, women to keep you company, a fleet of ships, and in return I need you to go raiding when I call upon you." Jareth and I looked at each other; our mouths fell wide open at such an epic offer. The Finn Commanders army was vast, his resources never ending. Jorma stood extending his arm for a hand shake agreement. "Gentleman, join me, rule the seas and the lands of the north with me. I have seen you fight, your bravery and determination far exceeds that of most of my men. They need leaders like you. I will offer my hand only once, will you join me?" Jareth and I looked at each other once more. I dropped my head and looked back up at Jareth, He recognized that look in my eye, the look of defiance.

"My lord, your offer is truly kind, but we cannot abandon our kin or our mission. It's not our way," I said confidently.

"So, then, there is no pleasing you. Brave men you are indeed." The Finn Commander pulled back his extended arm and stood quickly. "Brave and foolish. Guards! Take them outside to the pit!" The guards burst in to the Finn Commanders tent with swords drawn. Jareth and I put our hands up to protect ourselves. Out of the corner of my eye I saw another guard come from behind, I quickly turned my head but before I could see the guards face a club hit the top of my head. *Thud!* Darkness had fallen upon me once again.

"Wake up, you stupid bastards." A guard poured water on our bodies with a bucket. Startled, bruised and battered we stood to our feet. Like an animal I charged at the guard. I was pulled by my neck to the ground. A collar and rope kept me attached to a stone on the ground; Jareth was attached to the same rock. Reeling from the pain in the back of my head the guard stood over my body and kicked me repeatedly. In a fit a rage I stood again to fight them off but there were too many and they knocked me to the ground once more. "You dumb fool. You should have taken m'lord's offer. Now you are both slaves, dead men." The guards laughed as they continued to kick our beaten bodies. "That's enough for now; tonight, you're going to be the entertainment." Spit landed on my face. I wiped it off and rolled to my side.

"Stay down, brother." Jareth grabbed my wrist. "If you get back up, they are only going to beat you down." I let my body fall back down into the wet ground, my mouth half covered by mud, I barely had the strength the turn myself upright. I opened my eyes and looked at Jareth. He had taken quite a beating. Above his brow a large gash with exposed flesh could be seen. Blood got into his eyes making it hard to see. Jareth winced, grabbing his side, which was probably a broken rib. I looked back up and saw nothing but fists. The soldiers surrounded me and pummeled me mercilessly until I could no longer breathe.

"That's enough, ease up, give him a moment of respite. We don't want him to die on us yet," a soldier joked. The unnamed soldier then leaned forward and pointed at Jareth and me. "Oh, don't you worry yourselves too much. We will return to skin you alive; you can count on it." Spit flew through the air and landed on my face. I was in so much pain the offense was barely noticeable.

"Let's feast and leave these cowards to bleed." The soldiers laughed and walked outside. I waited until I could hear them no more. Perhaps it was a trick, perhaps they were waiting on us to move as an excuse to come back and pummel us. I crawled and squirmed like a worm; spit rolling out of my mouth. I couldn't see anything clearly, my eyes watered and burned. One solider had punched me repeatedly in the ear, as they leaned over me yelling and screaming. Jareth moved his lips slowly; I couldn't make it out, all I could hear was the ringing of bells. Squeezing and flexing my stomach muscles I finally reached Jareth and grabbed his hand for comfort.

"We will get through this brother, you and I together." Blood filled my mouth once more; turning my head, I relieved myself of the taste of it and spit a volley of red liquid. Jareth would not last this time. His flesh ashen white, he was very near death.

"Rest, brother, rest. We cannot escape in this condition," Jareth scoffed.

"Escape. The only escape from this is death, brother, the sweet release into the Valkyries loving arms." Jareth peered upwards through his blood soaked bangs. "Hear me, Odin, take me as a man, as a warrior, let me fight to the death so I may enter your..." Jareth's words failed him, his head falling to his chest.

"Jareth, Jareth!" I cried. Jareth began to snore, as he slumbered. Lying my head on the dirt I contemplated sleeping here but knew if they found me asleep next to my brother the beating I would take would be far more severe. I crawled back to my post, my ribs crunching and cracking. Each breath was worse than the last. How was I to escape this place? The Draugrs did not finish me, but the Finns certainly would if we stayed much longer.

I fought the urge to sleep, but the body's needs won over my own will power. I stared at Jareth and his blurry and bloodied figure. My head slowly nodded, eyes blinking more rapidly. Darkness, the warm blanket of slumber fell over me like a comforting tidal wave. Floating in the waters of my own mind I saw terrible visions. A child, sitting on a log in the middle of a dark forest.

"Come, Audan," he called to me. Without control of my own limbs I floated towards the child. A dark and inescapably haunting feeling came over me. I needed to stay away from this child, but why? There was nothing threatening about him. "Audan," he called to me again. "You are not welcome here. This place, your soul, you cannot be amongst us." He spoke to me in such a way, as if, as if he knew me.

"Who are you child? Tell me your name. Where are your parents?" His skin was ashen pale, his feet and hands a purplish black.

"You are playing with forces you cannot possibly comprehend," he said in a raspy tone.

"Who are you? I want answers, where am I? What is this place?" I demanded.

"This place?" The child looked up at me swiftly, his face, his face was gone! Nothing but a blank canvas of pale white lay before me and yet the child spoke. I stepped back quickly, startled, but I could not get away. "Do I frighten you, Audan? Do you find this place uncomforting? This is the middle place, the place in between agonizing Helheim and glorious Valhalla. This is where men go who cannot carry out their destiny." The boy grew silent for a moment twiddling his fingers. "Are you incapable of carrying out the tasks that the gods have set before you? Are you so inept that you would die and relinquish your very soul to this place?"

Without a second's hesitation I answered, "No, but why am I here?" The faceless specter nodded its head and turned away, speaking once more.

"You were sent here as a warning, Audan. The gods favor you, but, the question is Audan, which ones? The gods that sent you here did so as a courtesy, to warn you to not cross them or take their good intentions lightly." I contemplated how my actions may have grasped the attention of the gods and how I might interpret the meaning of this dark place.

"Then tell me, who favors me? Odin, Thor, Freya, Loki? Tell me now, child, or I'll…" I was angry, furious; I was tired of the games. The child turned fiercely and pointed his claw like fingers into my face.

"You demand nothing here, mortal! Here you are but a slave, here you are not permitted to experience glory nor pain. Here you simply suffer an existence of just being, there is no forward, no behind, and if I so choose I can keep you here to suffer in silence!"

The child's voice was harsh now, that of an old man. "You're no child, what are you?" The child creature sat down once more upon the log.

"I am neither dead nor living. I am the caretaker of this middle place, but in your case Audan, I am also a guide, perhaps even your salvation. The gods take interest in your affairs amongst the realm of men. Take heed mortal, you must choose your side wisely." He lifted his finger into the air now. "And, oh yes, like tribes at war the gods will force you to choose amongst them." No longer did I concern myself with the appearance of this thing, his words struck me deeply.

"What shall I do? Who can I trust?" I asked.

"That is not for me to decide, Audan. Do not perish this night or you will return to this place for an eternity. Finish the path that is set before you." I felt myself being pulled away, the child specter drifted away from me and before I could ask another question he echoed this final phrase. "In fear, you will find death, in bravery, eternal life." The dark forest was gone and without even knowing the name of the specter child he too disappeared from my sight.

Thrown once more into the warm liquid ocean of sleep, I floated there, hoping to never leave. The cold and pain slowly reminded me that I was asleep, that life was still mine to be had.

Closing my hands I could feel them fill with cold thick dirt. My eyes began to flutter and open once more. Hours had passed, but morning was still far off. I stared for a moment blankly at a pile of chains and thought to myself how wicked they looked. My nostril blew sending dirt into my eyes. Turning and twisting my body to sit back up right I was reminded of the beating I had taken. Why had they not returned to finish us off in our slumber? A momentary panic set in as I looked for my brother. He had not moved, and was still caught in his own deep sleep. There was no waking him at this moment, best to let him sleep and regain his strength. The vision of the mutilated child haunted me. Was it real? Did the gods once again visit me? It was hard to focus on the dream while coming to grips with the reality of our current predicament.

The soldiers returned to the tent once more, laughing, horns of mead in hand. The largest of the soldiers, the only one who continued to speak to us laid his eyes upon Jareth and I.

"I am in a particularly pleasant mood this night, my friends. Perhaps it's the mead talking, that liquid gold filling my belly, or the whore woman I just ravaged. In any case, I have decided, I'm not going to kill you, my friends. We're going to stay together just a little longer. My Commander thinks that perhaps he can still persuade you, that maybe your loyalties can still be altered through a little coaxing." The soldier knelt down next to me and raised my head up gently. "Are you still with me, my friend?" I barely opened my eyes and blinked. "You blinked, excellent, you are still with me. Then we have some time to get to know each other better, yes?" The soldier kept asking questions but he expected no answer.

The sound of metal scratching against a rock or whetstone; our torture was far from over. The soldier spoke once more with delight in his voice, "I have to admit, my friends, I am a little rusty at this. So many of our battles have been, less than pleasurable. It's always over so quickly, we run in, we sack a town, catch your people by surprise, you die, we take your things, your women, your children, and we move on before your allies are the wiser. But today, oh, today is a glorious day; blood will be spilt, slowly, elegantly for All-Father Odin. He will bathe in your blood and I will rejoice in his happiness." The soldier approached Jareth as I watched through half shut eyes. Laid gently to the ground, Jareth was now prostrate without the strength to fight back.

My every bone screamed out but words would not escape my lips. Jareth writhed in agony, moaning and crying. The soldier took his time, not cutting too deeply, only enough to inflict pain in the most sensitive of areas. Placing the knife on Jareth's chest, the soldier gently dragged the dull edge along his body. "Where are you most vulnerable?" the soldier asked. Jareth squirmed when the knife reached his rib cage. "Ah, and there it is." said the soldier. "To spare you the thought of hope, I want you to know, that this will hurt a lot but I will be here with you." The knife plunged a shallow gash into Jareth's rib cage, the soldier dragging the blade slowing, so not to tear the flesh. Blood spilled like tears flowing from Jareth's bottom rib. Once the soldier reached the end of the rib the gag fell from Jareth's mouth. "So friend, how do you find yourself now?"

Jareth cried out quickly, "Fuck you! Just kill me already!" and spit on the soldier. The soldier did not react beyond placing the gag back into Jareth's mouth, and then moved to the other side of his rib cage, dug the blade in once more. Slowly, the blade made its way along Jareth's rib. I watched hopeless in horror, moving my arms back and forth on the ropes that bound me but there was no hope of getting out now. No chance to save my brother from this pain. Suddenly, Jareth stopped moving, and no sounds came from him. The soldier looked at Jareth and smacked his face several times. "My friend, do you sleep? You know you can't die on me yet. Hello?" The solider smacked Jareth on both sides of the face. Jareth had blacked out from the pain and loss of blood.

"Ah, well, no matter. I need a respite from all this excitement. I feel invigorated but I fear the mead has left me drained." The soldier filled two large clay cups with water. "Here you are my friend, this cup is for you and this cup is for your friend when he awakes. He will need these fluids so I can continue my work.

We still have much to do." The soldier once again knelt down, this time looking at me. "Don't you worry. I will be back for you shortly, you can count on it." The soldier stood up and grabbed his knives. "Good night, my friends, get plenty of rest. This evening was just a taste of what I have in store for you, unless of course you take my Commander's offer."

At last, the torturous and blood thirsty fiend had left our side and we were once again left to bleed in the dirt. Staring at the ground I seriously contemplated accepting Jorma's offer to end our plight but my pride won me over. I can't give in.

Nine
Against All Hope

The dark skies appeared calm as the moon hung low overhead just above the outstretched cliffs. Jareth and I, still bloodied and beaten, lay very near death's door, doomed to spend an eternity in Helheim without an honorable death, without the chance to fight and die for our rightful place amongst the brave warriors of Valhalla. *Surely there must be a Valkyrie nearby*, I thought to myself, but none came. Tight ropes bound our hands and feet preventing any chance of escape. I tugged on the lines from time to time, pulling on the rock they were latched upon, turning and twisting my wrists until strands cut at the flesh. Blood sprung forth; I felt hopeless. The ropes were solid, recently made even. I was sadly impressed by the quality of the craftsmanship. I wheezed and coughed up blood, holding back tears of pain, and hiding my weakness as best I could. Small drops of blood flowed along the rope until they dropped to the cold dirt below. Spitting to clear my throat, I scooted along the dirt, leaned against Jareth and forced out speech.

"Brother..., if we don't get out of here...they...will execute us by sunrise. We need to come up with a plan. What say you?" Jareth did not speak, bereft of strength and will. He sat there motionless, cold and quiet. I reached out and lifted Jareth's swaying

141

head and nodded to myself in understanding of his weakness. "I'm going to get us out of here, brother. We're going to make it out. Do you hear me? I will not let us die like this." I felt around the cold dark ground blindly for anything that could be used as a weapon. Out of the corner of my eye I could see Jareth slowly lift his arm into the air, holding a small long rock in his hand. A crooked smile found its way upon my face. "What do you expect me to do with that?" I asked.

"Sharpen it upon the rock. We can use it to cut the rope to set us free, now get to work and stop wasting time." Jareth seemed as if his wits had suddenly returned, but as soon as he ceased to speak, his head and arm slumped back down to the dirt. I reached out with tired arms and retrieved the stone from Jareth's once again motionless limb, scooted back up to the stone and started the long slow process of running the rock back and forth to work an edge. *Slowly now,* I thought to myself, *slowly now.* If I tried to sharpen the stone too quickly it would chip and become brittle, I needed a sharp edge, and our lives depended on a sharp edge. A minute seemed like an hour, an hour an eternity. My thumbs became raw; the skin peeling backward from working the stone, my hands froze and stung in the open air. I nervously looked around, hoping the guards would not find me working towards our freedom. I wiped the sweat from my brow; looking down upon the stone, I could see that an edge began to form. What luck!

"How's it coming along brother? Is it ready?" asked Jareth without lifting his head.

"Almost there. Be patient, just a little more." Pausing to look back at Jareth, I wondered if he had actually spoken at all. He looked unconscious. Shaking off the thought, I spent what seemed like hours on that little stone until it was finally properly edged. I pulled the rope towards me and twisted my arm to get the proper angle. Moving my hands at great speed, the strands began to splinter and cut. I scooted up next to Jareth's back using his body to conceal what I was doing.

"Listen, brother, you need to come back now, find the rage deep within you because when they return, they will end our lives. I need you to distract him so I can jump him from behind." Jareth made no noise, no movement. I balled up my fist and punched Jareth in the back in frustration. "Brother!" I said through my teeth. "I need you alert if we're going to make it out of here. We will make it out of here." A noise, the sounds of feet trudging through the loose dirt headed our way.

"A guard is coming. Hide the stone," whispered Jareth. I had only begun to cut the ropes and now it seemed our escape would never happen. We scooted away from one another and looked towards the ground, pretending to be in a deep slumber. I clutched the stone and frayed strands in my hands hoping to hide them from our captors. The guard stood above us for what seemed like an eternity without any movement. What was he waiting for? He knelt down quietly and examined the ropes. Inspecting each strand until he came upon a section covered in a white powder, the remnants from the edged stone. The Guards eyes opened wide and he stood over Jareth and me once more.

"Open your hands, dog!" We sat motionless still hoping our rouse would be effective. "I said open them!" The guard removed a stick from his brown leather belt; kicking Jareth in the head, he opened his hands slowly showing he had nothing. Jareth looked up in defiance.

"Go fuck a swine." He spit on the guard's hide boots.

"You call me a swine! I'll show you, slave!" Jareth was clubbed over the head with the guards stick; his back arching and then flinging to the ground. Jareth rolled over and looked up at his aggressor as he beat him.

"What is your name, guard?" The guard perplexed by the question of a beaten man cracked a grin and crossed his arms.

"And why would you want to know my name?"

"Because I want to know the name of the man I'm going to kill." Jareth smiled wildly and laughed madly through his blood stained teeth. The guards face turned a deep red as a murderous rage came over him.

"My name is Erno and you will learn to obey your masters, slave!" Repeatedly and mercilessly, Erno struck Jareth with great anger; he curled up in a ball flexing his muscles trying to absorb the blows. No longer able to take the pain, Jareth lay there in surrender, his arms out to his side. "That's better. Now stay there while I introduce your friend to the same measure." Erno now turned his anger towards me.

"And you, what have you got for me?" I lifted my head slowly and spit on the guard's leg, smiling from ear to ear. Erno swiftly lifted his leg, kicking me in the forehead; I fell flat to the ground. He removed the rock from my clenched fist.

"Perhaps we need to get the iron puller and take out all those pearly white teeth of yours. It would be a waste to let you rot in the ground with those intact," remarked Erno, as he yanked violently on my lower jaw. Our captor paused for a moment to examine the rock, running his finger along the sharpened edge he drew some blood from his thumb. "Just as I thought, you thought you would actually escape, stupid fools. You will die here like the rest of your dog brethren." I opened my eyes just long enough to see the pommel of the guard's sword in his sheath. It was so close, almost in arm's reach; this was my chance, perhaps my only chance, to escape alive. My heart pounded furiously inside my chest and the blood surged through my body awakening every muscle for what could be my final act.

"Aaaahhhh!" I rose violently, my thighs exploding upward into the action. The top of my skull cracked against the guard's jaw. Erno's head and neck flew back and in one swift movement, I stepped behind him and wrapped the rope around his neck twice. No sound, perfectly silent. I tugged and pulled; the rope tightened and tore at his skin. Erno tried desperately to loosen the line from his neck to alert the other guards, the color of his face shifting from red, purple, and then to blue, his eyes protruding from his skull. Jareth stood up and, grabbing the sword from the guards sheath, he ran the blade into the guard's mouth through the back of his skull. Completely silent; a good kill. I stared in surprise at the blood covered tip of the sword that spilled forth a stream of gore and watched it slow to no more than a trickle. *Drip, drip, drip.*

Jareth breathed heavily, his chest rising and dropping rapidly. He gripped the now lifeless Erno by the shoulder and quickly removed the sword. Erno's body slumped forward; still on its knees. Jareth wiped the blood from out of his eyes. "What a fool, I can't believe how careless he was," said Jareth.

Still stunned by what had just transpired, I shook my head to gather my senses. "No matter. We need to go before the other guards find out their friend is no longer breathing. Use the sword to free us." Jareth quickly severed us of our bonds; the relief was instant as we rubbed our wrists to wipe away the physical memory of imprisonment.

"Check him," Jareth said, looking at the lifeless Erno. I reached down and ran my hands down Erno's body until I found a dagger hiding in his boot; it was better than nothing. Thinking of freedom, I well understood that we could not just walk out the front entrance. There would be more guards waiting just outside the dirt pit. I pointed to the opposite side hoping we would be less conspicuous. Crawling and digging into the dirt we slowly dragged ourselves to the top. Jareth peeked cautiously over the mound. "I think it's safe," Jareth said. No guards, not even a sound; the camp was eerily quiet. It appeared that the whole camp was fast asleep.

Jareth brought his head back into the pit. "We're clear. Everyone is asleep. Let's be on our way." One at a time, we climbed out of the pit; the cold air dulled our wounds but awoke the senses.

I pointed ahead to alert Jareth to the drunken guards who lay dormant next to the smoldering fire pit. "We need to kill them. If they hear us they will alert the others. If they find out we are gone, they will chase us." Jareth nodded in agreement; perhaps we needed to thin out the flock before we left. We crawled like snakes behind the guards, silently sliding our bellies on the cold, hard ground. Jareth and I looked at each other counting to three before making the kill. "One, two, three." I plunged my dagger into a guard's throat, the blade stopping his screams, the blood choking his breath. The guard's arms only rose up half way before he was robbed of his strength, he didn't even have time to fight back. Jareth covered his foe's mouth with his hands and stabbed him over and over in the back until he fell silent.

"Quickly, get their feet." I remarked. Bending down I grasped a guard's body by the ankles while Jareth grabbed his by the hands; we dragged them to a nearby empty tent and concealed their presence as best we could. Jareth stepped back outside and kicked dirt over the trail of blood to aid in covering our tracks. Picking up the guard's weapons added two spears and a battle axe to our stockpile before leaving the camp.

The safety of the woods beckoned, and as we approached the tree line, I spotted a familiar sight ahead. Just to the left of us, I noticed more stone boulders with slaves shackled to them. They were fast asleep, completely unaware of our presence. By the appearance of their small frames and heavily tattooed bodies they were wild things, dwellers of the mountains and ice. I initially ignored them and planned to sneak right past, but then something stopped me in my tracks; a heaviness. I suddenly felt the urge to help these poor bastards but couldn't for the life of me figure out why. We needed to escape and I didn't know if aiding them would help or hinder our cause. Jareth looked back at me. "What the hell are you doing? The gods set us free, so let's go. The sun will be up sooner than you think," exclaimed Jareth.

I snapped back, "The gods had nothing to do with it. We set ourselves free." I looked at the slaves again and turned back to Jareth. "Let's free them." My heart turned from darkness to near weightlessness in an instant. "Let's set them free." Jareth was furious and confused.

"What? Why? Let's get the hell out of here before we get caught and they tear us to shreds. Have you gone mad? We need to put some distance from this wretched place." Jareth looked concerned for once. Perhaps all the beatings and pain finally made him realize how much he really favors his own skin.

"Hear me out, brother. If we free them, we can use them to aid us in our escape. Arm each of them; they can help with the long journey home." Jareth clenched his fist tightly and looked up at the sky in frustration, perhaps hoping his answer would drop from the heavens. "Why are you hesitating? We don't have time for any inaction," I complained.

"Agreed, brother, but I'm not risking my neck for a flock of savages. We're getting home. If they can't keep up, then they die," argued Jareth.

"Very well. Trust me on this brother, I have an instinct," I said.

"You and your instincts are going to get me on the wrong end of an axe. All right, then, let's get them freed so we can get the hell out of here."

Jareth and I crouched down from behind the tents and made our way to the dirt pit where the slaves slumbered peacefully. We moved swiftly and quietly to wake the slaves. I cautiously placed my hands over the mouths of a boy and a young women. The first slave, a young woman, stood quickly with eyes wide in terror. "Shh, shh, be still my friend. We're getting you out of here." The look of shock on the woman's face, her eyes widened to the size of a fist in her disbelief. The boy awoke as well and looked to the young woman for how to react.

"Why should we go with you? You're part of the war band, you'll probably just kill me or make me a slave. I'm not going

147

anywhere with you, you barbarian." I understood her doubt to trust us but was running out of time to convince her otherwise.

"Here, take this as a sign of my trust and honor." Reaching in my belt I handed the slave girl a dagger. She leaned back thinking I was going to stab her but when she realized it was a peace offering, she reached out slowly, cautiously, waiting for me to pull it away and stab her as if it was some cruel trick. She wrapped her palm around the handle and placed the dagger close to her waist.

The boy was terrified; the young woman looked back at him, "It's alright, Ulvar. We will go with him," said the slave girl. I worked expediently to remove the chains that held them. Around their necks was a collar adorned with rune symbols that said, "PROPERTY OF JORMA." They were slaves of the Finn Commander. I worked the collar out from around their necks and quietly placed them on the ground. Ulvar and the young woman rubbed their necks vigorously, and a smile crept up the sides of the woman's face. By the brands on her skin I could see that all her life she had known the weight of a collar, ownership by a master, and now she was free to live, fight, and die her way.

Jareth had already freed two others and armed each of them with a spear. The last slave to be awoken was an old man with long, silver hair that ran down his back and tattoos that started at his feet and stretched to his neck.

"Old man," I said as I shook him from his deep slumber. "Old man, rouse yourself." The old man startled swung out his arm and looked about for the one that was calling him. Rubbing his eyes, he focused in on me.

"Wha..? Who are you young man."

"I am Audan and we're here to free you." The old man thought it was some kind of joke or trick, but when he saw the other slaves removing his shackles, he knew it was no jest.

"Quickly now, brother, we are overstaying our welcome and the gods will only grant us so much luck," said Jareth. He put the old man's arm over his shoulder and lifted him to his feet. We led the way out of the camp and into the tree line with the slaves following eagerly behind.

We only made it around one hillside, when the young woman reached out and grabbed me by the forearm. "Why?"

"Why what? Why free you?" I asked. The women nodded yes and looked up at me with watery eyes.

"Because we were in the very place you were, and we need your help to get home." She stared at me as I had never seen anyone stare at me before, as if I was Thor himself, come down from the heavens with the mighty Mjölnir, Thor's hammer, to rescue her from the depths of her despair. "What is your name?"

The young woman pushed her brown bangs behind her ear. "I am Evy."

"Very well then Evy. Let's get on with it."

"Thank, thank you," she said as tears streamed down her face.

"Don't thank me just yet. Make haste girl, now gather you wits so we can go."

A panic erupted in the camp; we heard the sounding of horns in the distance. Soldiers could be heard yelling, "The prisoners are escaping, the prisoners are escaping! To arms, to arms! Get the hounds ready!" It wouldn't be long now until they would catch up and track us down in the woods. Jareth took up the rear to keep the slaves moving at pace. Making it to a valley surrounded by steep hillsides we ran straight through the middle hoping to make expedient our escape. The old man stopped and knelt down placing his hands on his knees, breathing heavily.

"Keep moving, old man, or they will catch us. Do you want to die here? Is that what you want?" The old man looked up at me with a serious and steady look.

"I don't have it in me to run anymore. I tire of running from them," said the old man. Looking up, I noticed the two slaves with spears had disappeared.

"Where did the other two go?" I asked Jareth as he shrugged his shoulders. I turned my attention back to the old man. "So you're just going to quit and be a slave again? They will torture you or worse; place your head upon a pole."

"No. No, they won't," the old man said quietly. He stood up and grasped my shield and axe.

"What are you doing?" I asked as I pulled away from his grasp.

"Give me your shield and axe. I will delay their advance so you can make good your escape." My heart sunk deep into my belly. Why was this old man willing to sacrifice himself for us?

"Why won't you run to freedom? You can still make it. We can help you." Jareth scrambled over to us.

"What the hell is going on here? If he can't make it then leave him. He's probably dead weight anyway."

"Just get the others out of here," I snapped back at Jareth. "I will catch up."

Jareth was hesitant and grabbed my arm in protest.

"I won't leave you behind brother," said Jareth.

"And you won't, brother, I promise. Now go. Get the hell out of here. I'll be right behind you." Jareth reluctantly turned away and led the slaves forward. I turned my attention back to the old man standing tall before me.

"Can I not convince you to take another course?" I asked.

"No, Audan, I'm too old and too slow, but I can still take a few of them with me. Give me your weapons. I will delay their advance whilst you and the others escape to safety." In disbelief and shock, I handed over my weapons to the old man one at a time.

He placed the shield on his left arm and secured the leather strap to his forearm tightly so it would not give. Next he grabbed the axe, and let it fall to his side to feel the weight of the weapon in his palm, analyzing the grip of the handle. The old man looked up at me with a steely calm. "Go now. Before it's too late." My warrior spirit ached to stay, fight, and even die with this old man who owed me nothing, yet he would sacrifice everything. Despite my distaste for the gods I could feel All-Father Odin commanding me to remain at this man's side and do battle.

"You will have your glory, young man. They have robbed you of your strength through torture and unspeakable pain," the old man said to me. "But today is not the day you visit the Great Hall. It is not your time to be with Odin. Morleo placed his arm on my shoulder, staring at me with the warm gaze of a father. "Now go. Go before it is too late!" Morleo released his grip and turned away. I turned and started to run toward Jareth and the other slaves, making it no more than several steps I stopped and turned back to see the old man once more.

"What is your name, old man? Whom should I give thanks to for saving my life?" Keeping his body proudly forward he barely turned his head and said,

"I am Morleo, son of the great tribal warrior, Taran, and I am a slave no more." Morleo stood taller now, bouncing the axe against his shield.

"I won't forget you, Morleo. I will honor your sacrifice," I replied.

"Then honor it by living the life that was denied to me. Freedom is the greatest gift any man could hope for. Be free and grant freedom to those less fortunate than you. Today I die, a free man!"

The soldiers could be heard making it round the bend, shields and armor in a clamor. Morleo looked back once more. "Run, boy! Go! Go!" Those were the last words of the freed slave Morleo whose bravery and courage very well saved my life and the lives of several others that day. Looking back, I could see the torches that lit the hill side. Sinister shadowy figures approached, like running giants, and then, there was the great Morleo, his shadow appeared most fearsome and menacing of all. No longer a subservient slave forced to do the will of others; he stood now and chose his own fate. With a mighty roar, he fearlessly charged forward into battle, first striking a solider to the ground with his shield and then hacking at a second soldier in a frenzy.

I stood, mesmerized and moved at this selfless gesture of a man who barely knew me. Morleo turned and buried his axe into the back of the solider he had bashed with his shield. The soldier shrieked and yelled, as Morleo plunged the axe once more into his skull cap silencing him forever more. More soldiers came, forming a small shield wall; taunting and cursing at the now victorious slave. Morleo turned round quickly and was met by bristling spears from three other men. He threw his axe into the belly of one last bastard that he would take to the afterlife with him. Iron fell upon his body and drove Morleo into the dirt, his final resting place. I watched helplessly as the shadows stabbed the ground relentless in their efforts to punish an honorable man. The Finn soldiers grunted and breathed heavily over Morleo's now lifeless body.

He may have been a wild thing, a savage, but I hope to see him again in the Halls of Valhalla and honor him as a brother, I thought to myself. What a glorious and epic death to face down so many of your foes alone, to lay down your life for others. I knew I could linger no more so I headed off into the darkness after my comrades. Looking back once more at the light of the torches I could see Jorma, the Finn Commander, approach Morleo's corpse that was now bleeding out in the dirt. Morleo's long silver hair stretched out upon the ground, shining brightly in the moon light giving off an almost Asgardian glow. Jorma looked up at the moon and then back down at Morleo, as if the moon was telling him something he should know about his now dead slave.

I ran without regard to my freezing lungs or the painful wounds. I rounded three more bends near a river, and caught up to Jareth and the others. Jareth initially leapt forward expecting to do battle with Finn soldiers but was met by my smiling face. Jareth looked relieved to see me alive.

"Brother, by the gods, you made it! Where is the old man, did he fall behind?" Jareth asked. I knelt down placing my hands on my knees trying to catch my breath. Looking up briefly through the bangs of my hair I replied.

"He's in Valhalla now. His name was Morleo and he saved my life. Let's not let his sacrifice go to waste. We must escape this place my brother." Jareth stood up straight.

"Right then, everyone, follow me and keep up or stay behind and die." We disappeared into the endless forests with our enemies in fevered pursuit.

With Morleo dead, only three slaves remained in our company; all wild things, the boy Ulvar, Evy and Irun. We continued to drive on into the dark woods, splashing across a stream. Evy slipped and stepped into a deeper portion of the stream, catching her leg between two rocks; I heard a terribly familiar crack followed by an agonizing scream. Evy shrieked in pain and the sound echoed between the trees. She reached out desperately for help, "Irun!" she cried.

Irun ran over and tried pulling on Evy's leg, but it was no use. Evy screamed in pain. The broken leg was completely stuck; lodged between the rocks.

"It won't budge," Irun cried. "I can't move it!"

The cold river water rushed over Evy's body. The guards could be heard in the distance getting closer. Jareth grabbed Irun trying to comfort her, "We have to go." Evy looked up at our worried faces and shook her head.

"Go without me. I'm not going to make it," she said.

I put my hand on Ulvar's shoulder. "Come, we must go." The slave girl pulled away from Jareth and grabbed hold of Evy trying to drag the dead weight of her body out of the stream.

"Evy, please, come with us!" the slave girl begged. Evy looked at Jareth,

"Get her out of here! Promise me you will keep her safe? Promise me you will get Irun and Ulvar to safety." Jareth knew he could not keep that promise but lied to Evy knowing full well she would die soon.

"I promise."

Leaving Evy behind in the deathly cold the four of us ran from the sounds of the guards until the clamor of weapons and armor fell silent.

"Stop," I commanded to the others. Voices could be heard in the distance. It was the guards talking to Evy. I climbed atop a small rock face where I could see a single torch and the out-lines of figures. Three guards stood over Evy talking and then fell silent. Evy's face was buried in the water by a soldiers boot pressing against the back of her neck. The cold rushed over her face, Evy fought and struggled but the weight of the man crushed her until her arms fell lifeless and floated in the water next to her corpse.

Irun grabbed me by the leg, "Can you see her? Is she alright?" I jumped down, looking at Irun shaking my head I placed my hand on her shoulders.

"We have to keep moving or your fate will be that of your friends." Ulvar walked up behind Jareth and ripped the sword from his belt.

"What are you doing?" yelled Jareth. Ulvar daringly pointed the sword at us.

"Get back! You call yourselves men, but you are all cowards. I will avenge my sister's death!" Ulvar ran back towards the stream, back towards the soldiers that now numbered six.

Irun quietly called out in desperation, "Ulvar. No. Don't do it." We were too weak to run back to stop the boy but restrained Irun.

"No, no, no, he's just a boy please, not my whole family. No," cried Irun. Jareth placed Irun's arm over his shoulder and guided her forward. I picked up the weapons Jareth could no longer carry and took up the rear. We needed to find safety, a place we could stop and rest.

I watched from a distance as Ulvar approached slowly at the river's edge hiding in the brush listening to the soldiers. "They are not far. You two, go back and get the dogs. The four of us will continue tracking until day break," said one soldier. Ulvar gave out a great yell and leapt from the bushes. He placed his sword into the back of the soldier giving commands.

"This is for my sister!" The soldier reached back helpless trying to remove the blade. Ulvar drove it deeper, and the soldier's arms went limp as he fell into the water with the sword sticking upright out of his back. The soldiers caught off guard reacted slowly until they realized who was attacking them.

"Kill the runt!" Iron spearheads fell towards Ulvar's small frame; Jareth darted out of the bushes with a heroic battle cry. He flung his body upon the remaining soldiers, knocking them to the ground. I jumped into the fray, slicing a soldier's neck open. The waters below now ran red with blood. Another guard pulled himself halfway out of the water. I kicked him down and quickly straddled his chest. We pushed and pulled against one another's weapons until I head-butted him. I reached for my dagger and pierced it through his heart. He screamed briefly until I placed his head back underwater.

I turned to see Jareth and Ulvar stabbing wildly at the last soldier who began falling backwards. "Are you ready to die for your lord, Jorma?" Jareth mocked. I picked up a spear from the dead hands of a Finn soldier and as Jareth and Ulvar swung their weapons from side to side I flung forth the spear. As the spear flew, time itself seemed to stand still. I watched as the iron bolt pulled itself through the air catching the soldier in the side of his chest and plunging deeply in his lungs. The soldier dropped his guard, as he screamed in pain gripping the wooden shaft that protruded upwards from his body. Jareth and Ulvar lunged forward sinking their blades into his belly. As the soldier dropped to the ground, Jareth removed his sword and looked back at me in amazement.

"A fine throw! He never saw it coming!" Jareth reveled in our momentary victory; Ulvar however had found the rage within. I looked over Jareth's shoulder to see the boy now a boy no more, but an animal, ferocious with fangs dripping. Ulvar hacked away at the soldier's unmoving body; the boy had lost all sense tearing and ripping at the man's flesh. I cautiously reached out my arm.

"Ulvar." The boy didn't hear me; his rage clouded everything around him. "Ulvar." *Hack, hack, hack, hack, hack!* "Ulvar!" Despite my calls, he ignored me. Ulvar reached back further this time, ready to sever limbs. He let out a great cry. Just as the boy swung his sword downward, I lunged in front of the corpse, dropping to one knee and taking the sword blow with my shield. The blade plunged deep into the top edge. Looking up at Ulvar from under my shield I could see the boy breathing heavily, his teeth clenched. "Ulvar, that's enough." The boy continued to breathe heavily as he stared through me with cold dead eyes. "Ulvar, he's dead. That's enough, boy."

The blood rushed back to his face, his eyes became soft and large. Ulvar dropped his sword, fell to the ground below and began to weep. I lowered my shield and cautiously put my arms around him, cupping his head in my grasp. "It's okay, boy, you did a fine job."

I pressed Ulvar's head back slightly. "Look at me, Ulvar. Look at me. You did well. Do you understand? It's okay. You're going to be fine." he was inconsolable.

"I'm... I'm... I'm sorry." Ulvar let out a wail this time. I placed my hand over his mouth.

"Ulvar, you did fine boy. Stop crying now. We have to go, okay? Now, just stand up." Ulvar began to stand slowly, one leg after the other. "That's it, nice and easy. Now, I want you to follow Jareth. Always stay just behind him." The shaken boy nodded and turned away from me to follow Jareth. Looking back at the corpse-strewn creek I imagined what may have been if we didn't come to the aide of Ulvar. In some ways it seemed that the boy we knew as Ulvar had died in that creek, and now we were accompanied by Ulvar the Brave.

Ten
The Hounds

Hearts pounding, legs aching, we ran for our very lives. "Go, Jareth, go! Let's pick up the pace. Those bastards are right on our arse!" I bawled as I cut through the forest floor, leaves and twigs smacking me in the face.

Jareth took up the rear keeping our slave companions Irun and Ulvar moving forward as fast as their tiny legs could carry them. Irun whimpered and moaned with each step, her calves giving into her frantic scramble. Hounds could be heard in the distance barking and breaking through the brush, hoping to catch a taste of the scent they followed so furiously and for so long. We didn't care where we were going, as long as it led us away from our former captors.

"You know this is all you fault, right?" accused Jareth.

"My fault! How the hell is any of this my fault?" I objected. Jareth pointed at me, his fingers held together in the shape of a knife.

"Yes, your fault. If you had let me do the talking we could have avoided this mess and maybe be in Jorma's good graces as his honored Generals leading his armies to victory." I could sense the light-heartedness in Jareth's tone; he was having a go at me.

An uncontrollable laughter broke through my teeth as I made a failed attempt to seem serious.

"What! You're telling me that you would have proudly served our father's enemies and followed them into battle? You would rather be a slave to Jorma's wishes than follow our own destiny?"

"Yes, brother, I would. It's better than being chased like foxes through the brush. If he catches us there will be no bartering this time. This time he'll skin us alive and hang us on his mantel. Valhalla will never have us if we die in this manner," replied Jareth.

I punched Jareth in the shoulder. "You might look good on his mantel, right next to his stag," I jested.

"Well, if he puts me on his mantle, I pray to Odin and brother Thor that he uses your skull for a goblet," retorted Jareth.

"If you had done all the talking, we'd already be dead."

Irun, already in great pain, became agitated at our friendly squabble. "Would the two of you just shut the hell up! I can't take any more of your—"

"Aaaahhh!" we all screamed as we tripped over a log and slid face first down a steep fern covered ravine. It was so dark outside, only the leaves and twigs smacking our faces could be seen on the way down. *Thwack, crack, boom!* Falling from a short drop and into a shallow creek, we made a loud splash on the way down. The cold water rushed over my head and down my neck, piercing the lungs and making my wounds ache. A hand reached down, grabbing me by the collar and pulling me from the dark abyss. My ears now removed from the rapids, rang at the sound of silence penetrating my skull. I squeezed my eyes shut and gritted my teeth, the unending pain was wearing on me.

"Stop mucking about. On your feet, brother. We must be off," said Jareth. I pulled myself up using Jareth's arm for leverage.

Tired and out of breath, the situation suddenly seemed very humorous to me.

"This is like the time you slept with the Jarl's Daughter and he was going to sever you from your man hood," I joked with a smile. Jareth laughed heartily while Ulvar and Irun looked on.

"Ah, yes, the Jarl's daughter. Now there was a prize to be had. At least that was enjoyable; this is just hard work. If we get caught I'll get my dick cut off for nothing." Irun frowned and was clearly not amused by our joking and finding it difficult to understand how we could make light of such a terrible circumstance. Torches could now be seen glowing in the distance, getting closer and closer. The sound of the hounds was growing louder and echoed between the trees, almost at our heels now.

Irun pulled on Ulvar's shoulder and stopped to regain her breath. "I can't run any longer! I just can't." Our new friends were completely exhausted. It was only a matter of time before the Finns caught up; a look of terror came over little Ulvar.

"Run or die girl; I'm sure the Draugrs would have you!" I said shrewdly to Irun. The more my pain weighed on me the less I cared about our new found companions. They had become dead weight and I felt a sudden urge to lighten the load.

"We can't out run those demon hounds, even without the slaves. Let's kill the dogs," said Jareth with a crooked smile. He had a good point. The soldiers had to be quite a distance behind their dogs. If we could take out the dogs, then we could cover our tracks, the soldiers would never be able to track us in the dark. I closed my eyes and took a deep breath before speaking.

"Ulvar, Irun, you two keep going, walk swiftly but whatever you do, whatever you hear, do not stop and do not turn back." I kneeled down in front of Ulvar and returned his sword to him. "You need to be a man now; Ulvar the Brave." Ulvar looked up with a fierce smile upon hearing his newly given name. I wanted his new name to give him strength and power in the face of great danger.

"No, no. Please come with us Audan." Tears ran down the boy's gaunt pale white cheeks.

"All will be well, Ulvar. We will catch up before you know it. In the meantime, I need you to protect yourself, and Irun, let no harm come to her. A warrior always carries a weapon. He does not place it on the ground, and he does not give it to others to carry for him. It is a tool that can be used for good or it can be used to subject others to the life you have known as a slave. Ulvar, use it for good." Ulvar looked down continuing to pout; I placed two fingers under his chin and lifted his head upward. His light blue eyes made contact with mine. "Do you understand what I'm asking of you?" Ulvar nodded and wiped the tears from his face.

"Yes. I understand."

"Good lad. Now be on your way. I will be right behind you." Irun said nothing. I think she knew what was to be done, the sacrifice that we may make. She approached Jareth and I, placing a gentle kiss on each of our cheeks.

"Odin protect and guide you both. Come back to us, in this life or the next." Our companions swiftly made their way through the forest, disappearing in the dense green brush. Jareth hacked away at the ferns handing me a small bundle of leaves.

"Time to dig in. Let's kill these fuckers." We rubbed dirt, mud, sticks and twigs onto our bodies, anything to hide our scent, hoping the dogs would not notice us. I dropped to the ground placing the fern leaves over my body. Pressing my ear to the ground I could hear the pounding of the hound's paws tearing at the dirt beneath them. Then I could see the hounds fast approaching through the brush. Jareth reached into his shirt removing his necklace, the hammer of Thor, he kissed it quickly and tucked it back away.

I looked over at Jareth once more, "Brother."

"What?" he replied.

"Are you ready?" Jareth rolled his eyes without moving his head.

"Does it matter?"

"Steady! Steady. Just wait until they are right on top of you." The hairy beasts were very near now and I spoke no more. They sniffed rapidly at the ground walking hurriedly in circles; their tails stood high in the air. A nose found its way to my leg and moved slowly up my thigh. *Shit, he found me,* I thought to myself but the hound did not bark or bite, his nose betrayed him. Our journey through the woods and creeks must have washed away all trace of our stench. The dog's wet black nose made its way to my crotch. I gritted my teeth at the thought of the dog striking at my manhood; his black eyes shined catching the moonlight, his protruding teeth glowed in the darkness.

"Now!" I yelled. We rose ferociously from the ground striking at the three dogs. Jareth plunged his spear into the front of the canine's chest; the beast let out a terrifying cry as it tried to pull away. Jareth stood swiftly to his feet, pulling his spear out of the dog and dropping the iron once more into his neck; the hound's body jerked and rolled on its backside. Flexing my stomach, I lunged forward with both my hands on my axe, burying it deep into the hound. They fell quickly and moved no more. The third hound dodged a spear thrust by Jareth and leapt on top of me. The dog bit and snapped feverishly, spit flew into my face and the hound's hot rancid breath filled my lungs.

"Jareth!" Unable to reach for my weapon, I yelled for help as the dog pressed upon me with tooth and nail. "Kill it, kill it!" Jareth leapt forward swiping the dog's rear leg with his sword. Blood shot forth; the beast let out a deafening wail and limped off into the forest, leaving a bloody trail in his wake. Jareth lunged forward once more hurling his spear as hard as he could at the hound. Missing his target, the iron buried itself into a tree trunk.

"Damn! He's getting away. Once they find that dog our trail will be known to them." Jareth said. We stood from our hiding places, stepping over the two dead hounds, their tongues hanging out of their mouths, the heat still rising from the freshly dead bodies.

"Fetch your spear. You are going to need it." Jareth sprinted to the tree and dislodged it from the bark. We moved on and followed the stream just ahead, running noisily as our feet slapped the water. The sound of weapons and armor was now replaced by hounds once more.

"No, no it can't be," Jareth said looking at me with great frustration.

In disbelief I said, "They brought more dogs. Where did they get all of these hounds? They're coming, get in the river; if we float in the water the hounds will lose our scent. Here give me your shirt." I tugged at Jareth's shirt and he pulled away from me.

"What for?" asked Jareth.

"There's no time, just give it to me." There was a fork in the stream up ahead. I quickly tied Jareth's shirt on a log and floated it down the stream hoping the hounds would follow it. I watched it for a moment as it bobbed and weaved in the current, passing tree roots and bouncing off rocks. "This way, hurry, hurry."

Jareth now shirtless looked about the dark wood for anything that moved. "Do you think that will work? Do you think they will catch the scent?" he asked.

"Do you have a better idea?" I replied. We came upon a small cove with thick brush carved into the river's edge. The cold of the open air was beginning to eat at our hands and toes. "Quickly, hide here. Get down. Don't make a sound," I commanded. Looking at Jareth's face, I could see he turned to a deathly pale. If he did not find warmth soon he would surely succumb to the bitter cold.

"Jareth," I said under my breath. "Stay with me, don't give in to the cold. Fight it."

"My hands… I can't stop shaking," he replied.

"Good, it means you're not dead yet." Jareth looked down at his chest.

"I don't think I'm in the mood for laughter anymore."

"I know, just stay with me. It won't be much longer and we can find you somewhere to warm up," I urged. "You can be cold or you can be dead. We're almost in the clear, now shut your hole." I could see the battle that Jareth waged on the inside. He must have been screaming in his head, begging for it to be all over. I don't think he had ever experienced the unforgiving nature of the wild to such a degree. His usually warm face had turned a pale white, his skin began to shine and his lips and eye lids a ghostly purple.

We stared blankly into the abyss, the sounds of the hounds reaching the fork in the river. They bounced and splashed about tracing and retracing the scents. The voices of soldiers could be made out barking orders to one another. I reached into the river bed searching for a root to pull me down further and conceal my body. Jareth looked over at me. Shaking and miserable, he smiled.

"Let's just kill them and be done with it. I don't know how much longer I can keep running and hiding in the dark like a coward." Jareth shook uncontrollably, his lips turning a pale shade of purple under his bristling beard.

"Just be ready. I'll crack their skulls if they get too close," I replied. The soldiers could be seen now, chain mail gleaming in the glow of their torches. The dogs barked and howled, running swiftly past their masters.

"Follow the dogs; they're still on the scent. They can't be far off now. We'll get those bastards. They've nowhere to run," one soldier said. Another soldier about to run past, paused for a moment, turned, and began to gaze in our direction.

"Keep walking; just keep walking you fucking ox," I cursed under my breath and gripped my axe tightly.

"What are you waiting for? Let's move. They're getting away. Jorma will have our heads if we come back empty-handed," yelled a soldier. The warrior leaned forward with his torch gazing for any movement, any sign of us. "What are you doing? Move on, you idiot. The dogs went this way." The scowling soldier took one last look and reluctantly turned and walked away.

We climbed out of the water reeds; the soldiers were no longer in sight. Jareth and I heaved a big sigh of relief. "By Odin's beard, I thought they had us for certain," Jareth exclaimed. "How much further?"

"I don't know. Just keep moving and stop asking questions." My usual sense of compassion began to fade. Now just trying to survive I focused on the moment at hand. The cold was beginning to get to me as well. It took more effort than usual to ball my hands into fists. My joints popped and every movement reminded me of the biting cold. We marched back in the direction of our companions until I heard a sound echo in the trees. I pressed my hand against Jareth's chest, stopping him in his tracks.

"Do you hear something? Is it the soldiers again?" Jareth dropped his arms to his side and readied his spear.

"No, brother, it's something else." I stepped lightly on the dirt floor looking behind each tree as I passed it until the sound became more obvious: heavy breathing. The light of the moon shone between the trees, revealing steam rising from behind a mossy mound. Looking back at Jareth, I said, "Prepare yourself." We readied our weapons and slowly made our way around the mound. As we inched closer, I heard a gasp. "Irun, Ulvar, is that you?" I called out quietly. Pairs of feet stuck out from under the mound and our companions slowly stood up.

"Audan, Jareth! Thank the gods you have returned to us. We thought for sure the dogs had taken you." Irun embraced us in her arms with little Ulvar standing just behind.

"What are you doing here? I told you to keep moving, no matter what."

"We were tired and scared. We needed to rest," replied Irun. Jareth took several steps forward and motioned us towards him.

"We need to keep moving. I do not think the gods will keep favoring us so."

"Jareth, what happened to your shirt?" Irun asked.

Jareth gazed at me with a look of frustration, "Audan had to borrow it." Irun approached Jareth and placed her hand on his shoulder.

"You're as cold as the grave. Here take this." Irun removed her black wool shawl and handed it to Jareth who happily received it. With his chilled blank stare, Jareth nodded his head in thanks. I looked down at Ulvar; his face still shaken since that mess at the creek. His little legs scampered and skipped quickly along the path.

"Are they gone? Are we safe?" asked Irun.

"We're not safe yet. We need to get to the beach and find a ship. A small fishing boat will suffice," I replied. It was early morning and the skies darkness was beginning to give way to the light of day. We approached a clearing in the forest and cautiously crept out of our hiding place. Looking around for any sign of soldiers, they now appeared to be long gone. Jareth and I grabbed our weapons at the ready and fashioned a long stick as a spear for Irun. "We may need these to take a ship. Do you know how to use a spear?" I asked Irun.

Clearly offended Irun replied, "Of course I do. I'm not ignorant."

My blood turned to a boil and I grabbed hold of the sharpened stick in Irun's hand pulling her close to me. "I never said you were ignorant. I asked if you knew how to use a spear and by that I mean when the time comes will you be ready to pierce a man's flesh and bleed him out like a stuck pig until he moves no more?" I was quite serious in my query. My intention was not to frighten or belittle Irun, but to prepare her for what may come.

"I am ready. Many apologies, Audan," said Irun, as she dropped her head.

Jareth looked back. "Don't be sorry. Just don't be dead."

Scurrying through the ferns like rabbits we made our way up a hill to get a better view of the surroundings. "Look there, Audan. That's it; that's our way home. That's our chariot." Jareth pointed to a grouping of torches in the distance, along the beaches edge was a makeshift dock with a small fishing boat. Their longship must have been out on a raid.

"That must be a resupply dock. Let's get on with it," I said. Making our way down the hill, I turned to Irun. "You need to stay in the shadows. Remain just behind us and always where my eyes can see you. When I give you the signal, move forward to meet with us. No matter what you see don't make a sound. Ulvar, the same goes for you. Do you understand?"

Irun and Ulvar both nodded. "I understand," she said. "Thank you, Audan."

"Don't thank me just yet, we're still a long way from home." Reaching the outside of the small encampment, we crept in quietly, moving one at a time giving each other the signal to move forward or stay put. Everyone at the dock appeared to be asleep, even the watchman was bereft of his post. The fog continued to be our ally and hung over the makeshift camp providing some much needed concealment. "Here, take these." I found some farming tools and handed them to our companions, better improvised weapons than the sticks I had given to Irun to carry around.

We couldn't just approach the dock head on, someone may spot us. "Let's get in the water and swim to the dock. We can take them by surprise," said Jareth.

"I'm not getting in that frigid water. I tired of being cold all the time. Why can't we just move down the dock?" I exclaimed. Hearing myself talk I began to sound like a whiney child.

"Nobody asked you. Do you want to get caught? The planks will be too loud. Now, get in. Consider it payment for taking the linen off my back," replied Jareth.

I dreaded the thought of being any colder than I already was, but it seemed like the only way to take a ship undetected. "Stay here," I commanded to Irun and Ulvar. Walking over to the beach's edge, we slowly made our way into the dark liquid, gritting our teeth, trying not to make a sound. Needles again. The water was so cold, the feeling of ice flowed into my veins and made my bones ache. I was suddenly very awake and very aware of my soreness. Jareth moved forward into the water with not only a look of disdain but pure hatred for the troubles he had faced this day. We swam under the dock looking for any sign of movement. Small waves began smashing against the wood pilings and covered any noise we made. Gripping the dock's edge, I raised my head upward and spotted a guard sleeping quietly. Tapping Jareth on the shoulder, we now both saw the man with sword in hand.

Jareth turned to me and whispered quietly, "Should we kill him or just sneak off with the ship? If he hears us, he'll alert the others."

"Kill him. We need time to signal Irun and get the hell out of here." I said to Jareth. Quietly we climbed up a ladder onto the dock. The watchman was asleep on top of a pile of fishing nets. I stood behind him, waiting to cover his mouth to muffle any screams. Jareth stood over the watchmen with a long dagger.

Looking at each other we counted with our fingers, *one, two, three.* I covered the watchman's mouth, gripping his head tightly in my arms. The watchman's eyes opened just long enough to spot Jareth driving the dagger into his chest. No sound; no whimpers. The watchman's body briefly tensed upwards and fell limp.

"Cover him with the nets." suggested Jareth. I waved my axe towards Irun giving her the signal to move towards us. Irun and Ulvar spotting me were overjoyed. They were going to make it after all. Irun ran down to the dock and grabbed my hand. Jareth took the watchmen's jacket and quickly covered his body; his arms shook as the body warmth from the coat surrounded his skin.

"That's much better," said Jareth.

"Good girl. Get on the boat," I said. Jareth unlashed the oars while I untied the boat from its mooring. Irun and Ulvar scrambled to the small fishing boat and pushed off from the dock. With no water, no food, or provisions, we started our way home. Jareth rowed silently into the darkness while I manned the rudder. Irun grabbed a cloth found on the deck and used it for a blanket, sharing it with Ulvar. We were all still so cold; shaking uncontrollably. I kept looking back at the village waiting to hear yelling and see the gathering of armed men, but it never happened. The village remained asleep and silent. They would find their dead watchman in the morning rotting amongst the fishing nets. By then the four of us would be a day of sailing away. Jareth continued to paddle aided by the hope of not dying or getting caught. The light of day was increasing. Jareth looked at Irun much in the same way I looked at Sada. Perhaps he had a realization that he never could have had in the darkness. I too thought she was beautiful, goddess like even.

Irun had been well-groomed by her previous masters. Her long black hair flowed effortlessly to her waistline and her brown eyes warmed the soul even at the briefest glance. Her long slender fingers wrapped around her arms trying to keep in the warmth. Irun looked up at Jareth through her bangs and Jareth smiled. For the first time in his life, Jareth found himself short on words.

"So, um, you're a pict, huh?" Irun nodded and Jareth just smiled.

"Jareth," I interrupted.

"What?" he replied.

"Ease up on the poor girl. Barely a moment has passed in the light and you're already trying to make her your next mistress." Irun blushed at the thought.

Turning to me she asked, "Am I free?" I moved my gaze off the horizon to acknowledge Irun.

"You are as free as you choose. When we get to Bjorgvin you may do as you wish." Irun's face lit up as she marveled at the thought but it was somewhat frightening for a lifetime slave.

"Where shall I go? What shall I do?" Irun asked.

"I know you're new to this freedom thing, but when we get to the motherland you're welcome to settle in with us until you feel comfortable to move on," said Jareth.

"I welcome the thought and will accept your most gracious offer," she said.

"Do you have kinsman anywhere near?" I asked.

Irun shook her head slowly. "No, they are all dead or traded as slaves long gone from this place."

Jareth picked up the pace, rowing faster and deeper in the ocean water. It wasn't fear of death that motivated him; it was fear of failure; of being caught again and dying in a way that was not honorable. What would we have done with our captors, placed them in the center of the village, slit their throats like sheep for all to see and hang their bodies in the air, letting the gulls pick at their flesh until only bone and rot remained.

Hours had gone by, and Jareth was beginning to tire and wince. "Let's trade places brother. I think you've paddled long enough."

"Where is the wind? Does Odin not wish us to see home?" exclaimed Jareth.

"The wind will come, for now we paddle," I said.

"Do you remember that time we snuck out to steal horses from the neighboring war band?" asked Jareth.

"Of course I do. I remember you talked me into it, and I got kicked off the horse."

"I told you to hang on, didn't I?" said Jareth. "It was a cool summer night just like this one, calm, quiet. I woke you and told you girls were waiting outside; I've never seen you jump up so fast. When we got outside I told you they were in the next valley. We picked up our daggers and ran into the night without a care in the world." said Jareth.

"Until we got there, then you told me what we were really doing. I was so scared to get into trouble."

"Trouble? They would have castrated us and fed us to the wolves. In any case, it was fear that made me fall. Fear was the reason I almost got caught that night, why I was so hesitant to steal the horses," I said.

"Well, you don't have that problem anymore. Look at what we have done, brother."

I began to breathe heavy, getting into a rhythm of rowing, trying not to tire too quickly. Suddenly in the distance, I saw a lamp. Jareth pointed towards the bouncing light in the distance.

"Brother, look there," said Jareth.

"Finn raiders! Everyone get down and shut your holes," I commanded. We peered over the boat railing and off in the distance saw three distinct lamps glowing just above the water's surface.

"Don't let them take me back," Irun pleaded. No longer a slave, she was now hunted prey, a feeling that she would have to come to tolerate if she wished to keep her freedom.

"Shut your mouth and you'll be fine," I whispered. Men could be heard laughing and drinking.

A longship, we mustn't let them find us. If the Finns caught us they will torture us for the pleasure of it. I thought to myself. Irun's face was now pale as the fear of capture consumed her. I looked about for a new course and pointed starboard.

171

"Get closer to shore, stay in the darkness." I rowed harder keeping my strokes silent, smooth, and low to the water as Jareth turned the rudder towards shore. Once we were far enough away we headed west again towards Bjorgvin. The long-ship of the Finnish raiders faded into darkness, no longer posing danger. No doubt, they would find their fallen comrades at the docks. It wouldn't be long before a raiding party headed towards our villages to claim retribution.

"Pick up the pace, brother, we need to get home and pre-pare defenses," urged Jareth. The sky cracked and crackled in the heavens. Thor was watching over us, or coming to drown us with lighting. Thor was funny that way; we all paid homage to him, and looked towards him for help in battle. Sometimes he was with you and other times, against. Making sense of the gods was never an easy task, so most Vikings didn't ask any questions. In my case, I still doubted their existence and merely hoped that if they were real that they were on my side. The wind began to howl tugging at the sail as the waves moved our boat further out to sea. I sat quietly pondering the connection between Sigr and the Draugrs we faced in the dark forest. Why did they not continue their chase and why would Sigr send us there? None of it made sense.

"Let's get the sail better secured." I said to Jareth. Jareth held on to the sail rigging as I pulled the rigging tighter, raising the sail up the mast until it could be raised no more. I tied the rigging down to a peg and latched it in place. The sail caught the wind and pulled our boat quickly over the waves.

Jareth began to laugh, "Ah ha ha! We did it, brother! We're going home! By the gods, nothing can stop us now!" I laughed and allowed my guard to drop momentarily at Jareth's sudden optimism. The Finns would send a raiding party back to us for revenge of what we had done. This was not over by any measure.

"Oh great, a mist, do you see that Audan? A fucking mist. It can never be easy can it?" A wall of fog headed straight for us that stretched the entire horizon. In all my years of sailing I had never seen a mist befall us with such speed.

"Get closer to shore or we will lose our bearing." Getting lost at sea was a fate worse than death, and we hoped to avoid such a calamity. A man can lose all sanity if he gets lost in the fog. Jareth turned the rudder starboard to get closer to shore. We were no more than several hundred yards from the coast line, but soon, there was no coast line to be seen, only fog, only silence. The wind and waves that had once carried us had subsided, and we were adrift as we had feared.

"Back to the oars, then. Slaves, if you want to live and be free you will help us," Jareth said reluctantly. "Are we cursed, brother? Does Thor or Odin not look after us?" he asked.

"Patience, brother. It's just fog. We will get through this," I replied.

"This must be that witch's doing, Sigr. She sent us on this errand. She has cursed us and removed us from Odin's sight." I thought back to the corpse goddess in the cave, and her message. Did she intend for all of this misery and terror to fall upon us?

After hours of rowing, there was still no coast line in sight, no sound, no wind; we were truly lost at sea. My strength had once again escaped me and I was in need of respite. "I tire, brother," I said to Jareth.

"Take a nap, it doesn't look like we're going anywhere. I'll pray to Aegir for a gentle current and safe return home. Perhaps the sea giants can still look out for us," replied Jareth.

I scoffed under my breath, "You do that, brother." I found a pile of ship line that one of the slaves was resting on. "Move," I said to Ulvar pointing at the other side of the boat. Without hesitation and mostly out of fear he removed himself. Lying down in the center of the boat I pressed my head into the ships line until it became bearable to sleep upon. My wounds still aching, some still bleeding, I began to fade away in the silence that surrounded us.

"Listen. Do you hear that?" Irun looked about trying to locate the sound.

"What is it, girl?"

"I don't know what it is. Rain perhaps?"

"I hear it too." The sound of rushing water was obvious now.

"We must be close to land. A waterfall perhaps." Irun smiled with optimism that was quickly wiped away.

"By the gods. Whirlpool! Get the oars, turn this thing around now!" Jareth yelled. I stood quickly and we paddled with all our might, but for every stroke, we were pulled back two more. I reached out to Ulvar and Irun with the ships line.

"Here, take these. Lash yourselves to the ship and don't let go!"

"Row, row!" Being pulled into the vortex, our small ship creaked and bowed. The front prow began to lean inward. We grabbed on to whatever we could to keep from falling out of the ship. Our weapons flew past us bouncing on the deck and into the water.

"Brace yourselves!" I yelled.

The ship capsized and broke apart and our bodies were swept away with the jagged splintered remnants. We were dragged under into the dark cold abyss. I grabbed Ulvar's arm as our bodies were tossed about the ocean floor. The whirlpool spit us back into the open sea; deep, deep into the depths of the ocean. The light above could be seen, but it was faint, and so very far away. My lungs burned, the water pressed upon my skull. As I swam upwards with Ulvar I couldn't see Jareth or Irun. I feared they were lost. The light became brighter and brighter. I looked down at Ulvar, he was already gone; his grip loosened from mine. He was already lifeless but I felt that I could still save him. I pulled and pulled using the last full measure of my strength and will; and then I stopped.

The pain had miraculously ceased, my chest no longer felt as if it would explode. The cold water no longer seemed endless or terrifying. Shadows overcame my body from above. I looked up, staring through the great blue blanket and a smile came over my face. Death was upon me and there would be no more pain, no more suffering. Shadows turned to a blinding light, hands reaching downward and tugged at our bodies, lifting us towards deliverance.

Eleven
Trust & Deceit

It had felt as if eons passed me by as I slowly drifted through the dark ether that surrounded me. Visions of Sada visited me in this murky place, her hand touching me gently; running her fingers though my beard. Her hair shined brightly in the light and as I looked upon her face, her smiled faded into the darkness; worry became evident upon her brow as she shed a tear down her flawless cheek. The hands that pulled upon me in my vision now grasped upon my collar and cradled my body gently carrying me upward. I felt safe, even rested, as I was softly placed on firm, solid ground.

"Awake, Audan," a soft voice called from somewhere in the obscurity, though I could not surmise who it was.

"Audan, it's time for you to awake and rise." A bright light shined from above, so intense, so warm, I squinted my eyes and clenched my teeth. Placing my hand over my eyes to block the intense light, I attempted to see clearly this gentle voice that summoned me as my sight adjusted to the magnificent brightness.

"Who calls upon me? Reveal yourself at once," I demanded.

A moment of silence followed and then a melodic voice called out ever so delicately, "You don't know my name, Audan? I certainly know yours, we all do." The replies were so mysterious; my mind raced with random flashes of memories from times past.

"Cease with your games spirit and reveal yourself!"

A burst of laughter echoed in the air and traveled along the whispering winds. "Calm yourself, brave marauder of the north. It was not my intention to anger you."

"If I knew whom you were, my lady, I would not be asking, now state your name and your purpose!" I became further agitated. Was I still captive? Was I about to be tortured once more by that mad bloodthirsty Finn? Death was becoming a welcome thought to the idea of continuing this never ending journey of pain.

"Open your eyes, Audan. No harm will befall you here. You are under my guardianship in this realm." My eyes began to adjust to the light; I saw blue, bright blue skies above. Clenching my fists I pulled something from the ground. *Grass?* I studied the green in my hand and found I was sitting on lush, green grass that was warm to the touch. The sweet air filled my lungs with the scent of flowers and awoke the senses in a way I had not experienced since days of youth. I rose to my feet in utter awe as I gazed upon the endless beauty that lay before me. The epic fields stretched as far as the eyes could see and into cosmic oblivion; the shadows of white clouds darted and raced along the bed of wild flowers beneath my feet. The inescapable cold of the north was now replaced by warmth I'd never felt before.

"What is this place? Where have you taken me?" I asked in amazement.

"You are in the realm of Fokvangr, my sanctuary and household. We welcome you, Audan, favored son of Rurik." My heart stopped for a brief moment and my muscles became cold. "Be still Audan, you are among friends here," the voice said. My mind raced and dashed back and forth knowing the answer in my heart to the character of this voice but I hesitated momentarily for sounding foolish.

"Dare I ask, Freya, is that you?" I asked with a weary voice. I remembered the stories I had been told as a child around the fire pit about the gods my brethren prayed to every day. Was this truly the home of legends our great ancestors spoke of? The voice circled me speaking in one ear and then the next. I turned my head from side to side following the sounds as they visited me.

"Ah, so you do know my name. I'm quite flattered considering how low in esteem you hold the gods these days. But, then again, who could blame you in all your mortal troubles?" replied Freya. I swallowed and looked in a panic for the right questions to ask.

"I hear you, my lady, but still cannot see your figure clearly. Where are you?" I asked. The winds shifted once more over my shoulder and in front of me.

"I am everywhere in the realm Fokvangr. I am the grass, the trees, the wind, and even in the very air that you breathe. But if you desire me to be something more familiar to your mortal sight…" The bright light appeared once again as gold dust floating in the air, circling in a vortex of wind until taking familiar shape revealing the voice. A woman appeared in front of me. "Now then, does that suit you, Audan?"

"If you are truly the goddess, then, am… am I dead? It must certainly be so?"

Freya smiled and giggled placing her jeweled fingers over her face. She swung her head back and forth, her flowing blonde hair waving gracefully in the wind.

"Heavens no, of course not. Well, not yet, anyway. What would make you think you're dead?" I pondered Freya's question but still found my head stuck in a fog. Only fragments, pieces of memories remained that floated about like embers from a fire.

"If I'm not departed then how did I get here? Why am I here?" I wanted answers and Freya did not seem to be in a rush to provide them. She appeared as a woman of thirty-five but with the demeanor of a much younger girl. Everything seemed to make her smile or giggle; everything was a game to her. She even moved about as a young girl, always bouncing about, never standing still in one place for very long.

"I summoned you here of course, as my honored guest. Let's just say you are neither dead nor alive at this moment. I have you in a middle place to put it plainly, but only for a brief time. You are also here to speak in confidence on a matter of great importance to me."

"And what may I ask am I here to discuss?" I reached down to my waist attempting to find my axe to rest my hand upon, but it was gone.

"About you, Audan, about your plans, your future. I also need something from you, a favor if you will and it seems that you are the right man for the task. You have a talent for staying alive and whether you like it or not, you have acquired a taste for blood."

In a panic I suddenly realized something very important was missing. "Where is my brother, Jareth? And Ulvar and Irun? Where are they? What have you done with them?" I demanded.

"Done? Don't be silly. Your friends are perfectly fine. They are safe, I assure you."

"So where are they?" I angrily stepped forward clenching my fists. Freya placed her hands upward to calm me.

"Safe, as I said. They slumber soundly under my protection. You must trust me in these matters."

"And my axe, where is my axe? Why have I been disarmed like a foolish child?"

"You won't be needing your weapons here; besides, your mortal instruments would do you a disservice if you turned them against your gods. What do you last remember, Audan?"

I looked about for answer, perhaps something familiar. "We were in a ship I think, a whirlpool appeared amidst a great fog and we were sucked in. I had Ulvar by the hand and swam upward towards, something, a floating light. I don't remember." The fog continued to cloud my thoughts, I rubbed my head; perhaps I had struck it upon a rock at the water's edge. Freya placed her hand gently on my shoulder; the warmth of her hand radiated through my body as she pressed her fingers against my skin.

"You have been through a great ordeal; it's only natural to feel a bit, forgetful. In time your wits will return to you."

"You asked for a favor? What sort of favor would a god ask of a man my lady? If you're a god can't you just fulfill your own wishes by speaking the words?" I asked like a true warrior, direct and to the point.

"Unfortunately, even the gods have their limitations in certain circumstances. Come now Audan, you must be hungry." Freya fixed her eyes on my grumbling stomach. "Let us feast before we discuss business. I don't like to talk on an empty stomach and everyone knows a warrior is only angry if he is hungry." I gazed upon the fields and vast meadows that lay before me. It was like nothing I had ever seen before. Flat green meadows that stretched out to the horizon, blue sky, not a single cloud, no fog, no ocean. The air was warm, with a light breeze carrying the smell of wild flowers.

"I must be dreaming. Is this real? Are you a witch?"

"So untrusting are we, Audan?"

"If you are Freya then you are most certainly a Valkyrie, and your wretched kind are not to be trusted," I said harshly. Freya circled me slowly, looking me up and down as a predator stalks its prey on the hunt. Her slight grimace suggested that she was offended by my remarks.

"I'll admit that some of my lesser sisters have been unruly in your realm, but don't think we are all alike. Some of us serve good, others evil, and some, well, some of us serve our needs and do as we please. That is, when All-Father is not looking with his ever watchful eye. I understand you met one of my servants, Sigr? She's one of my more trusted maidens, which is why I sent her to you to deliver my invitation."

Freya was beautiful, inescapably beautiful, hair gold like the sun, skin as white and fair as freshly fallen snow, tall and slender. She wore a white robe and carried a gold decorated sword on her waist.

"If you are the goddess, then why do you carry a sword? Are you not immortal? What do you have to fear from me?" I asked. She laughed once more placing her slender fingers around her swords decorated pommel.

"Even the gods have enemies who look to destroy us, just as you, Audan. We must be ready for anything that comes our way." Freya looked down lifting her hand and briefly gripping the sword handle. "I grow tired of this game. Are you ready to eat or are you going to continue to question me like a captured soldier?" Freya tilted her head down, shifting her eyes upward looking at me with curiosity. "No? Wonderful, follow me."

Freya extended her open hand in front of her as gold dust swirled and danced just above her palm. A dark ram's horn emerged. Gripping the horn gently, she blew a great call into the air three times. I looked about waiting to hear a response from another horn until suddenly the ground beneath my feet began to shake and tremble. It became louder, and more intense. Looking up at Freya I asked, "What is it?"

"Why do you look frightened, Audan?" Freya did not turn her head; she merely looked forward smiling in anticipation of what was to come.

"I'm not frightened." I was lying. I reached to my side only to be reminded that my axe was gone. With no axe to protect me, I felt completely vulnerable to the creature that was about to approach us. What beast of old had she summoned?

"Abandon your worries, Audan. It is only Virnir." In the distance just beyond the rolling hills, giant antlers became visible, as tall as trees that stretched to the heavens. The head of Virnir was now plainly seen as he called out to Freya with a great playful bellow. She giggled and laughed at the cries of this beast. Closer this massive creature came until its neck and head briefly blocked out the sun. I placed my hand above my eyes to get a good look at this great elk. Freya stepped forward towards the hooved beast. "Come down, Virnir," she commanded.

The great beast lowered its head to the ground and placed one of its antlers directly in front of us. Freya stepped lightly onto the Antler, turned and extended her arm towards me. "Well, Audan. Come along. Or do you prefer to walk? My household is a great distance from here and we have little time to discuss my plans." I stood in place completely in awe of the majestic beast that bowed before us.

'This... this is incredible! We have nothing like this in all the lands of Midgard." I looked at Virnir's enormous body as his chest rose and lowered with every breath. His gigantic deep brown eyes shifted and fixed upon me as if he was giving me permission to join Freya. Stepping forward, I grasped Freya's hand and guardedly made my way on top of Virnir's enormous antlers.

"Grab a horn; it's a long way down once he starts moving. The Great Elk let out a cry and lifted his head swiftly upward. I gripped the horn as tightly as I could; the air rushed around my body until his head came to a stop. As Virnir began to move, his horns gently swayed us back and forth. I could see the endless green for immeasurable distances.

"How ever did you tame this beast?" I asked Freya.

"All creatures of this land belong to me. Even the wind and sun heed to my commands. I can move the stars, turn spring to fall or cast ice over all I see. Today I'm in a spring mood." Freya waved her hand outwards with outstretched fingers and wild flowers began to appear and blossom everywhere she gestured. I no longer had any doubts of her powers; I only questioned the way in which she wished to use them on me.

"I can hear you," Freya said. I turned my head towards her with a confused look. "Your thoughts, Audan, I can hear them. Sigr was merely the messenger; I am the master," she said as she smiled.

"Can all corpse goddesses hear the thoughts of men?"

"Corpse goddess?" Freya replied clearly angered. "What an awful epithet. That's such a disparaging way to describe my kind. You men of Midgard can be so cruel sometimes. I prefer a more regal term befitting my ancestors, Valkyrie, if you please."

"Valkyrie it is then. So, do you share this gift with all your sisters?"

"Nay. Our magic is unique to the individual. Some are quite talented with the gift of foresight, the ability to conceal themselves amongst the forests, or even to take on other mortal forms.

"So if you can read my thoughts are you suggesting I stop thinking?"

"I wouldn't think that would be terribly difficult for you, Audan." I smirked at Freya's jest.

"I see I will need to guard myself in your presence."

"No, I merely ask that you control your thoughts. I never understood how mortal minds work, always jumping from one vision to the next. It's so primitive."

"So, what do you see in my mind?" Freya fixed her gaze upon me; it appeared cold this time, harsh and unforgiving. Her childish nature disappearing in an instant, even the color of her skin appeared to grow darker.

"Shall I describe the things you already see or explain to you the truth you cannot accept? The great and horrible things that lurk in your beating heart, the desires of your black soul?" I nodded with confidence.

"Try me."

"Very well, then. Your thoughts are terribly dark, Audan: selfish, vain, and cruel. Your mind is filled with murder drenched in the lifeblood of your fallen foes. Carnal thoughts find their way between your violent visions; ecstasy and lust permeate through your every dream. In your mind you have already had carnal knowledge of me twice despite the love you hold for Sada. And yet…"

I hesitantly asked for more. "Yes?"

"And yet, you do not act on these specters. Your thoughts betray you and reveal the true nature within your soul. You only lack the freedom with which you need to take action on your deepest desires. As gods, we do not ask for permission to take action, we merely do as we please. For now, I ask that you discipline your mind."

"I'll do my best but I cannot make any promises. How do you suggest I clear my mind of this fog?"

"Focus not on what was, what may have been or what is yet to be. Focus on what is in the realm before you. Here you will find truth in every moment and every action." We approached a wooded area covered in birch trees that rose high into the sky. Freya tugged back on Virnir's horn.

"Virnir, stop here." Virnir took one more step and quickly stopped. "Down, Virnir." I tightened my grasp on the horn as we quickly descended to the forest floor; the air rushing past my body. Freya and I stepped down from the great antlers that had carried us so very far away. Freya approached Virnir's face and began to pet his fur as one would a hound. "Thank you, my child. Be on your way." Virnir rose up once more and departed from us, disappearing quickly somewhere over the horizon. Freya skipped ahead several steps before turning back to me. "This way, Audan, and keep by my side."

Heading towards a large wall of blackberry bushes, I quickly caught up. Freya motioned her hands and the thorny bushes removed themselves opening like a doorway, curling and looping in one another until a path had been cleared before us. I stopped briefly, once again in utter amazement at this display of sorcery. As I passed the thorny walls I hesitated for a moment and looked back, but it was too late, the walls had already closed behind me. Nowhere to go but forward from here on out.

Freya strode to a large rune stone in the middle of a grassy courtyard, her white robe dragging lightly on the grass beneath her bare feet. She placed her hand on the inscription covered stone and looked back to me. "Take my hand, Audan."

"Where are you taking me?" I asked cautiously.

"This isn't an exercise in trust and I wasn't asking. Now, take my hand." Freya extended her long elegant fingers outward, a slight white glow emanated from her palms. I reached outward slowly and gripped her hand. At the moment our hands touched warm light shot upwards from beneath our feet. A blue glow surrounded us, buzzing and dancing around our bodies. I released my grip of Freya's hand, and in the blink of an eye, the large rune stone was gone from sight, and the grassy field no longer lay beneath my boots.

"You see, that wasn't so bad now was it?" We had now entered a hall the likes of which no warrior had set eyes upon in all of Midgard. Great columns of living trees that stretched endlessly into the sky, the table was made of dark smooth stone that grew from the ground itself; everything here was alive and connected to the earth.

"Please, Audan, sit. Welcome to my home." Freya motioned to a chair made of vines. The chair moved towards me. I sat down suspiciously, waiting for the earth to swallow me whole or take hold of my neck. "May I offer you a drink? You must be parched after your long journey." Another Valkyrie, as fair and beautiful as all the rest, appeared suddenly from the shadows with a large silver goblet and placed it in front of me. "I am assuming that honey mead will suffice to quench your thirst?" The Valkyrie generously poured the mead into my goblet. I looked up at her and through her chestnut brown hair I could see her pale blue eyes. She turned to look at me briefly and I saw a flicker of light, like fire, dash across her eyes. She looked away and then stepped back into the shadows. I looked at the mead for a moment, hesitant to drink. It was perfect, golden, clean, and most certainly poisoned. I looked over at Freya suspicious of her every move as I rolled the goblet in my hands.

"Poison?" Freya exclaimed. "Why would I poison you, you're already in Fokvangr! There would be no point in killing you in a land of honored dead. Besides, I'm quite fond of you and still have need of your particular skill set. We've yet to discuss my proposal for you future." Freya raised her arm and snapped her fingers; several Valkyries entered the chamber with silver serving dishes and a roasted wild boar on a spit. Almost in unison they placed the feast on the table before us. Savory smells filled the air making my belly grumble.

"This is a feast befitting a king. Is all this for me?" I asked. Freya leaned inward placing her hand on her chin.

"We have been expecting you Audan, for quite some time. It's not often that we have a hero in our chamber, at least not a living one."

"A hero? I'm no hero. I'm just a warrior trying to survive."

"Is that so?" Freya leaned on the table running her finger along the brim of her goblet. "Then why do you move against the Jarl of Bjorgvin?"

"I have done no such thing."

"Perhaps not willfully, but in your mind you are already gathering your forces, recruiting men for war."

"The raid on the Finns was ordered by the Jarl. It had nothing to do with what I desired."

"But the men are loyal to you and your father, are they not? It was you that led them into battle, not the Jarl, and it was you they fought for. How many friends have you lost to battle Audan, how many? How many more are you willing to sacrifice, to put to the sword for your glory?"

Pain overcame my mind; the great ocean depths— that was the last thing I remembered. The fog in my head cleared for a moment, once again reminding me of my lost companions. "What have you done to me? Why can't I remember clearly?" A pounding in my head came on as flashes of Jareth, Ulvar, and Irun hit me like a hammer.

"Drink, Audan. Your pains will subside but you must drink." Freya grasped the cup in my hand and helped lift it to my lips. Looking down at the cup, it moved and shook in place, everything was distorted.

"Drink," I whispered under my breath. With a shaking hand I raised the goblet and heartily consumed my mead. The pain quickly vanished and my worries were no more.

"'Thank you, will suffice," said Freya.

"Thank you." I reached for the bread rolls in front of me and stirred them in my stew. The aroma of the food was intoxicating, almost too much so. I drank the mead waiting for it to kill me, but all I found was satisfaction.

"Is the food and drink to your liking? I had it especially prepared for you," Freya said.

Speaking with a mouthful of salty pork I replied, "Yes, very much so. I can't recall a time when I was presented a feast more glorious than this."

"Well, it must be difficult for you; always scurrying about the dark corners of Midgard, fighting, killing, running, hunting."

Looking upwards, I saw Freya sitting on her throne. It appeared soft, comfortable, not like something you would see a King or Jarl sitting on. There was no gold on this throne, nor silver, or shiny things. Freya seemed smaller now, less formal. She slouched in her giant throne and laid her legs over the side as she bounced them back and forth. To my great surprise her thrown was flanked by great beasts; on each side of her lay a cat, large and black with eyes that glowed bright yellow. They seemed content but kept a watchful eye on me as I swayed back and forth in my seat.

"So back to business. I have something you want, and you have something I want."

"And what could you have in your possession that I desire?" The drink had completely overcome me now. My speech was sloppy, slow, and I knew it. Barely through one glass and I was already more inebriated than the village drunkard.

"Foresight, I can see into your future, Audan, or your possible future, but there are obstacles in your way. You wish to be Jarl is it not so?" My tongue now loosened by the mead spout forth words without thought.

"Yes! Or, perhaps one day." I stood now trying to relieve the many pains in my body.

"Well, I have much greater plans for you, I wish for you to be King of the North." Freya rose with her hands extended in great seriousness and excitement. I fell back into my chair and laughed deeply. I slapped my leg and my eyes teared from great amusement.

Wiping the tears of laughter from my eyes I replied, "King? Are you mad? I'd have to slay half the Kingdom to attain the throne." Freya remained poised and confident in her statement.

"Mad? Show a little decorum Audan. With you in the seat of power there's no telling where the Viking nations could go. You could rule over all Midgard." I took another drink from my goblet and wiped my chin with my forearm.

"And how do you plan to make this happen?"

"You will need to silence those, both living and dead, that would work against you."

"The living I can kill, how do you expect me to kill a dead man?"

"That's where the favor comes in. You will need to venture to Asgard and retrieve a weapon for me. The journey is fraught with peril; I have sent many men before you, none have come back alive."

"And what weapon will I be bringing to you from Asgard, Thor's hammer?" I asked sarcastically.

"No, no, you couldn't possibly get away with that. No, I need you to get into the grand armory inside the Great Hall, Valhalla. There is a sword that resides there, a sword forged in fire and ice in a time before the gods of your people. Only this weapon can vanquish the dead."

"And what will you do with this gift that I will bring you? What do you have to gain, Freya?" She was hiding something, I could tell but she was very good at keeping it discreet.

"That's my business and mine alone. Let me worry about the details and you stay to your task."

"And in return for running the gauntlet and bringing you this slayer of the dead?"

"I will assist you in your effort to become all powerful King of Midgard. I will conceal your armies while you gather in strength and you can move undetected to each of your foes."

"How do I know this isn't some kind of trick?"

"You don't, but if you wish I can simply wake you up at the bottom of the ocean. If the sharks don't devour you I'm sure the clans will figure out something to do with you once you have been caught again. Although I don't think you'll be rotting in a pit this time. They'll probably castrate you and feed your corpse to the wolves, or better yet, they will torture you first and slowly grind your body into stew."

"That's enough." I knew she was taunting me and I didn't much care for it. My happiness brought on by spirits was quickly turning to fire in my belly.

"Or separate your limbs from your body and put them on displ..."

"I said that's enough!" I stood quickly slamming my goblet on the table and spilling my mead on to the floor. "I will not hear any more of this. I will aide you but no tricks, corpse goddess."

"Wonderful."

Twirling the now empty goblet in my hand I asked, "So how do you plan on getting me into Valhalla? Do you intend for me to walk right in through the golden gates? Ask for permission to be let in?"

"I will get you to the plain of Asgard, but as for the method of entry into Valhalla, that will require your own doing, Audan."

"Is it guarded?"

"It is Valhalla, home of the gods! Of course it's guarded."

"Is it dangerous?"

"Of course."

"Good." I burped and lay back heavily in my chair.

"You will take my chariot. My Valkyries are preparing it for you now. You will need to conceal yourself and appear as one of the fallen warriors. I shall cast a spell that will alter your appearance but be warned that this magic will only work on other undead. If the gods spot you, they will plainly see through my ruse. Once inside, you will have to find a more creative way to get to the armory."

"And when I have done this for you, you will send me back and free my friends? Then I can go home?"

"I will send you back to your ship, along with Jareth, Ulvar, and Irun. But know this mortal, if you are caught, I will not be able to save you from the bowels of Helheim that they will most certainly throw you in to. Traitors of gods are not treated mercifully in Helheim by Hel the goddess. She'll probably feed you to her vile hounds." Freya laughed, lifting her head up towards the sky. "Now, do we have an arrangement?"

Freya reached out her hand. I paused for a moment, wondering if touching a god one too many times would kill me, but then again, I was already in Fokvangr. I reached out and gripped the hand of a goddess. Warm light surged through my body once again and the sensations were beyond my understanding. Opening my eyes, I noticed Freya looking at me in an all too familiar a way.

"Excellent!" exclaimed Freya. "Let us celebrate our newly found partnership. I bid you good fortune, Audan and should you succeed, the world as you know it, will be yours."

Twelve
We Were Mortal Once

Placing her goblet firmly on the stone slab table, Freya clapped her hands and jumped upright. "I have a surprise for you."

"Well, then, bring it forth so I can have a look," I replied merrily. The fabled chariot of Freya entered loudly into the hall. Small though it was, the chariot possessed a splendid dark oak frame, perfect in every way, with neither knots nor splinters to be found in this wood. Gold trim followed the unusually rounded curves of the rails. But what was most unusual and almost breath-taking was not the chariot itself, but what pulled it. To my surprise there was no horse, no mule nor ox that would convey my method of travel this day. No, Freya's chariot was pulled by something bearing tooth and claw of the feline variety, something feminine that would complement the personality of the goddess herself. These, house cats, you might call them, were the size of large hunting hounds. One of the purest white, and the other of the deepest black. Their coats glistened even in the dim light of the halls of Freya's home. Such piercing features these creatures had; sharp ears, long, pointed chin-hair akin to a beard and whiskers that stretched far beyond their faces.

"What magnificent beasts! What are they called?" I asked with excitement.

"The white one I named Flurry and the black one is Raven. They are the most precious things in all of creation to me and the only ones of their kind in all the realms."

I slowly approached the chariot with my hands purposely at my sides; both cats turned their attention to me straightaway. Their faces perfectly chiseled along their feline bone lines, they were a menacing sight to behold up close. A slight green glow, much like the Draugrs of the dark forest, radiated from their all-seeing eyes. I paused momentarily, wondering if they were wild and would consume me but the cats did nothing beyond watch my movement, obviously domesticated to the extent that you can domesticate a giant feline. Freya approached gracefully behind me with a cloth barely draped over her perfectly-formed body.

"Do not be concerned. They will take you to Valhalla safely, and when you succeed in your task, they will return you back to me to deliver my prize," said Freya.

"And if I fail? What then? Will you feed me to your pets?" I asked as I mounted the chariot. Freya walked to the front of the chariot and gently stroked the faces of her feline companions with the back of her hand. They leaned in to her touch, purring loudly.

"The honored Viking dead of Valhalla are not known for welcoming trespassers to their Great Hall. It is an unforgivable insult to walk amongst such heroes without having yet earned the title. Focus on the task at hand, Audan, and all will be well. Now go." Freya's eyes glowed warm like embers from a fire. I found myself momentarily under her control. She approached me, grabbing the top of my tunic and pulled me downward for a passionate kiss. Her lips, warm and inviting pressed hard against mine; perhaps a final goodbye for a doomed soul. Smiling, I suddenly felt invincible but heavy with the guilt of betraying Sada in the name of survival.

"Thank you for your favor, Freya. Your kindness is not easily forgotten," I said. Freya nodded and with a wide smile, turned, and walked seductively back to her chambers without another word.

I reached to grab the leather reins and wrapped them around my hands. I snapped them against the backs of the giant felines; they hissed and moaned. Digging their claws into the ground, they pulled the chariot effortlessly forward. We picked up speed expeditiously and as I looked back for a final glimpse of Fokvangr, Freya and her fortress disappeared into a dark foggy mist. The chariot no longer bounced or rattled rolling on the ground. The ride was unusually smooth for the wooden wheels of a chariot and eerily quiet. The cats did not seem to notice or mind.

Are we on the ocean? I thought to myself. Looking over the rails there was no water to be seen, or earth for that matter, just the grey and white fog that encircled the chariot. The air grew colder and colder; I could smell the ice and felt the freeze creep into my bones.

Tucking in my shirt to find some warmth I began looking about the chariot for something that would provide respite from this cold. I reached downward, finding a white fur, and draped it over my shoulders. The chill quickly subsided as I shook in place. *Where was I? Why was it so cold?* Looking down at the reins in my freezing hands, a glimmer of a small white speck floated about and then fell upon my arm.

Snow? Was it not still summer in the land of the North? Looking forward the white cat Flurry seemed all but gone and the black cat Raven was now a spotted white.

"Perhaps you two fur balls know where we are?" I asked the cats in vain. They did not respond and continued their trek forward.

"We must be up in the mountains somewhere?" I wanted to know not just that I was going to Valhalla, but also how to get there. Perhaps, for the living, it was not meant for us to know such a thing, for only the honored dead could travel all seeing to the Great Halls.

The fog began to thin out and clear up ahead. "A light, at last!" I said to myself. Through the dark patches of cloud, I could see glimpses of snowcapped trees and rocks. Just then, a blinding light pierced the fog, I covered my eyes with my hands for a moment peeking through my rigid frozen fingers.

"Damn, I can't see!" The fog cleared and the blinding light slowly subsided. A silence fell over the sky, my eyes widened and my jaw dropped at the vision that lay before me. There it was, there ahead lay the epic and great home of the honored dead, the home of the Norse Gods of old, the ancient ones; Valhalla.

It was not the single great fortress as I had envisioned since I was a small child but it was an entire city atop an epic snowy peaked mountain. *If only Jareth could see this.* The great mountain towered so tall it appeared to float above the clouds looking down upon what I thought was Midgard, the realm of humans, my home. If the mountain did indeed reach the ground, no man could ever surmount its peak for the edges of this peak were entirely sheer, jagged, and inhospitable even to a mountain goat. The great fog that clouded my view for so long surrounded the city as a solid wall. What lay just beyond the fog was a mystery to me, but perhaps here I would find the answers I sought. I leaned casually into the chariot's rail looking down over the side, when I realized that I was not gliding on a path but soaring in the air.

"By the Gods! Where is the ground?" startled, I fell back into the chariot and held on for dear life. "Freya! Freya what have you done, you witch?" I yelled as I slowly pulled myself back up and marveled at the site of the great city below my feet.

"My brothers and sisters will never believe this if I tell them. By the gods, how did we ever get up here?" I suddenly felt ill; a sweat came over me while the cold air rushed over my head.

I was not fond of heights and I don't believe that any man of Midgard had ever ridden the sky. Raven turned back to look at me with his snaggletooth and grumbled loudly. "Raven, be silent you cursed cat!" I yelled at the monstrous feline. The cats gave out a hiss in unison as I spitefully slapped the reins against their hides.

Out of the corner of my eye, I caught a glimpse of great stone statues of two Viking warriors clad in armor and carrying weapons that guarded the four entrances to the city. The statues loomed high into the sky and well above the monumental doors, covered in ornate rune inscriptions that remained secured. At the foot of the statues flowed raging rivers that plunged into the sky, turning great falls of water into clouds and fog. Between each statue was a tower with watchmen dressed in the most spectacular battle suits. There was so much to gaze upon that I found it difficult to focus on the task at hand.

Suddenly, a cold shadow crept forward and fell over my chariot. Looking upward, I saw another chariot, much larger than my own and pulled by a monstrous golden eagle. The chariot soared past and it's riders looked back upon me. They were heavily armed with bows, sword, and axe; a patrol perhaps? Now realizing I was not the only one in the sky, I knelt down slightly, trying to keep a low profile. The armor clad riders moved on, paying little attention to me as they dove into the city below. Straight ahead, there lay a great fortress of wood and stone encircled by a massive flock of crows flying overhead, swirling and looping in all directions.

The Great Hall was now before me. Adorning the top of the Great Hall wall a massive Viking Ship, built into the Hall itself, the oversized, longship appeared to be the personal quarters of the Gods, perhaps even All-Father Odin himself. In the center of the ship was a wooden tower that spiraled high into the heavens above, decorated with flags and fearsome dragon's heads carved of wood. What a sight to behold! I longed to be a welcomed guest in this place but knew very well I must go un-detected. I found a dark passageway behind several longhouses near the fortress and coaxed the cats to a safe landing. The chariot's wheels slammed hard against the paved cobble stone and scraped to a blaring stop. Stepping down from the chariot, I expected the ground to be cold and hard, but it was neither. I felt light, almost joyful to walk on the surface of Valhalla. Despite the snowcapped buildings and streets, the air was pleasant, not cold, nor hot. The snow itself even appeared different than that of the snow from my homeland. I knelt down to pick up a handful of ice, expecting to see it melt in my hand, but alas it did not. The snow was like powder, neither cold nor wet; I turned my hand over and watched it fall to the ground softly as it sparkled in the dim sunlight.

Thankfully, I had made it alive. I knelt down and kissed the ground, reluctantly thanking Odin, whom I realized may be very near. I reached down into Freya's chariot and removed a leather cloak from a sack-cloth. Hesitant and somewhat in doubt, I placed the cloak around my body and over my head, hoping that it would shield me from the gaze of the dead warriors. The magic that built this kingdom was everywhere: the air, the snow, in the buildings themselves. Even my wounds no longer caused me ache or pain. This was a place of great healing and I now lamented at the mission that Freya had sent me upon. I walked up to the cats who were then eagerly cleaning themselves with legs shot in the air.

"Remain here and I shall return shortly, do you understand?" Raven hissed while the white cat paid no attention to me at all. "Wicked creatures. Why am I talking to the cats?" I remarked as I shook my head and set forth down the streets of Valhalla.

Scouting the fortress ahead, there appeared to be one entry and one exit to the Great Hall, an appropriate design for a defense, but defense against what I wondered? Peering from behind several barrels of mead I gazed upon the great hordes of

Vikings carelessly feasting, fighting, and fucking in the court-yard. *What a spectacle!* It was no wonder warriors were risking all to enter Valhalla; the never ending celebration of manhood and endless supply of lusty ladies, the former slave girls of the honored dead, was a prize well worth the cost.

Somebody will surely see or hear me if I don't get inside soon, I thought to myself. Gripping the side of the barrels, I reluctantly released my grasp and hurriedly moved behind a massive statue in the center of the courtyard. Looking upward, I was suddenly startled at the realistic look of the stone beast staring down upon me. The statue depicted a brave Viking warrior piercing the chest of a great and fearsome cave giant. So it was true, the Giants truly did exist; perhaps all but wiped out by the gods. Looking about at the wall and great gates of the fortress, it now made sense why the defenses were so large. The gods were not trying to keep out man. The fortress was designed to keep out and defend against an army of Giants. No army of man could ever hope to reach this place, much less breech the defenses if they did.

I was startled when a voice called out from behind me.

"You there!" the booming voice called. I turned to find a particularly intimidating tattooed warrior standing in front of me. The man was well-armed with a sword, dagger, axe, bow and arrows. His long silver hair extended past his waist. The hair of an old man, but his face and body appeared youthful, that of a warrior not yet past his third raiding season.

"Greetings, fellow warrior!" I replied confidently to avoid rousing suspicion.

"Do you make your way to the hall for the feast?" he asked.

"Is there not always a feast?" I said as the warrior gave me a hard stare and then exploded into laughter.

"Well met brother! Well met! Enough with idle banter. I am parched and require the gods honey. Until the Ragnarok!"

"Until the Ragnarok!" I replied. The seasoned warrior stumbled forward and headed to the Great Hall without delay. I watched him closely for a way to get inside, but with the watchman standing their posts it seemed impossible. Another loud noise caught my attention, causing me to turn my head to find a small group of revelers, loud and boisterous, heading to the feast. If I could blend in with the crowd I could make my way inside without alerting the guards. I waited until they were nearly against the statue.

Wait for it. My heart raced inside my chest; I took a deep breath to calm myself as I counted the moments. *Now!* Darting between the party goers I wedged myself within the group. I sang and danced a merry tune, doing my best to appear off kilter with the rest of the crowd. As we danced, passing the massive stone walls adorned with red and gold flags, it appeared that we would walk effortlessly past the guards.

"Halt!" shouted one of the guards. *Damn! They found me.* I kept my head low sticking closely to the crowd as the guard spoke to the group's leader. "Just where do you think you are going?" asked the guard.

"Where the hell does it look like we are going!" responded the group's leader angrily. "To feast of course, you dumb ox!" *He's insulting the guard, why is he insulting the guard?* It appeared that I had picked the wrong group to use as a cover and was moving ever so quickly to an untimely death. The guard stared sternly for a moment.

"If you're going to the feast, you must be properly equipped." Reaching behind his post the guard pulled up drinking horns full of mead; the group cheered and danced. "Drink and be merry my brothers and sisters! Welcome, welcome, come in." I cautiously took a horn of mead from the guards hand and followed my unsuspecting companions inside. As we made our way further inside I held back and let the group pass me so I could find the armory. They danced and cheered until their laughter faded into the warmth of the Great Hall.

"This way…" a woman whispered. I looked behind me but no one was there. I whispered back.

"Freya. Freya is that you?" I looked for a sign, a bright light, but it was nowhere to be found. Sticking my finger in my ear, I attempted to clean it out thinking I must be hearing things.

"The staircase…" There it was again, the whisper. I looked over my right shoulder where the voice was coming from. A narrow and dark staircase that led down into the bowels of the Great Hall was before me. *This must be it.* Quietly, I crept down the stone steps until I reached another long hallway lit by torches leading to a giant door. *There it is*, I thought to myself. *The armory of Valhalla at long last.* The door to the armory was the height of a wild oak and just as thick, covered in iron bars and adorned with murals of great warrior battles against terrible monsters.

"Perhaps there is a magical property to this door," I said to myself. I must be cautious. Kneeling down, I picked up a pebble and threw it at the door. Nothing. This is far too simple; there must be something here that I cannot see. I walked closer to the great door and felt around running my hands on the iron bars. There was no handle, no key hole. How does one enter a door that has no handle nor key hole? I pressed upon the door and it would not budge. Below the murals were inscriptions, the same riddle repeated over and over again.

The quickness of a hare, the boldness of a bear, pass ye not lesser souls, keeper of the brave and bold.

What did this mean? Why wouldn't it open for me? A dull sound began to echo in the distance. Footsteps! I quickly hid behind a chest in the hall. Two guards marched by laughing and drinking as their armor clanked in unison. I could feel the sweat dripping down my forehead until the guards stopped nearly in front of me.

"Check the armory." Peeking around the chest I could see one of the guards taking off at a sprint and he ran straight into the door. He was going to crash into it, what is this fool doing? Without a sound his body passed through the door as one passes through a waterfall. That's it! I have to run through the door. I waited eagerly for the guard to return so I could give it a try. He popped his head through the door, looked about and then caught up with the other guard.

"All clear, now where were we?" They returned to their laughter and drinking without hesitation. They wandered out of sight.

Alright, I can do this, I can do this. I ran straight for the door and just before reaching it I closed my eyes in anticipation of the hit.

Slam!

My body fell upon the door and I bounced to the ground like a fallen tree. Why did it not work?

The quickness of a hare, the boldness of a bear, pass ye not lesser souls, keeper of the brave and bold.

I did that, didn't I? Thinking back to the deceased Viking warrior he did not flinch; he didn't even contemplate the thought of hitting the door. He just knew he could run through it. That's it. I have to know I can get through the door, not just think that I can. I picked myself up off the ground, my ego more bruised then my body. I stepped back several paces and ran at a sprint straight for the door.

"There is no door, there is no door, there is no door," I chanted to myself as I approached the door. With no doubt in my heart, I passed through like a Draugr through stone.

Relief washed over me as I patted down my body making sure everything was in its rightful place. Looking at the door and walking backwards into the armory I celebrated this small victory, but it was not to last. A growl erupted from behind me and echoed off the weapons that lay strewn about. The hairs on my neck stood up straight, and I knew I was in trouble. Slowly turning, I found myself confronted by a menacing looking beast of fur and fang. A great Grey Wolf now blocked my way to the weapons inside the armory.

I had seen and hunted many wolves in my time in Bjorgvin but never had I encountered a wolf of such size. On all four legs, the beast stood the height of a man, and a head the size of my chest. I reached for a torch, but before I could grasp it the beast closed the gap between us. The breath of the wolf blew hot on my face, the smell of decaying meat logged between his teeth.

"Ah, I can smell what you had for breakfast. They feed you fish?" The guardian wolf bared his teeth and dropped his head getting ready to strike. Without a choice I reached for the torch as the wolf leapt forward. *Clank!* The wolf stopped suddenly just short of sinking his teeth into me, and I saw a chain hiding under the thick fur of the creature's neck.

"So, you are a prisoner here? And here I thought this armory was yours." I smiled at newly found fortune but the wolf found no amusement as it snarled and drooled at the thought of ripping me limb from limb. I looked about the room and noticed a stash of bones and weapons just behind the creature where other victims, perhaps men much like me, once tried to tangle with the beast. "Poor bastards." The armory was small but the wolf had just enough chain to make a meal of these men. *Now how to get past him?*

I gazed about the armory and saw no tool to aide me in my passing of the ferocious beast; no tool but the wolf's chain itself. *That's it!* "Alright beasty, are you ready?" The wolf snarled and snapped waiting for my first move. I flexed and shook searching for the speed and strength inside to overcome what must be done. Charging forward the beast knelt down and snapped at my head. I threw myself to the ground sliding under the wolf's belly and snatching the chain on the other side. The beast turned quickly but found himself tangled in the chains falling over. As he kicked his legs wildly on the smooth stone to get back up I leapt atop his back and wrapped the chain around his neck. The wolf pulled and fought with every ounce of his strength but soon his power failed him as he succumbed to a lack of breath and slumped over. He slumbered and breathed heavily as I loosened the chain that bound his neck.

"The case…" The whisper returned. Atop a shelf, I saw a long wooden case covered in layers of dust and cob webs. Wiping back the decay with my hand revealed a plain dark wood, nothing special about it. I opened the case and a faint hum could be heard and quickly faded away. Inside the case sat an old, rusted sword of the poorest quality.

"Who would want this piece of junk?" A breeze traveled across my hand and along my arm. This must be the sword Freya sent me for, but I didn't understand why. Tucking the sword into my belt I turned my attention to the wolf that was slowly awakening behind me.

Time to take my leave. I quickly made my way past the wolf once more, tiptoeing over his limp body. "Thanks for the sword," I said to the wolf that no longer barked or snapped. I quickly turned towards the door and ran into something directly behind me.

"What is your purpose here mortal? What are you doing in the armory?" The voice belonged to Thor, who appeared before me in his armor with the great hammer in his hand. "I asked you a question, mortal. Now answer me or I shall be forced to destroy you."

"My lord, I was sent on behalf of one who is much like yourself."

"You mean a god? You were sent here by another god to break into my armory and take this sword?" Thor reached out with his hand. "Give it to me." Without hesitation I handed over the weapon. "I see you bested my hound, not many can, especially not a mortal. What is your name?"

"I am Audan, son of Rurik, Chieftain to the people of Bjorgvin."

"So, you are a warrior then."

"I am," I answered confidently.

"So, warrior, which one of my kin sent you here? Was it Loki? He's always up to his tricks."

"I don't care to share my lord or it would surely mean my undoing." Thor leapt at me placing his hammer against my neck.

"Tell me or I will grind you into my stew!"

Barely able to breath I spoke these words, "It was Freya, my lord." Thor surprised by my response, pulled back his hammer and cocked his head.

"Freya? She dares defy our great father, Odin. What use does she have for this sword?"

"I know not, my lord. She would not share her intentions, nor divulge any secret to me. She merely promised me a great fortune if I would return it to her."

"And why did she choose you?"

"I know not, my lord."

"There is a lot you do not know and yet you were willing to carry out this dangerous task for her. What was she going to give you in return for you services?"

I hesitated to answer, not knowing how the mighty Thor would react.

"A king's title," I responded. Thor became agitated and stepped closer to me.

"King? King of whom?"

"King of the North."

Thor became enraged; his eyes turning bloodshot. In an explosion of blinding light an old man, tall and hooded, appeared placing his staff between us and faced Thor.

"Calm yourself, son. I do not think this is the doing of your sister, Freya. Nor is Audan the lone culprit in the matter. We cannot discuss this matter here; they may be watching. Quickly, to the throne room." We exited the armory; Thor dragging me by my collar until we reached a tall wooden door with two guards standing in front of it. "Bar the door and let no one pass." the old man ordered.

"Yes Odin!" replied the guards. *Odin? The old man was Odin?* We entered the throne room; the guards slamming the doors shut and locking it from the outside. Odin and Thor continued their discussion as if they had never ceased.

"How do you mean father? Has she not sent this man to retrieve this sword and return it to her?"

"Perhaps, but she cannot wield it. No god can, expect for maybe one." Odin's words were ominous, leaving the hairs on the back of my neck standing upright.

"Of whom do you speak father?"

Odin lowered his head resting it in the palm of his hand.

"Long ago, before the time of man, before the time of gods, there were great creatures of the elements of Midgard: earth, fire, water and ice. These creatures ruled the cosmos for eons before the first god appeared. One such creature, so named Surt, resided in the fiery realm of Muspellheim. Surt forged a great sword in the very fires of Muspellheim that he would use at his discretion to end existence as we know it when he felt the realm of Midgard had become spoiled and corrupt."

Thor placed his hands upon his hips and laughed heartily.

"That's just a fable, father. A story we tell the other gods to keep them in line." A smirk appeared under Odin's hood.

"Aye, is it? You know there are mortals down there that think the same of you and I? That we are merely tales told to children to maintain peace and order." Odin seemed calm and understanding of my predicament and so I felt compelled to ask a question.

"Is this the sword I was sent to retrieve for Freya? The fire sword?" I asked.

"I'm afraid it is, Audan. You see, Surt did come down upon Midgard many generations ago and was met by my grandfather, Buri, the first of our kind from Asgard. Buri knew of Surt's plan for destruction and so loved Midgard and the beings that inhabited it that he waged war against Surt. The battle was brief as Surt rained down molten rock from the heavens and spit forth ash to choke out all life. All was nearly lost as Buri lay bloodied and beaten. Surt raised the fire sword high into the air standing over Elivigar, the heart of Midgard, but, in a moment of sacrifice, Buri removed the fire sword from Surt's grasp and thrust it upon the fire demon. A great light appeared. Surt was blasted back to his fiery realm and encased in molten rock where he would plan his revenge for an eternity."

"So what of Buri?" asked Thor.

"Buri perished in the explosion, or so we thought. Buri suffered greatly by gripping the sword even for a moment; he now slumbers eternally in the great ice. I believe that Freya, or whoever controls her, intends to free Surt so he may once again wield the sword and destroy Midgard. Freya cannot travel to Muspellheim and Surt cannot leave his tomb; he must be freed, but Buri can accomplish these tasks. If Freya can awaken Buri and turn his will, the fire sword could find its way to Surt's hands, destroying Midgard and the Gods.

"Gods cannot die. We are not mortal and do not suffer the same as men." Odin stood placing his hands on the table in front of him.

"Do you think that everything is so plain, my son? That the reality which exists before you was brought on in such simple terms? No, it is not as unassuming as all that." Thor inched closer to his father.

"What are you saying, father?"

Odin stood upright now, slowly removing his dark hooded cloak he replied, "There are many dark secrets that we gods have protected throughout the ages. Now with the survival of the realms at stake perhaps it is time we shed one of our secrets. Man has long worshipped us, some out of fear, and some out of respect or tradition. Most because they believe we are inherently different than man. They believe in us and worship us because we are immortal, because we have power beyond them. If they knew the truth the realms could very well become a different place. The truth is that the mortals are not so different from you and I."

"Father, you speak in tongues. Speak plainly to us. What secret? What is it that men are not to know?"

The weight of these dark secrets could be seen upon the brow of Odin. His wrinkled forehead appeared to get heavier as he contemplated his response. Odin turned away once more placing his arms behind his back, staring at his throne.

"My son, we were mortal once."

Thirteen
Exposed

Odin sat heavy in his great stone throne. Grinding the bottom of his staff into the ground he continued to explain the ancient tale of the Norse gods. "The pair of you seem shocked beyond reason. Does it surprise you that the light of men which burns out in such short time once dwelled within us, within our ancestors as well?" Thor stepped back, dropping his hammer to the stone floor; lightening crashing outside as it struck the ground.

"No, how can this be? To speak of such things is to desecrate the very existence of our ancestors. This man was sent here to steal from us, nothing more. We should treat him the way criminals are supposed to be treated. Hang him from the highest tower; gut his belly and let his entrails hang low for all to gaze upon." Thor pointed angrily at me with fire in his eyes. I dreaded the thought of the many ways in which he sought to murder me. Odin lifted his hand above his arm rest, signaling Thor to cease his angered banter. Thor lowered his flexed arms and relaxed his stance once more.

"Gather around, children, I have a tale to tell you both. Tales few remember and even fewer believe to be true." I took a half step forward before Thor quickly stopped me with his massive hand.

"Father, I must protest. This thief should not be given any of our wisdom. He may betray us. This is no place for a mortal." Odin lowered his head into his palm and shook his head several times before looking back up through his long hair.

"Have you not heard anything I have told you my son? I understand your concern, but I think Audan is an unwilling pawn in this game of deceit." Odin turned towards me, his face shadowed by his dark cloak. "I will ask you only once, so speak truthfully so that I may spare your life. Are you going to betray us, my mortal child or will you swear your loyalty and hear what I have to say before I allow you to leave this place?" I was thankful that Odin was reasonable and willing to take a chance on my honor. If it were up to Thor, I would be pounded into the ground by now, a bloody stain on the cold cobble stone floor.

"I'd like to hear what you have to say All-Father," I replied humbly. Odin leaned forward in his throne balancing on his staff with both hands.

"Very well; when Buri, your great grandfather, sacrificed himself on that most divine of days there was another ancient creature of the elements that witnessed his glorious sacrifice. Augelmir, the great giant of earth and ice, so ancient was he that he knew the names of every rock and every iceberg of Midgard. With his massive icy arms he lifted Buri's lifeless body and vowed that his surviving kinsman would be forever immortal, eternal guardians of the realm of Midgard. This was to be the gift for Buri's sacrifice. Augelmir encased Buri along with the fire sword in a great glacier where he would sleep until his wounds were healed, until the Ragnarok. Augelmir then blew a great icy wind that carried with it the gift of eternal life; that wind reached Asgard and we have been protectors of the realms ever since."

"So he slumbers peacefully within the ice. Why were we told that he died that day? Why did you lie to us?" asked Thor.

"Because your mother and I were troubled that one day some-one would go looking for Buri and find the sword of legend. We took it upon ourselves to seek out his icy crypt and removed the sword with the help of an enchantment. The sword, much like Buri, is dormant. Bereft of its fiery glow, it is merely a sword now and should remain so."

"Does this mean that the final battle is here? Is the Ragnarok upon us?" I asked. Odin turned to me looking upon my figure with his one good eye.

"The Ragnarok is not merely a single event, Audan, but a se-ries of events that must take place at the proper moment and in the proper place. Only the elders who reside in the frozen watery realm of Elivigar can know if the signs have appeared. We must seek out their wisdom and guidance if we are to understand our adversary's intent." Thor's anger grew, black clouds emerged through the windows of the fortress and thun-der cracked loudly above, shaking the very foundation below our feet. He knelt down, picking up his hammer and raised it high in the air.

"We must warn the others of Freya's treachery. Call the coun-cil and have her arrested. Justice must be done; it is the way of our people." It appeared that Thor held the moral high ground but not the wisdom with which to aptly apply it.

"No, my son, we do not yet know who else may be in league with Freya. She may merely be a puppet, but if so, who is the puppeteer, I wonder? Who controls the strings? Audan, what else have you seen on your adventures?" Despite all my battles and suffering, I still hesitated to speak to Odin, and I chose my words carefully for fear of what they may bring.

"My lord, in the dark forest, my brother and I came upon the undead. They rose from their graves and committed to battle." Odin quickly turned to me with a stunned look upon his face.

"Draugrs! Are you absolutely sure?"

"I am, All-Father. I've never seen the dead walk amongst the living but I know a rotting corpse when I see one."

"Why were they after you? Did you remove treasure from their hallowed ground?" he asked demandingly.

"I know not, my lord. We took nothing from the graves and gave no offense to the dead. We were sent upon that dark place by Freya's messenger, Sigr. She visited us in the cave after the battle on the beach."

"And your brother, where is he now?"

"Freya has him and several of my companions in her safe keeping. She says they slumber safely under her protection. What that means, I know not."

"It's not like the Draugrs to attack without provocation. Something is driving them, leading them on beyond their purpose. I fear there are dark forces at work here." Odin tugged upward at his long grey beard while in deep thought. He began to hum a tune I had never heard before, perhaps a warrior's song. I looked over at Thor and could see him getting impatient, gripping the handle of his hammer tightly, ready to pounce on me at any moment and end my existence. Thor was pacing intolerantly between the towering columns of the Great Hall. He stopped and took another step towards Odin.

"We must act against this offense, father. What shall we do?" asked Thor. Odin continued to stroke his beard as he stared into oblivion.

"Do? Yes indeed, what shall we do? What can we do?" Odin paused for a moment from stroking his long pointed beard and turned towards us. "We shall do nothing until we can get to the heart of this treachery. This villain is beyond my sight, my all-seeing eye is clouded. We must tread lightly or fall prey to this hunter's trap." Odin approached me, placing his arm around my shoulders as a father would to a son. "Listen to me, Audan, and listen closely, the very fate of your realm is at stake. I cannot intervene for fear of setting things into motion before I can hope to halt them. But you, you may be the key to unlocking this mystery."

I was honored to have such trust bestowed upon me by the King of Gods. Nodding my head I replied, "I will do whatever you require of me. My life and the lives of my men are yours."

"Let us hope it does not come to that. If we are going to be victorious we will need to keep you alive; you're the only one with access to Freya. Now, on to more pressing matters. You cannot be seen leaving this place. If you are found it may alert whoever is consorting in this affair; even our guards are not to be entrusted with this secret. You will take the back passage. Thor will meet you at the end of a culvert and guide you safely to your chariot. Speak of this to no one until you are free of Freya. She must believe beyond disbelief that you have fulfilled your task without being compromised. Do you understand?" Odin now had his hands on both of my shoulders.

"I do, my lord, but how may I ask am I to deceive Freya? She has the power to read the darkest thoughts of men. She will find me out." Odin smiled as he stroked his beard, the crow's feet appearing deep around his eyes.

"Well, that is a conundrum now, isn't it? I may have just the remedy!" Odin turned to a bookshelf filled with colored vessels and strange objects. "Now where did I put it? Ah yes, there it is." Odin said with great enthusiasm. He grasped a large dark bottle and handed it to me. "Here, Audan, take this with you."

"Is this mead?" I asked curiously.

"Yes, but not just any mead, mead from my halls, my own private reserve that I keep locked away for special occasions. Present it to Freya as a gift to drink, it will cloud her mind temporarily, but be forewarned, if you drink from this vessel, your lips will loosen and all we have discussed will pour out of your mouth faster than you can pour mead from this bottle." I gripped the bottle placing it up to the light of a torch, examining the clean crimson liquid that flowed inside. I never thought of the gods dabbling in witchcraft, potions, and spells. Perhaps I still had much to learn.

"I will not fail you, All-Father." A heavy hand slammed my shoulder from behind and pulled me back. Thor's hot breath fell uncomfortably on my neck and ear as he spoke.

"Listen and listen well, mortal! You may go, Audan of Bjorgvin. But know this; if you deceive me in any way, I will destroy you and send you to the fiery pit that is Helheim."

I nodded my head, ready to be free of his shadow. "Yes, my Lord, I understand and will carry out this task you have put before me." Odin gently pushed Thor aside and spoke to me once more.

"You have doubted us for a very long time, Audan. Perhaps it's time we help you rebuild that trust in your gods that you lost so long ago." Odin grasped me by the shoulder and turned me towards a wall. He slammed his crooked staff to the ground three times, the echo bouncing loudly off the walls. *Knock, knock, knock!*

"Was something supposed to happen?" I asked curiously as we stared at the stone wall. Odin cracked a wide smile through his grey beard.

"Wait for it." The wall shifted and stones moved to one side until a wooden door became visible; pure magic! The mystical powers shown before my very eyes began to wash away any doubts I had of the god's powers; the doubts I had held all my life. No matter how hard I tried I could not deny the fantastic sights that now revealed themselves.

"You truly are the gods of legend." I quickly stepped off but was stopped by the hand of Odin.

"One last thing, Audan, once you escape Freya and return to Midgard you must venture forth to Elivigar, the heart of your realm, and seek the council of the elders. I know you and your companions have been through a great ordeal but if what you said is true, then our troubles have only just begun." Odin reached out with his hand, opening his fingers, he revealed a golden necklace encrusted with precious stones. Why was Odin handing me a necklace?

"Is this for me? Is it magic?" I asked. Odin laughed deeply.

"Your time for treasure and riches will come. No, this is tribute for the elders. Greedy old bastards that they are, they will not converse with you unless you have brought payment. Do not give up the necklace so easily, they may be tempted to limit what they are willing to share unless you grease their palms further. Now go, Audan, run and do not turn back." Odin lifted his arm, reached upward and removed his black eye patch. I cringed for a moment thinking of the empty and deformed eye socket he was about to reveal. "I will be watching you." Words could not escape my open mouth, for under the eye patch of Odin laid the entirety of all the realms. I stared uncontrollably as I spotted stars and the ancestors of old, streaking across the dark sky in his eye, realms and places never seen before. Odin released the eye patch, snapping it back into place and began to chuckle loudly, throwing his head back and placing his hands on his stomach. "Well, boy, be gone."

I nodded and quickly ran down a dark stone hallway before me. Torches lit themselves as I sprinted towards them, lighting the way down what seemed an endless path. My feet slammed and echoed against paved stone floor. I stopped momentarily and looked back; the path was gone, only darkness remained. I cared not for this place, the cold and eternal darkness left me feeling that I would be consumed by oblivion, never to return home. I shook off the thought and continuing forward, I finally came upon a spiraling staircase. Beyond the staircase lay nothing, just emptiness. I picked up a small pebble and tossed it off the edge waiting, waiting, and waiting for a sound but none came forth. I nervously swallowed my spit and looked away as beads of sweat fell from my forehead.

"I think I'll take my time," I said to myself. Slowly, I made my way down the never-ending staircase, seconds turned to minutes and minutes into an hour. My mind began to wonder about home, about my fellow kinsman, and of course about Sada. Sada, I missed above all else; her warm soft touch would be comforting in these times of uncertainty. I wondered how many men attempted to lay with her in my absence? "Scoundrels..." I said under my breath as my blood began to boil at the thought of another man touching Sada. I'd have their fucking heads on a spear head.

I'm sure everyone thought I had died back on that beach with the rest of my brothers in arms. I wanted to get home to reassure my love that I was alive and well. I sat down and looked over the edge once more. Nothing, still just oblivion lay below my feet. A passing thought crossed my mind about ending it all, about throwing myself off the edge of this staircase to stop my suffering. Would it hurt? Would I feel the blow, the crushing of my bones, the cracking of my skull? I didn't know if there was a bottom to this place, perhaps if I fell I would merely fall for an eternity until I died of thirst and hunger.

"Do it..." a small voice called out.

"Who's there? Who said that? Show yourself." I demanded looking about the blackness.

"Do it you coward, kill yourself and end your suffering. Your love betrays you! She thinks you are dead and has already found another to take your place."

"Lies!" I yelled into the darkness, "All lies! Now show yourself!"

"Do it, Audan, why suffer any longer, ease your pain and end your miserable existence. Odin is using you. Even if you do make it to the end of this staircase, Thor will see your blood run cold down his hands." The voice seemed to be closer now, but I knew this voice. Who was it that urged me on to my death?

"I know your name, spirit. Now show yourself!" A cold air blew across my shoulders, the hairs on my arms now stood straight.

"We are one in the same, Audan. You need only to look at your reflection." It was my voice? How? The darkness was playing tricks on me, perhaps a test. I closed my eyes for a moment.

"Leave me be!"

"And why would I do such a thing? You're never going to get out of this alive and you will never see Sada again. Don't you see this is the only way?" My stomach twisted and turned; I suddenly felt deathly ill.

"No. Stop it! I'll not hear any more of this! Do you hear me dark spirit? You have no power over me!" The voice gave a sinister laugh.

"Do it, Audan. Kill yourself. It's so easy, just take one little step over the edge and let go. Your freedom is closer than you think." The voice was not coming from the darkness, it was from within. In my head, I could hear the voice yelling and screaming at me.

"No!" I yelled as I grasped my head. "I will not yield! I will never yield!"

"Every man yields one way or another. Eventually you will break." I knelt down and sat on the steps.

"No, stop. It's not real! You're not real! Be gone, dark spirit!" A silence fell over me once more and the cold wind ceased to blow. As quickly as it arrived the voice had now disappeared. Wiping the sweat from my brow I asked myself, "What happened?" I lifted my head and looked about, the darkness still remained but the voice and its presence was no more.

After a moments rest I shook off those dark thoughts and rose once more continuing my unending descent, step by dreary step until a soft light could be seen in the distance. The bottom of the staircase was within reach and just beyond was a doorway leading to another hall; at last! All my dark thoughts, all my hopelessness vanished without a trace. My heart beat quickly,

216

overjoyed by the sign of hope! I walked towards the stone archway cautiously walking on my toes. The soft glow of candlelight could be seen flicking in the well-furnished hallway ahead.

Turning the corner, I quickly stopped in my tracks. I could hear a large clamor, a squawking of birds. Crows, perhaps? I peeked around the corner and to my eye's surprise I gazed upon an enormous flock of crows crowded in the hall. They pecked, hopped and cawed at one another.

"What the hell are you doing here?" I asked aloud. I needed to get past them if I wanted to get out of here. I rounded the corner and the crows did not peck, they did not hop, nor did they caw. Snapping their necks in my direction they were very much aware of my presence and very interested in what I was doing. I stood still, straightening my body, hoping they would not attract any attention. The largest of the crows slowly hopped forward, bouncing it's dark beak with each step until it reached my feet.

He turned his head to the left and tilted it up as if to get a better look at me. He blinked twice and cawed, pecking at my feet. "What was that for you, stupid bird?" I took this as a sign from the gods and slowly removed my hood. The crow took a step back as the others looked on.

"Caw!" I jumped back startled. Was this crow trying to talk to me? Again he cawed and then uncontrollably, the crow began to violently choke on something. I felt compelled to come to his aid but did not know why.

"Cough it up, you stupid bird." I kneeled down smacking his feathery back gently.

"Cawwwwph!" A shiny bronze key covered in spit emerged from the beak of the crow and bounced twice before resting firmly on the ground. Stunned and confused I stared at the key curiously. The large crow quickly hopped forward; leaning over, he pushed the key towards me with his beak. "You want me to take this?" I cautiously picked it up thinking the crow would peck at my hand, but he did not move. The key was pure bronze;

it even seemed to glow as I twirled it in front of my face. This was no ordinary key. Besides the golden glow it was intricate, carefully carved and inscribed upon.

"What is it for?" I asked the crow. *Wonderful, I'm talking to a crow now*, I thought to myself. The crow just cocked his head to one side and cawed again. I stood up. "Thank you. I think." I stood and tiptoed between the flock of crows as their heads followed my every movement. Looking back one last time the large crow bowed, then hopped away.

What was this key for? Was there something here in Valhalla that I was meant to find? I did not want to invite the wrath of Thor once more. He already let me go once; I do not think he would be so merciful if I attempted another break in to something else. Beyond the hall and the flock of birds a wooden door with an iron ring lay before me. I slowly opened it as it creaked loudly. I placed my hood over my head once more to conceal my face. Looking outside at the stony walkway I could see the culvert in the distance.

I quietly walked forward, arriving at the culvert I could see Thor sitting down next to Freya's Chariot. I kicked a small pebble over to make some noise so not to startle him.

"Fear not, mortal. I knew you were there," announced Thor. I rolled my eyes.

"Of course you did." Thor rose slowly, facing me. He was no longer wearing his armor, but a brown tunic more than likely trying to conceal himself as well from the legion of honored dead and the guards of Valhalla.

"I see that you made it past the staircase," Thor said with surprise in his voice.

"Was there ever any doubt?" I asked curiously. Thor lowered his head and smiled up at me through the strands of hair hanging on his face.

"The staircase is not just a secret passage out of Valhalla, Audan. It's a test of mortal and god alike. Many whom have ventured into that staircase have gone mad, never to return."

"You knew about the voices? Why send me?"

"Indeed, I did. I did not think you strong enough. I was wrong about you, Audan. Father and I do not always see eye to eye but you have proven yourself strong enough to carry out this task." Thor reached into the chariot handing me the leather reins. "You are ready."

"What was it?" I asked.

"The voice?" Thor replied.

"Yes, what was it?"

"The voice was you, Audan. It was your inner enemy, your doubts, hatred, malice and cowardice. Everything that is evil within you. It attacks you weaknesses, tries to urge you towards the path of least resistance. What did it ask of you?"

"It asked for death. To kill myself in that dark place," I said ashamed, lowering my head.

"And did the voice get to you?"

"For a moment, yes. The thought of death was comforting, even inviting. I wanted it all to end. Just one small step could have stopped all of this."

"And what stopped you?" asked Thor. A smiled erupted on my face.

"The thought of better days. When the darkness runs from the light. When I can stand tall amongst my people as a better man than those who seek to undo me."

"You're a better mortal than most, Audan. Take comfort in that. I wish you farewell, we will be watching from a distance." The more I came to know the gods, the more I saw them as mortals. They exhibited all of our traits and in many cases more so than we men: anger, pride, deceit, honor, kindness and lust. I looked back at Thor, wondering if I would ever see him again. I never even thought to ask him if my fate was set down by the gods. Perhaps he was helping me on my journey, perhaps he was helping himself.

I felt a sinking feeling in my heart. I longed to stay at Valhalla and here in Asgard, but it was not my time. I had not earned the right to drink and feast amongst the brave men. Gripping the reins in my hands, I whipped Freya's beasts once and we took flight back amongst the stars. It seemed like such a desolate, foreboding, and inhuman place. The skies were so beautifully lit, but the air was thin and cold. A man had to force himself to breath in such a climate.

Into a foggy mist we sailed further towards Freya's home. Freya's beast Flurry once again disappeared in front of me. Only Raven could be seen as a spotted cat. Looking into the chariot I stared intensely at the sword given to me by Odin. What was Freya's purpose with the sword from the armory of Valhalla? Did she indeed seek to bring the Ragnarok upon us all? I still had more questions than answers. With the Army of Valkyries at her disposal, she could have sent any number of them to do her bidding. The fog began to break away and rays of sunshine shot through the clouds. We had returned to the realm of Freya. We landed gently in the grass and pulled alongside the great thorn bushes that lined Freya's home. I stepped down from the chariot and began removing the items I had taken with me from Valhalla. From behind I could hear steps making their way towards me.

"Welcome back, Audan. Do you bring me what I asked for?"

Fourteen
The Puzzle

"You return to me Audan, unscathed and unharmed. You had been absent for so long I was beginning to worry that you may have failed in your quest," remarked Freya as she walked towards me clad in a long dark robe that seemed to glow as the stars do in the night time sky.

"I have my lady." I bowed my head slightly as Freya gracefully approached me with her arm extended.

"And did you bring me what I asked for? Did you bring me the sword from the armory of Valhalla? Or did you fail like so many others did?" I wondered to myself who the others were; probably just soldiers in Freya's game. I momentarily recalled the pile of bones and armor that rested just behind the grey wolf but the thought passed quickly as I returned to the present state of affairs. I did not have any time to ponder what the results of these failed attempts were. Reaching behind my back, I removed the leather cloth tucked under my belt. Freya began to laugh with excitement and placed her hands over her mouth in utter surprise. I slowly unlashed the leather cloth and revealed the ancient sword that lay beneath.

"You did it! You actually, truly did it. Well done! I knew you could do it. I have such faith in you, Audan. Where so many others have failed you have proven your worth to me and to our cause." Freya quickly reached down and removed the sword from my grasp holding it high in the air. She turned in place angling the sword to catch light upon the blade. "Remarkable, is it not? That such a simple thing could harness such great power?"

"Our cause?" I questioned. I wanted to know who else would be a party to Freya's plans but was careful to shield my intentions. Freya dismissed the question placing her hand gently on my shoulder.

"Do not bother yourself with such details. All will be revealed in good time." Freya clapped her hands twice. "Sigr! Sigr, where are you, you foolish girl?" A bright light appeared and quickly diminished revealing my former acquaintance from the sea shore cave.

"Here, my lady." With a look of shock, Sigr greeted me with her eyes averted. "Greetings, Audan. How do you fair?"

I wanted to question her about the forest, about the sword, about everything. But, now was not the time.

"I am well, Sigr. And you?" Before she could answer, Freya interrupted her.

"Sigr, take this with all care and lock it away. I'm sure you know where to put it." Sigr bowed her head slightly.

"I am at your service, my queen." Her eyes glanced upward; the look of worry betrayed her. What did she know? She once again vanished in a bright blue light and Freya turned her attention back to me.

"Well then, where were we?" asked Freya.

"I was merely questioning if your faith was not misplaced in me for 'our cause' my lady?" I asked while emphasizing the word 'our'.

"Do not cause worry to that pretty face of yours. It would be a shame to see it wrinkled so. I see great things in your future, and I will assist you in making them happen." Freya ran her slender fingers through my hair and lifted her gaze upwards. "Audan, you are amongst friends here. Let's not trouble ourselves with customs. Make yourself at home. What is mine, is yours. Stay as long as you like." I felt light, fulfilled even. As if all my cares and worries in this world had slipped away. Suddenly recalling Thor's warning of Freya and of her hidden scheme I thought it may be best to distract her and find the perfect moment to serve Odin's mead.

"My lady, would you care to play a game?" Freya smirked and turned her head slowly to one side staring intently at me.

"A game? I love games, Audan, but how are you going to beat me if I can read your thoughts? You seem to be at quite the disadvantage." Freya squirmed excitedly at the thought of a game.

"Ah, but that is just it my lady, the game is very simple. We shall take turns." I walked over to a tall chair and plopped myself down, crossing my leg and leaning back in a manner that made me seem daring, or so I thought. "I will think of something and you guess what it is. Then I will take a turn and try to guess what you are thinking. The first of us to guess right may ask a request of the other." I seemed over confident, even to Freya.

"And how do you intend on beating me Audan?" Freya asked curiously.

"Did I happen to mention that this would also be a drinking game?" From beneath my shirt I removed the bottle of dark crimson mead and held it up for Freya to see.

"Where did you get that?"

"I stole it while sneaking about in Valhalla. Perhaps, you would like to share?" I handed Freya the bottle and watched as she examined it for a moment.

"Is it mead?" she asked curiously as she examined the container.

"It is."

"Wonderful." Freya removed the cork and began to smell the vapors leaving the bottle. "It smells magnificent, a fine vintage." Leaning back she took a drink straight from the bottle. "Oh my!"

"Well, what do you think? Is it to your liking?" I asked.

"I don't think I have ever had anything quite like it." She smiled wildly from ear to ear, her eyes wide with excitement.

"Let's have a warm up then, shall we? What am I thinking right now?" Freya slinked over to me and sat down in my lap draping her arms around my neck. I tried to maintain my composure as I stared blankly at Freya.

"Curious," Freya stated.

"What do you find curious, my lady?" I began to sweat thinking perhaps she noticed something odd about the drink.

"Your mind appears to be empty; perhaps it's true what they say about you warrior types. Although, despite your mind being empty your body language speaks volumes about you. Perhaps it's all the blood rushing to your cock that's keeping you from thinking of anything clearly." Freya began inching her hand down my thigh from my knee.

"What say we try this again." I quickly lifted Freya and placed her in the chair across from me. "I will start and you can follow, agreed?" Freya, like a child, placed her hands on her chin, her elbows on her knees and leaned forward with absolute enthusiasm.

"Well, stop stalling. Let's play the game so I can beat you already," Freya said through a wide-eyed smile, fanning her hand towards me.

"Very well. You're not thinking of me or any of your subjects for that matter. You're not thinking of any animals or monsters of the deep." Freya nodded as I fired off my deductions one by one. "You're thinking about yourself." Freya, shocked, leaned back and shrugged trying to hold back her smile.

"Well, of course, I'm thinking about myself but could you perhaps be more specific. What about myself am I thinking about, Audan?" Freya lowered her head and through her long eyelashes looked up at me with her piercing ice blue eyes.

"You're thinking about pleasing yourself and what you will do next to make yourself feel pleasure." Freya stood, walking towards me with a look of lust. She began to run her fingers through my hair once more.

"Close enough, Audan. Now, it is my turn." Freya quickly took another drink from the bottle as I cleared my mind, thinking of the black, the darkness, focusing on the void that lay in every man's mind and every man's nightmares. Freya sat back into her chair looking not at me but through me. Her ice blue eyes grew dark and the darkness spread until her eyes were consumed by what look liked disease or pain. "Audan, try as you must to clear your mind, I can see within it; your darkest secrets, your deepest fears."

"Then what do you see, my lady?" I now released my mind to the void of feelings, my muscles going numb, almost floating, and suddenly, light. I stood in a wet green field. Looking at my feet and then my hands noticing I was armed with spear and shield. When I looked up, I saw the massacre that lay before me, the piles of Viking dead that littered the battlefield. The smell, sights and sounds were all so familiar and then a voice echoed amongst the air.

"Audan, you may clear your immediate thoughts but I can still see within you, your past, your present, and sometimes your future. Shall we continue playing this game or have you had enough?"

"Freya! Why did you bring me back to this place?" I listened closely for Freya's answer but no response was returned. The taste of rocks in my mouth, blood, and not my blood, but that of the men I had slain many years ago on this battlefield. The haunting memories, the smells, tastes, sights, sounds, and horrors of what I had done that day all flowed back into me. "This was not what I was thinking, Freya, now get me the hell out of here!" My heart raced as I began to question what was real and what was in my mind.

"What's wrong, Audan? You don't like this memory? Was this not a glorious victory for you and your men?" snickered Freya.

"It's a memory, Freya, nothing more. Now get me out of here. This is not the game we were playing." Then suddenly, as if awoken from a bad dream, I returned back to my chair in Freya's home. "What the hell did you do to me?" Freya crossed her legs and leaned back defensively.

"I merely showed you what was hiding in your mind. Your immediate thoughts seem broken to me so I had to find something of use," argued Freya.

"It wasn't on my mind. It was in my head, back there somewhere tucked away and you brought it back. Why?" I was distraught, my hands trembled, the taste of blood and death still on my lips.

"Audan, if you can't be bold in the games that you play, then why play at all?"

I suddenly became so enraged that I lunged forward at Freya. I gripped her throat tightly, wrapping my fingers half way around her neck.

Freya stood with me still gripping her throat, now becoming just as enraged as I. She suspended me in the air and threw me effortlessly across the room and shouted "Do that again and my face will be the last thing you lay your eyes upon." I knocked the back of my head against the wall. Reaching behind my head I felt something warm running down my neck. I found a bit of blood oozing out of my skull.

"You forget your place, Audan of Bjorgvin; I am Freya, a God born to reign above you. You will serve me, Audan, or I will dispatch you in the manner that I see fit." Freya, seeing the blood upon my hand instantly gained her composure once more. "Oh, you're hurt. You mortals are silly little things, always getting bloodied and dying." Freya's reaction seemed a genuine surprise. She kneeled down and inspected the fresh wound to the back of my head, placing blood on the tip of her finger. Freya then licked the blood from her hand, closing her eyes to savor the taste. "It's a marvel that you survive at all," she remarked. Handing me a strand of her hair Freya said, "Rub this on your wound and all will be well." I reluctantly took her long blonde hair and rubbed it on my head. The wound began to tingle and warm; I reached up and found that it was healed and gone.

"Thank you, I think."

Freya now looked upon me with a look of curiosity and hunger. "Would you stay and dine with me, Audan, before you leave back to Midgard?" She extended her open hand to help me off the floor. I took it and stood. As she helped me up she pulled me in close to her, eagerly awaiting my response.

"I think I can stay for an evening meal. Why not?" I said slightly changing my demeanor to entice her. Freya leaned into me, pressing her body slightly against mine, content with my answer and took another drink from the bottle. "Perhaps... perhaps it's not food that I crave," I said as I looked upon her with a mock sense of desire, hoping she would take the bait. She was an epic beauty; there was no doubting that fact. Knowing her poisonous nature she was a tainted and terrible beauty that I hoped to be free of shortly.

"What then? What is it you crave, my dear Audan?" Freya replied, clearly entering a state she was not accustomed to. I had not seen her look this way before, the way of intoxication; and not just from the mead, but from her obvious sexual appetite.

"Perhaps we should drink a bit more mead and you can help me figure out what it is I crave." Freya quickly took another drink and then held the bottle to my mouth urging me to drink as well. I tried to think of something fast as to not draw her attention to why I would not drink. I suddenly leaned in and kissed her, hoping it would distract her. I pulled back a moment later to see her reaction. Opening my eyes, I could see the look of lust igniting within her.

"Oh my, we certainly do have an appetite tonight, don't we, Audan?" Freya said as she slowly began skimming off part of her cloak to reveal her bright bare skin underneath. I could do nothing but stare and wonder what I had just begun. Freya wrapped her arms around the back of my head and quickly pulled me into her lips. She kissed me hard, much harder than I was used to with Sada. I could feel Freya's tongue run across my lips and slip into my mouth. Her breath was cool, her body hot.

I decided I should play into her desires if I had any chance of returning home. I pulled back from her kiss to see her gazing at me anxiously. "Lose your appetite?" Freya said with a slight smirk on her face. I reached over and pulled the rest of her cloak off, almost ripping it on the way down.

"Just want to see what is being served." I extended my hands out to wrap them around her waist, then moving one down her back side, the other around to her breast. She gasped in surprise, taken aback by my actions. She quickly regained herself and began kissing me passionately once again. I continued to run my hands all over her milky white, smooth body.

She removed her hands from around my neck and ran them down my broad shoulders, working her way onto my chest and stomach. She started to undress me as fast as she could, all while trying to savor the taste of my mouth on hers. I wondered how long it had been since she had another mortal man. I attempted to put that thought out of my head as quick as I could.

After shaking off the thought, I suddenly realized her hands were removing my pants and she was no longer kissing me. She was down on her knees fulfilling her appetite. I looked down at her and she back at me; a look of fierce fire in her eyes. She quickly stood and pushed me down onto the floor. Though my enemy, I couldn't help but be enticed by her supple breasts, long glowing hair and perfectly round rear. Her body was unmarked, no scars, no flaws, clearly the body of an immortal. She climbed on top of my naked body and began to sway and grind her body against mine.

I reached up and caressed her breasts, feeling how soft they were. I sat up and placed one in my mouth. Sucking on her nipple, she moaned out in pleasure, tugging at my hair, urging me not to stop. She finally pulled me away and pushed her tongue into my mouth. Suddenly I was inside her; she grinded back and forth on my cock, rubbing her breasts against my chest.

I flipped her onto her back but she rolled me back over, obviously needing to feel in control. I grabbed the bottle of mead and placing my fingers into her mouth, opened it up and poured some more in. She guzzled it down as if it was the most delicious thing she had ever tasted. I could tell it was working its magic on her as Freya became less aggressive in our encounter as time passed.

Flipping her around I entered her from behind while on my knees. I thrust into her as hard as I could. She screamed out in sheer pleasure, begging me to not stop. I reached around to grab one of her breasts and used the other hard to grab a handful of her long blonde hair. As I yanked on it, she only seemed to get more enjoyment. We continued for hours, Freya not tiring as a mere mortal woman would. It wasn't until Freya rolled over and looked at me with satisfaction that I realized my plan may have worked. With a motion of her hand, Freya dismissed me. I then realized I would be permitted to return home. "Are you content and full now?" I asked with slight amusement, hoping Freya would stay lying down.

"I am. You may go now," she said waving her hand in the dim light of the fire. She was content, perhaps even tired, as tired as a goddess could possibly get. I stood placing my clothing back upon my body.

"Then I shall take my leave. Thank you for your kindness." Freya sat up from her resting place keeping a cloth draped over her chest.

"Will you return and visit me, Audan? I get quite lonely here amongst my hordes of Valkyries. Women can be, entertaining but I have other…cravings." Looking down at her as I put my pants back on, I tried my best so seem interested at the thought of returning.

"Is that so? How will I get back here?"

"All you have to do is say my name, and I am yours." I warmed at the thought of another sexual conquest but a twinge crept up my spine knowing that I had betrayed Sada. How long would it be until she found out?

"Shall I use your chariot to return to Midgard?"

"No," said Freya. "You need to get back to the mortal world. This will require something different entirely." Freya stood walking towards me seductively as she let the cloth fall off her body. "I'm not going to be untruthful to you Audan. This is going to be painful." I scowled and turned my head not knowing what she meant but before I could answer her hand was around my throat, I couldn't breathe. Try as I might, I could not remove Freya's grip upon me. The harder I struggled the faster my strength left me. The darkness began to consume me, Freya disappeared from my sight. When I realized I was no longer in her chambers, I was in the water. A hand reached down and grabbed my collar pulling me from the depths.

My head exploded out of the sea and I gasped intensely forcing air into my body. *Cough, cough, cough, ahhhhh!* I looked up to find Jareth pulling me upwards into the boat.

"Come on, brother; get the water out of your chest." As Jareth pulled upon me I felt a weight dragging me down.

"Ulvar? Ulvar! Jareth help!" I realized Ulvar was still in my icy grip. I lifted my arm upward revealing the still pale body of the brave boy.

"No!" Irun shrieked and helped pull Ulvar into the boat. His body lay lifeless, cold, and wet. Jareth pulled me into the boat as

I dragged myself upwards rolling onto the hard wooden deck. Jareth slapped Ulvar across the face several times.

"Wake up, boy! Damnit! Wake the hell up!" Irun grabbed Ulvar by the shoulders shaking his body, his head swinging back and forth. I crawled over to his body and propped myself upwards.

"Move!" I pushed Jareth and Irun aside and grabbed Ulvar by the ankles, lifting his body upwards and shaking him violently. "Don't die, boy! Come back, come back!" I closed my eyes, completely exhausted as I lifted his little body up and down begging for something to happen. I could hear Irun shrieking in the background, with Jareth attempting to console her until at long last salt water exploded from Ulvar's mouth.

"He's alive!" Irun stood and rushed to Ulvar taking him from my grasp and resting him on the deck. Ulvar coughed and wheezed; the light returned to his once dead eyes. Jareth reached over and grabbed a wool blanket placing it atop the boy.

"Keep him warm or the cold will take him." Irun tucked the blanket around his frail little body. She smiled and cried, pulling Ulvar's hair away from his eyes. "Audan, are you okay?" asked Jareth.

"I'm fine. I just need to dry off. Do we have anything I can change into?" Jareth looked about as I stood still with my arms wrapped tight around myself.

"Get your clothes off. Take my coat." Jareth took off his coat while I pulled off my wet cloths. The coat was warm taking the chill off. Irun wrung the water from my cloths and hung them from the sails.

"Where the hell are we?" I asked.

"I know not, brother. The fog has consumed us for many hours now. We are adrift without the stars," replied Jareth.

"How did Ulvar and I fall into the water?" I asked.

"What are you talking about?" Irun asked. There was a great wave; you and Ulvar were knocked overboard." She said looking slightly confused. "Are you alright, Audan? What vexes you?" I stared around in disbelief. Was it all just a dream? Or were the gods speaking to me? Jareth looked at me, puzzled.

"Maybe you got bit by one of those Draugrs. You're not going to turn on me are you?"

"Shut up, fool. Let's get a move on and get home before someone catches up to us." The mist began to clear up ahead. The light shone brightly upon the ice and frozen landscape. Icebergs floated quietly as we all gazed at the frozen cold.

"Where are we?" asked Irun.

"This is the heart of Midgard, Elivagar," I said as I suddenly realized that my visions of the gods were not visions at all.

"Have you been here before brother?" Jareth asked.

"No."

"So how do you know this is Elivigar?"

"The gods told me." The trio looked back at me astonished at the words that escaped my mouth. Jareth scooted closer towards me.

"I don't think I heard you clearly, brother, the gods?"

"I was in Asgard, in Valhalla. The gods told me to find this place and here we are."

"Are you mad, brother? You hardly believe in the gods. What made you change your mind on this matter?" Jareth grasped my arm; he looked at me as if I had lost all sense of myself. *The necklace!* I reached into my pants and searched nervously until I stumbled upon what I was looking for. I slowly removed the gold necklace that Odin had given me as the others watched me intently. "Where did you get that?"

"I have been there, brother; I have seen it. It's real. It's all real."

"I believe you, but why are we here?"

"To see the elders, the ancient ones. Only they can determine if the signs of the Ragnarok have appeared. Our quest has become more perilous than we thought." I gazed upon the frozen landscape of water and ice as Jareth rowed slowly avoiding the icebergs. "There, do you see that?" I pointed to a dark cave of ice. "Row there."

"But there's nothing there," remarked Irun.

"No, no it's there. I can feel it in my bones. That's where we will find the elders."

"Well, you heard the man. Let's get moving." Jareth adjusted his oars and moved us towards the cavern. As we approached the entrance, this haunting feeling washed over me like a tide. I feared that we may never again see the light of day. The cave appeared to go on into infinity as Jareth rowed slowly into the darkness. Ulvar stood and looked back at the light of the entrance now about to disappear.

"What if we can't find our way back? Will we be lost?"

"All will be well; Jareth and Audan will protect us." Irun responded. The icy walls slowly began to change revealing stone wall that lay beneath.

"Irun, give us a torch," I commanded. Irun began to strike a rock against the blade of my axe until sparks flew landing into a shredded cloth. She blew on the embers slowly until they caught ablaze and wrapped them around a stick. Irun approached me and leaned over the side of the boat illuminating the walls that surrounded us.

"By the gods! It's everywhere," exclaimed Jareth. Lining the walls under the light of the torch an emerald glow of rune inscriptions could be seen; great murals depicting ancient battles of gods, monsters, and elementals.

"What do they say?" asked Irun. I looked up and down at the inscriptions but could not make out any of the symbols.

"These symbols are foreign to me. They look like ours but none of them make sense." I was confused. Were the elders so ancient that even their language differed from ours? A tongue lost millennia ago when the elementals still walked Midgard? The glowing inscriptions spread to the stone ceiling above our heads, lighting the tunnel's path. "This must be old magic. I've never seen anything like this, not even in Valhalla."

We reached a small dock made of stone and pulled the boat next to it. Ulvar leaned out grabbing the stone cleats we would lash the ship upon. "There it is, Elivagar, home of the Elders." A great staircase of stone rose high up in the caverns ending at a massive wooden longhouse. Smoke billowed from the stacks above the straw covered roof top.

"It appears we are not the only ones here," remarked Jareth. "Shall we finish this?"

"Let's get this over with. I don't want to be here any longer than required."

"Audan?"

"What?"

"You may want to clothe yourself."

"Right." I removed Jareth's jacket grabbing my now slightly damp cloths from the sail. "Irun, Ulvar, you're coming with us. I'm not taking any chances leaving you behind." Everyone exited the boat and began the long ascent to the Elders home. The caverns were eerily silent. Great pointed rocks hung low from the ceiling and the walls glistened like snow.

"Do you suppose there will be food?" Ulvar asked desperately as his stomach grumbled loudly echoing against the stone walls.

"I don't know. I will be satisfied if they don't welcome us at sword point," I remarked. We arrived at the door of the longhouse; it was surprisingly small and simple. I looked about for any sign of occupancy but none could be found.

"Maybe we should knock?" asked Irun. I turned back and smirked. Gripping my axe handle, I was ready for anything. *Knock, knock, knock.* The sound echoed in the cavern but no one replied.

"Perhaps they are not home?" Jareth remarked.

"I doubt it brother. They must be here." I knocked harder, this time the door creaked loudly as it opened. I entered cautiously.

"Hello? Is anyone here? We seek the wisdom of the elders." The towering hall was vacant and had been for centuries. Dust and debris scattered about littering the floor and paths. In the very center of the room was a small stone alter. I approached it hoping to find something to lead me in the right direction but alas it was just filled with water.

"This place is rank with death, brother. I think we should leave," said Jareth. I ignored his warnings. Odin sent us here so this must be the right place.

"We seek the elders. I was sent by Odin himself." The room began to shake and the ground rumbled beneath our feet.

"Who disturbs the slumber of the elders?" a thundering voice called out. We were startled looking all around for the source but saw nothing.

"I am Audan, son of Rurik. I was sent by Odin to seek your wisdom and counsel."

"A mortal? Here in Elivagar? We have not had mortals here since their creation." I looked about the empty hall but could not see the elders.

"May I ask where you are?"

"Gaze upon the altar." Looking downward into a water-filled alter, ripples flowed until an image of three old men could be seen clearly. I looked up from what I thought was a reflection and yet the room was still empty.

"Do not be alarmed, Audan. We are not within your realm at the present. Elivagar exists both in Midgard and its own realm. Now, tell us, why have you come before the council of the elders?" Jareth, Irun, and Ulvar quickly encircled the altar looking down at the water.

"I seek guidance on the Ragnarok." The men looked at each other and began speaking quietly and whispering on private matters.

"The end of times, yes, it is foretold that one day Midgard would be consumed in combat, blood, and fire. Your question however is not direct enough. What do you wish to know about the Ragnarok?"

"Is it upon us? Have the signs revealed themselves?"

"Signs. What do you know of the signs?"

"I know nothing, that's why I'm here. I need your help."

"And do you bring us tribute?" I slowly reached into my pocket and removed the gold necklace given to me by Odin. The old men leaned forward to get a better glimpse of what I had brought before them.

"I do but I need your oath that you will help me."

"He lies, he lies! He came to take it from us." The old man to the left ranted randomly as the others attempted to calm him. Any trust I may have had for them was now completely washed away.

"Silence!" The old man at the forefront turned his head towards me again. "My apologies, young Audan. Yes, we give you our oath and solemn promise." A hand, old, wrinkled and worn rose from the water of the altar; its fingers outstretched ready to receive the necklace. I didn't trust them, the elders in the background appeared nervous, even angry. Quickly reaching out I grasped the hand tightly and pulled my dagger up to the wrist. The old man shrieked and yelled in pain.

"Don't try to trick me, old man!" I yelled.

"What is this, how dare you dishonor these sacred halls with your insolent accusations." I bent his wrist harder to one side; the elder winced in pain begging me to stop.

"I want each of you to swear upon your lives or so help me I will cut off your wrist and destroy this altar."

"No! You wouldn't dare! This altar is sacred, our only path to the mortal world!" I had the elders right where I wanted them. They were scared and hesitant now, no longer making demands. I could see the fear is their eyes.

"Tell me what I need to know and the tribute is yours to take!" The three men looked at each other once more speaking in private. In unison they replied.

"We swear."

"Very well." I removed my dagger from his wrist and placed the necklace in his palm. He quickly grasped it with his gaunt fingers and long nails, pulling it back into the altar. The elder held it up for the others to see as they examined it.

"This is from the halls of Valhalla itself is it not?"

"It is."

"Of the finest quality I see. It will be an excellent addition to our collection." The elder handed the necklace back to the others and returned his gaze forward.

"Fine. Now, tell me of the signs."

"Yes, the signs, the signs. In order for the end of days to commence the ancient signs must be revealed. There are but four, no more, no less. A great army will appear, not of blood and bone but of decay and rot."

"You mean the Draugrs?"

"Do not interrupt! Secondly, the gods will become evident to man, no longer just symbols of faith and they shall walk upon Midgard blazing a path of death and destruction. Armies will rise and fall in the blink of an eye. The third sign precedes the fourth: darkness will fall upon Midgard; the sun will be choked out by an ashen cloud.

"And the final sign?"

"He will return to finish what he once started. If the dark one retrieves the sword of fire the age of man shall be undone. Not even the elders can escape his justice."

"Do you speak of Surt?"

The elders gasped in fear.

"Insolent boy! We do not utter his name. It is forbidden, forsaken! To call his name is to knock upon his very prison."

"Is that all?" The elders once again turned away conversing in private. Sweat began to run down my forehead. I did not like where this was going.

"There is one last detail we forgot to mention."

"Which is?" The old man laughed wickedly.

"You are not the only one seeking the signs." At the end of the hall footsteps now made themselves heard. The smell of death and decay permeated the air, a smell most familiar.

"Draugrs!" I shouted. "Get to the boat! Go, go, go!"

They screeched and screamed, their menacing howls echoing in the halls, chilling the bone.

"Keep up, Ulvar!" Jareth yelled.

"Just pick him up!" I cried. Jareth grunted and leaned down to pick up Ulvar.

"You're heavy for a runt!" I got behind Jareth to help push him forward. The Draugrs were slowly catching up. We exited the longhouse and I turned to shut the door.

"Irun, give me your sword!" I jammed her sword in the door handle barring it shut but it would only hold for so long. "That might buy us some time. Run!" We made a mad dash down the stone steps until arriving at the dock.

"Cowards!" Five Viking Draugrs stood between us and the boat with many more following quickly behind us.

"Jareth, put Ulvar down. Ulvar, Irun, we will dispatch them. Get in the boat when it's clear." Ulvar and Irun side stepped the five Draugrs while we protected their path.

"Are you ready to die, mortal?" the lead Draugr said with blood dripping from his face. Jareth drew his sword while I bounced my axe handle in my hand.

"Until the Ragnarok?" asked Jareth.

"Until Ragnarok." We turned once more to the decaying Draugrs. "Glory!" We lunged forward, ducking and side-stepping a Draugr's swing. I severed his leg at the calf, cutting his tendons and knocking him the ground as blood spewed forth. I could see

Jareth out of the corner of my eye, fighting off two others as I moved on to the next. A spear thrust flew past my head cutting my ear; the sting enraging me! Stepping forward, I grabbed the spear pressing my head against the Draugr's rotting chest. "You foul creature!" He shrieked trying to free his spear. With my free hand, I swung my axe into his side, getting the iron stuck in his ribs.

"Fool, you will die in this place. All of Midgard will burn! Your family, your kinsman, all will burn!"

"Not if I can help it!" I pulled at my axe to no avail. Breaking the spear free of the Draugr's grasp, I thrust it upwards under his chin, the point bursting through his head. I stepped and pulled my axe with all my might; his rib cage giving way, cracking and splitting until it was free. The final Draugr was in front of us now, moving backwards as Jareth and I put his back to the water.

"Audan! Jareth! Please hurry, more are coming!" urged Irun. The screams from the longhouse were getting louder; they must have knocked down the barred door. We were running out of time.

"Let's finish this beast!" We charged forward at amazing speed, the Draugr still pulling his sword back to swing when we landed our blows. A sword point to the face, and axe blow to the knee. The creature was pummeled, collapsing to the ground like a scarecrow. We ran quickly towards Ulvar and Irun jumping aboard our small boat. We paddled away from the docks. Ulvar pointed from the bow of the boat.

"They're here!" Corpses clamored loudly down the stair way and onto the dock, flinging axe, spear, and arrow towards us raining iron death.

"Get down!" I shielded Ulvar as best I could, stretching my body over him. Bladed instruments flew all around, as Jareth rowed lying prostrate on the boats deck. "Row faster, faster, faster!"

"I'm trying!" exclaimed Jareth as he paddled furiously. The beasts leapt and fell from the edge of the dock reaching out with blade, nail and tooth.

"No!" My arms grew cold and my heart pounded ferociously. I stood in the boat swinging my axe wildly, knocking Draugrs into the icy depths below, cutting limb and finger. Flesh and dark blood exploded in the air soaking everything on the boat. Tirelessly, I swung my arms back and forth, back and forth, my body giving in to the blood rage. With each piercing of their decrepit flesh, I craved more as I watched their bodies give way to my onslaught. One by one, they fell into the murky waters, Irun hacking at the fingers and outstretched arms of the Draugrs struggling to get out of the water. Jareth put more distance between us and the dock and the Draugrs gave chase no more as they paced back and forth.

The light of Elivagar began to dim as we ventured further into the icy tunnel, making good on our escape. "Is everyone alright?" I asked. The trio nodded their heads. Irun was clearly shaken; the blood of the undead staining her skin. She dipped her arms in the frigid water trying to cleanse herself.

"Why won't it come off!" she screamed as she feverously rubbed her arms and hands until the skin became raw.

"Irun!" shouted Ulvar but she gave him no acknowledgement. "Irun! Stop it!" Ulvar pulled Irun's arms into the boat as she fought back.

"No! No! It won't come off! It won't come off..." cried Irun. Ulvar squeezed his little arms around her and held tight.

"It's okay, Irun. Their gone. We're safe now. We're safe." Irun leaned into his shoulder and let out a wail as she cried aloud. The light of the world outside was now visible and we slowly made our way back outside of the tunnel.

"Why do the gods punish us so? What offense have we given to deserve these endless trials?" asked Irun.

"It's not all the gods, Irun," I remarked.

"Where to now, brother?" asked Jareth with a weary look upon his face.

"We go home, we must warn the others." I looked upwards at the clouded heavens, "Odin! Odin, hear me, All-Father! Grant us a strong current home so we may be free of this place." The air was deathly silent as I gripped the boats rail, "Damn you, Odin! Are you there? Do you hear me, Odin! I'm asking you, for once in my lifetime, help me! Do not leave us to death and despair!"

A cold wind blew softly across my face tugging at my hair. I looked to the waters as they began to push our tired boat forward through the ice and fog.

"The gods answer your prayers, brother. So it is true; you have seen them," said Jareth.

"Praise Odin!" I cheered aloud. "We haven't much time; everyone take rest."

"All of us? Who's going to watch the boat?"

"Odin will get us safely home. We need to rest to prepare for what's next." I waited as the others settled in and closed their eyes. Jareth lay down, opening his right eye to stare at me suspiciously. "I said close your eyes and rest. All will be well."

"You've gone mad. You know that, right? I like this new Audan." Jareth finally closed his eyes. No more than a few moments had passed until everyone was asleep. I gazed once more at the foggy horizon and slowly laid down for my own deep slumber.

Fifteen
Thief of Hearts

"Audan." Something shook my shoulder repeatedly. I tried to brush it off but there it was again disturbing my peaceful slumber. "Audan, wake up, brother."

Without opening my tired eyes I asked, "What is it, Jareth?" I wanted nothing more than to continue sleeping on the cold hard deck of the boat but Jareth was having none of it.

"We are here." remarked Jareth.

"We are where brother?" I opened my eyes looking upwards at the clear blue sky. Hungry gulls circled overhead just below the sun that now hung high. Sitting up quickly, I found myself awestruck at the pebble-laden beach our boat now rested upon; the familiar smells and sights flooded my thoughts with warm memories.

"We're home!" I yelled in utter excitement. Jumping up from my resting place, I threw myself onto the shore stumbling over the boat's railing. The cold dark pebbles burrowed themselves into my bruised and battered body, but I cared not. I was home at long last!

"Who goes there?" A forceful voice yelled in the distance. I quickly rolled on my stomach, looking upwards. Atop the sandy berm sat a scout on his horse with spear drawn. "I said, 'who

goes there!' Make yourselves known or make yourselves dead!"
I did not recognize this warrior but his clothing was all too familiar.

"Tell your Chieftain that the sons of Bjorgvin have returned!"
The warrior's horse bucked back and forth.

"There are many sons of Bjorgvin. What makes you so special?"

"We are Audan and Jareth." The warrior quickly lowered his spear and squinted his eyes tightly.

"By the gods! Don't move, I'll send for help." The warrior rode at great speed on his auburn steed towards the village. In the distance I could hear him shouting wildly. "Rurik! Rurik! They have returned! Your sons have returned!" A great clamor could be heard moving closer to the beach as I gathered the strength to stand. I slowly raised myself to my knees staring at Jareth, Ulvar, and Irun who helped each other up from the pebbles. Jareth walked towards me and knelt down to lift me up.

"Do I always have to..."

"No!" I commanded extending my arm. "Not this time." I slammed my fists into the ground and with every ounce of my strength, lifted myself upright. My vision darkened as I caught my breath, squinting in the brightness of the sunlight. Ulvar slowly walked towards me with sadness in his eyes.

"Is this your home? Are we safe Audan?" I looked away from Ulvar and took a deep breath catching the scent of freshly cut pine. Placing my hands gently on his shoulders, I replied.

"Yes, Ulvar the Brave, we are safe now." Ulvar wrapped his arms around my waist and held me tightly. I patted his back firmly to reassure him that everything would be all right.

"I am in your debt for saving us. I will serve you and your family if you wish?" Ulvar bowed his head like a servant would his master. I knelt down and gripped the boys shoulders once more.

"No, Ulvar, it was you and Irun that saved me. I don't know if I would have made it without you. Here you will be my brother until the end of days. Here, you will be free until the end of yours." The boy, overcome with joy, let out a cry of victory and threw his fist high into the air. Irun jumped upwards sprinting to Ulvar and grabbed his arms swinging him in a circle on the beach.

"Brother! Our kinsmen have arrived!" The ground shook with the sound of thunder as an entire village descended upon us from the beach head. Fathers, mothers, siblings and children cried in excitement lead by Rurik who charged forward on a black horse that tore at the ground beneath.

"Sons!" yelled Rurik as he stood upright from his steed. I could see him pulling back on the reins as he approached us; leaping from his horse just before it stopped. "Boys, thank the gods almighty you are safe!"

"Father!" I yelled. We held each other in a great embrace. Rurik leaned back grabbing Jareth from behind the neck, pulling him into his arms.

"My boys, my boys! I thought you had been lost to our enemies on that cursed beach. I never should have left you. Can you ever forgive a proud and foolish old man?" Rurik eyes welled up with tears as he lowered his head in shame.

"No forgiveness is required father," replied Jareth.

"But I don't understand. What happened to you boys? Where did you go?" I thought for a moment on how I could possibly convey our adventure to our father but danger was very near and I needed to prepare our village.

"Father, we are all in grave peril. As we speak an enemy of unspeakable power descends upon us with the intention to destroy every man, woman, and child of our clan." Rurik's face quickly turned to determined anger. He puffed out his chest and gripped his sword appearing ready for battle.

"The Finns return to finish us off?"

"No father, not the Finns. I think they are the least of our concerns."

"Well, if not the Finns, then who, my son?" I didn't want to sound foolish in front of the rest of the village, for I knew how this would sound like madness.

"We must speak in private father but you must place the men on guard. I don't have time to explain now I just need you to trust me." Jareth looked intensely at father and nodded his head.

"Of course, my sons, of course." Rurik turned to his guards. "Men! Rouse all of our warriors, man the walls. Arm the women and children and place them in the servant's quarters next to the long house."

"Yes, my lord! You heard your Chieftain. Let's move sharply now!" Bear barked at everyone.

"Audan!" a familiar voice cried out from behind the crowd. "Audan, my love!" I lifted my head searching for the voice and found my woman.

"Sada!" pushing Rurik and the villager's aside, I moved my way towards Sada until she jumped into my arms. She wrapped her strong legs around my waist and embraced me briefly with her arms until she pulled back to press her lips heavily against mine. Her long and wild hair wrapped around my head as I filled my chest with the flowery scent of her beauty.

"My love, you return to me!" She looked over my face seeing the many scars, cuts, and bruises the journey had left upon me. "What have the gods done to you? Were you captured?" I pulled her in for another kiss, pushing our tongues deeply into each other's mouths. The taste of her was sweet like mead. I wanted nothing more than to drop her to the ground and take her now.

"There's no time to talk now, my love. You need to get the woman and children into the servant's quarters. Arm yourself and the others, close and bar the doors." Sada's great joy quickly soured to disdain at the sound of poor tidings. Kenna approached as well with her slave girls following behind.

"Boys! You've come home to us!" Kenna hugged us both and looked to Rurik recognizing the frustration on his face. "What do you need me to do?"

"Help Sada get the women and children to safety. We need to ready our defense." Kenna kissed Rurik on the cheek and bowed.

"As you will my love. Sada, let's go." said Kenna as she pulled Sada away. Sada resisted and ran back into my arms.

"Why? Are we in danger? I won't let you leave me again." A hand jerked my arm from behind; I turned back to find Rurik pulling on me.

"We need to go, son. Sada, do as your man says." Sada nodded her head and reluctantly headed back towards to the village with Kenna.

"Sada! I won't leave you again. I will be right here!" Sada blew me a kiss and turned away once again. Irun and Ulvar looked confused and frightened. I approached Irun to reassure her all would be well, "I want you to take Ulvar and go with Sada. Stay with the villagers and do as you're told. I promise we will protect you." Irun stood and threw her arms around me.

"I know you will. Just bring Jareth back to me alive, do you understand me?"

"On my honor, I swear it." Irun kissed me gently on my cheek and turned to Jareth to say her goodbyes. We left quickly to speak alone in the Great Hall escorted by father's guard. When we arrived father ordered the guards to remain outside while Jareth and I eagerly sat down at the table covered in half eaten food.

"Feast, drink, you must be famished." ordered father. Without hesitation we ripped and tore at plates of meat and drank heartily from the drinking horns. I could feel my belly warm quickly as the food made its way into my body; it wasn't long before I was satisfied. "I eternally thank All-Father Odin for your safe return. Now, I need you to tell me why we have put every warrior at our disposal on guard. What danger has followed you to our shores?"

"Father, I am tired beyond measure so I will speak plainly. A vast army of Draugrs have been awoken under the command of an unknown evil. The gods, Odin and Thor, fear that Freya is leading them at the behest of another to destroy all of Midgard." Father stood there silent, his eyes wide and mouth hanging open without a sound. I waited patiently for him to laugh or burst out in anger but alas he said nothing. "I know it sounds mad, but it's true." Rurik turned to Jareth as he sat down heavily in his chair.

"Jareth, what know you of this?"

"What he says is true father, all of it. When we were forced to leave the beach a Valkyrie visited us and sent us on a quest. We have been visited by the gods on more than one occasion and have been chased by their monsters. Audan was forced to deceive Freya. I don't know how long we have until her wrath is unleashed upon us." Rurik slammed his fist on his arm rest.

"Guards!" Two well-armed Vikings entered the room and stood waiting for orders. "Convene my war counsel and send our fastest rider to warn the Jarl. We are at war."

"Right away, my lord." replied the guards sharply as they departed the hall.

"So you believe us?' I asked.

"Do I have a choice my son? Clearly something is coming whether it be the gods or something more sinister. In either circumstance, we will be ready to fight and die honorably."

"Thank you, father." A loud crash came from behind. The longhouse door swung open and the veteran soldiers came flooding in to hear the orders from my father.

"Take your seats!" The warriors sat with a loud bang as their armor and weapons shuffled in their seats. "My sons have returned with a message from the gods and that message is war. An unspeakable terror is headed our way. The gods have seen fit to release their monsters upon us. For what reason, I know not.

I know to some of you this may seem absurd but to those who know of the old ways, we have seen our fair share of frightening things. If Audan and Jareth say we must prepare, then I will not doubt them!"

"Until the Ragnarok!" shouted a warrior.

"If any man oppose this calling of the guard speak now." The room fell silent as warriors looked back and forth over the fire pit for the one that would go against Rurik's wishes but no one dared to object. "Very well, brothers, it is settled. To your posts! Prepare for battle! Until the Ragnarok!" the room erupted into a furious cheer of men and iron. All but the most senior members of the war council stood and returned to their battle posts.

I stood slowly, my muscles still weary from the long expedition, and approached my father. "And where shall I be posted?" Rurik raised one eyebrow and smiled, placing his arms on my shoulders.

"You are dedicated and brave, my son, but you and Jareth are far too weary to engage in combat. I would ask that you stay here and rest until you are ready to lead our men." Despite my disappointment, I was relieved to know I could get some rest for the moment.

"Thank you, father," I said bowing my head. Just outside a horn sounded loudly near the front gates.

"To arms! To arms!" a guard yelled. Disregarding my father's wishes we ran outside to the gates only to witness our brothers already engaged with an army of Draugrs climbing up the wood palisades. Warriors atop the wall hack and slashed at the beasts keeping them from getting to the other side. The air was ripe with the stench of rotting flesh and father covered his mouth because it offended him so.

"By the gods! What are those?" exclaimed Rurik.

"The undead father. Freya's monsters descend upon us." We turned our heads to a loud banging sound and could see the main gate beginning to give way as the lifeless warriors pressed their bodies against it in mass.

"Jareth, get the men to reinforce the gate! If they break it down all is lost." I ordered with haste.

"On my way!" Jareth sprinted away as I rushed up the rampart with Rurik to aid my fellow warriors. Before moving up the wooden steps a half cleaved Draugr body fell in front of me. I dropped my axe swiftly on his neck splashing my face with dark rancid blood and his green essence erupted to the sky.

"Hurry son get up the steps!" Our archers worked diligently firing without rest but the arrows were not enough. Draugrs littered with arrows scaled the walls with tooth and nail and slowly hacked their way towards us. I picked up a spear from a fallen warrior and flung it forward hitting a Draugr in the chest and knocking him off the wall. Another Draugr climbed up in his place and lunged forward stabbing a warrior in the gut and kicking him off the rampart. I gazed over the wall to witness a sea of monsters pushing at our gates.

"Die beasts!" Rurik yelled, hacking away the rotting limbs of a Draugr.

"Father! Cut off their heads!" Rurik pushed the armless Draugr downward cleanly lopping off his head. Green lights poured out of the creature and Rurik watched them shoot skyward. The sounds of striking iron and wood were deafening. I picked up a shield and charged three Draugrs coming for our archers; two fell over the edge, the other lay below my shield. As I stood over him, he reached over my shield and clawed my back. I screamed in pain and anger. I pushed my body downwards and leaned in towards the decrepit beast's face burying my blade into his neck; sawing through bone back and forth until his essence poured out.

"Brother! Father!" Jareth yelled from the main gate. "We can't hold any longer. They are breaking through!"

"Rally! Rally! To the hall! To the hall!" screamed Rurik. The archers stepped backward still firing arrows as quickly as their arms could take them. Our warriors flooded the hall; standing in the doorway, I ushered everyone inside until the last man entered.

"Bar the doors!" ordered Rurik. I placed my weapons down to help move tables and lumber to wedge against the door as we heard the gates being bashed down.

"It's too late. They are already upon us." I turned and knelt down to grasp my axe and shield when suddenly I felt something rigid against the bottom of my chin. A sword point was barely a hair away from my throat. Every warrior rose like lightening to his feet, knocking furniture about the hall and reaching for their blades. The Valkyries were too great in number and far too quick for them. From the very air we breathe they came, appearing from nothingness with a sword point hovering in front of each warrior's chest ready for the bloody plunge.

"Be still, men of Bjorgvin. Calm yourselves. We bear you no ill will. It is your son, Audan, we seek," said Freya.

"Take your hands from your blades or face our wrath," called out another Valkyrie. The men held fast and looked to me for a sign or signal to attack. I looked about the hall and dropped my head as if already defeated.

"Do as they say men. They're too swift for us. I'll not have harm come to anyone else for this." I commanded. Slowly, each warrior removed hand from blade handle and placed their hands at their sides.

"Now isn't that easier than putting up a fight? I thought perhaps we could handle this in a civilized manner." said Freya as she walked about the room. *Crash!* Rurik threw over a wooden table in anger.

"What is the meaning of this? Who are you wicked women? Speak now or so help me, I'll send you back to the dark place whence you came, demon!" Rurik demanded holding an axe in one hand and a dagger in the other ready to strike down Freya and her comrades.

Freya quickly turned her gaze upon Rurik, extending her elegant fingers towards him while keeping her sword point on me. "Calm yourself, Rurik. I wouldn't want to shorten your reign as ruler of Bjorgvin, brief as it may be. I am the one who carries you to the next world, the one that you pray to for travel to your final salvation in Valhalla. The one you pathetic mortals depend upon for your final journey to prepare for the last great battle, the Ragnarok." Freya smirked and looked about the shocked faces of the long bearded Vikings.

"By the gods, it cannot be. Freya, is it truly you?" asked Rurik, his voice shaking as he slowly lowered his weapons. Freya smiled from ear to ear.

"It is I, Rurik, Chieftain of Bjorgvin. I'm here for your wayward son, Audan. He has been quite active of late and we have some unfinished business to discuss and a debt to be repaid." Freya turned to me once more. "Don't we, my estranged lover?" Freya stepped closer, her breath hot on my neck. Out of the corner of my eye I could see her waving a dagger. Freya dragged the dull edge of the blade along my neck, down to my now pulsating chest. No matter what I did, I could not calm myself. My heart raced, sweat poured from my brow. I raised my arms to my shoulders with my palms open facing outward in submission to Freya's will.

"Freya, allow me to explain my intent before you lay judgment upon me or anyone of my house. These are good men and they don't need any part in your plans. I'm the one you want. So take me, take me and leave this place be..." Freya quickly stepped back and extended her sword once more, still clutching the dagger in her other hand.

"Silence, you fool! I gave you the chance of a life time and you betray me. How dare you, an insignificant mortal, betray Freya, Goddess of the Valkyries? I will not be made a fool of by you or any other man of Midgard! You will do as you are commanded! You will finish the tasks I give you! Do you understand me, human?!" Freya's emotions burned and writhed within her. Tears of a Goddess; drips began to run down the flawless pale white skin of her face. As the tears fell, they smoldered into hot steam on her chin line and disappeared without ever touching the ground. Her hands and sword trembled, making me question her ability to control the situation. This could be my chance. *Odd*, I thought to myself, such human emotion for a god.

"Why do you cry, my goddess? What troubles you?" I asked sounding as genuine as possible. Freya shook the blade of her sword and pressed the tip hard into my chest.

"I am not your goddess. I will ask the questions here and you will answer them or I will have your life much sooner than I intended," shrieked Freya. Her eyes grew bloodshot, strained even. For a moment she appeared faint, briefly closing her eyes and then once more gaining her composure. Once again she was focused, her eyes sharp and direct towards her intent.

"Freya, if you have a quarrel with my son then you quarrel with me. Perhaps we can make reparations. Just don't harm my son. We can make great sacrifices in your honor." Rurik stepped closer as he spoke, no doubt hoping to put himself in striking distance of Freya. Freya dropped her arms to the side in frustration.

"Don't harm your son? Such arrogance, who do you think you are? Mere mortals! I am a goddess and will do as I please. I could wipe out your pathetic little village in the blink of an eye. Is that what you want for your people? A land of smoldering fire and ash?" remarked Freya.

"I would advise against such a bold move against those you seek to rule. You are not the only god that we hold sacred," I said boldly.

"Silence! I gave you no permission to speak." Freya paced the room once more, placing her sword behind her neck, bouncing it off of her shoulder in contemplation. "So Audan, what will it be? Are you going to tell me where the true fire sword is or do I have to coax it out of you? Do you recall what the Finns did to you after your capture? I could do much worse and make it last for an eternity. I could grant you immortality until you have experienced every measure of pain that a man could possibly experience."

I smirked and stood their silent looking to the sky and thinking to myself, *Thor, where are you in my moment of need?* I was beginning to doubt the resolve of Odin and Thor as I could hear the cries of combat; the screams of pain just outside.

"Why do you attack my men?" asked Rurik.

"My Draugrs were told not to attack you. Perhaps it is your men that instigated the battle? Now I won't be able to order them back, the blood thirst, you know. Once they begin, they must continue until they have consumed all." The shrieking screams of the beasts were haunting; with each shrill I twitched and writhed inside in anger.

"Damn you, Freya. I'll give you nothing!" I said in utter defiance.

"Very well, if you don't wish to speak with me then I will force the words from you." Freya turned towards the fire pit and grabbed a hot iron from the coals, stoking it for a moment before removing it and placing it in front of me.

"What do you plan on doing with that?" I asked sarcastically.

"You promised me, Audan. You gave me your word as an honorable man that you would bring me the fire sword, and then you tricked me. You made me feel something for you that I have never felt before." Freya briefly looked down with a lost and sad expression upon her face. Her sadness now grew to anger and fury. "We could have ruled this realm and mine together." Freya leaned forward next to my ear and whispered ever so gently. "You broke my heart... Now I'm going to break your spirit." Freya raised the hot iron glowing red and plunged the iron into my chest, the smoke billowing upwards from my seared skin and blood. My head flung back, screaming in unrelenting pain; the smell of my own flesh burning and rotting, filling the air of the hall with a rank stench. Rurik leapt forward screaming and yelling; attempting to come to my aide he was restrained by his men for fear he would be slain.

"This is your last chance, Audan. Join me or fall!" Enraged and angered Freya's eyes were a piercing red, her face of contempt turned a bright red as she held her blade to my throat. I spat at her feet in utter defiance.

"Never." Freya turned her head to one side in absolute disbelief, pressing the blade harder against my throat as she leaned into me.

"What? What did you say Audan?" Freya heard me clearly. She was daring me to be so bold to repeat my defiant statement.

"I said 'never.' I will never join you, nor will the people of Bjorgvin. Now, finish this. Take my life. I will gladly go to Helheim if it means disappointing you." I relaxed my body and released myself to the idea of knowing my death was now certain.

"Very well, mortal. I'll see you in hell!" An axe flew across the room plunging into a Valkyries back. She shrieked, kneeling to the ground and reaching behind her trying to remove it. Her beautiful face changed, turning dark and scarred. No longer a gorgeous creature but a demon woman with long fangs and dead black eyes. The Valkyries had turned into hideous winged ghouls from the depths of hell. Rurik leapt into the air in celebration at his perfect throw.

"Die you foul beast!"

"You're no Valkyrie! What are you?" I asked in shock.

"Beasts! Demons! To arms men, to arms! Kill those fucking creatures!" commanded Rurik. Vikings lifted their weapons and began to struggle with the Valkyries. As blade pierced flesh, the Valkyries transformed into the horrid things of nightmares. Their blood ran black and stunk of decay, now bereft of their former glorious visions. Despite our best efforts, the creatures were too fast, striking down man after man with blade, tooth, and claw. Jareth and Rurik attempted to come to my aid as I lay on the ground in excruciating pain, but they were struck down by the shield blows of Valkyries. A spear thrust aimed for Jareth narrowly missed its mark as he spun his body to avoid a steely death. Jareth returned with his sword and injured a Valkyrie, leaving an oozing gash across her shoulder. The Valkyrie paused and stared at her wound. Jareth delivered a final blow, severing the beast's head and turning it into ash and embers.

"They can die?" asked Jareth quietly in amazement. "They can die! Take off their heads brothers!" I propped myself up to see a Valkyrie lunging atop Bear and sinking her fangs into his neck ripping out flesh and tendon. She had cut deep and blood shot out into the air from Bear's neck.

"No!" I screamed with outstretched arms. As Bear fell to the ground other Valkyries piled atop his body, devouring his flesh until he went cold and lifeless. Rurik returned with axe in hand removing the heads of two Valkyries that knelt above Bear. Their bodies fell quickly turning to ash and ember only moments after death.

"Die you foul creatures!" As Rurik swung violently, more Vikings poured into the hall. For each Valkyrie we slayed they would kill four of our men. I stood slowly using every ounce of strength I had, screaming inside for the power to slay the evil beasts. Looking to my left I saw Freya staring at me with tears in her eyes.

"I will kill all of you." I said in vein. Freya pulled her sword behind her back about to strike me when suddenly lighting and volleys of thunder cracked down from the great heavens. The sky and earth shook; one, two, three cracks overhead. The Valkyries ceased their onslaught and once again we found ourselves at a standstill. Freya looked behind her and up towards the black clouds now overhead, shaking her head.

"No, no this cannot be. This is not supposed to be this way" she cried.

"What's the matter Freya? Does your kin bellow for you?" I asked.

"So I see you were caught by Brother Thor were you? You failed to mention that to me, didn't you my love." A bright light filled the room blinding all around; I placed my hands upwards to cover my face until it dimmed away. A dark cloaked figure with a wooden staff and a crow on his shoulder appeared; Odin was now amongst us.

"Odin! What are you doing here?" demanded Freya. All warriors in the room immediately dropped to their knees and bowed their heads.

"I will not have any more bloodshed Freya. Stop this madness. Return to Asgard and I will see to it that you receive fair treatment." Freya turned her gaze back to me.

"You bring Thor and Odin against me! I will end you!" Freya raised her sword once more about to strike me down when Odin slammed his staff to the ground twice and a great wind threw Freya to the ground.

Freya stood and pointed her sword at Odin. "All-Father, you will not stop me. This realm is mine and mine alone! I will destroy you if I must!" Odin's body moved like the breeze towards Freya. He grasped her tightly by the neck and lifted her from the ground throwing her to my feet. She lifted her head slowly and stared at me with great fury.

"Go ahead Audan. Tell her why I am here."

"I was sworn by oath to Odin not to speak of it to a soul or spend the rest of eternity in Helheim. Surely even you can understand. My loyalty and allegiance are to them and them alone."

Freya stood quickly placing her blade against my neck. "So you would swear yourself to Odin but not to me. You coward of a man. Am I not your favorite God Audan? We've shared so much together, I feel as if we have always known each other." Freya slowly dragged her blade down to my hip and applied enough pressure for me to grit my teeth; I waited for the plunge.

"Freya! Drop your blade!" shouted Odin while thunder cracked outside. She raised the blade to my neck once more. My eyes turned to meet hers and she smirked before pressing the edge of the blade into my neck. Blood trickled down my side and my legs went cold as I began to fall uncontrollably. She held me up and turned my head towards her to savor every bit of my final moments. Her fingers gripped the blade tightly ready to tear across my throat. "Freya!" Odin yelled once more but this time it was a deafening sound that brought everyone to their knees. Freya gritted her teeth fighting back the pain until she dropped her blade releasing me from her grasp She touch the side of her face directly beneath her ear and lifted blood on her fingertips that had poured out from her ear. She appeared in shock at the sight of her own crimson fluid.

"Very well Audan, but be forewarned. War is coming, not only in the heavens but on Midgard as well. You should choose your allies wisely for I will choose those I favor, and those I disfavor." Just as Sada entered the room, Freya placed her hand on my face with regret in her eyes.

"I'm sorry my love. I could have given you the world if only you stood by me but you betrayed me." I stared at Freya's eyes and it felt like eternity. The color of glaciers, flawless and eternal, I felt lost within them.

"Audan? What is she talking about?" Sada asked. Freya laughed wickedly.

"Foolish girl! In life or death Audan will be mine. He's already tasted the purity of a goddess. Haven't you my love?"

Sada charged forward in a rage, "You bitch! I'll kill you!" Sada grasping a sword from a nearby table, swung at Freya with all her might. Freya reached upward and caught the descending blade with her bare hand. Slowly turning her head towards Sada her face changed once more to the ghoulish creature in her soul letting out a shriek. She swung her other arm knocking Sada to the floor.

With her sword point still on my neck, Freya turned her attention back to me to see my face full of anger and rage as I covered the fresh neck wound with my hand. "Sada! Are you alright?" Sada did not respond as she lay motionless on the floor. "Freya, mark my words I will be your undoing for that!"

Freya laughed dismissing my threat. "We will return mortal. When the gods take their winter slumber and we are once again free of our bonds we shall be back to rain hell fire on you and those you love. There will come a time when we no longer bow to the crack of lightening! You will regret turning your back on us!" Freya and her Valkyries vanished, disappearing into the air leaving the carnage and death they unleashed behind.

Father rushed to my side, "Are you alright?" I gently gripped my chest where a brand had now burned its mark.

"I think so father. Help me outside. Jareth, attend to Sada. See that she is taken care of." I placed my arm over father's shoulders and hobbled outside to take account for what had happened. Bodies, blood, armor and weapons were strewn about. My brothers had fought valiantly to hold off the undead. A guard stood atop the palisade.

"Thank you All-Father for not letting my people perish this day." I said to Odin with much thanks in my heart.

"You are an honorable man Audan. I could not stand idly by while Freya unleashed her hate upon this place. However, my power wanes every moment I spend on Midgard. I must make haste to Asgard."

"Will I see you again?" I asked.

"Perhaps. For now, I need you to get well and wait for us to call upon you. I bid you farewell." Odin smiled and before I could say goodbye to him, a bright streak of light appeared and he vanished back to his realm.

"Did the Draugrs vanish as well?" I asked.

"No brother. Look to the horizon. They nearly breached our defenses entirely until retiring from battle. The day was surely theirs." In the distance I could see the small army of Draugrs heading into a fog. No doubt they would return, but when, I knew not. I looked upward for a sign.

"Odin and Thor, hear my plea. What shall I do? Where shall I take my people from here?" Someone approached me from behind; it was Sada, her robe lightly brushing the dirt trail.

"Thank the gods you are alive!" I said in sheer excitement.

"And you as well my love!" Sada said as she wrapped her arms tightly around me. "What happened in the hall?"

"Freya happened. I fear what she has planned for me, for you. She's not like the other gods. She's very much like us; she feels, wants, needs. Her anger and wrath is beyond compare."

"Are we safe?" Sada asked nervously.

I cautiously approached the main gate staring out into the ocean's horizon, "All-Father Odin, Mighty Thor! I swore an oath to you and it has been honored. And yet, your kin threaten war and death upon my people. What shall I do? Command me, lead me and I will gladly follow!" The skies grew darker, the clouds billowing and growing in the evening air. Lightning began to strike all around charging the very air. Sada grabbed onto me tightly in fear and reverence of the lightning god. A reply fell down upon Midgard, with a single word no more than a whisper carried upon the wind.

"Prepare..."

Ready for more Marauder?
Read an excerpt from the second book in the series;

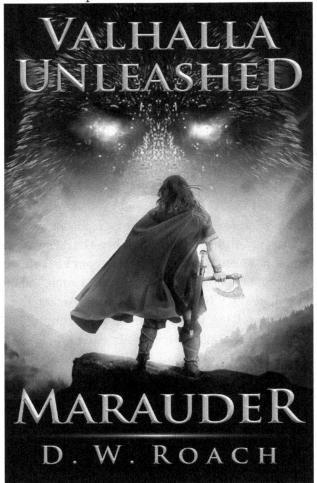

One
Healing Wounds

Death, glorious death…

The lifeblood of one's clan is built upon a field of corpses strewn about a magnificent battlefield. We stand upon death, that of our foes and our great Norse ancestors. Their flesh, blood, and bone have been beaten, grinded to dust beneath our feet, building the very pathways to our destiny's end. Sharpen you blades, fierce warriors of Odin, make your hearts hard like iron, and focus on the tasks the gods have set before you this day. Death will be your song, your banner, your resolve. Become the things you fear, the things that linger in the darkest corners of your miserable soul, become…

Death.

The destruction had been done by the Draugr despite them fleeing the battlefield of Bjorgvin at the behest of their dark winged masters, the Valkyries. Most of the village lay in ash and ruin, embers floated amongst the smoke filled skies and all was lost, save the Great Hall. Jareth and I eagerly returned to what remained of our households and tended to our wounds. The weeks ahead were filled with a constant aching and an un-nerving feeling that our enemies would return in the dead of night. Through burning sun and blistering cold, men of Bjorgvin stood at their posts and watched the tree lines endlessly. Our enemies never returned to finish what they had started, lest they temp the rage of the All-Father. As we rebuilt our homes and mended ties with loved ones, we reflected on those who had moved on to the glory of Valhalla. Many a night, I stared upwards at the burning lights in the darkened sky and wondered if they were torches leading us to Asgard. When I was a child, sitting around the fire my father told me great and wondrous tales: that the lights were the shine from the weapons of our ancestors, that our loved ones kept them sharp and brilliant so we could one day find our way to them. A soft voice suddenly emerged pulling me back from my night time gaze.

"It's cold, my love. What are you doing awake so late with the door open?" I looked back to see Sada, the concern on her brow evident. Turning back, I gazed outside at the crescent moon that slowly fell behind the snowcapped mountains. The streaks of light bouncing off the white powder lit our village nearly as bright as morning. I sighed deeply.

"They will return for us. I hear the mountains groaning; the gods are restless but they do not show themselves. I fear our new found allies may have forgotten us already." Sada stood from our fur draped bedding; walking to me, she placed her hands around my waist resting her head on my shoulder.

"Do not despair, my love. Odin has a plan; our destinies have already been woven for us. When the time is right he will be here to guide your hand to victory or Valhalla. Until then we must be strong; the gods demand strength. Are you not just happy to be home?" Sada cocked her head to one side with a slight frown upon her face as she moved her hands to my bare chest. She had worked hard to be a good women and any unhappiness from me only made her question her usefulness.

"Of course I am. This time of peace is greatly cherished but I am haunted by the fact that it will not last much longer. Each sweet moment is one I cannot reclaim and soon they will be but memories faded into dust." I paused to take in a deep breath, the air cooling my lungs. "Do you feel it, Sada? The frost is returning to Bjorgvin. The mountain passes will be snowed in presently." Sada's chin sank deeper into my shoulder.

"And I am glad for it. We have enough to worry about always gazing at the sea." Sada was right. With the passes closing, we only had one route for our enemies to strike. I pulled a small axe from my belt and ran my thumb along the blades edge several times. The blade of the axe was still pitted from our previous battles; perhaps it was time to visit the blacksmith to renew its edge.

"I should go check on the watchman; see if they require anything." As I stepped out of our home Sada grasped my wrist and pulled me back towards her, pressing her warm body against mine.

"Stop worrying and come to bed. The men can handle themselves for one night. You have worked hard for many days and are in need of respite."

"I suppose you're right, as always," I said reluctantly and returned quietly to our bed. As I lay down a sigh left my lips. Sada began rubbing my chest and rested her head next to mine.

"You're a complicated man, Audan. You worry too much. Put your fate in the hands of the gods and all will be well." Sada's words echoed in my head bouncing from ear to ear as I lay awake staring at the straw covered ceiling. I turned to my side and uneasily let sleep come over me as I twisted and turned hearing the words *prepare* over and over again in my skull.

* * *

"Audan," a voice called loudly from outside my home. "Audan, wake up." I rubbed my face coarsely; slowly opening one eye I reluctantly replied.

"Who..., who is it?"

"Who do you think? It's Jareth. Get up!" I turned to my side and exhaled deeply in frustration.

"Go away!" I said in protest.

"We have business to attend to."

"It is early, brother. What the hell do you want?"

"It's not what I want, it's Father. He demands your presence in the Great Hall."

"Now?" Jareth popped the door open slightly, peeking his head in.

"Now." Finally opening my eyes, I could see the suns light peaking in. I had slept soundly after all; no bad dreams. The corner of my lip was cold and as I wiped my face, I noticed I had drooled all over myself. Perhaps the first night of good rest in a long while. I looked over at Sada who barely moved, her beautiful pale feet stuck out from beneath the furs. Leaning over, I gently bit her heel, smiling as I did so. She pulled her feet quickly underneath the furs and cocked her head back to look at me through her long messy hair.

"What do you want, my love? Is something a matter?" she asked.

"I have to go see Father. Have food ready when I return." Sada moaned and went back to sleep. Standing up, the cold air greeted my body. My muscles ached as I stretched about looking for my clothes. Once dressed, I quietly headed outside to greet the day. The village was silent as the mornings light beat away the dew left by the evening mist.

As I made my way towards the Great Hall, no more than several ships length from my hovel I saw the watchmen standing alert at their post with shield and spear in hand.

"Good morning," I said. The young men popped up rapidly to return the greeting.

"Good morning, Audan," they said in unison.

"I take it the evening was uneventful?"

"Quiet as the grave. Not a soul to speak of." I looked about the village turning my neck slowly left to right.

"Where is your relief? Should he not have been here by now?"

"They are due in any moment. Probably still washing their balls." We laughed quietly under our breath, everyone was dreadfully tired. A bright color form the watchmen's shield suddenly caught my eye.

"What is that?" Reaching for the man's shield I turned the front towards me to see a newly painted scheme. "The head of the serpent. Is this the one I slayed in the North Sea?"

"The very same. We wanted to strike fear into the Draugr should they return. Do you approve of it, Audan?" I cracked a smile and handed the shield back to the watchman.

"It looks more terrifying than I remember," I said enthusiastically. "I'm putting you in charge of painting everyone's shield just the same. Can you do that for me?" The watchman looked at the other guard and then back to me.

"It would be an honor brother. I will begin right away."

"Very well, back to your duties then." The watchmen resumed their patrols, keeping a wary eye on the tree line. The Great Hall was now in sight, a warm glow emanated from the fire inside. I pounded my fist on the thick wooden doors and a meek voice called out from inside.

"What's your business?"

"It's Audan. I'm here to see my father. Just open the damn door." The door swung open slowly; as I stepped forward I could now see the guard that was inside. Father was just ahead sitting in his chair with furs draped over him keeping off the cold.

"Hello, Father." He turned, looked up, and smiled at me.

"My son. I'm sorry to have awoken you so early. I trust you slept well?"

"I did, Father."

"No nightmares?" he asked.

"No, Father. No nightmares. Not this time anyway." He motioned to the wooden chair draped in furs next to him.

"Please, sit. Stay by my side for a time. Perhaps we can share a meal together." He looked up at his guard by the door. "Tibor, leave us please and send the slave girls to fetch us some breakfast. My son must be hungry." Tibor nodded his head.

"Yes, Rurik." He briskly stepped outside. The door closed loudly behind Tibor echoing in the Great Hall.

"So what is it that you want to speak with me about?" I asked curiously. Father tugged roughly at his auburn colored beard over and over again; I thought perhaps he may pull it out.

"Tell me again, son, what was it that attacked us on the day that you and your brother returned home from your absence?" I was puzzled by this question.

"I don't understand, Father. You were here fighting with us." Father slammed his fist on his arm rest.

"Just answer the damn question!" he yelled staring at me with wide, angry eyes. I stood in frustration placing my hands on my belt. It was too early for yelling in my opinion.

"How many times must I tell you, Father! It was the Valkyries and the Draugr that besieged us that day. You were not seeing visions or dreams." Father rubbed his face vigorously with both hands as if to wipe away the memory from his blue eyes. Lowering his arms and grasping the decorated leather bracers on his wrist, he turned and looked at me with disbelief.

"I saw it with my own eyes and still to this day I cannot believe what I have seen. Undead creatures, flesh hanging from their bone walking amongst those that still draw breath. Beautiful winged women turned to skin eating demons before my very eyes. How could such a thing be true? Why would Odin allow such creatures to be released upon my people?"

"What troubles you, Father?" Rurik was clearly vexed by something closer to home.

"The Jarl, my son. The Jarl troubles me, his scheming and plotting behind closed doors vexes me terribly and I fear this may be our last winter in Bjorgvin. Damn Steinar that arrogant fool!" Father kicked another chair next to him in anger knocking it over.

"We sent messengers. What do they say?" Father laughed sarcastically under his breath lifting his head towards the sky.

"Ha! They say nothing because Steinar has given them nothing to say. They send no message, no sign of good faith that our alliance will be maintained."

"What of the other Chieftains? Surely they will..." I was cut off quickly.

"No word, not even trade or commerce from our usual companions. The Volsung Clan, ScyIding Clan, and the Wylfings have all been completely silent to our calls for aide. I fear we have been everlastingly cut off from the Jarls good graces." Father stood now, stroking his beard as he stepped away from his chair. "We have done well these last few months to repair our village, to fortify our defenses and prepare what men we have for another attack, but I fear it's not enough to hold off the living and the dead." Dropping his head father kicked about a small patch of dirt at his feet.

"So we are alone then. We must continue to prepare for an attack, double our efforts." Father turned to me and crossed his arms atop his blood red tunic.

"It is good to hear you say that, son. Just last season you would have suggested we raid Steinar before he had a chance to attack us. You have matured beyond your years and for that I am grateful both as a chieftain and father. You will make a fine leader of your people one day."

"Thank you, Father." I tried to think of a way out of our troubles but nothing I could conceive of seemed realistic. "Father."

"Yes, my son; please, speak freely." Father moved in front of the fire pit at the center of the Great Hall, slowly moving his hands closer to the flame to catch some warmth. A knock suddenly came at the door. "Yes, what is it?"

"Breakfast, my lord," Tibor spoke from the other side of the door.

"Very well, come in and set it down." The door slowly opened and Tibor entered first. Following behind him were two well-dressed slave girls with braided blonde hair. Keeping their heads down, they quickly placed two wooden blocks at our table with food. "Thank you Tibor, you may leave us." Tibor bowed his head.

"Yes my lord." Tibor waved to the girls to depart the room and they did so without hesitation. Tibor closed the door once more and we began picking at our breakfast of freshly made bread, dried herring, and apples from a nearby orchard.

"Apologies, son, for the interruption. Please continue and enjoy your meal." I picked apart some food, stuffing small pieces into my mouth as I spoke.

"What if I were to appeal to some of our neighbors, lavish them with gifts or perhaps invite them to a great feast in our glorious hall. Would that not sway them? Perhaps even pull them away from the influence of Steinar?" It was rare for me to speak in such a way. Politics! Oh, how I detested the thought. My ramblings made me tired and I longed for the chance to drive the tip of a spear violently through Steinar's balls!

"You're thinking like a chieftain; regrettably, I've already tried all of it. While you and your brother have been working hard to rebuild our home I have sent goodwill as far as the Ice Lands. Word of your great adventures has spread throughout the kingdom and now the other Chieftains think we are either great liars or that I am old and have lost my wits." Father scratched at his salt and pepper hair nervously. "This is exactly what Steinar wants, our allies thinking we are weak and incompetent. The Draugr may be the least of our worries. In any case, any fortunes of ours pale in comparison to that which the Jarl contains in his coffers. Competing with him will take cunning."

"So if our lord turns against us and our neighbors shun us, what are we to do, Father?" Looking out a small opening in the wall of the Great Hall, Father gazed upon the majestic mountainside of *De syv fjell* or the Seven Mountains.

"The great snows are coming, yes. Soon the mountain passes will be closed and the ocean channels frozen. We must hold out for the long freeze and prepare for the battles to come. No raids shall be had by us in the coming spring." Father stood and removed a dagger from his belt. "This time we shall spill the blood of our brothers," he said as he violently stabbed the blade into a wooden table. The blade glistened in the darkness of the hall reflecting the light from the roaring fire as it swayed back and forth on its point. Placing one foot atop a stool, father raised a wooden mug from the table taking a hearty drink of the day old mead and then slamming it back down.

"A little early for drinking, don't you think, Father?" He emptied the mug and placed it loudly on the table. Father returned a dirty look bearing some of his teeth.

"What are you, my mother? Get me another drink if you're going to lecture me. By the gods..." I smiled and quickly grabbed his cup. "Pour one for yourself as well. There's something else I wanted to speak with you about." My heart felt heavy at the thought of even more poor tidings.

"What is it this time?" I asked reluctantly.

"Come, sit with me and finish your breakfast before it gets cold." I sat hurriedly placing our mugs in front of us and shoving more food into my mouth.

"Tell me again, my son, what was it like?" I knew exactly what he was referring to. I cleared my throat and took a drink of my mead before speaking.

"Valhalla?" I asked. Father nodded and I continued. "From what I saw it was the most beautiful thing I had ever laid my eyes upon, next to Sada that is." Father chuckled taking another swig of his drink.

"Beautiful, is that all you have to say of our afterlife?" I looked up at Rurik, and saw his attention fully fixated upon me. I crossed my arms and rested my elbows on the table.

"The ice does not sting, the mead flows endlessly from great fountains, song is heard everywhere, but…"

"But what, my son?" I looked about the Great Hall hesitantly trying to find the right words to convey to Father.

"Valhalla, there is much we do not know, Father. A war is brewing amongst our gods. We must tread lightly." Father looked at me sharply.

"Now is not the time for hesitation. Surely, we have allies amongst the gods that can come to our aid. Can you not call forth Odin? He assisted us once; he can surely do it again." I shook my head several times, swallowing another piece of herring.

"It's not that simple, Father."

Rurik slammed his fist on the table. "Well why the hell not?" A chilling breeze suddenly came over me.

"Where is your humility, chieftain!" The Seer quickly entered the hall appearing out of from the darkest corner of the Great Hall.

"Seer, how did you get in here? I told the guard no visitors!" demanded Rurik.

"How I entered is not important. It is the why you should concern yourself with."

"Enough with your riddles, old man; get to the point or get the fuck out!" Rurik pointed to the door with drink in hand.

"Your impertinence is staggering. Even in the face of insurmountable odds you would rather hide out in your winter cave and drink yourself senseless. Did you not see with your own eyes the immortal beings and undead creatures that came forth for your own sons?" Rurik placed his cup upon the table and tucked his thumbs under his aged belt buckle.

"I did and I still don't believe what my eyes have seen."

"If you doubt your eyes, then you doubt our gods, and if you doubt our gods you are no man of Odin."

"Old man, get to your point. I will not have you enter my Hall and show disrespect." Father gripped his mug tightly and I turned my eyes to the Seer awaiting his wise response.

"Very well. The Ragnarok approaches. The signs are becoming clear as day," said the Seer as he pointed towards the sky.

"What signs?" Rurik asked.

"The ones your son knows all too well."

"Son? What is he talking about?"

"The Elders, Father. The Elders said there would be signs of the final battle to come," I said.

"As we speak, Surt is planning his escape from his rocky tomb." The Seer sat down using his driftwood staff to brace his weary bones.

"Surt? You must be joking, old man. Surt is an ancient god, a myth; even if he exists he holds no weight over the All-Father." The Seer became enraged slamming his staff to the ground.

"This is no joke, chieftain! Do you not feel the presence of death everywhere? Can you not smell the rotting corpses in the wind? The Draugr and Valkyries descend upon us and yet you narrow your focus. You are blinded by your own ego and arrogance." Father sat back in his chair now opening his hands in submission.

"Seer, my father is troubled by politics and means no disrespect. Please, stay with us and grace us with your counsel." The Seer grinned and gladly remained sitting.

"Your son seems to have more sense about him than you. Take note, good chieftain, he may even be king one day." The Seer looked about the table and lifted his gaze to Rurik. "Were you not about to offer me a drink?" Rurik stood reluctantly as he walked away to fill a wooden mug for the Seer. "It is time to gather you allies, Rurik. Time is not on your side. You may be safe while the snows fall but once the ice has receded your enemies will come at you by land, by sea, and from the heavens." Father placed the mug in front of the Seer and sat down.

Taking a deep breath he replied, "What shall we do?"

"Tribute and treasure will not spare you from the sword this time. It's time for a lesson in humility." The Seer quietly laughed under his breath knowing full well Rurik would struggle with this.

"Humility? And who am I to be humble towards?" demanded Father.

"It's time to call upon your father-in-law." Rurik stood there speechless for a moment simply glaring at the Seer. I waited tensely for a response that never seemed to come until Father burst out laughing.

"I've never known you to have a sense of humor, Seer. Perhaps the drink has already gotten to your mind." The Seer, however, did not appear to be amused.

"Call upon your wife, send her to retrieve her father and his army. They can open new supply lines and help fortify Bjorgvin." Rurik was furious, his brow was heavy and turned a bright red. Running his thumb up and down the handle of his axe, it seemed he would wear it down to splinters at a moment's notice.

"Kenna will do no such thing. I forbid it!" he yelled.

"Is this you talking or your vanity, chieftain?" asked the Seer. Rurik paced the room back and forth; his rough hands balled up in a fist.

"I will not open my doors to that arrogant, insolent, bag of wind! He is not welcome in my halls."

"And why not?" A soft voice asked. We turned our necks to find Kenna standing in the doorway of her chamber.

"My love. I thought you were foraging in the wood with the other women?" asked Rurik. Kenna wore a simple red dress of wool with a grey overcoat. She slowly removed her hood, revealing her stern gaze.

"I was but then my ears began to burn. I thought perhaps the gods needed me to return home. It seems I was right."

"These matters do not concern you. I'd ask that you return to your duties," Rurik commanded.

"What matters could concern me more than the welfare of our family, of our people?" Kenna strode gently up to Rurik, placing her hand on his bearded cheeks. Her hands were freezing from the outdoors. Rurik grasped both her hands placing them in his to provide warmth.

"The Seer was providing us his counsel," said Rurik. Kenna raised her eyebrows, turning to the old man in curiosity.

"Oh, and what do you have to tell us. Have the gods sent a sign." The Seer lowered his head out of respect for Kenna.

"The gods send many signs, my lady. I merely interpret their meaning and humbly attempt to convey their will. The bones have spoken to me and they speak of your father, Jerrik." The room became silent; Kenna's eyes opened wide as she turned her head to one side and smiled.

"My father and I have not spoken for a very long time. Why would I waste breath on him now?" Kenna crossed her arms waiting for the Seer to respond.

"My dear, I don't presume to fully understand the meaning but I would assume it has something to do with our current predicament." Kenna looked back and forth between Rurik and the Seer.

"What predicament? Rurik? What is he talking about? What are you keeping from me?" Rurik stood upright wiping the mead from his bearded chin.

"Sit down, my love. We have much to discuss." Sitting at the table, Kenna straightened out her dress and neatly placed her hands in her lap. "We are in need of new allies. We have fallen from our Jarls good graces. Steinar no longer receives our messengers nor does he accept our tribute." Kenna turned her head to one side seeming perplexed.

"Perhaps he is dead," she exclaimed. Rurik smiled, reaching into his waist, he slowly produced a knife that he used to whittle at the table.

"If only that were true. Then our troubles would surely be at an end, but I fear that they have just begun. Even our neighboring Chieftains will not send word of their loyalty. We have been cutoff with only the snow and ice to protect us now. I believe what the Seer is saying is that it's time to make peace with your father and ask him for his help. It's been a long time Kenna, old wounds will heal." Kenna pursed her lips and clenched her jaw.

"After the dishonor, I caused, you expect me just to saunter into his hall and have him accept me with open arms?" I was puzzled as I had never met my mother's father before. I just assumed he had perished in the raids long ago.

"Mother, of what dishonor do you speak?" I asked. Kenna's eyes were stern and cold. She turned to Rurik for some guidance on how to respond to my question.

"It's alright dear. I think it's time you tell the boy the truth. He's a man, he can handle it," Rurik said calmly.

"I was hoping it would never come to this my son but it appears your father is out of choices. Long ago when I was just a girl my father Jerrik told me that it was time to be given to a proper suitor. Longships with emissaries came from all the tribes bearing furs, treasure, and riches of every kind to secure my hand. Father sent the emissaries back asking for the suitors to reveal themselves in person to be judged fit. The men came and soon father made a bargain with a Lord in the South Lands.

"I was to wed his son, a much older man named Finn. Finn was a warrior like your father, but unlike Rurik he was cruel and motivated only by his selfish glory. Finn was joined by many men including another I recall seeing standing at the back of my father's hall; a man with a handsome and kind face.

"I just had to meet him before Finn took me away, no matter the cost. One evening I snuck out from my chambers to find him standing watch at their longship. It was love at first sight; we ran away together in the darkness taking only what we could carry. We traveled by foot for many weeks living off the land until finding a small village that took us in. That man was your father, Rurik, who then was known as Tate." Sitting in astonishment, I did not blink even once.

Clearing my throat I asked, "And all these years, your father has not found you?"

"I think for a time my father and Finn went searching for me, driven by their anger and shame that I had caused. Eventually, they gave up. We stayed here and built a strong community and created new families for us to love and look after." Kenna wiped a single tear from the left side of her cheek. "Is this truly what you need? If it is I shall do as you wish." Rurik smiled placing his hand lovingly on Kenna's shoulder.

"Then it is settled. Tomorrow we shall gather a small but bold group of men to escort you on your journey to see Jerrik." said Rurik.

"You're not coming with me?" protested Kenna.

"Sadly no. We already have too few men. I need to look after our people."

"So not only must I relive this unpleasantness but I'm being asked to do it alone?" Kenna was on the verge of anger as her eyes began to redden with frustration.

"No, my love, not alone. Audan will accompany you in this quest." Mother looked at me and shook her head violently.

"Absolutely not! You can't do that. They will look at him as a bastard. They may even try to murder him." Rurik turned to me pointing with a rigid finger.

"Take your best men, Jareth, Gunnar, anyone you wish. Arm yourselves well and whatever you do, do not separate yourselves under any circumstance. Do you understand?" I nodded sharply.

"I do, Father. I will guard her with my life and the life of our warriors." Father slapped his hand on my shoulder and smiled widely.

"That's a good lad. I'll make arrangements for you to bring tribute as well. I'm still uncertain on how Jerrik will respond to Kenna's unexpected arrival. Let's hope that a beautiful daughter can melt the ice in an old man's heart."

"Do you suppose that Finn is still amongst my father's company?" asked Kenna.

"I don't know much about your father other than where his home was the day we left it. If Finn is still alive after all these years surely he has found another woman to call his own. More likely he is drinking in Valhalla." Kenna stood and leaned into the open arms of Rurik. Stroking her long hair, he said "All will be well, my love. You will see. The gods will protect us."

"I ask to take my leave, my lord," said the Seer. Rurik dropped his head and swatted open his hand towards the Seer, dismissing him.

"Audan, I'd like to share a word with you in private if you would honor me." Without replying, I left Kenna and Rurik to their discussion. Stepping out of the hall, Tibor remained standing guard outside.

"You can head back in Tibor." Tibor nodded raising his shield and spear slightly as he turned to resume his post. Looking back, I could still see Mother and Father in a warm embrace. Once outside, the cold air greeted my face as I followed the fast footed Seer.

"Are you armed, young man?" he asked.

"Of course, but why do you ask? Are you expecting an attack?" I was suspicious of the Seer's questions.

"No, young Audan, but I carry no weapons so it is wise to keep company that does." The Seer picked up the pace and moved faster down a sloped grassy hill covered in a thick fog.

"Old man, why are you moving so fast?" The Seer did not respond. "Old man? Do you hear me?" At a light run, we headed towards torches at the edge of our village. "Where are you taking me?" Reaching the torches, the Seer stopped abruptly and slowly turned towards me. "I didn't know you could move like that," I exclaimed.

"We needed to put distance between our voices and the ears of men." Something was different about his voice, the raspy tone had vanished and a clearly deep voice was now present.

"Are you well, old man? You sound strange to me."

"Of what old man do you refer?" The Seer lifted his arm and gently removed his cloak revealing his never before seen appearance. I braced myself to see the rumored grotesque features of the Seer's face. Slowly raising his head, I could see a long grey beard, hair that extended passed his shoulders and as his gaze met mine, astonishment came over me when I beheld a familiar missing eye that contained the stars of the night time sky.

"Odin..."

The Marauder Series

- Marauder

- Valhalla Unleashed

- Realm of Fire

All of these books are available on Amazon.

About the Author

I live in the Bay Area with my gorgeous wife, my beautiful children, a crazy black cat and a sweet black lab. Marauder Valhalla Unleashed is the second book I've released in what is anticipated to be a series of eight books.

I've had an amazing life growing up on a small farm, working on ships in Alaska, joining the Marine Corps, and for the last ten years I've been working as a Global Security Professional.

For fun I like to go shooting, play hockey, go camping, have BBQs, and hang out with my family. Over the last few years I started brewing my own beer, mead, wine, and hard cider (hard cider is my favorite.)

I chose to write a book for a number of reasons, and in the end, it was for the love of the story. As I put words to paper the characters came to life for me. I remember at one point going to bed and all I could dream about was the adventures the main characters were going on. It became exciting and very real.

In many ways I incorporated much of my own life experiences into the books I write. I wanted to convey what it was like for the warrior, the guy on the ground, fighting against nature with the odds stacked against him. I also wanted to show readers and fans of Norse mythology something they haven't seen before.

I hope you enjoy the Marauder Series as much as I enjoyed writing it!

You can find Marauder books and social media at the below links;

Main Web Page
http://marauderseries.blogspot.com/

Book Series Page
http://www.amazon.com/gp/bookseries/B019SCYN26/

Facebook
https://www.facebook.com/marauderbook

Amazon Authors Page
http://www.amazon.com/David-Roach/e/B00QBBZDNQ/

Tumblr
https://www.tumblr.com/blog/marauderseries

Lightning Source UK Ltd.
Milton Keynes UK
UKHW010050141020
371533UK00011B/227

9 781715 594183